MAN,KIND

A Climate Fiction Adventure
BY C.C. BERKE

SODAK
PUBLISHING

Man, Kind is a work of fiction. Names, characters, places, and incidents are the products of the author's imagination or are used fictitiously. Any semblance to actual events, locales, or persons, living or dead, is entirely coincidental.

Copyright © 2020 by Christopher C. Berke

All rights reserved. No portion of this book may be reproduced in any form without permission from the author, except as permitted by U.S. copyright law. For permissions contact Sodak Publishing, LLC.

Published in the United States by Sodak Publishing, LLC.
www.sodakpublishing.com

Originally published in hardback in December of 2020

Hardback ISBN: 978-1-7362335-0-4

Paperback ISBN: 978-1-7362335-1-1

Ebook ISBN: 978-1-7362335-2-8

Cover Design by Brent Plooster (www.brentiisdesign.com)

Interior Design by Christopher C. Berke

www.ccberke.com

Instagram: @ccberke
Twitter: @thechrisberke
Facebook: /ccberke
Goodreads: C.C. Berke

FIRST EDITION PAPERBACK

For every strong woman in my life.

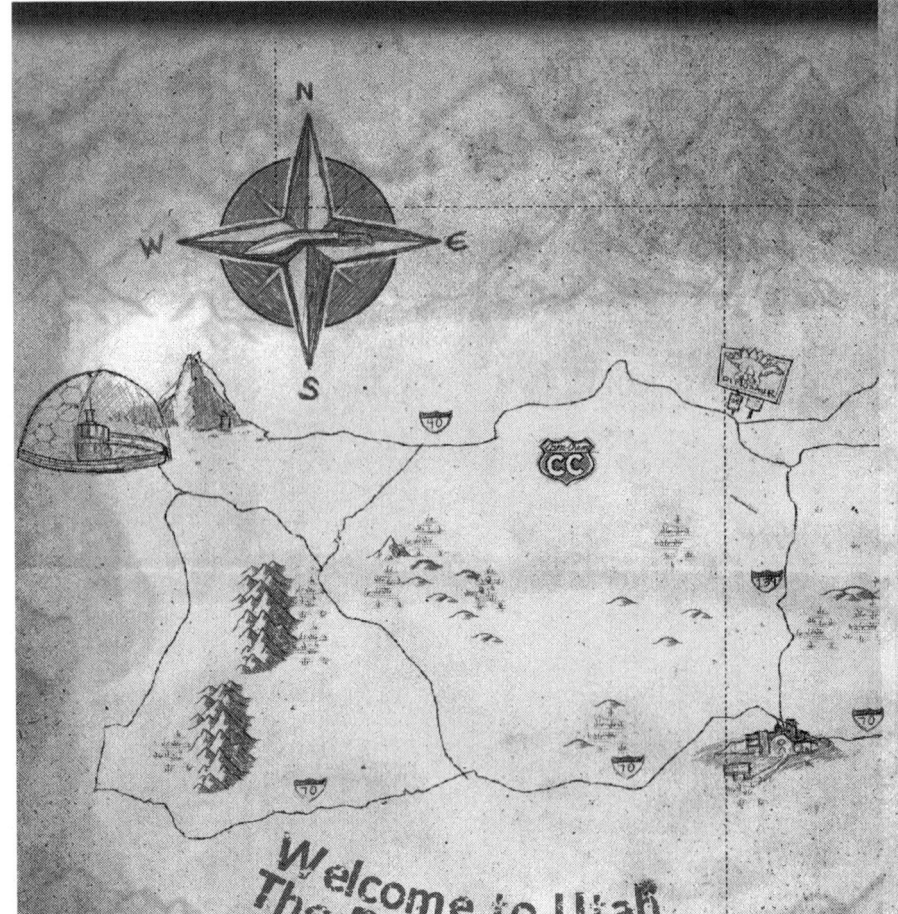

MAN,KIND

In front of ten thousand tons of concrete wall, a woman collapsed to the earth with an outstretched arm.

"Please!" she screamed through blood-filled lungs, peppering the air with a red mist. "I'm begging you!"

There was no answer.

Not far behind a trio of warped, wrathful men were advancing towards her. The woman thought she had lost them during a frantic escape in the darkest hours, but the salacious laughter bouncing off nearby ruins told her otherwise. She called out once more with a weakening breath.

Still nothing.

The woman's neck craned. An intricate, almost impossible domed complex could narrowly be seen rising from the inside of the towering wall's ridge. She squinted. The dome appeared to be shifting silently in the sky. Or was it just the dancing of heat on top of its surface?

A biting twinge in her abdomen pulled her focus away so she checked the hand cupping it; dark and damp. Life was rapidly draining from her body and, along with it, a desperate message.

The echoes of amusement faded and were soon replaced with unobstructed heckling. They could see her now. Each of them were tossing taunts her way like bitter throwing knives. "You can't get away from Him that easy!" one would shout, while another mocked her stupidity.

In mere moments they had reached the helpless woman lying face-down in the sand-swallowed road. One menacing assailant licked his lips at the sight of a stained trail, snickering at her attempts to crawl farther. Another circled around to the woman's head. She reached out, grasping for rescue, only to find the top of a worn boot. Disgusted, the man kicked the hand away like a stubborn cockroach. "Ain't no one behind that wall who gives a shit about you, lady."

One of the others grabbed the woman's legs and tugged on them, touting his willingness to drag her the whole way back if he had to. To the group's pleasure she let out a hollow scream in agony.

"Still plenty'a guys who ain't had a go yet!" the last of the three jeered.

The sunburnt sky sizzled with insidious laughter. Cupping his crotch, the man standing nearest the woman's head declared, "I'm gettin' hard just thinkin' abou—"

Crack!

A deafening sound snapped the words from the man's mouth with deadly precision. An eerie silence followed the pulsating echoes of the gunshot that left all three men standing frozen. Not one dared move as if it would make the hole in their companion's head a reality if they did. Within seconds, however, the lifeless body crumpled to the ground, leaking a crimson trail of its own.

The remaining two spun wildly to locate the origin of their partner's demise. Down the buckled street, through shattered windows, behind mangled cars, but there was nothing. The surrounding area was completely desolate of life. And then they saw them. Two cloaked figures brandishing large rifles were positioned on top of the bastioned wall protecting the dome, each scoped directly at them.

The two men took the brief moment of silence as a not-so-friendly signal to make a run for it. One broke off into a dead sprint while the other had to relinquish the woman's ankles before joining after. Fifteen steps later, however, two more deafening cracks dropped them stiff to the ground like fallen planks. Nothing remained in the air but a swirl of sand lifted by a gentle breeze.

Nearly half an hour passed before a steel gate at the foot of the cement-slab fortress rumbled to life and split at the center. Out stepped a figure, a pale hood and robe shrouding their face and feet, that floated across the dusty road like a hurried specter to corroborate the fallen visitor's intent. Once next to the woman, the figure removed their hood with both hands, giving a mistrustful scan of the near-distant mountains before kneeling, and checked for a pulse. It was slight, but not enough.

The robed figure shifted weight and dug a hand into a small leather satchel draped around their right shoulder. Out came a syringe donning a bright orange cap. After inspecting it briefly, the figure removed the cap and jammed the needle into the visitor's pulseless neck.

A sudden, deathly gasp of air contorted the woman and she flung up to her feet with a racing heart. "Where am..." she wheezed, "...am I alive?"

"Please, take a deep breath."

To the visitor's surprise, it was another woman who had replied. She had not heard a voice this poised, this heavenly, in so long that she began to question whether or not she was actually conscious. However, a quick glance around the arid environment assured her she was still, in fact, where she intended to be. She had made it.

"Who are you?" she asked frantically.

The robed woman rose to meet her eye-to-eye. "Please. You need to take a deep breath."

A sharp pain spasmed inside the visitor's gut and she looked down at her blood-soaked clothes. "What's...what's going on?"

"Listen." The robed woman took the other's frail hands into her own and held eye contact. "We cannot save you. The adrenaline in that shot I injected will only last a few more moments, then you will die. Now, what have you ventured all this way to risk telling us?"

A deluge of realizations flooded the dying woman's cognizant. Her pupils dilated, her head jittered, her mind scrutinized every memory she had ever made. But the stinging sun forced a hand to shield her eyes, turning her gaze to the massive wall. Something magnificent flourished safely behind that open gate. Something vital. Something that reinforced the hardest decision she had ever had to make. Then, calm as a leaf slowly swaying to the earth, she remembered the single thing that mattered most in the entire world.

"I found...I mean, I have..." she tried to say, but did not know which combination of words to use with her remaining seconds. "My child... the solution..."

The woman's legs gave out and she slumped to her knees. Her borrowed time was being reclaimed. As she fell to her side she reached into the breast pocket of her filthy jacket and retrieved a crumpled piece of paper. A smile etched itself into her lifeless face before she exhaled her final breath.

"Damn," cursed the robed woman before flicking the hood back over her head. She knelt back down to respectfully close the deceased's eyes, then plucked the piece of paper from between two stained fingers.

On the walk back to the gate dividing ten thousand tons of concrete wall wrapped around an intricate domed complex, the robed woman unfolded the paper and stopped dead in her tracks. Written down was the location of a building, a single name, and an age.

Entry 1

She said someone would come for me. That she couldn't take care of me anymore. That it was time to say goodbye.

Then she kissed my forehead and whispered, "You must wait here. No matter what."

I hadn't even taken off my coat before she rushed over to the door and slipped through the crack like a shadow. Now I'm all alone in a place I've never been before. I wish this was just a bad dream, that I'd wake up and be back at home, but I'm too scared to fall asleep.

So I guess I'll wait. It's only been one day so I'm not too worried about her yet. Besides, we'll be back together as soon as this mysterious someone comes and rescues me, right? Of course I'm right. That's how things are supposed to work out.

Anyway, the moonlight is leaving me now so I think I'll close my notebook and just... keep waiting.

"No matter what," she said.

Between four walls of steel beams and splintered sheetrock, and atop a floor of cracked concrete, Juno rested on a smattering of seat cushions and salvaged jackets. Her delicate fingers slid a worn out pen she used for journaling down the convenient space in the spiral binding of her frayed notebook, then set it nearby. She rolled onto her right side and met a lonely wall with her nose. Inanimate and cold, she decided she was not yet desperate enough to make friends with construction material, so she rolled back over and tucked her long hair behind her ear.

Juno's entire life had just been frantically collected and shoved into this tiny room. Using the lingering moonlight still creeping underneath the door, she began taking stock in what she had been able to grab. At the adjacent corner from her makeshift bed was a chair tucked neatly under a small desk. Spread across the top of the desk was her tattered backpack, a couple month's worth of what passed for food, a pile of large plastic water bottles, and a small tactical folding knife she had never even seen before last night.

On the floor next to the desk was a paltry stack of weathered books that Juno had managed to snag in the scramble. It was a sad sample of the collection she had acquired over the years. In the limited aura she could make out a torn technology magazine, a collection of young adult romance novels, and, her favorite by default, a field guide on local wildlife missing its cover.

In the far corner, as far away from her nose as possible, was an empty plastic bucket Juno was told to use to relieve herself. She hated that bucket. The blue cylinder taunted her from the shadows, laughed at her pathetic pile of what could hardly be considered luxuries, and pushed an overwhelming rush of resentment out from her teary eyes. Before succumbing to the sobs, she immediately sprawled onto her back and sighed at the ceiling.

Why was it suddenly too dangerous to stay home? Juno wondered, abhorring her new accommodations. *It's not like* anything *changed.*

Yet for some reason life was uprooted and scurried into the city where her new existence was made perilously clear: stay in the room, stay silent, and stay out of sight. No room for exceptions. And still, despite the warnings, all she wanted to do was scream out at the top of her lungs. But Juno was not dumb. She knew the risk of screaming. So instead she forced her eyelids closed and tried to sleep her new nightmare away.

Entry 2

I was flipping through the reptile part of this field guide and did you know that a tortoise is attached to its shell? It also said that a tortoise is a turtle but a turtle is not a tortoise and that a group of them together is called a creep and that the scales on their shells are called scutes. So weird!

I really hope I get to see one someday.

Or any animal really.

P.S. I'm gonna need to find a real bathroom soon. Like tomorrow morning soon. This bucket stinks.

The sun shared its first glow with Juno as she tip-toed from behind the door of her tiny prison. It was the first time she had seen the greater area of the building basked in daylight. A quick scan of the room revealed many desks and chairs, much like the set in her own room, all separated by short walls that came up to her nose. She made a mental note to explore their secrets soon, but the tingling between her legs demanded urgency.

At the far edge of the expansive room was a wall comprised of massive glass panels that still allowed most of the morning to shine through their dusty surfaces. To the right of the desks just outside her door were two large, glass-walled rooms. Assuming neither housed a toilet, she cautiously ventured to the left.

After slinking through the labyrinth of half-walls, Juno soon spotted the double steel doors she had arrived through two nights prior hiding in a corner. Closer to the middle of the wall was another fancier pair of double doors with a small gap of textured stone between them. Printed above was the word ELEVATOR in bold metallic letters. On either side of the elevators were two more doors tucked inside small hallways; one reading ENTER and the other EXIT. Desperately, she rushed over to ENTER so she could relieve herself.

Inside was not at all what she expected. There was a sink, which was familiar, and two elongated toilets hanging vertically on the wall, which were not. Juno inched closer while simultaneously digging deep within her brain to unearth the instructions on how to operate these foreign objects. She was acclimated to something that more-or-less resembled a chair, but the pressure in her bladder told her that the time for thinking was over, and demanded improvisation. Immediately, she dropped her pants to her ankles, spun around, and backed into the wall-mounted toilets. The alleviation outweighed any embarrassment and she started to giggle, realizing the situation hilariously mirrored a shaped peg-and-hole game she played with as a child.

Juno left the restroom with a bit of happiness reclaimed from the previous nights of discomfort and depression. She stood in the open room for a while, relatively upbeat, and listened for any indication that something other than the breath from her lungs was making a sound. Nothing. She then looked both ways as if crossing a street, zipped straight back into the tiny room containing her bag and books and makeshift bed, and promptly returned into the open hugging a big blue bucket. If she was going to be living here from now on, it was *not* going to be next to her own sewage.

Beneath the hazy glow of the Oasis, an entire room of thirsty patrons turned a suspicious eye towards a pale-robed woman who had just emerged from outside. Intentful stares scanned the supple curvature of her body as she removed a hood and laid it across her shoulders. It took a few uncomfortable moments for her vision to adjust to the rusty atmosphere of the establishment, but she eventually spotted who she had chanced a meeting with towards the back of the room. Strange, she noted, that it only took the dusty silhouette of someone she once knew to make her consider this reunion a mistake.

Once down the rickety staircase, traversing through the tight path between packed chairs and tables, the robed woman took notice of a handwritten sign behind the bar. It read Oasis Forecast in choppy letters. Directly below was the message: Cloudy: Low Power.

The bartender ducked underneath the cobbled sign and began operating a squeaky hand crank. Lightbulbs above suddenly regained enough strength to properly display the decrepit shape the Oasis had fallen into. The furnishings were rough, grey, and rotted, and the people were even moreso. A slight twinge of guilt tugged at the woman's heart, but she had already arrived at her table. All emotion would need to be sidelined during the forthcoming conversation. It was too important.

"You know I despise meeting in public, Lexa," the robed woman began.

The sojourner she had ventured to meet in the middle of the night was drinking from a clear glass of premium water; an extravagant purchase considering the Oasis's clientele. Lexa wiped a dribble from her chin and returned with, "Pan. How's it feel to be somewhere you're not wanted?"

"Keep your grievances to a minimum," Pan warned, wary of all the piercing eyes acutely displaying the opposite of adoration. It was already uncomfortable enough for her to be out in the world, much less amongst drunkards in the depths of a darkened bar, without the stale air of resentment hovering between the two as well. A resentment she especially wished to avoid at this time. "I have something of extreme importance to share with you and I don't want it floating into the ears of these...people."

"Relax," Lexa scoffed, "they all know you're with me."

Lexa winked at the bartender and Pan followed the line of sight. The bartender had finished pouring a brown liquid from a dusty glass bottle, slid the drink over to a dusty old patron, and then turned around to flip over an equally dusty vinyl record. Brief crackling was followed by a twangy guitar. The lights dimmed again so the bartender resumed his duty at the crank. Once both music and lights were in full operation, most of the patrons went back to happily drinking away their sorrows and ignored the only two women at the corner of the room.

Pan, now feeling more or less shrouded from being overheard, resumed speaking. "I have a mission for you. A retrieval."

"Another one?" Lexa rolled her eyes so hard her head flicked backwards. "We've been through this hundreds of times. They always turn up missing, pinned dead to a wall, or conveniently nonexistent in the first place."

Pan interlaced her fingers and leaned her elbows on the table. " I know we've had our fair share of setbacks, but my intuition tells me this one is different."

"Different how? One less scab? Blegh! Everyone thinks they're so damn special..."

Lexa threw back another swig of crisp, costly water while Pan pried on. "Different as in she was *born*."

If only for a second, Lexa took pause at the word *born*, but clung tightly to her skepticism. "So what? I was born, too."

"Those were," Pan sighed, "unique circumstances. Judging by the mother's age, this one was born within the last decade or so."

Mother was as foreign a word to Lexa as *born*. "And that means what to me, exactly?"

Pan dipped her head as an invitation for Lexa to lean in. Stretching the final thread of remaining respect, Lexa caved and dragged her chair in closer.

"A young woman..." Pan paused to find the correct phrasing, "...arrived at my doorstep a few days ago. She said she had a child. We brought her in for testing and the results came back positive. Overwhelmingly. Do you know how substantial this finding is? The odds of there being a second generation are microscopic; a *third* is infinitesimal. This child could be immune."

Lexa's eyes narrowed. "And you want me to, what, somehow track down the only ten-year-old girl on the planet, hold her hand, and skip her right back to you without complication?"

"She's closer than you think."

Pan reached into a leather satchel wrapped around her shoulder to retrieve a crumpled piece of paper and slid it across the table. A small drip of dried blood stained the corner. Lexa shook her head at the theatrics and snatched the note from under Pan's fingers. When she flattened the folds out and read the three lines of scribbled text, her spine straightened.

"So what happened to the mom?"

"I think you can guess."

Lamentingly, Lexa grazed with rough fingertips a thick scar that ran from her right cheek up to her forehead, then casually slid them through her buzzed hair. "This is too dangerous. Even for me. Once word gets out that—"

"Keep your voice down," Pan interjected. "I have reason to believe that whispers have already traveled. When the young woman—the mother—arrived, her entire body was bruised and battered with the addition of a deadly stab wound to the abdomen. We had to use our waning supply of ammunition to put down three of His..." she paused to feign cringing, "...*acolytes*. It was a miracle she made it as far as she did."

After a few moments of what Pan perceived as reflection, and what Lexa perceived as an awkward silence, Lexa scoffed again. "I think mankind has more than proved to itself that miracles don't exist."

Exhausted, Pan chose to ignore the animosity. "Believe me, if I thought anyone else was capable of bringing this girl, this child, back alive, I wouldn't be sitting across from you."

Another moment of silent chess followed between them; each studying the other's eyes to see who would reveal an opening. Eventually Lexa stopped tapping her fingers on the table and spoke. "Let me come back home and I'll consider it."

"You know I can't do that, Lexa."

The tone between the two suddenly switched from civil to war. Lexa seethed. "After every scar I've acquired while freelancing for your hopeless pursuit, you still won't let me back into that conceited dome? Arcadia is nothing more than a group of terrified elitists who get off on watching a desperate world burn behind the safety of their fancy wall."

"Please don't do this," Pan urged. "Not here. You know exactly why we must remain secluded. Even from you."

Lexa took another pull of pricey water while looking Pan dead in the eyes. "Even from me, huh?" She leaned in even closer to her ally-turned-adversary. "I've fought, scavenged, killed, and suffered for you and those assholes for far too long, and the only thanks I ever received was a boot out the door."

"Your habit of truancy could have destroyed the inviolable research we've been working on for the last half century. We simply could not house someone who decided they were no longer committed to our pursuit after one small mishap. Besides, the contaminants alone you risked bringing back night after night..." Pan suddenly realized she had been baited, cleared her throat, and pivoted the conversation. "I *know* you understand the importance of this—"

The empty glass slammed with a *thunk!* and Lexa stood up. She tossed two AA batteries on the table; doubling as gratuity *and* the signal that their time was at an end.

Desperate, Pan racked her brain. *How could Lexa ever appreciate what a mother is willing to go through for her child?*

"Wait!" she called out, grabbing Lexa's forearm. Lexa paused, then leaned back reluctantly onto the edge of the table. "If the young girl is in fact immune, and she arrives to us with breath in her lungs, then I will try to convince the council to allow your return."

With a heavy head, Lexa slunk back into the empty chair and extinguished her spiteful tongue with a long sigh. "This is a suicide mission. Everyone will be after her. Everyone. You know that, right?"

"Please," Pan continued to beg. She knew she had regained Lexa's attention, but the deal would never be sealed without the use of one final bargaining chip. The only prybar strong enough to open Lexa's locked heart. Reaching out across the table, Pan placed a forlorn hand on top of her adversary's. "For Rodan."

Lexa recoiled, leaned back to the safety of distance, and the two decidedly steeped in silence for an eternity. Eventually the music slowed, the lights flickered, and the familiar squeak of a tired crank filled the Oasis. It was not until the lyrics of the next song began aerating some tension when Lexa finally spoke again. "If I risk my life for this little brat, then you're going to have to do a lot better than *try*."

Entry 12

I'm so stupid! I've been using those goofy wall-toilets for weeks before I realized it was a bathroom for boys. Duh! So guess what? I went up to the next floor and immediately found one for girls. They even still flush!

Upstairs is crazy. It's like whoever built my floor (that's right, this is MY floor) got bored halfway through building the next one. It kind of looks the same as mine, but I can see all the big metal bones and there aren't many walls. It's basically just a bunch of desks and chairs and trash scattered everywhere. One time a plastic bag flew by me like a ghost and I freaked out!

I also only counted three big windows at the edge and the rest are missing. Gulp! But in the blank spots there are these little floors with railings that stick out past the walls. It's really scary feeling the wind this high up in the air, but I kind of liked it. Makes me feel tall.

Anyways, I can't wait to see what I find on my next bathroom break.

A month had passed since Juno had been condemned to her new refuge alone. Although she was ordered to stay put in her room, she could not help but take the longest routes to and from the bathroom upstairs. To her, staying out of sight always meant the same thing as long as no one saw her.

Over time Juno came to the conclusion that she was inside some form of workplace mainly because no house would ever require this many desks, chairs, and half-walls up to her nose. And since there had been no time for a tour when she arrived, she was left to assemble every piece of the building's puzzle on her own.

Juno had also inferred that this particular building was more important than the ones outside the windows because the tops of them could not be seen unless her nose was pressed to the glass. She enjoyed looking down on the dusty skyline and imagining what people did inside their individual offices. Were they working or playing? Did they write the books she had been able to read? Did they, too, walk up and down the stairs every day? Or was there a faster, easier way to scale a building this tall? Seventy-four floors; that was the number she had recalled running up a month ago. Her legs had never burned so much.

Despite the layers of mystery, Juno's confidence in her new hideaway was at an all-time high. It had not been long until her trips outside of the tiny room lasted anywhere from an hour to the better part of an afternoon. She used these opportunities to forage through the floors and learn about the people that once occupied them. Each mission, as she labeled them in her head, produced equal parts answers and questions.

Why would people want to work here? Juno asked herself as she sat down at a desk she had yet to sift through. There were still a surprising number of them left even after the weeks she had been at it. The first thing she liked to do when manning a station was open every drawer and inspect the contents. Like most, the top drawer of this one was disappointingly filled with dried up pens, yellow notepads with curled corners, and funny plastic clips. By this point she knew the good stuff was always stashed in the larger one below.

A framed photograph of a smiling family greeted Juno as she pulled out the bottom drawer. Though she had never seen the actual taking of a picture, the concept of how a digital camera captured them was explained within the pages of her old technology magazine. She delicately picked the frame up and wiped a streak of dust away with her thumb so she could see the once-happy faces. Looking back at her was a man, a woman, two daughters, and a cat; another animal she hoped to one day meet. Sadness unexpectedly began to burn her eyes, but was just as soon extinguished by a chuckle once she realized the family was all wearing the same ugly green and red sweater. Even the cat.

Juno carefully set the merry clan aside and reached further into the drawer. What she recovered looked to her to be another frame, only heavier and more reflective. There were three buttons on the edge of one side. She pressed one button that had a little red dot at its center, then nearly dropped the device as it played a startling four note chime. To her amazement, an image lit up in the shape of four equal sized squares that transformed to fill the entire surface with a breathtaking meadow of wild grasses, blossoming flowers, and flying butterflies. Juno gawked at the level of succulent color being presented to her. It was like staring through an imaginary window. Every green blade, every purple petal, and every orange wing transcended her to another time and place.

Juno's heart felt like it had emptied and refilled itself. She could have stared at the image of the field forever, wondering what it would be like to pluck a soft flower and breathe it in, but was disappointedly interrupted when a small black box appeared signaling the device was entering BAT-TERY SAVER MODE. The meadow faded to solid black and left strange little icons behind.

Her short time in the flourishing field may have been over, but, perhaps, Juno thought, she could discover something more about the building if she touched one of the icons with her finger. What opened was what looked to her like a piece of paper with the title GENESYS Q3 LIQUIDATION REPORT. Juno sighed. She had no idea why one would report how much liquid a company possessed and tapped on another icon with the word MEMO labeling it. Her eyes scanned the document and none of it made any sense. Some phrases popped out such as, The technology still needs testing, and, There just isn't enough time, but, in contrast, she had no idea what Bankrupt or Under Federal Investigation meant.

Then, just as she was about to click another icon, the words on the screen slowly faded into nothingness and could not be resurrected with any number of button pushes.

. . .

Entry 13

I had another boring day of searching desks but at least I found a new writing slash reading spot! Remember those missing windows on the floor above mine? Well it turns out it's not so dangerous if you stay on one of the sections with the railings. Sometimes I like to lay on my tummy and just stick my head through the bars. It's not the best during the day, though. Everything is so hot and dusty and I can't see very far around me. Some days I can't even see the street below.

Night time is usually the best since the world seems to calm down before bed. One thing I love is when my hair falls over the edge of the building. The way the warm breeze lifts it up and sets it back down is comforting. She used to do that when I couldn't sleep.

You know, all the boys in those silly romance books seem to like the long haired girls. Do you think they'd like mine too? Even if they didn't mine still makes me feel pretty. I don't know why, it just does.

Thirteen blocks away and seventy-four floors down from Genesys headquarters, two acolytes dragged an unconscious elder from a crumbling apartment complex in the darkest hour of night. An hour in which only shadows operated unseen; unchecked. A third acolyte dressed in a black duster that draped down to his black boots emerged slowly behind them. He sparked a match to light a crinkled cigarette and acclaimed with a puff of smoke, "At least this wretched soul offers *some* value to us."

The two in front dropped the old man like a diseased sandbag at the edge of the sidewalk and turned to face each other.

"Can you believe the boss has us goose chasin' in this fuckin' city again?"

Mildly annoyed, the other scoffed, "I don't think that's how the expression goes, Laity."

"Well fuck you, Deacon. And fuck this mission, too," Laity sneered, scratching a scab on the back of his neck. "We've been out here for weeks and still nothin' but—" Then, suddenly distracted, he turned to the third man in all black. "Toss me one of those cigs, eh Abbot?"

"Bishop," Abbot corrected before taking a long drag. The pale smoke he exhaled was taken swiftly by the night sky. "If I've rectified you once, I've rectified you a thousand times: He christened me Bishop. And since you are both members of my hand-selected clergy, Bishop is how you will address me."

Laity rolled his eyes. "Fine. Toss me one of those cigs, eh Bishop?"

Bishop paused as an assertion of newly-ordained power. It was an essential formality to prove not only to himself, but his clergy as well, that he controlled this situation and all that followed. Deacon and Laity both shuffled impatiently before eventually drooping their heads at the ground. Satisfied with their realized submittance, Bishop slid a cigarette from the carton and flicked it towards his brethren. The white cylinder landed between their feet.

"Christ," Laity sighed and begrudgingly leaned over to snatch his smoke. As his fingers pinched the soft white paper the crumpled old man abruptly sprang to life, grabbed Laity's hand like a viper, pulled it into his toothy mouth, and bit down. Hard. The shock of the attack threw Laity's balance off just enough for the old man to bring him to the ground under his own momentum.

"Fucker's got me!" Laity cried.

Deacon swiftly ran over to his partner's aid. "Hold still, I got ya!"

But the old man's clutch was a vice grip.

With Laity flailing on his side, and Deacon trying to pull him free, the old man clenched his remaining teeth with everything he had until his mouth cut loose from the hand. Deacon and Laity went tumbling backwards into the empty street; the former bumping his head on the blacktop and the latter wailing into the night sky.

Certain he was not yet free from danger, the old man spit the warm finger out at the two men who yanked him from his home and jumped up to face the third. But the final assailant had vanished. *Must've scared him off*, the old man considered foolheartedly, though the last drops of adrenaline coursing through his aged veins urged him to make an escape while opportunity was still in his favor. Listening to fortune, he turned to flee.

Unfortunately Bishop had not disappeared. Instead he was waiting patiently for the old man to run directly into a short, hooked knife. The sharp blade entered the skin as easily as the shirt in front. Hot blood slid along the silver edge. Woefully out of options, the old man exhaled a knowing breath.

"Now, now," Bishop grinned as the skewered man slowly leaned his dying weight into him. "Just where do you think you're off to?"

Bishop stepped backwards to let his casualty collapse to the ground. The old man felt warmth oozing between his fingers, but did not bother to check the source. It was only a matter of time.

Laity and Deacon had recovered from their fits and scuttled back to the scene mad with rage.

"He bit my fuckin' finger off!" Laity yelled. He raised a vengeful boot above the elder's head.

"Quell your tantrum," Bishop barked back. "This was no fault but your own. You were careless."

Laity backed away obediently while Deacon decided it best to keep his own mouth shut. After Bishop wiped off his dripping knife with a section of the old man's fretted shirt, he kneeled down next to him. There was a brief moment of cold silence on the sidewalk. The type of silence that was always followed by a storm.

Eventually Bishop took the final drag from his cigarette and extinguished it directly in the fresh stab wound. The elder howled in agony, then began to weep.

"Silence," Bishop demanded, grabbing the old man's neck. "This is your final moment to reveal the truth and redeem your pathetic soul. Now... Where. Is. The. Girl?"

Terror and confusion repleted the old man's final thoughts. He had always kept to himself, had never hurt anyone. Tears streamed from his innocent, grey eyes. All he could do was shake his head and mumble, "I t...t...told you. There ain't been n...n...no girls around here for decades!"

"Shame," said Bishop heavily. He knew the old man no longer had any reason to keep such a secret, that their search would continue for as long as required, but he also understood a leader's duty in keeping the morale of his men lifted. "Because if there were a girl, your final moments would have been significantly less painful." Then, after standing up to light another cigarette, he flicked his head and added, "Boys."

Deacon and Laity cracked their eager knuckles and moved in.

Time was growing stale with each day inside the office becoming more and more like the last. Nearly every desk had been rifled through with none offering any more pieces to the puzzle that was Juno's new life. Everything she collected was an uninteresting tool used for work. If she recovered one more pen or notepad or dead electronic she would have to scream. The only things stopping her from breaking down were the forbidden secrets still hiding behind the two rooms surrounded by glass walls.

Every day Juno would peer through one of the broken slats in the blinds and hope the offices would divulge at least one of their many mysteries. But because of the dust caked on both the outside and inside of the windows, details were impossible to clarify. So she jiggled the unmoving handle for the hundredth time, huffed at the door's inaccessibility, and left once again for her daily bathroom break.

When she came back down from the floor above, Juno suddenly

found a red box hanging between the two metal doors labeled ELEVA-TOR. The light of a rogue sunbeam must have been angled just so because she had never noticed the crimson container before. Yet today it caught her eye, and she strutted over to inspect it closely.

"In case of emergency," she read the bold words on the casing aloud, baffled at how she had not been drawn to them earlier. The box was made of strong metal that had a long door with a small window at its center. Like the first brush stroke on a fresh canvas, Juno wiped away a streak of dust with her fingers to reveal what was inside. Her grin widened as much as her eyes.

With a large axe now in hand, or hands, rather, because of its weight, Juno stormed over to the rebellious glass offices with spiteful purpose. The biggest room looked the fanciest so it would be the first to feel her wrath. Both scrawny arms raised the heavy weapon high above her head, then, without a second thought, drove the blade down onto the handle. It did not break. Instead it sent a deafening *clank!* echoing throughout the building. A moment of panic tightened all of her muscles like a drawstring as she waited ashamedly for the reverberations to subside. *How could you be so stupid*! she scolded herself, then bolted to the safety of her room.

An hour later she re-emerged still craving access to the glass office, now understanding she had to gain it quietly so as not to foolishly forfeit her location. But she had a plan. This time she wrapped one of the old jackets she had been sleeping on around the handle. Then she gave it another good wack with the axe.

Thunk!

To her delight, the muffled sound could no longer travel *and* the handle loosened a little.

Thunk! Thunk!

After around the seventh strike, the handle released its grip on the door and dropped to the carpet with a satisfying *clink*! She was in.

Juno wiped the sweat from her forehead, set the heavy axe on top of the nearest half-wall in case she would need it later, and entered the forbidden room.

Her first stop was a cart filled with colorful liquids. The cart was constructed of gold tubes supporting a large mirrored tray and the liquids were housed in etched crystal bottles without labels; all of which were covered in a thin veil of dust that hid their former glint. The entire presentation looked gaudy to Juno, like a display of misguided extravagance from a time of excess. She picked up one crystal decanter that left behind a perfect square of reflective mirror and removed the clear plug at the top. The burn of alcohol climbed into her nose and poked at her eyes. "That stuff is poison," she remembered being told, and set it back down where she found it.

Next she plopped down into a leather high-backed chair. A small cloud of dust escaped from under her rear that warranted an upbeat snort. Then, using foot propulsion, she wheeled over to a massive wooden desk.

"Cameron Friedrich," she read aloud from a crystal nameplate embossed with gold letters. "Wait, Freed-rich. Fried-rick? Whatever."

The name of the person who once occupied the desk did not carry much weight with Juno as she had seen more names than she could remember over the past weeks. What did matter to her were the interesting items this person might have kept to himself. She pulled open the top drawer and enjoyed how much smoother it slid on its track versus the desks in the greater area. *Cameron must have been important*, she thought with a curious smile.

Like all the others, the first drawer contained a yellow notepad, a few pens, and something similar to the electronic picture frame except with raised buttons of numbers and symbols. But there was also something that clattered inside; a small orangish bottle with a label wrapped around. "Fer-til-a-mol," Juno sounded out as she spun the small container with her fingers. "Please take one pill after injections twice a day to increase sperm count." Juno scrunched her face and threw the bottle back into the drawer as if it had spontaneously caught fire. Whatever was inside, she wanted nothing to do with it.

Then, like always, she found the real prize housed inside the larger drawer below. Elated, she lifted an emerald plastic bag of pure delight into the air and gazed at it like a long lost friend. `Wint O Green` in big white letters stared back at her, inviting her to tear into it and devour its contents.

Yes, the risk *was* worth the reward, she concluded, and retired for the night to enjoy her bounty.

Entry 21

Ugh!

It's been almost two months since she dumped me here and I'm almost out of food. When is someone coming for me? When will we be reunited? Why are these Life Savers individually wrapped in plastic? Seems so wasteful.

Anyways, I'm doing a little writing upstairs at my balcony spot before I get too sleepy and I just noticed that for the first time I can see mountains in the distance! The sun just dropped behind them and now they're this beautiful purply color! (My favorite, by the way.) The fog or dust or whatever is always in the air must have blown away for the night.

You know what? It'd be awesome to climb a mountain someday. I wonder what it would be like to look down on everything. Probably a lot like up here but with way less trash.

Well my eyes are getting heavy. Gotta rest up for another day of being all alone.

. . .

At the crest of the final mountain in her path, Lexa dropped her brimming backpack on the ground and leaned against a large rock, taking note of the unusually clear skyline this evening. She lowered the hood around her head and let out a sigh of exhaustion that created a pocket of steam in the barren atmosphere. At this elevation the air had a refreshing nip. And it would be her last night to enjoy it alone.

Lexa reached into her bag and pulled out a cylindrical canteen of water, an MRE, and a small, lightweight pot. She mixed just enough of the ingredients to get her through the night and neatly packed away the rest. As the food absorbed the moisture, she leaned back and admired the cooling eastern sky once again. Her destination was easy to pinpoint because it was the tallest building in the decaying city, jutting out like a gold-capped fang in a jaw stuffed with too many cracked teeth.

"Genesys," she read the enormous metal placard aloud with a smirk. "How ironic."

When the food was ready she spooned the paste into her mouth with grim disinterest. Flavor was hard to come by these days. The one thing that could make the prepackaged meal slightly more tolerable was heat, but she would not chance lighting a fire to cook it.

Not out here.

A large plume of dust sent Juno's lungs into a fit after diving onto a stagnant sofa. The extra long couch had collected enough dust over the years to fill an entire floor. Ten floors below her own, to be exact.

Juno's confidence in her absolute seclusion grew by the day. Since she had dissected every nook and cranny of the top two floors weeks ago, she decided to head the opposite direction after each morning's bathroom visit. Down. And immediately she found the layout of this one much more interesting than all the others. Half-walled-in desks were replaced with ornate couches and small tables. On top of tall benches surrounded by stools rested styrofoam cups and stagnant cords hanging from attached outlets. An assortment of miniature fridges were scattered strategically throughout the ample space, all empty, unfortunately. Lifeless screens lined two of the walls. And, at the center of everything, sat a massive desk in the shape of a ring cut in half. Behind the crescent desk was a large stone wall garnished with fake rocks and plastic plants that gave the impression that water once flowed over them.

At least they're green, Juno thought.

A metallic sign at the forefront of the dusty stone slab caught her attention. `Genesys: Teeming With Life` glistened in once-lustrous gold letters. Down at the desk was a slightly smaller sign reading `Reception`. Juno studied the hazy reflection on the letters and imagined for a moment who might have been receiving her.

A table to her left held a pile of untouched magazines carefully fanned out like a deck of cards. The peculiar alignment swept Juno away until she was suddenly in a candlelit cellar soaked with rare laughter. A queen of hearts hit the table, then the three of clubs, then the nine of spades, and then... "Slapjack!" Two hands slapped each other on the way to cover the jack, sending cards and much needed bliss into the cramped atmosphere.

Juno wiped an unexpected tear across the grime on her cheek and lifted up a magazine that somewhat resembled the royalty of playing cards. On the cover was a close-up of a man's bust bordered by a thick red rectangle housing the word `TIME` emboldened at the top. At first glance the man looked rather ordinary—slick black hair, a crocodile grin, steadfast eyes; generically handsome in his own right—and that he was just the unfortunate victim of an old, rotting page. But after closer inspection something started burrowing into the pit of Juno's stomach. One clear and one bloodshot eye stared directly at her, begging her to look away, but the request was futile. Hers were already glued.

Craggy veins slithered between pockets of pink sores dispersed all across the man's once-smooth face. Deep, welted lines had been clawed into his neck by irritated fingernails. And, in a failed attempt at concealment, the blackened char of dried scabbing protruded just above his shirt collar. Below were six chilling words: `How Cameron Friedrich` `doomed us all.`

Juno gagged inside her own mouth and flipped to a random page immediately. *Why would they put something so horrible on the cover?*

She spent a minute erasing the image from her mind before reopening her eyes. Luckily, the new page she landed on was the exact opposite of the horror she had just witnessed. A bright, almost luminous kitchen of all-white and stainless steel welcomed a three-piece family flashing equally shimmering smiles. A middle-aged woman was happily placing a plate in front of a young girl while a man stood behind with his hands on her shoulders, giving a generous wink of approval. On the flawless plate, which Juno noticed as the only dish on the table, was a serving of fresh and vibrant food. "The secret to feeding your family with less," she read the caption aloud, genuinely enthralled by this picture-perfect family.

Through the puff piece Juno paged and mentally swapped places with the inanimate daughter. This was what a real family was supposed to look like: a spotless home, fresh-cooked meals, bright conversation, unending...

Juno bit her lower lip searching for another word that appropriately described her feelings. *Support.* A family showed unending support. They always showed up, always came through. They did *not* abandon you at the top of a skyscraper.

Tears blurred the staged actors inside the kitchen. Juno shot up from the couch and threw the magazine of lies as hard as she could, except the friction of the air grabbed the pages and dropped it straight to the floor, infuriating her even more. She was on the brink of doing the one thing she was absolutely not allowed to do: scream at the top of her lungs. Instead she snatched the source of her projected anger from the floor and tore it into as many pieces as her small hands could grip onto. Then, with a final fling of her arms, she tossed the scraps into the air and let the relief rain down like confetti.

Juno was already feeling better about herself when she heard a loud clang in the distance and ran for her life.

. . .

Entry 24

Something hilarious happened this morning! I was reading this magazine like ten floors down when I heard a loud noise coming from somewhere else. I very calmly walked back up the stairs to scope out the situation.

I was NOT scared.

Yep, I knew right away the metal box that I found the axe in had fallen off the wall. It must've gotten too old and couldn't hold on any longer. Once that was solved, I went back to my room to lay low for the day.

I repeat, I was NOT scared.

By the way, where did I put that axe?

Juno closed her notebook and set it down. She felt distracted. Something in the air was different tonight. Or, rather, a lack of something in the air. It was the final eve of her second month of internment and the film had graciously vacated the atmosphere, allowing a number of twinkling dots to attend the unwanted milestone.

She rolled onto her back to try and make the best of another lonely night. The balcony's cement cooled her skin through her shirt as she began stabbing at stars in the sky.

"...10...11...12...13..." she counted with her index finger.

Juno sighed. *Thirteen.* That was how old she would be in the morning. It was only two months ago that it was two months away. Now it was finally here and no one was around to notice. No one was around to care. She knew she would be alone when she woke up and she knew her desk would not display its annual gift. On her balcony of solitude she could not help but reflect on past birthdays. Lighting scented candles, eating all the expired candy she could stomach, playing card games, cracking open a fresh notebook, spending an entire day with...

Juno furrowed her brow and let out a huff of air. *No one is coming for me. I should just accept it.* She told herself to wake up. That this was only the first of many birthdays that would be spent alone. That, because of her dwindling food and water supply, she might not even survive to see the next one. But, frustrating as it was, she also told herself that there was nothing she could do about it right now, and slowly let it go.

Eventually Juno reached in and slipped the final Life Saver from her pocket. After pulling the minty-white candy from its clear plastic wrapper by pinching it with her teeth, she returned her attention to the stars. She marveled at the sheer number of them. How many of them shined on Earths like hers? Earth like it was in the old books; full of vivid color and ambitious life. And how many girls on their own Earths were looking up at the same stars as Juno and wondering if someone...anyone...else could be out there, too? Someone they could trust, could talk to, could laugh with. Just so none of them would have to do it all alone. Even someone who would cough—

"Huh?"

Juno shot up like a lightning bolt. The distant hacking came from outside the building, not inside. She flipped to her stomach and crawled until her head poked out between the balusters of the balcony's railing. Her long hair fell over her face as she leaned, forcing her to pull the strands back with one hand like a curtain, then her eyes darted frantically across rooftops, then windows, and then down the road...

There! On a corner just up the street a strange silhouette dashed between the shadows like a slippery specter.

Juno ducked lower and watched the unusual behavior of the featureless being. It moved so gracefully, without fear, but also kept to the darkest path, clearly not wanting to be noticed. And once the figure was directly in front of her building it paused for a while before hurling a glass bottle into the middle of the street. The shatter echoed, pulling an involuntary gasp from Juno's mouth.

The figure's posture angled up towards the balcony.

Juno instantly pulled her head back through the balusters, snagging her soft ears on the hard metal. It hurt, but the pain would have to wait while she sat gasping for silent air through fingers clamped around her mouth. She counted thirteen breaths, calmed, then gently returned to her hands and knees. Back at the edge, Juno carefully stretched her neck outward from her body like one of the tortoises in her field guide.

The street was empty.

Minutes went by until Juno gained enough courage to stretch out farther. Her entire head was now bravely exposed in the unusually clear night sky. Then, while scouring the sidewalk, a strong gust of wind pulled her hair, diverting her attention westward. No longer were the twinkling stars visible above the mountains on the horizon. Her brief moments of serenity were, like always, interrupted by the fear that always followed. But at least someone *might* have been there for her birthday, she thought, even if they vanished, leaving only a ring of shattered glass as a gift.

It was not shattering glass that startled Juno awake the following morning, but a twisted echo from somewhere inside the building. She shot up, got dressed, and cracked the door of her room. The sun had just wrapped its rosy arms around the skyscraper so little could be seen. It took time for her heart to slow, but, once it did, she slunk across the office floor to investigate the stairwell.

On the other side of the double steel doors Juno leaned and tilted her head over the railing. A clatter came from far below; ten or so floors down by her guess. *Good*, she thought, for now, and remained out of sight.

Juno's next thought was perhaps this was the person from last night, or, even better, the one who had been sent to find her. And on her birthday of all days! The brief flash of easement allowed her mind to fantasize. Suddenly she was lying on a mattress back home. Not a pile of coats and awkward chair cushions, but a *real* mattress. A half-melted candle fluttered warm shadows against a windowless wall. At the far end of her bedroom someone climbed down a ladder. Someone comforting. Someone who would protect her. The silhouette approached the side of the bed and slipped its arms underneath her, careful not to disturb. But Juno was already awake. Waiting with closed eyes...

Tightly, Juno gripped the metal railing and flung her head over the edge, ready to scream, "I'm up here!" when a door eleven floors below blasted open, and from behind bellowed a deep voice. She recognized it not as the upbeat tempo she would prefer from a would-be savior, but a trepidatious grumble that came from illness.

"They're sick," Juno whispered. She remembered hearing voices like this from beneath the floorboards. Occasionally a wanderer would enter their home uninvited, forcing her to sit in utter stasis as hard soles crossed the hatch above, and hope the haggard rug hiding it would be enough. The worst were the muffled struggles that always followed. All the yelling, the stumbling footsteps, the abrupt silence... then waiting days for the hatch to reopen, wondering if she would ever be seen again.

"Why can't I ever see the people that visit?" Juno asked one time when the tension had been stretched to the seams. All she got was, "Because they're sick, sweetie."

Half a torso appeared in the aperture of the stairwell. Startled, Juno gasped the tiniest puff of air that somehow gained enough strength to travel eleven floors below and into the figure's ears. All at once the tattered stranger rushed into the opening and looked upwards. Juno, having only seen the top of a hairless head, reeled her own back quickly enough not to be seen. Her shoulders slammed into the hard cement wall behind.

Making herself as skinny as possible, Juno held in her panicked breaths with one hand while the other shook like a rattle. She listened silently for the imminent approach of the stranger. Below, each foot slapped the next stair louder than the last. *Seven...eight...nine...* She counted the steps like a clock ticking down to her fate. Only the feet paused on the tenth. To her relief, a new door flung open and the steps faded through it.

They didn't hear me!

Juno used the stroke of luck to sprint back to her room so she could begin concocting a plan of escape. *This person must be searching the floors for something else*, she convinced herself, lapping the confined space over and over as she considered her options. She could lock the door, stay silent, and hope her handle would be miraculously passed over. Or she could wait for them to enter another floor and make a seventy-four floor dash to freedom. But where would she go? She did not know the city and, other than the mountains, had no idea in which direction anything might be. Frustratingly, she came no closer to an answer on the tenth lap than the first.

How am I gonna get out of this? Think, Juno!

A distant crash accompanied by more grumbling piqued Juno's ears. Her instincts darted her to the door. *Whew, still locked!* Though, oddly, the clamor was coming in even clearer than before. She froze in place and listened. *There!* Underneath the desk was a rectangular hole in the wall shrouded by a grate. Dropping down on all fours, she crawled over and pressed her cheek against the metallic lattice.

"I think I seen someone," a graveled voice echoed.

"Where?" a second voice asked.

There's two of them!

"Out there. Top of the stairs. Could be our missin' girl!"

"You're outta your mind, Laity. If she was real we'd've found her by now."

"Shut yer ugly mouth, Deacon. I know what I—Goddammit my fuckin' hand! What'd you do that for? You *know* my finger just got bit off!"

Something crashed to the floor and the one called Deacon laughed a sinister laugh. Juno held her breath even more tightly.

"Are you two quite finished?"

There's three!

"Fellas, I swear I seen her! Second to last floor."

"We've been in the city over a month and ain't seen nothin' but an old man," Deacon asserted. "Besides, you said it yourself the other night. Somethin' about a goose chase? Just look for booze and cigs so we can get the hell outta here."

"Seriously!" Laity defended. "Think I saw long hair, too. Could be a perdy one."

Juno covered her mouth. If she willed it hard enough, maybe they would not believe him.

The unnamed third voice chimed back in. "If He calls upon us to pursue a girl, we pursue a girl; for the one who seeks, always finds."

The cryptic manner in which that one spoke sent a new kind of fear bubbling underneath Juno's skin. She started to tremble.

After a short pause down below, the crassest one, Laity, spoke again. "Hey Deacon. What'll ya give me if I'm right?"

"Nothin'. Cause you ain't seen nothin'. Now quit wastin' ti—."

"I *know* I seen 'er, Bishop," Laity pleaded. "Just lemme go check. And if I'm right, I got dibs on gettin' the first go."

An insidious chuckle followed. Juno could almost hear saliva dripping from disgusting lips while an even longer block of silence wedged its way between the three interlopers and herself. Finally the third, whom Juno had just heard dubbed Bishop, spoke again.

"So be it," he sighed. "We will consider the ring of glass a sign of good fortune. Carry out your investigation. We shall wait here." Laity quickly jeered something towards Deacon before Bishop finished his instructions. "...Keep in mind our directive is to deliver the girl alive and unscathed. I would not like to imagine His wrath if we presented her otherwise."

The seconds between "otherwise" and the door blasting open into the stairwell could have been counted on one hand. It slammed into the concrete chamber with such a startling *bang!* that Juno's head clunked against the underbelly of the desk. "What was that?" she might have heard, but all sound was lost to the welt throbbing itself into existence.

While rubbing the bump Juno begged the tiny room for answers to her situation. How much time did she have? Where else could she hide? How thorough would these three men be? What did Laity mean by *gettin' the first go*? The simple truth was there were too many unknowns to answer before a visitor would be knocking on her door.

With one part bravery, and two parts desperation, Juno snatched the tactical knife from the top of her desk and unfolded it for the first time in her life. A hysterical heart pumped sweat from every single one of her pores. Her body was both overheating and freezing at the same time. Then, to add to the disillusionment, the door Laity had burst through automatically closed, sealing away all sound from the stairwell. Time was only a guess now. All she could do was try to ready herself with a weapon she had never used before.

Prying open the double steel doors had not seemed so difficult after the seventy-four story climb up a decrepit elevator shaft.

Lexa had slipped into Genesys headquarters just before the final stars blinked away and spent the early hours invisibly scaling its floors. It had also not been long before she picked up the foul scent of three acolytes stumbling across the same path. Her lure had worked. And although she and the men both had their compasses aimed in the same direction, it appeared the acolytes had little to no specifics about *where* exactly they were looking or *who* exactly they were looking for.

Each floor the three men blindly turned inside out only solidified the foundation of Lexa's intuition. So, during spells of fruitless ransacking, she would confidently ascend the powerless shaft of Genesys, only resting when the men took to the stairwells. Now at the top, the only thing left to do was wait for an opportunity to present itself.

Once she was sure the elevator doors would stay open on their own, Lexa silently slid into the office to survey the layout. A window-lined wall glazed countless cubicles with the warm outlines of late morning. Golden dust hung quietly in the air. At the opposite end of the office were two ostentatious glass enclosures designed to simulate importance, and around the final edge was a wall housing many closed doors. To her immediate right, before the door-lined wall began, was the entrance to the stairwell.

"No doubt *they'll* come from there," she whispered, moving softly onto the faded carpet. "Now where is *she* hiding?"

Always study your environment, an unwelcomed voice suddenly echoed while she shuffled between the individually walled-off desks. Lexa shook the condescending comment away like an old cobweb, then continued on.

Soon she spotted a peculiar object resting on top of a cubicle wall near the glass offices. It was an axe. She approached the weapon, but before picking it up her foot tapped a busted metal knob lying on the ground. "Must be getting warmer." When she lifted a piece of the handle to inspect, nervous shuffles came from behind a nearby door.

"Bingo."

But that was not the only noise inside the building. Down below, the faint ramblings of irritated acolytes could now be heard. They were getting closer as well. Lexa quickly slunk over to a vent in the wall and pressed her ear against it.

"—to deliver the girl alive and unscathed. I would not like to imagine His wrath if we presented her otherwise."

Shortly after, a door in the stairwell crashed open. Lexa lunged for the axe, then froze. Clearly something so enticing would be much more valuable as a distraction than as a weapon. Her years of training had taught her such a large, slow, inaccurate device would put her opponent at a disadvantage nine times out of ten. Confident in her decision, she ducked behind an adjacent cubicle to wait for her unsuspecting prey.

The acolyte's slow, breathy advancement up the stairs gave Lexa a few moments to review the plan she had hatched up the previous night. When the unusually clear evening sky had brought her attention upwards, the one thing she had been resenting since stepping foot outside the Oasis was staring right at her. There, on the second-to-last floor of Genesys headquarters, a young girl's hair billowed in the breeze. She was as real as the name on the blood-stained note. And that was when it clicked. There was no foreseeable outcome where Lexa could successfully smuggle a young, fertile female across hundreds of miles of populated and perilous terrain. *But a male...*

With that solved, one more issue still loomed over her shoulders: getting a head start on the acolytes. They would surely be keen towards anything that moved. Who knew an empty glass bottle lying in the street would offer the answer to part two? If she could lure those madmen into the Genesys building with a loud noise, shadow them to the top floor, then make an escape before they knew which way was up, she could feasibly disappear into the city unnoticed. Figuring it was as good a strategy as any, she gripped the bottle tightly in her hand and strolled down the street.

But just before she made her position known, Lexa took one last glance up at the balcony. For a brief moment she tried to put herself in the girl's shoes. How terrified she must be. Confused. Alone. But the breeze of sympathy was swiftly stifled by a deep indignation in the pit of her heart.

"This better be worth it," Lexa said. Then she took a deep breath and tossed the empty bottle into the air.

Before long the stairway doors that led to the seventy-fourth floor flung open. Instantly Juno could hear the clunking footsteps outside, but could not discern in which direction they were headed. She nervously shifted her weight back and forth while attempting to study the knife's handle with her palm. All she could gather was that the gridlike impression from the metal was starting to dig into her soft skin.

Glass shattered and Juno's whole body flinched. One of the two offices was certainly now in shambles. Then there was a relentless pause. Silence equalled uncertainty and, to Juno, uncertainty was the most terrifying feeling of all. But the footsteps started up again. They marched around in a menacing pattern, always followed by aggressive jiggling of handles. The intruder was only a few doors away.

Another office burst open and the feet disappeared inside. There was a long pause, then, "What's this? Gah! Damned bucket'a piss!" The container toppled and liquid splashed out. "Little bitch better be close…"

One by one Juno listened to the rest of the doors open and slam shut until the only one left was the one she stood behind. This was confirmed by two sudden foot-sized breaks in the strip of light at the door's base, reaching inward like malefic arms. The handle clicked without budging. Juno swallowed a lump of what felt like a hundred Life Savers at once, except mint was not today's flavor. Then the handle clicked harder, the lock still holding firm. Stinging sweat dripped into teary eyes. Yet another violent shake of the handle turned her breaths into panting.

"Come out little girl. I know yer in there!" the one called Laity snarled.

She was seconds away from screaming when a sharp *thunk!* jolted her stiff. *What was that?* she wondered.

Another *thunk!* came. Then another, and another, and another, until a splinter of wood dislodged itself at the center of her door, revealing a silver edge.

The axe!

Juno was vehemently reminded of where she had left it. That she had just hand-delivered a weapon used for breaking barriers. *How could I be so stupid?* But shame was not enough to slow the blade. Swing after swing the shiny end of the axe became more visible through the fracturing wood. Juno willed every last ounce of energy trying to focus on the knife in hand. She would have to act fast. Only one more swing and the axe would be through.

But the silver edge never returned.

"Who the fuck're you?" spat the man. His voice sounded startled before he yelped.

Juno rushed to the newly-splintered peephole to try and get an eye on the sudden turmoil, but the sun was shining directly through the office windows now, blinding her view. All she could make out were two shadows circling each other.

"I can't wait to kiss your neck with this blade!" Laity boasted.

Juno's eyes slowly adjusted to the bright light and she could now make out silhouettes of the two strangers. One was short and malformed like a hastily-drawn sketch. The other was taller, slender, and shockingly graceful; starkly reminiscent of the shadow she saw on the street last night.

Laity took one swing with the axe and the new stranger danced effortlessly around it. Then he heaved it around once more, missing by a body's length. On the third pass the stranger slipped underneath the lumbered swing, grabbed Laity by the throat, and slammed him backwards onto the floor. As they both fell out of sight, Juno could only listen to what followed.

"He'll...never...stop..." Laity seemed to warn, gasping between each word. Then there was a metallic slide as the dropped weapon was lifted off the ground. A fleshy *thwack!* came next, silencing the belligerent, heaving man for good. Finally, after all was still, the sound of twisted meat and cracked bone ushered the removal of cold steel from warm body.

Now most afraid of the mysterious fourth intruder, Juno stepped away from the door, fighting the urge to vomit.

Thunk!

The incoming light through the door's gash suddenly turned to darkness.

Thunk!

Her fate was at the end of a wooden handle.

Thunk!

She had no idea what to do with the blade slipping in her sweaty palm.

Thunk!

...

A breath-long calm came and went before the door split open as if it were prepped with explosives. Then, in a blind, adrenaline-fueled spasm, Juno charged knife-first.

"Ahhh!"

Instantly her wrist was snatched out of the air, her body was twirled, and she was plunged backwards into the smattering of seat cushions and old coats by a massive boot.

Juno spent a few breathless moments gasping for air and staring up at the ceiling. She could not breathe. She could not fight. Maybe, she considered, this was always how it was supposed to end for her: abandoned at the top of a skyscraper where she could no longer be a burden.

When the air started pulling back into her lungs, Juno's head fell over towards the intruder that so leisurely knocked the wind from her. After squeezing the vision-blurring tears from her eyes, what, or rather who, Juno witnessed jerked her limp body upright with both excitement and dread. *A woman?*

Time halted as she absorbed the mysterious figure from top to bottom. The stranger had extremely short hair that barely concealed a hatchwork of scrapes in her scalp. Dark, austere eyes that scanned the room quickly split a long scar that ran from the top of her forehead to the middle of her right cheek. Her skin was a dusky mixture of grime and pigment that naturally absorbed the intense sun attractively. But what was most striking was her stature. This woman was not only over a head taller than herself, but had a muscular, femanine curvature to her body that Juno could only dream about. She was, in a word, stunning.

"Juno?" the woman more told than asked.

Still catching up to her breath, the dazed girl nodded complacently.

"We need to leave. Grab only the essentials."

The woman slung the large axe onto her shoulder with ease while Juno remained frozen. She was still studying every inch of the dangerous and captivating stranger. Her outfit looked as if it were meticulously pieced together over many years with every garment serving a specific purpose. She had rugged brown boots, dark pants with a light shirt that looked worn yet durable, and a hooded duster that hung past her powerful waist. Strapped around her bust was a sturdy leather harness that sheathed the scariest looking knife Juno had ever seen. Completing the outfit was a rugged backpack filled with who-knows-what hooked around her shoulders. Juno had not realized how her studious gaze kept moving upwards until her eyes met the woman's.

"Now!"

Juno shook away her trance and ran over to the desk. She propped open her own empty backpack, then leaned over to scoop up her pile of books.

"Leave them."

She froze mid-lean and hovered back to the top of the desk. First she dumped what was left of her food supply in the bottom, then a few articles of tattered clothing, and finally reached for the cluster of plastic water bottles.

"Leave those, too."

Juno paused. This was all she had. Without her books and essential water supply she was down to little more than the clothes on her back and a few extremely expired granola bars. She wanted to cry. But before she could zip up her depressingly empty bag, voices returned from the vent below the desk.

"What the hell's takin' Laity so long?" one asked.

"I sense something has intercepted him," the other replied. "Or perhaps someone."

"He better not be fuc—"

The men's words were cut off by the closing door of the stairwell. Juno turned and the woman had gone. Frantically, she grabbed her backpack and darted for the doorway. There she saw the woman at the edge of the room shoving the axe grip-first through the steel handles of the stairwell door.

"Let's go!" the woman commanded.

Juno took one step forward before nearly forgetting the most important thing in the world to her. The final relic of her previous life. Her one personal expression of freedom. She rushed back into the room she had reluctantly called home for months to secure it. Notebook now safely in hand, she delicately slipped it into the designated pocket of her backpack and zipped it up.

When Juno exited for the second time, the imposing woman had already cleared the entire distance of the room. She clamped Juno's shoulders and lifted her off the ground.

"Do you think this is some sort of game?"

Juno twitched her head left and right.

"Do you know what those men will do if they find you?"

Juno shook her head again.

"Then quit fuckin' around and do as I say!"

The woman dropped Juno and started back towards the door she had just barred. Heart now pumping out even more angst, Juno followed until she saw something so terrifying she had to rub her eyes to accept its existence. The man that had infiltrated her floor to get the first go was now lying on his back with an open axe wound splitting his sternum. But that was not the detail that disturbed her. Nor was the fact that one of his arms was oddly shorter than the other. What really crawled under her skin was the myriad of scabs and sores littered across his exposed flesh. How was this possible? What had he done to deserve such a thrashing? Just as with the Time magazine cover, Juno forced the new nightmare from her mind and scurried over to the demanding woman.

"Hold this," she commanded, handing her backpack over with one arm.

Juno took the bag with both hands and nearly fell to the ground under its heft. When she mustered the strength to lift it back up she nervously asked, "W...What are you doing?"

The woman did not respond. Instead she hopped into the empty elevator shaft and grabbed hold of a thick cable with both arms. Then she wrapped her legs firmly around the cable and slackened her grip. After carefully studying the layout of the shaft for a moment, she said, "Come here."

Juno inched up to the edge of the shaft and, afraid to look down, closed her eyes.

"Here's what we're going to do," the woman instructed. "You see that elevator about ten floors down?" Juno opened one eye and nodded. "You're going to hand me my bag. Then you're going to grab onto me and we're going to slide dow—"

The instructions were violently interrupted by a burst of chaos coming from the stairwell. Juno spun to her left and saw the doors swing open as far as the wooden axe handle would allow. There was now enough of a gap for two arms squeeze through. Like unruly tentacles, they felt around for the obstruction, attempting to remove it. Fortunately the pressure from the doors being pushed against the axe bought valuable seconds, though arms were soon replaced with glimpses of weathered faces with fiendish eyes fixed directly on her.

"Well I'll be damned. Laity was right!"

"Juno, focus," the woman urged, unseen by the men. "You need to—"

"Step away from the shaft, little girl. We're here to save you!"

"Ignore them. Jump to me."

"Don't do anythin' foolish now!"

Juno stood petrified. Every word coming into her ears added a hundred pounds to her body. The demands swirled around like a tornado of fear, devouring her uncertainty as fuel. Who were all of these people? How could she know these men were not the ones sent to rescue her? How could she trust the woman that had already killed one?

The doors retracted and slammed open again like thunder inside the fear-fueled storm.

Boom! Boom! Boom! Crack!

The axe's handle was starting to splinter.

Juno crouched down and hugged her knees. All of the banging... all of the yelling...all she wanted to do was go home. She closed her eyes and sobbed.

Suddenly the axe split in two and the doors burst open. The two madmen bolted in, but a powerful arm yanked Juno into the elevator shaft before they could grab her. The next thing she knew she was gripping the woman's waist with all the strength left in her body as they slid down into the darkness.

"Well I'll be damned!" a voice from ten floors above taunted. Juno looked upwards and saw the two men standing on the edge. Something was anomalous about them. "There'll be no distance you can run after He finds out *you're* involved!"

"Wh...who are they talking about?" Juno mustered up the courage to ask.

"Ignore them," the woman asserted, prying Juno from her waist, then guiding her small hands to the thick cable attached to the elevator. She kneeled down and met the young girl's eyes with her own. "Look at me. Hold onto this as tightly as you can. Do not let go. No matter what."

No matter what? Juno had been told that before. The last time she saw—

"Understood?"

She gave a frightful nod and tightened her grip. The woman removed the massive knife from the holster on her chest and began loosening a large steel pin with it. The blade looked tantalizing now that its angled shape gleamed out in the open.

"Stop this nonsense now and we may avoid reporting your involvement," the other man's voice echoed. Bishop. Juno felt her skin crawl again at the way he spoke. "Unless you would prefer another scar to match the first, hm?"

The insults enticed Juno's attention back upwards but a hand intercepted her chin and diverted her gaze. The woman was standing now, even more intimidating this close in proximity, and staring directly into the girl's eyes once again. "Are you holding on?"

Juno wiped a tear from her delicate cheek, grabbed back onto the cable, and nodded.

"Then here we go."

With a swift kick of her boot the woman fully dislodged the large pin, sending themselves and the elevator into free fall.

. . .

They had been walking all day.

As the sun moved their shadows from west to east, not a word was exchanged between the woman and the young girl. The woman kept up a tireless pace to create as much distance between themselves and the Genesys building as possible. Juno struggled to keep up, panting and sweating the entire time. She had forgotten just how hot the world outside could get.

From the ground, Juno could now see the severe condition of the dead city as they zigzagged between crumbling skyscrapers. The midday sun spotlighted the webs of cracks crawling up concrete faces like elderly veins. Countless sandstorms had beaten the bricks from buildings and tossed them through innocent glass panes. Stagnant trash piled up in mounds behind pillars and inside alleys and underneath walkways. It was as if the residents completely disappeared and left behind everything they had ever made.

The woman crossed a wide, empty street before hugging tightly against a decayed light rail train. Juno followed blindly like a lost ship to a star. Once up close, the young girl could see the vengeance time had exacted on the vehicle. As if in a fit of rage, it had chewed through much of the vibrant red paint and punched out every window, leaving them gaped like toothy mouths.

While Juno tried not to cut herself on something sharp, one of the train cars lurched, startling her. The woman had effortlessly climbed up on top and was pulling something out of her bag. Then she held the unusual device up to her eyes, quickly scanned the area, and hopped back down. "This way," she said, rushing towards a barren cross street.

I really don't think I can keep this up, Juno sighed as her lungs continued to ask for more air.

Later in the afternoon, as corporate buildings shrank and single homes grew by the hundreds, Juno realized she had not walked this far since arriving in the city. But for some reason that final night only came back to her in fragments. She recalled fleeing in the evening, just as the sun passed the horizon, the seventy-four floor climb of agony as the moon came out, then suddenly finding herself alone before the sun rose again. The splitting fatigue she suffered that night felt like nails underneath her feet, fire inside her legs, but was quickly extinguished by heartbreak. Now, as the prickling flame slowly spread again, the pain fell inches from unbearable. She had to break the silence. Juno halted and said, "My feet hurt!"

The woman neglected to turn around. "Keep moving."

Reluctantly, Juno continued to follow for another hour, cursing silently the entire time. Already the sun was melting over the peaks in the distance and the woman showed no signs of slowing to address Juno's feet or, as she just now realized, her thirst. She had not had a single drop of water since the night before. And to make matters worse she was forced to leave her only bottles behind.

Juno was licking the dryness from her chapped lips when they happened upon a rickety wooden sign that she felt the need to read aloud. "Crown Hill Lake. Is there water there?"

"A long time ago," the woman passively replied. Then she abruptly turned off the street and up an unsuspecting alley. Juno, now even more confused, had to run up behind her just to keep up. They turned right down a smaller alley and then took a sharp left into a moldering, fenced-in backyard. Behind the fence was a large yellow house with boards hammered across every window. Remnants of grey vines still clung to the siding like ghostly tendrils. They swiftly crossed the yard. But before entering the house, the woman stopped them both on the back porch to carefully examine their tail. "We're staying here for the night," she finally said.

Once inside, the woman instructed Juno to stay put by the door while she checked inside every room. Only when she returned did she allow the young girl to come further into the house. The entryway led directly into the kitchen. Juno set her bag down on a table, then admired the old decorations. A cabinet filled with flower-patterned plates, a wooden bowl containing weaved orbs, identical lidded jars that descended in size, all frosted with settled dust. When she started towards an adjacent living room, a hand stopped her and groped her chest.

"Lift your shirt up," the woman said.

Hot blood rushed to Juno's face, boiling beneath the skin. She crossed her arms tightly against her breast and asked, "Why?"

"I'm not going to ask again."

When Juno chose not to comply, the woman impatiently separated her crossed arms and tugged the shirt up over her head. She inspected the exposed torso for what felt to Juno like an eternity, then pulled the shirt back down to reveal brick-red cheeks. "They are starting to show. How old are you?"

In the chaos Juno had completely forgotten what day it was. What it meant to her. But instead of feeling excited to be one year older, she felt ashamed to be alive. "Th...Thirteen. Today."

The pause for consideration was nonexistent. The woman dropped her own bag on the table next to Juno's and unzipped it. What she pulled out was a small black garment with two straps and a hooded duster jacket similar to her own. "You'll need to hide them from now on. Here, wear these."

The items were tossed at Juno and she caught them with clumsy arms. Holding them up she understood the jacket, but was confused about the strapped thing. "How do I wear this?"

Slightly irked, the woman replied, "It used to be called a sports bra. It's tight around your chest and you wear it under your shirt." Then, unexpectedly, she slid a chair out from under the table and spun it around with one hand. "Come here and sit down."

Still embarrassed from a moment ago, Juno hesitated. "Why?"

The woman's patience was wearing as thin as the yellow paint on the house. She stormed over, grabbed Juno's arm, and pulled her onto the chair. "Sit."

In the small amount of evening light that squeezed between the boarded windows, Juno watched the shadow of the woman behind her on the wall. The dark silhouette ran its fingers through her long hair. The momentary tingle took Juno's mind off the horrors of the day and she trustfully closed her eyes. She was a little girl again, her hair being braided between delicate fingers while a candle emitted the soft scent of wild flowers. The memory soothed the pain in her body like a warm bath. Maybe today would not be a total loss.

Juno allowed a smile as the bulk of her hair was pulled tightly into a ponytail. She felt one hand grip the bundle of dark strands while the other left her scalp. Then came the subtle scrape of metal against leather, a sharp sound that sent a shiver down her spine like an ice cube. What followed was another familiar noise. It reminded her of tearing paper...

Juno's eyes shot open to reveal an image against the wall that sunk her heart into her stomach. The wicked shadow was holding an angled knife in one hand, and a dangling clump of long hair in the other.

"What did you do!" Juno screamed. She catapulted from the chair and clutched what remained on her head.

"Relax," the woman spoke directly. "It'll grow back."

Juno's face swelled. "How could you!"

"You need to remain quiet."

"I don't even know you!" she cried. "You were supposed to come rescue me, not ruin my life!"

Surprising herself, the woman was taken aback. For the first time that day she considered her brashness and decided to kneel next to the chair in an attempt to look less intimidating. "Look. Those men from this morning...those aren't the only ones out there. If any one of them sees you, your chest, or your long hair, then you'll wish I had used that knife on your throat instead."

"B...but," Juno sniffled, "how do you know that?"

The woman turned her head slightly to think. The cooling twilight caught the edge of her scar. Juno traced the long blemish with her eyes and wondered if that was part of the story.

"Just trust me," the woman continued. "They have a sickness that cannot be cured. Now, please, sit in the chair so I can finish."

Resentfully, Juno sat again and leaned back. She clenched her eyes and cried through each snip of surviving hair. When the deed was finished, Juno grabbed her belongings, left the kitchen, and bolted up a nearby staircase. There she entered the first room that contained a bed and slammed the door.

Inside, a vanity quietly beckoned Juno from across the room. She used the sleeve of the jacket given to her to wipe clean a section of mirror. In the dim reflection she twisted her head to scrutinize her new haircut. The top was short, barely longer than the width of her fingers, and the sides were even shorter. She had never seen herself like this. Then she held up the so-called sports bra and squeezed it with rage. In one evening her entire identity was either being cut away or covered up. "Some birthday," she grunted.

But before Juno sauntered over to the bed in defeat, she spotted a shelf floating over a tiny caged cot in the opposite corner. On top of the shelf were three frames with discolored pictures inside. The photo on the left showed a man dressed in a dark suit kissing a woman in a flowing white gown. In the center was the same couple, only they were casually dressed in some sort of grassy field. The man had his arms around the woman while they both cradled her large stomach with their hands. The final picture on the right revealed a third member of the family. They were in a small white room with a bulky plastic bed. The woman was lying down and the man was leaning over to kiss the tiny baby in her arms. Juno's eyes wandered down to the empty crib. Resting inside was a small pillow, a neatly folded blanket, and a stuffed tortoise.

What happened to them?

Before her emotions could swallow her whole, Juno snatched the tortoise up and dove onto the nearby bed. She curled up under the covers and clenched the stuffed animal close to her body. She knew she would have to be stronger from now on; that thirteen was only going to get harder from here. However, at least for tonight, she would embrace her last few hours of childhood in a warm bed with a soft friend.

• • •

Downstairs, Lexa lit a candle that slowly warmed some water. "Jambalaya," she read out loud as the MRE packet sent stale rice and dried beans clinking into the pot, followed by some flavored dust.

While the meal heated, she tossed the empty packaging in a plastic trash bin along with the young girl's hair clippings, returned all the gear to her bag, and slid her knife back into the holster on her chest with a *click*. Next she searched the kitchen for two bowls, two glasses, and two metal spoons that might still be intact. Fortunately there were plenty inside the cabinet of hideous china. Finally she checked the faucet for running water; dry as the mountain air.

Once the food had finished cooking, Lexa split it equally between both bowls and filled two glasses halfway with water from one of her cylindrical aluminum flasks. Cup and bowl in hand, she moved for the stairwell. At the top were three doors, one of which was closed. She figured the girl was behind it and knocked three times.

"I'm sorry, Juno. I know this is hard. I've made us some dinner if you want to come eat with me and get to know each other," is what Lexa's heart urged her to say, but her head told her to remain focused. Stay distant, detached. For both their sakes. What eventually came out was, "Food," said as blandly as the meal itself.

She set the bowl and glass on the dingy carpet just outside the door and went back downstairs. Once in the kitchen she dug into her own helping alone. Like always. As she chewed the cardboard-like food, her shoulders slumped forward with an unwanted weight.

"Thirteen," Lexa mumbled. "There's no way she's going to make it."

The following morning consisted of more walking and more silence. Mile after mile Juno gritted her teeth through the pain in both her feet and her heart. Her head felt naked. Her chest felt constricted. The only things keeping her sane were the incredible structures sprawling across the desolate city. It turned out that a life lived in seclusion had left nearly everything to the imagination.

Oddly, her favorite landmark came in the form of a colossal group of intertwining streets suspended high above that all curled together in the shape of a crude butterfly. Juno remembered reading about the colorful winged things in the field guide she was forced to leave behind. She also remembered that monarchs could travel up to one hundred miles in a day. However far a hundred miles was, she considered, was probably nowhere near the distance she had already been forced to walk.

Once underneath the curled overpass, the woman stopped them for a quick snack. A pocket of shade cast by a massive chunk of concrete that had fallen from the wing-shaped bridges provided a perfect oasis. While they sat chewing on some sort of nutrient bar, Juno cranked her neck upwards and tried to imagine a swarm of cars buzzing around them. How fast did they go? Where were they all headed? Did they actually buzz? Or hum? Or growl? All questions she was far too afraid to ask of her new companion.

By midafternoon Juno's shoes had transitioned from needle-filled to numbing. She looked down at her old sneakers and noticed the worn rubber soles peeling away. With each step they flapped harder against her feet, even when she tried to adjust her gait.

But shoes were not the only thing rubbing Juno the wrong way. Constantly she was pinching at her shirt to adjust the restrictive band now squeezing her chest, and the collar of the stiff canvas jacket she was told to wear kept rubbing against her newly exposed neck. Toss in the unforgiving heat of the sun and the recipe for discomfort was complete. When it seemed nothing could calm her nerves, Juno decided enough was enough. "I'm hot. I'm sweaty. And my feet hurt!"

The woman groaned. "We need to keep moving."

Juno, whose animosity towards the stranger who cut her hair was about to boil over, spat, "Maybe I'll just stay here instead!" She halted and sat down on the dented hood of a nearby car. Then she crossed her arms with an audible, "hmph!"

Without so much as a hitch in her step, the woman said, "Go ahead. I'll move much faster without you slowing me down."

The response took Juno by surprise. To her, it came as an unnecessary insult and an uninvited challenge. Fine, she thought, and laid back, pretending to carelessly gaze at the monochrome sky.

Obstructing her clear view from the corner of her eye was a strange billboard. She turned her head towards it and saw an image split in two. On the left quarter was a red background housing a prominent logo. The logo was in the form of a large white shield, the inside also split in two, with the word CamChem printed in bold black letters at the top and two bright red C's filling in the bottom. To the right of the red section was a man sticking something into the side of his shiny new car with an extra wide smile. The viewer was also told to Create The Perfect Family Getaway! in gigantic yellow print stretched across the top.

But the longer Juno stared at the unusual billboard the stranger it became. Much of it had been altered by a hasty vandal with black spray paint. The word Getaway had a thick line crossed through it and the "e" at the end of Create was replaced with OR. Then there was the man standing happily by the car. Though his eyes had also been blacked out, the face still looked familiar somehow…

The absence of the woman's footsteps suddenly brought Juno back to reality and she shot back up from the car hood. *Where'd she go?*

Not willing to give in quite yet, Juno bought time by inspecting her sneakers. She removed the worst shoe from her left foot and peeled back the rubber bottom. Few sections of the sole clung to the body by stubborn glue alone. She set what remained of the disintegrating footwear aside, then yanked off her hole-filled sock, only to tear them further in the process. Her foot had grown a garden of white blisters. She repeated the process with her right foot before squeezing them both with tired hands.

Relief only lasted a few pleasant minutes when something started stinging her face. Juno's eyes squinted for the invisible intrusion, unable to locate its source. Then she looked farther away. A mouth of swirling wind, sand, and debris was swallowing houses in the nearby distance. Fast. There would not be much time for her to find cover. Frantically Juno pulled on her torn socks, haphazardly tied her stretched laces around the entirety of each shoe to keep the soles attached, and hopped off the hood of the car.

She ran in the direction the woman had continued on in, but was rapidly absorbed by the storm of sand. Tiny granules peppered Juno's delicate face and neck, forcing her to pull the duster's hood over her head. Visibility reduced from a couple blocks, to a couple streets, to a couple of feet. She cried out for help but the tempest swept away her voice with its momentum. Lost, all Juno could do was crouch to the ground and cover her head.

Growing chunks of debris slapped the side of the canvas coat, each hurting more than the last. There was no choice; Juno had to get inside... something. With all her might she stood up and ran blindly. Her shoes filled up with sand that grinded into her blisters. Her cries for help evaporated along with her tears.

The winds continued to pick up strength and Juno now struggled to maintain balance. A tumble over an unseen curb scraped through her pants and knees, but not before spotting something in the distance. A darkened shape was fast approaching. *Could it be?* Juno willed herself back to her feet, ran three steps, then was knocked out cold in the middle of the street.

The door splintered inward from the impact of a powerful kick. Four more and the frame broke completely free and crashed into the entryway. A wave of dust greeted the two acolytes. They entered, searching every last room only to find them exactly as time had left them: barren. Empty-handed yet again, they went back outside to try the house next door.

"How long are we gonna be doin' this, boss?"

Bishop dabbed beads of sweat from his brow, careful not to rub any salt into his irritated mange. "As long as we must, Deacon. For how will we reap our harvest if we concede?"

"Uh huh..."

They walked up the front porch of the neighboring home and kicked the door in as they had the last. Seven rooms searched, seven rooms without answers. They left and tried another. Then another. Then another.

"I mean, seriously," Deacon continued his plight, "There's gotta be a million houses in this damn city. And there's only two of us since Laity got split in half. Let's just head back."

Bishop shook his head slowly. He grabbed Deacon by the collar and stared deep into his bloodshot eyes. "And tell Him what, exactly?"

Deacon winced at the fabric scraping against his scabbed neck. "That we didn't find the girl. That's all!"

"But we *did* find the girl! And we know who aids her. If He ever discovered 'twas Lexa who foiled us…" Bishop loosened his grip around Deacon, suddenly distracted by the distance. A storm was rising. "It appears we are trapped here for the night anyway."

Bringing a hand to his freed neck, Deacon turned to match Bishop's gaze. "Damn! There's always another one."

"Indeed," Bishop acknowledged before returning to the task at hand. "Listen, we both saw them enter this neighborhood. They must have grown careless, left something behind. We'll search as many homes as the sky will allow before taking cover."

They continued to infiltrate weather-beaten houses until the storm eventually closed in. Sweeping sand began nipping at the open sores covering their exposed skin. They knew they would not survive long outside.

"The yellow one!" Bishop shouted over the gales. "Over there!"

The two men darted across the street and put their shoulders into the entrance of an unassuming yellow house with dead vines clinging to its side. The door gave way as if it were made of rot, sending them tumbling into the foyer. Deacon found his feet first and heaved what was still attached to the hinges back against the angering wind. "Whew!"

Then he helped Bishop up and added, "All I was tryin' to say is He'd never have to know. We could just tell Him Laity got too drunk and fell down an elevator shaft."

Bishop moved out of the hall and sat down in a living room across from the kitchen. He rubbed his forehead carefully with both hands. "The prudent see danger and take refuge," he recited, just over his breath. "The simple keep going and pay the penalty."

"The hell does that mean?" Deacon asked from the kitchen, already rifling through cupboards.

"It means—"

But something cut Bishop's response short. Something in the air of this house was unique to all the others; as if it still had a fragment of life lingering inside. Maybe it was a faint smell, maybe it was a brush of premonition, or maybe it was a language only the shadows spoke. He could never quite explain in words these sudden feelings of clairvoyance, but they had earned him his prestigious rank and title, and they were beckoning to him now. "Someone's been here."

Silently, the hunch grabbed Bishop's hand, lifted him from his seat, and led him up to the second floor. There was a room behind a cracked door that he stepped into. Greeting him was a clear reflection of hisself from a dusty mirror. A streak had been freshly taken out of its layers of grime. As he inched closer, the mirror offered even more intrigue. Reflected from behind, on top of the bed, laid an empty bowl and stuffed tortoise.

"Hey boss!" Deacon called up from downstairs.

Bishop ran his finger across the bottom of the bowl; still moist. They were here. He could feel it.

"Boss!" cried Deacon again.

Agitated footsteps stomped towards the top of the stairs. "I'm in the middle of—"

But Bishop was no longer annoyed by the interruption below once he laid eyes on his partner. Clutched in Deacon's hand was a long clump of hair the exact same color as their missing girl's.

When Juno awoke she was lying down, basked in the flicker of a half-melted candle. Wax was pooled around its base. There was no more wind, sand, or sky, nor was there a sun or moon or stars. She looked around. Her surroundings felt vast in their emptiness. Hollow, even. She squinted and a sea of empty shelves came into view.

Juno sat up and immediately winced from a throbbing pain in her temple. When she reached up to touch it, she felt a bandage neatly dressing a wound.

"The first scar's always the hardest," a voice in the darkness said. The woman stepped into the soft candlelight and checked the wrap around the young girl's head. She would be fine. "Still want to go it alone? Or do you need another rock to the head to wake up?"

Flush with embarrassment, Juno let out a small whimper and laid back on the ground. A line of deep blue windows sat high up on the wall. Night had fallen. Her stubbornness had cost them an entire day.

"You'll be safe here for the night," the woman said, slinging her bag around her shoulder.

"Where are you going?" Juno sniveled.

She did not hear an answer. Instead she heard footsteps leaving her yet again. The woman slipped through a crack in a door like a shadow, then slammed it shut with bitter regret.

Entry 25

I can't sleep. My feet are torn up. My shoes fell apart. My pants have holes in the knees. I'm going to have a scar above my right eye. And I just got ditched for the second time... TODAY!

Sorry. This has been the worst two days of my entire life and I don't know how to explain how mad and scared and worried and frustrated I am.

Yesterday morning four people came for me. Just like I was promised, I guess. Three scary men and one extra scary woman. They all thought

I belonged to them. One wanted to 'have the first go', whatever that means. Anyways, the woman won in the end by killing one of the men and pulling me into an elevator shaft without somehow dying.

And get this. We finally escape the building and she basically makes me run all day until we get to this yellow house where she decided it was time to CUT OFF MY HAIR! That's right. She cut it all off with a knife.

Plus she also lifted up my shirt (not cool!) and forced me to wear a tight thing over my chest. No boy will ever think I'm cute now because I basically look like a boy!

And if all that wasn't already the worst, she doesn't even talk. We walk and walk without a single word. All she's told me so far is that men are bad and I look too much like a girl. I don't know where she's from. I don't know what she plans to do with me. I don't even know her name! How can I trust her?

Ok, calm down Juno. Think of the good things.

She doesn't seem to want to hurt me. She's given me food and water. And she rescued me from the sand storm earlier, but ONLY after she ditched me. I might have even thanked her if she hadn't cut my hair.

Seriously never forgiving her for that.

A streak of morning sunlight grazed Juno's face, waking her, and she found herself wrapped snugly in a light blanket. She rolled her stiff body over like a fallen log and sat up. Her head was only mildly throbbing. A few feet away the woman whom she thought had left her was still asleep, lying on her side with one arm under her head and the other gripping the knife that was always attached to her chest. Juno made a face of speculation and unfurled the blanket from around her legs. Small bandages had patched up her bare feet where the blisters had been.

Shaking her head in disbelief, Juno looked around for her socks and shoes. They were nowhere to be found. But in their place was a mysteriously unscathed box lying next to a backpack she had never seen before. Careful not to disturb the hard-nosed beast, she crawled on all fours over to the package and opened it. What was inside dropped her jaw to the floor. A brand new pair of rugged hiking boots and a bundle of wool socks—all in her size—awaited their new home on her sore feet. Both grateful and stunned, she looked over at the sleeping woman with a slightly smaller chip on her shoulder.

Next was the bag. It was taller and far more durable than her old backpack. There were useful pockets and clips and straps all over the outside. And, if the box of shoes was any indication of what it contained, she was in for a treat. Juno reached inside and pulled out new pants and shirts, another sports bra, a few lightweight metal canteens already filled with water, matches, her old granola bars, and several other odds and ends.

With everything laid out across the floor Juno shook the bag for any straggling presents. Something solid was still tucked away. On the side was a tall pouch with a peculiar bulge. She unzipped it and froze. Sticking out was the unmistakable black handle of a new knife. This was not something she wished to become familiar with right now so she zipped it back up as if she had never seen it.

As for the rest of her new wardrobe, Juno could not wait any longer. This was the first time in her life she had ever received brand new clothes and shoes. Where had the woman found them? First she slipped the top pair of wool socks out of their plastic wrapping and pulled them over her feet. They felt like a warm hug from a new friend. Then, after peeking at the woman's closed eyes first, she undressed. The new pants were a thick nylon material that was gentle on her skin and the shirts were a very tough, breathable fabric; all in shades of tan, grey, and brown, of course. Next Juno sat cross-legged on the concrete floor and placed the first hiking boot in her lap. She especially liked a little imprint of a tree stamped near the heel. Absorbing every gleeful moment, she threaded the thick laces through the loopholes with careful precision.

Now it was time. Juno hopped up and plunged her wool-hugged feet inside each boot. After tying them nice and snug, she rocked back and forth quietly to test their fit. *Perfect!*

From the windows high above, orange light began crawling its way deeper into the warehouse. Juno could now make out more of the empty space. Some handwritten signs were haphazardly strewn about a nearby shelf, their clear plastic casings catching both the sun's reflection and her eye. She walked over quietly, making sure to appreciate the comfort of her new footwear along the way, and picked up a few to read.

"Everything must go," she read quietly, then moved the top sign to the back of the stack. "Going out of business. Eighty percent off. The end is...nigh? All stock reduced. May God have mercy on—"

"Time to go," the woman called out.

Startled, Juno dropped the stack and they all clattered loudly on the ground. It was not until the humiliating echo subsided did she slacken her seized body and rejoin the indoor camp. The woman was rolling up her blanket and motioned for Juno to do the same. As she picked up her own she realized it had been brand new as well.

While Juno packed she contemplated whether or not to thank the strange woman. *Let's see...she hasn't tried to kill me yet...but she did cut off all my hair...but she did rescue me from the storm...but only after abandoning me...* In the end, gratitude outweighed the fear.

"Thank you for the new boots and stuff," Juno said, slightly hoping she had not been heard.

The woman, kneeling down to make room for the blanket in her backpack, never looked up. "Happy birthday," she said flatly. "Take care of them."

With a stunned smirk, Juno did as she was told and closed the top of her bag once it was filled. When she stood up the woman was slipping on her duster. Juno sensed the urgency and mimicked by putting on her own. But as she fished her arms through the sleeves the hood fell down, swallowing her head whole. This caused her to stumble in the unfamiliar boots and she went crashing sideways into something soft yet lumpy. Things unknown ticked and tapped across the ground.

Two hands immediately yanked Juno back to her feet and ripped the hood from her head. "Careful!" was barked at her and she squinched her face as if it had come too close to fire.

Mortified, Juno watched the woman return the scattered items into the fallen backpack. It must not have been fully zipped. Deciding it best not to say anything else, the young girl picked up her own bag, revealing something small lying at her feet. It was a clear cylinder with a bright orange cap at one end. She pinched it between her two fingers and raised it curiously to eye level. A translucent fluid caught the yellowing light. "What's this for?" she blurted.

The forgiving demeanor, if there ever was one, had completely vacated the woman. She snatched the device from Juno's hand, slipped it back into its designated pocket, and zipped her backpack closed with finality. "For emergencies only," she warned.

Seconds later Juno found herself following head-down as the woman stormed over to the exit. The door screeched as it was pulled open part way, letting in a rectangle of late-morning light and a yawn of tired dust. Juno coughed, then, without indication, they both slipped out into the rising heat.

As they crossed the vacant field of simmering concrete and continued down a buckled highway, Juno came to realize how quickly she was starting to resemble her escort. *Bodyguard? Companion?* Whatever she was, she had certainly made an imprint; and not the endearing type. It was more like how being exposed to the sun for too long could turn anything grey. Both had short hair, long jackets, big boots, functional clothes of a depressing palette...even the fresh scar forming on the young girl's forehead had her echoing the woman a bit more than she would like.

Couldn't I at least have her body? Juno solicited, then chuckled to herself.

Hours passed and the space between buildings and houses expanded, eventually thinning into sand-ridden highways lined with downed electrical poles. Snapped wires littered the streets like dried up snakes. Juno had read that there were once over three thousand species of the slithering serpents and every single one of them were gross. She was happy they were all dead, but stepped lightly around the wires anyways. Just in case.

The view of the distant mountain range they were headed towards was now disappearing behind the rocky terrain growing upwards on either side of them. Juno read every faded road sign along the way to distract her thoughts. One in particular stood out to her.

"Now leaving Denver," she read aloud. The big green sign overhead grabbed her for some reason. Perhaps it was the large white letters. Or maybe it was the number 70 stamped in a big blue shield. Either way she was enticed to ask, "Is that the city's name?"

"It was," the woman answered with uninterest, more focused on keeping the pace brisk.

She did *answer*, Juno mused, and prepared to capitalize on the moment. "How'd you know the elevator thingy would stop?"

The question managed to coax the woman into turning her head. "What?"

"At the building. We were falling really fast and then we weren't. How'd you know we wouldn't die?"

The woman's attention returned forward. "They're designed that way."

"Interesting." Juno was two-for-two on received answers, albeit vague ones. "How?"

"What?"

"How are they designed?"

"With a hydraulic braking system."

Juno shrugged. *Good enough.* "Where were we sleeping last night?"

"An old mall."

"Woah!" Juno's voice perked and she eagerly skipped forward to the woman's side. "In one of my books there's this boy. His name is Dean and he's the captain of his whole school. Anyways, Dean likes this girl, whose name is Eleanor, but all her friends call her Ellie. She has long yellow hair and she's also a captain, but for cheer—"

"Is there a point to this?"

Cut short, Juno looked up to a severe side-eye. She swallowed and continued carefully. "Well at the end of the story they go on a date to a mall. I was wondering if it was kind of like this mall."

"Maybe," the woman said, then added bitterly, "You should empty that trash from your brain before it rots."

Juno muttered defeatedly, "Yeah, those books are kinda dumb I guess," then looked down. Over time she gradually fell a few paces behind the woman. A bead of sweat trickled down the stubble on her head, reminding her yet again of the atrocity from two nights before. "Why did you cut my hair?"

The woman let her wait a bit before answering. "To minimize distractions and to conceal your identity."

Juno crinkled her nose behind the woman's back before continuing on with her list of questions. "What did you do to that man back in the building?"

"I killed him with an axe."

"Not that. I mean the stuff all over his body."

The woman stopped walking and Juno nearly ran into her backside. Then she took a heavy breath and said, "He did that to himself."

"What do you me—"

But Juno was stopped short by the woman turning to face her. "Listen to me. Do you see that out there?" She gestured towards the infinite landscape of rocks and roads and mountains and the nothingness in between. Juno swallowed. "We need to cross over all of that and we need to do it quickly. The more time and energy we waste with this incessant questioning, the more danger we'll be in. Now let's go."

After a brief staredown the woman resumed her jaunt along the abandoned road. Juno stayed put, trying to summon enough strength for one last question.

"Wait!" Juno called out.

The woman halted one final time and turned to face her interrogator with exasperation. "What now?"

"Can...Can you at least tell me your name?"

The two found themselves in a standoff of silence, neither willing to draw. A hot gust of wind flapped their loose jackets. Juno crossed her arms as if the signal could intimidate the words into leaving the woman's mouth. It did not. Instead, the woman turned and continued west.

Juno watched until the woman was just out of sight before running after her. The truth was her greatest fear was being left alone. She would do anything to prevent it from happening again. Even if her only option was a nameless wayfarer who had sheared her head.

Rapid footsteps soon rejoined the woman's graceful stride and they continued down the highway side by side. After enough time of wordless walking, the woman glanced down at the young girl and said, "Lexa."

Two dark figures stood in the empty parking lot like floating logs in a smoldering sea. Their clothes were heavy with heat and the bottoms of their boots were melting.

"Over there, Deacon. Do you see it?"

More interested in a sole-shaped imprint sizzling on the concrete, Deacon replied, "See what?"

"That door is ajar."

"What door?"

Bishop cupped the top of Deacon's head and turned it upwards. In front of them was the north wing of a moldering mall. More specifically, the object of Bishop's concern was in the worn face of an old storefront whose sign had long since faded away.

Deacon ducked his head away reflexively. "Easy on the hair," he rebuked. "I ain't got much left."

They entered through the enticing doorway to see what secrets it might reveal, and to escape the blistering sun, if only for a few moments. A strip of windows high above took in the early afternoon light and shared it with the vast interior. What they found spotlighted was a barren department store littered with empty shelves. There were signs of sales, but none of life.

"Some molemen probably skittered through here," Deacon said, trying not to let his voice carry. "Bastards are gettin' desperate."

Bishop did not reply. Instead he ventured deeper into the empty warehouse to hunt down a careless clue. Of course, he used his eyes and ears to scan the darkness, but he also relied on how the room *felt*. Shadows sometimes told him stories when he took the time to listen. He closed his eyes and walked forward, breathing carefully.

Shcrat!

Something was under Bishop's boot. He pulled it back and kneeled down to find a pile of plastic signs. They were not quite in an orderly stack and not quite in a disorderly scatter. They had been dropped.

Picking up the sign on top, Bishop read the scribbled message. "May God have mercy on our souls," he said in a deep tone of disapproval.

Deacon overheard and cooed, "Our poor little souls!" while kicking some loose dirt into the air.

"Mercy," Bishop continued. "They were cleansed of their sins. What greater gift of mercy could they desi—Stop!"

Deacon froze at the edge of where shadow met sunlight. A guilty cloud of dust hovering near his scabbed face was swirling to the floor as if it were pointing at something. Bishop hurried over to inspect.

"Uh, boss? You okay?"

"Silence!" Bishop said, dropping on all fours to find the sediment's beacon. He placed a hand flat on the ground and lightly slid it across the cement floor. It was cool to the touch and very smooth...until it was not. Grazing his fingertips was a malleable mass of melted wax.

Bishop sprung to his feet and searched the surrounding area. If a candle had indeed been used for light, then...there! On opposing sides of the telling drip were two body-sized clearings swept out of the aging dust; one large and one small. He palmed Deacon's head once again and turned it. This time his partner did not recoil, and instead smiled at the outlined proof.

"May He have mercy on *their* souls."

Juno's new boots had brought her dying feet back to life. The purpose-built clothes whisked away her sweat and the bag fit comfortably against her back. Everything, it seemed, was working together to stabilize her spirit during today's unrelenting trudge.

The landscape drolled on. Hills gradually stretched into longer and taller hills, but everything else remained identical. The seething sun cast its monochromatic light across the neverending stretch of highway, causing ripples in the distance. Cracked concrete, downed power lines, and the occasional rusted-out vehicle all melted together inside a boiling mirage.

By mid-morning Juno had a stroke of thirst to go along with her boredom. Daring not to slow down, she slipped her backpack around to her chest and removed a half-empty canteen. It was her last one. She took a mouthful, then wiped the sweat from her forehead with the sleeve of her new duster. "Can I ask you something if I promise to keep walking?"

"Fine," Lexa said, her eyes fixed forward.

Juno returned her pack to her back and tightened the straps before starting. "Why are we wearing coats?"

"To protect our skin."

A slight gust of wind pressed the canvas jacket into Juno's body, the hot fabric evoking the sun's intensity on her skin. She sucked in through her clenched teeth and asked, "Well, then, where are you from?"

"Far from here."

"Where are we going?"

"Far from here."

"Are they the same?"

Lexa sighed. "I suppose."

"What's it called?"

"What's what called?"

"The place far from here!"

"Arcadia."

"Ar-cay-dee-uh…" Juno mouthed slowly. She liked how the word flowed over her tongue. She would be sure to write it down later. "So how did you know where I was?"

"Lucky guess."

"Yeah, right!" Juno said playfully. She watched closely for a reaction from Lexa, but none came, so she changed direction. "What's with that scary knife on your chest?"

"It's called a kukri."

That was another interesting word Juno told herself to remember. "Where do you get a kukri?"

Lexa was quiet for a while before deciding to humor the young girl. "The kukri originated in a country called India. It has many uses." Then, startling Juno, she pulled the knife from its sheath, exposing the bottom half. It reflected the sun harshly. "See the notch at the heel? It *can* be used for cutting, but its real purpose is to divert liquid away from the handle, always ensuring a secure grip."

Juno's eyes widened until they hurt. "Woah! Can I hold it?"

Lexa snapped the kukri back into its holster and continued on saying nothing.

After a time, a tender question materialized in Juno's head. One that had retreated into the dark corners of her mind after their escape from the Genesys building, slowly building enough courage to step back out into the light. Juno bit her lower lip, then looked up to Lexa. "Do you know where my mom is?"

Lexa's gaze pulled from the melting horizon and fell to the ground. "I—" She cut herself off.

The question had caused a slight shift of power in the conversation. Even though Juno was young, she still had the right to know what happened to the only other person in the world she had ever known. But then again, after all she had seen in the last few days, maybe it was better if nothing was said at all.

"She—" Lexa was fumbling for the right words when she looked up and spotted something dark emerging from a sun-rippled mirage up the road. Her cold edge returned. "Get behind me. Stay silent."

Juno obliged. She ducked behind Lexa's legs and stole a peek from around her waist. There *was* something coming towards them. It was large and made a faint rattling noise as it traveled. Slowly it grew in size until she could see that the bulk of its rounded figure was composed of many equal sized...*scutes?*

"It's a tortoise!" Juno blurted.

The creature stopped.

"Shit," Lexa huffed. After carelessly jumping out from behind cover, she had to yank Juno back by the arm. She put both hands on the girl's shoulders and spoke very sternly. "Do you have your knife?"

Juno felt around her pockets for her old folding knife and nodded, though Lexa probably meant the newer, scarier one still hiding in her backpack.

"Stay next to me, don't say a word, and keep your hand on it."

When they approached the creature Juno saw that it was not a tortoise at all. To her disappointment, the body was just a rusty shopping cart with an orb of umbrellas attached to it for shade; only resembling her favorite animal's shell from a distance.

Pushing the cart, however, was a tortoise-like man. He was stout and hairless with cracked, scaly skin. Pitch black goggles covered his eyes and a dusty trench coat draped down his body, stopping just short of two hideously bulbous clubbed feet. They looked like fat, twisted tree trunks with five knotted branches protruding out of each. Behind him was a line of nine other men, all naked except for burlap sacks covering their heads and hips. They were skeletal, scorched red by the sun, and chained to each other by the wrists.

Breakfast crawled up Juno's throat while Lexa spoke to the tortoise man.

"Water?"

"Eh, I might got some t'spare," the tortoise man said with a rickety voice. He shoved his arms into the junk-filled cart and pulled out two plastic bottles filled with cloudy liquid. "For th'right price, 'at is."

"Not those. Any others?" Lexa asked with stonelike cadence. She pulled a handful of silver batteries from her pocket and displayed them palm-up.

The tortoise man feigned noninterest and turned his attention to Juno instead. The girl took one step back as he leaned over in her direction. He focused one of his black lenses with a twist of the frame and presented a craggy smile. "'Ow much for the boy?"

Juno snapped a quick look at Lexa. *Boy?*

"Not for sale," Lexa said, maintaining her composure. "Any other water?"

An uncomfortable amount of time went by until the tortoise man straightened back up. "Shame, that." He tossed the plastic bottles back into his cart of salvage and lifted out a large, tubular canteen. "A boy'd fetch a lotta water."

Lexa remained calm. "I'm willing to pay for whatever you have to spare."

Juno's eyes moved from Lexa, to the tortoise man, to the chained up line, then back to the tortoise man. She nearly jumped. His black goggles were still fixated on her, reflecting her shaved head.

"Tell ya what. I'll give ya two'a these canteens and two'a these slaves for the boy." He jerked on the leading chain and the men all shuffled forward awkwardly. "They still got a bitta life in 'em."

Lexa reached out and pulled Juno back behind her legs. "Not interested. I'll pay money for water or we'll be on our way." Then she slowly moved her handful of batteries back towards her pocket until the tortoise man caved.

"Now let's not be hasty!" he interrupted. His focus was now glued to her palm. "I spose we can do one for twenny."

Lexa clenched her fist around the batteries as if they were about to fly away. "Twenty? I can get four bottles for that on the dryest day!"

The tortoise man ticked the adjustment ring on his goggles once more. "Five for the water..." He flashed his crumbling teeth. "...and fiteen for keepin' quiet 'bout the boy."

Pride eventually faded and Lexa's grip slackened. She counted out two D's, four AA's, and two Buttons, then said, "Fine."

The tortoise man's dirt-crusted fingers snatched the batteries up like a spring-trap and brought them close to his goggles. "All of 'em still work?"

"Yes."

Only after he touched his tongue to the prongs of a D did the tortoise man release his clutch on the canteen. Lexa took it with repugnance and clipped its handle to a carabiner hanging from a strap on her backpack. Then she grabbed the girl by the arm and led her hastily to the far side of the cracked highway.

Once they were a safe distance away, Lexa stopped Juno and unhooked the metal flask she had just purchased. She unscrewed the top and took a small pull, immediately spitting it out. "Ach!" she coughed as the liquid splattered onto the pavement. "Half vodka."

She tipped the bottle over and let its contents be absorbed by thirsty sand. When it was empty, she clipped the container back to her bag, grabbed Juno yet again, and ushered her off the concrete and down into a ditch. "Come. The road isn't safe anymore."

The bordering hill was a lot steeper than Juno had expected. She had to use both hands and feet to gain any sort of traction. Within a few steps, however, she slipped on a rock and tumbled backwards, rolling head over heels. But before she hit the bottom her whole body wrenched. Lexa had been quick to grab the sturdy handle at the top of her new backpack.

Suspended in air, legs dangling, Juno caught one last glimpse of the tortoise man. He was still staring at her from behind his black, soulless goggles.

Entry 28

    Today was really scary.
    A creepy man that looked like a tortoise tried to buy me! He had a bunch of starving people chained together that he called slaves. Their heads were covered with bags but I know their faces were sad because mine was sad too. He also thought I was a boy. That means Lexa was right about the hair and sports bra, but I'm still not happy about it.
    Speaking of Lexa, she told me some things today. She's from a place called Arcadia (I love that word!) and I think that's also where we might be going. I've never heard of it. But I had also never heard of Denver even though I grew up somewhere near it.
    I wonder what Arcadia is like. Maybe that's where my mom is waiting. Do you think there are any Deans there? Or Ellies? Nevermind. I'm not supposed to think about that kid stuff anymore.
    Lexa also told me her big knife was a kookry (or however you spell it). It has a special thing that keeps liquid away from the handle. Do you think she meant blood? Ew!
    The sun is almost down. Lexa is scouting around somewhere while I'm crunched in the backseat of an old car. It's really uncomfortable but at least it's keeping the sandy wind out. I wonder what it was like to ride in one of these.

> Fast? I can't imagine anything moving very fast in this heat.

The sign read `Welcome to Silver Plume, Visit Main Street`.

Lexa explained to Juno that despite their gained exhaustion from climbing all day, they had to bypass the larger Georgetown to avoid risk.

"What risk?" Juno exhaled before they meandered into town.

"Where there is shelter, there is always risk," Lexa stated matter-of-factly. "And bigger towns have bigger risk."

Juno had not understood the logic behind skipping one town for another until she saw the size of Silver Plume. About thirty buildings were all that stood and only half of those still had roofs. The architecture was primordial to her, as if the town had been built by an ancient civilization. Wooden plank sidewalks, wooden plank storefronts, wooden plank awnings, wooden plank roofs, all moldering along the street labelled `Main`.

An eerie silence welcomed them like a passive tour guide as they entered the small town—if it could be called that anymore. The guide directed Juno's curiosity back and forth to the square-shaped structures on either side of the road, leaving no explanation of their purpose. None had even offered up so much as a hint until one building in particular jutted out from the rest. It was a tall, triangular structure with cement stairs leading up to an arched doorway. There were additional arched windows on either side of the door and a circular one floating just above, all void of the glass they once framed.

Clinging to the large wooden door was some sort of poster that, despite the elements' best efforts at removal, had somehow survived all these years. Large golden letters read `OUR SAVIOR IS COME`. Behind the typeface was a suited man with the same wide smile as in the billboard back in Denver. Further down were the words `Guest Speaker: Cameron Friedrich`. A startling magazine cover flashed behind

Juno's eyes.

She shook the image of the man from her head and followed the steeple upwards. At the tip sat a symbol she was not familiar with. It was essentially a gigantic lowercase "t" with something dangling from its center. When Juno lifted a hand to shield the sun from her eyes she soon realized it was not a some*thing*, but a some*one*. Half of someone, to be exact, swaying in the stale breeze.

"Lexa!" Juno squeaked.

Lexa, who was just exiting a building from across the street, briefly glanced at the windswept torso and stepped over to Juno. "What?"

There was an anxious crack in Juno's voice. "Why is there a skeleton up there?"

"Just some unlucky bastard."

When the young girl eventually peeled her eyes away she realized that Lexa had already left down the road. She rushed after to catch up. The veil of innocence over Silver Plume had now been lifted. Horrors of the past oozed from every corner. Between two buildings on the right was a pile of empty shoes caked with layers of sediment. Across the street was a pile of their former occupants. A plastic bag tumbled across the street until getting snagged inside an empty shop that had been converted into a haphazard landfill. Before Juno knew it, she had bumped straight into Lexa.

"I don't like this place."

"Tough," Lexa consoled in her flat demeanor. "It's too hot to climb mountains at midday and we're low on water."

They turned and crossed a quaint little bridge with a railing that Juno paused to lean over. Below was a riverbed of dry stones, bleached bone-white by the sun, thirsty for the blood that once gave the river life. But the stones were not alone in their destitution. Littered throughout were fragments of colored glass, plastic, and other items of trash that had all found their way inside the nooks and crannies, each a worthless gem dropped into a dead setting. The young girl's soul felt heavy.

"Over here!" Lexa suddenly called out from a nearby building.

The two slipped inside a two-story apartment complex and removed their hoods to let their eyes adjust to the darkness. Lexa started up the stairs and Juno followed.

"You need to learn how to find your own water," Lexa said when entering a bathroom. She went over to the toilet and lifted the tank lid. "And this is always the first place to look."

Juno peered over the top of the tank and saw it half-full of clear liquid. She made a face and asked, "But doesn't that water have pee in it?"

Lexa rolled her eyes before looking into Juno's. "Not until you flush. Up here is relatively fresh if the plumbing is intact." She unclipped the deceitful canteen she had bought from the tortoise man. Then she dipped the neck inside the tank and watched it slowly guzzle up water. "See what I'm doing? Now go downstairs and fill yours up as much as you can."

A short while later, Juno returned with two canteens filled mostly to the top with clear water. Lexa had three. They combined their bounty into four completely full containers and then headed back downstairs with the empties. Lexa beelined to the room beneath the bathroom and tapped her knuckles along the wall. She went from one end to the other and back until she stopped somewhere in the middle.

"Come here," Lexa instructed, then began knocking again once Juno was at her side. "Do you hear how it sounds less hollow than the other spots?" Juno nodded as best she could with an ear pressed against the sheetrock. "Now go find something that can put a hole in this wall."

Juno returned after a few minutes brandishing a long skinny piece of fiberglass with one pointed end and a plastic boot attached at the center.

"Where did you get that?" Lexa asked.

Juno shrugged. "There's a bunch of these in a closet full of coats and stuff."

Lexa had already marked an X in the wall with her knife and motioned for the young girl to begin. Juno gave a curious look, then swung the awkward thing she had found. A fragment of sheetrock ricocheted from the wall and landed on the floor. So did the heavy board.

"If you want to survive out here, you need to be strong," Lexa said.

With one arm, she assisted Juno in re-lifting the board and held it in place. "Go again."

Lexa released and Juno swung, this time with a grunt. A new chunk of sheetrock flung off.

"Again."

A crack slithered down the wall.

"Again."

Panting, Juno wearily raised the board and swung from a different angle. The impact ripped the board from her hands again and it clunked loudly across the floor. She kicked at it with her feet and sighed. "I can't do it."

Lexa picked up the board and inspected it. On the lower half, just behind the boot, was a lever. She squeezed it down with her palm and the boot popped off. Now half as heavy, she shoved it back into Juno's arms and commanded, "Use your anger."

Juno wiped the tear of defeat bubbling under her eye and tried to think of something that made her angry. Immediately she was back on the seventy-fourth floor of the Genesys building. The impenetrable door of Cameron Friedrich's office was laughing at her. She *had* to find out what was inside...

With a battle cry, Juno raised the board and rammed the angled tip straight into the wall like a spear. The crack split wide open. Then she yanked the board out and a satisfying pile of debris came with it.

"Keep going!" Lexa encouraged.

The young girl chopped and stabbed and yelled and spat while a bare pipe gradually came into view. Juno was losing control. "That's enough!" she heard from somewhere, but the words were not enough to stop her. She was still angry.

The chopping continued until Lexa grabbed the girl by the scruff with one arm and removed the board with the other. Only when Juno stopped kicking at the air was she released. "Do you think you got it?"

Juno wiped the dripping sweat from her forehead and saw the gaping crater she had just created. A final chunk dropped with a thud. "Sorry."

Lexa did not say anything. Instead she went over to the wall and gripped one of the pipes. "Still cool," she muttered keenly, then reached down and pulled a channellock from her bag. "Get the empties ready," she said while twisting loose a pipe connector.

Cold, clear water dripped from a gap into one of the empty canteens Juno was holding up. Lexa made an adjustment and the trickle turned into a stream. "Fill every one to the brim. I'll be right back."

Giddy and triumphant, Juno loaded up each bottle with the refreshing fruit of her hard work. She was proud of the strength she had been forced to realize and felt a gratifying sense of accomplishment. She had contributed to the team.

When Lexa returned she was carrying an empty five-gallon bucket, a towel, and a bar of soap. She set the bucket down to catch the drip from Juno's final canteen. As Juno screwed on the last lid, Lexa told her to drink as much water as her body would hold, then use what was left to wash up. Finally, before closing the door, she added, "I'll fix us something to eat."

This was the first time Juno had removed her clothes in days. She peeled them off like a grungy vacuum seal and hung them over the backs of two chairs. Luckily there were no mirrors in this room so she would not have to witness how filthy she was. With the soap bar in hand, she stood under the gentle drip of the pipe and improvised a shower. Once she got to her head her fingers paused. They ran through her hair so easily now. *Maybe this short hair thing has its perks*, she wondered, but quickly rinsed the thought from her mind.

In the kitchen Lexa was heating up some canned food over a tiny propane bottle. The fact that she was cooking something on a stovetop without actually using the stovetop was grimly ironic. A door behind her creaked and she turned, knife handle gripped tightly, then relaxed. It was only Juno entering with clean skin and ruffled wet hair. Seeing the young girl like this sent a foreign pang through her heart. Not a stinging pang, more of a warm tug, but one she needed to keep under control.

Juno sat at the rickety table and asked, "What's for dinner?"

"You're in luck," Lexa mocked. "Today we have pinto *and* black beans." She poured the black and brown mixture onto two plates that were set out and slid one over to Juno. "Eat up."

Juno spooned some into her mouth and was pleasantly surprised. It had been a while since she had moist food cooked so thoroughly.

For most of the meal they sat quietly across from each other, stealing quick glances from time to time. The only sounds came from chewing or spoons tapping plates, though Juno was about to open her mouth when Lexa suddenly asked, "So, do you actually know how to use that knife of yours?"

Juno's shoulders went all the way up to her ears, then dropped. "Point and stab?"

"And how did that work out for you the other day?"

Red-faced, Juno took another quiet bite.

"You know," Lexa continued, aiming her spoon across the table, "There might come a time when I'm not around to fight for you." Juno shuddered at the thought of being alone again and looked up to Lexa staring. "Finish up and I'll show you a few basics."

In the adjacent family room, Lexa and Juno pushed some furniture out of the way and stood across from each other like duelists.

"Now, where do you keep your knife?" Lexa asked. Juno reached into her pocket and wiggled the knife free from some bunched up fabric. Lexa lunged across the room, kukri already at the girl's throat. "Too slow. Always keep your weapon where you can grab it without thinking. Never where it can snag." She backed away and started the next lesson. "Show me how you hold it."

Juno unfolded the blade of her tactical folding knife with her thumb, but Lexa snatched it from her hand. "I could have killed you twice already. Where is the new one?"

Tail between her legs, Juno left to get the knife tucked untouched in the side of her backpack. It was twice the length of the one left to her by her mom, and came with its own sheath and straps. Back in the living room with Lexa, she pulled the black-handled gift from its housing and winced as the solid black blade swallowed any light that touched it. It was petrifying.

"Ok, come at me," Lexa taunted.

Juno stood how she imagined she was supposed to: feet shoulder-width apart with the knife clenched firmly down by her waist. Then she lunged forward, immediately floored by an outstretched boot once again.

"Slow learner, huh? Keep your knife extended at all times. Anyone attacking from the front will automatically put themselves at risk. This also gives you time to create the distance needed to study your surroundings. Try it now."

Juno nodded and rehearsed what she had just been told. She held the knife outwards and circled the room thrusting at imaginary attackers. It gave her a dark sense of power.

"Alright," Lexa interrupted. "Now what would you do if someone attacked you?"

With a flick of her arm, Juno made a slashing movement while simultaneously jumping backwards. Lexa was able to rush and grab the front of the girl's shirt before she tripped over a coffee table and stabbed herself.

"Never put yourself off balance. If someone's careless enough to charge you, you have control of the fight." They recentered in the room and Lexa demonstrated how to stand properly. "Make yourself as skinny as possible by turning sideways. Good. Now you are a much smaller target. Also balance your weight between both feet. Exactly."

Over and over and over the next hour Lexa ran drills with Juno. They took turns attacking and being attacked. She showed the young girl how to parry inwards and outwards so she could target and expose an assailant's weakness. She demonstrated how to thrust a knife and what parts of the body to aim for. Slight improvements were made, but Lexa knew more training would be imperative in case... Well, she did not want to think about *in case*.

As the exercise percolated through time, warm light started beaming through the blinds of a west-facing window. Lexa halted Juno mid-jab and went over to separate two slats with her fingers. The sun was just about to kiss the mountain peaks. "Pack up," she said. "We're heading out."

An eclectic collection of junk crashed across the pavement when Deacon kicked over the shopping cart. The goggled man attempted a run for his life, but tripped over his own inflated feet and slammed face-first into the ground. Blood seeped from his craggy scalp and sizzled on the concrete.

Deacon slammed a boot onto the man's chest before he could crawl any farther. Then he leaned over and yanked the pitch dark goggles from the bald head, exposing one pale eye and one blackened socket. Twirling the eyewear in his finger, he teased, "You know these things make you look like a turtle?"

"I ain't seen nothin'!"

Bishop approached and took command of the interrogation. His palm was filled with shiny objects. "Your newly acquired wealth says otherwise," he said, slipping the batteries into his own pocket. "And the lack of available water in your humble storefront."

"Road's been em'ty fer weeks."

"Is that so?" Bishop hummed, scanning the nearby hills. He picked at an irritating scab on his neck before looking back down at the tortoise man. "I assume you're familiar with our patriarch, correct?"

The tortoise man spasmed.

"So you must also know that He punishes those who withhold truths, correct?"

Like an upturned tortoise stuck on its shell, the scaly man rocked towards his interrogator. He grabbed the back of Bishop's boot, pulled, and tripped him to the ground. Then he rocked the other way, using the momentum to roll to his feet. Five steps later Deacon had already seized the man's collar and yanked him back to the ground.

"I ain't lyin'!" the tortoise man cried. "I din't see nothin!"

Deacon's fist was raised above, ready to drop like a piston. "You didn't see noth—"

"Come now, Deacon," Bishop interrupted, shooing his partner away with flapping hands. "That's no way to coerce cooperation."

Bishop kneeled onto the tortoise man's chest with all his weight to make sure he stayed put. Once he caught the attention of the pale eye, he removed a short, hooked knife from his pocket. It flashed in the sun. He then pinched the end of the handle and swung the tip of the blade over both of the tortoise man's eye sockets like a deadly pendulum. "Do you favor a game?"

The deformed, hairless man yanked his head away.

Grinning, Bishop clutched the man's chin to hold him still. "Perfect. Now if the knife happens to drop into your eye, you have told us the truth, for the blind could not have seen. However, if it drops into your vacant socket, well, His wrath will be just. You have ten seconds to divulge before it's decided for you. One..."

The knife swung from one peripheral to the other.

"I swear!"

"Two..."

"I ain't seen no one for weeks!"

"Three...four...five..." The sharp pendulum swung back and forth. "Six..."

"I'll never tell you 'n those fuckin' crazies nothin! I swear to—"

"Now we're getting somewhere," Bishop taunted. "Seven..."

"You can tell the Scab King to kiss my—"

Bishop let the knife slip just enough to be noticed. "You know He despises that name. Eight...Nine..."

"Alright!" The tortoise man screamed at the top of his lungs, which quickly deflated into a whimper. "Alright. I'll tell ya what ya want. Just get that thing outta my face."

The knife halted. "Go on."

The man was panting. "Few days ago. Woman an' a boy. They bought a bottle'a my water 'n moved on. That's it, I swear!"

Bishop raised an eyebrow. "A boy? How old?"

"Fuck if I know." The tortoise man squirmed again. Deacon came from behind and leaned a boot onto his swollen foot. He seethed through a clenched jaw. "Youngest I ever seen!"

"Long brown hair?"

"Nah. Both were buzzed."

"Hm." Bishop flipped the knife and grabbed the handle in his fist. Then he stood up to confide in Deacon. "That explains the haircut. We're following the right path."

Deacon nodded in agreement and pressed down harder with his foot. The pain-filled cry brought a grin to his face. Bishop rolled his eyes and glanced back at the turned over cart. The slaves had long gone. Given their bagged heads, none would be worth the effort spent tracking down for answers. Most would not even make it to nightfall.

"Where were they headed?" Bishop asked, interrupting his own thoughts. He nudged Deacon with an elbow so he paid attention.

The scorching pavement had already climbed through the tortoise man's trench coat. "Southwest," he winced. "Up the mount'ns."

The two acolytes looked at each other.

"You think they're goin'..."

"I do," Bishop confirmed.

"That means they'll have to..."

"Precisely."

"So there's no sense in..."

"I'm afraid not."

"Then we should just..."

"Agreed," Bishop finalized. "Collect anything useful from the cart and set fire to the rest."

Deacon skipped over with ferocious delight

"No!" the tortoise man pleaded. "My wares!"

Bishop dropped a knee back into the tortoise man's chest and looked him square in the eye. His mouth stretched ear to ear. "Deacon?"

His partner was already filling packs with bottles of water, food, and batteries when he replied, "Yeah?"

"What does the scripture say? An eye for a lie?"

Deacon tipped a small can of gas over and struck a match against the torrid pavement. As he flicked the flame into the junkpile he replied, "Close enough."

Entry 33

I'm exhausted!

We've been climbing all day and the higher up we go the harder it is to breathe. Lexa tried explaining sea level and elevation to me. It kind of makes sense. Basically the closer you get to the sky, the less air there is to breathe. Seems backwards, huh?

Speaking of elevation, tomorrow we're headed to a place called Leadville. Lexa says it's two miles above sea level which is one mile higher than Denver (where we started)! Also a mile is a certain measurement for how far you've walked, if you didn't know. Five thousand two hundred eighty steps to be exact.

Lexa says she has a friend in Leadville that can help us with supplies. Can you imagine what a friend of Lexa would be like? In my books friends always made other friends laugh and I've never even seen Lexa smile. I almost teased her about it until I remembered how many friends I have. <u>Zero</u>. I've had a mom and a Lexa and that's it. No boys. No girls. No one my age that even got to see my long hair before it got cut off.

Ugh! I'm probably so ugly now!

> Anyways, knife fighting lessons have been going on every day. I'd say I'm getting pretty good, but she keeps showing me that I'm not. I gotta keep practicing. Who knows, maybe I'll be the one rescuing her someday!
>
> In other news, I'm sleeping on top of my first mountain tonight! How cool is that? Lexa says we need to ack-lim-ate (can't spell that word) to the elevation up here. I asked her what that means and she said something like, "Gets your lungs used to the air." Who knew climbing mountains came with so many rules!
>
> But there is one downside to being way up in the clouds: it's freaking cold at night! Lexa says it's not safe yet to start a fire so I guess I'll just go ahead and freeze to death.
>
> Kidding!
>
> Maybe.

Leadville was an old trading town and an even older mining town. It was also one of the last bastions of commerce and inclusivity due to its remoteness. Pilgrims had to brave elements as well as elevation to migrate there, and arriving was a euphoric release of hate's cold, stony weight on the soul. Exhausted civility kept the edge at bay like a steadfast cliff against an ocean storm. Plus, as the residents knew, prejudice never turned a profit on the free market.

"Still the highest elevated town in America," Lexa told Juno as they crested the final mountain that morning. "Whatever that's worth."

From the cliff's edge Leadville looked like a nice little town. Even under the hazy filter of the browning sun, sections of colorful buildings and houses still made themselves known with pride. Juno saw a number of roads, hills, houses, and shops. There was also a single building with a triangular steeple ten times the height as the one in Silver Plume, but not nearly as ominous.

The night before, Juno had imagined she would quite like to live among the hustle and bustle of a thriving trade town, where she could talk to all sorts of people coming and going as the wind. But her hopes had given up once she laid eyes on the true Leadville. Not a soul was in sight.

Farther west was a fitting backdrop to the lifeless town. A boundless graveyard of black tree stumps climbed the titanous mountains like charred scabs. As the elevation grew, the sickly stumps diluted into cold, grey rock. A select few of the tallest mountains wore bald caps on the tips of their peaks. Juno had never seen anything so tremendous, so unmoving, in her entire life. The range stretched endlessly below the sky like a silent, impassable wall.

The scarred landscape briefly reminded Juno of the face that had been following her. The poster, the billboard, the magazine cover. Those scabs crawling up his neck… She shivered from the chill in her spine and returned her attention to the vastness of it all. *What could be on the other side?* the young girl wondered, hoping she would not have to scale them to find out.

Lexa noticed Juno gawking. "The Rocky Mountains," she said, then started her descent towards the town. "Should be there in a few days' time."

"What!" Juno snapped as she slid down after on some loose rock. She hopped at the bottom and took a small leap towards Lexa. "You mean we're gonna go *up* those?"

"Do you see a way around?"

Juno oscillated her head left, right, and left again. The mountains went on forever. "Well there's gotta be some sort of path between them."

"Great idea!" Lexa chided. "I bet no one else has thought of that."

Juno's scowl at the back of Lexa's head was becoming a procedural habit. Maybe now was the time to put her newfound knife skills to work…

"See the bare peaks of the tallest mountains?" Lexa asked before Juno could live out her thoughts. Juno *had* been wondering about them, but was sour about the sarcasm and pretended not to care. "Yeah."

"They used to be covered in white snow—that's frozen water that falls like rain—untouched by man. Even this whole town would be blanketed in the stuff during this time of year." She paused for a regretful moment, then added, "But that was long before me."

Lexa's whole description was difficult for Juno to imagine. She knew frozen meant extremely cold, but had never actually encountered anything in that state. And the only thing that ever fell from the sky was sand that had been lifted by the wind.

They continued down the cliff face until the land leveled out. From what Juno could tell, only one road entered the town and only one road left, and Lexa made sure they avoided it. Instead, they slipped through a small drain that passed under the highway and ducked between some buildings.

Lexa explained how to use structures as cover by staying tight to the walls and monitoring vantage points. Most of the lesson was lost on Juno because every building they snuck by was completely void of life. In fact, if it were not for the physical buildings themselves, there would be no evidence that anyone had ever lived there in the first place.

"We heart," Juno read aloud as they passed a long brick wall that had writing on it. She knew the word was supposed to say "Leadville", but something had been scribbled over the top. "Deadville?"

"That's odd," Lexa stated more to herself than Juno. "Stay close to me."

Things did not change inside the heart of the city. Vacant buildings lined a weathered street, unmoving like a snapshot in time. The front doors of every shop creaked in the hot breeze.

They kept on until they reached a storefront with a facade much taller than the building itself. A derelict wooden awning hung over the entryway and above it were five windows and a placard. `Silver Dollar Supply`, Juno read in her mind, amused that the `u-p-p-l-y` were not the original letters, and were instead pieces cobbled together from other signs.

When they entered the Silver Dollar Supply it was devoid of all light aside from a losing battle between the sun and some dust-caked windows. Behind them, the door slapped against its weathered frame and a dusty rectangle filled its place as the whole room turned to shadow. "Wait here," Lexa said, then disappeared into the darkness.

Juno took a few creaky steps inward while her eyes slowly adjusted. The air smelled sweet and musky, like one of her old books still in a stack back at Genesys. She always enjoyed the scent that escaped each time she turned a page.

Half blind and lost to curiosity, Juno bumped into something that rattled immensely. She reached out a hand to calm the noise when some of her fingers unexpectedly gripped a cold metal lattice. "Huh?"

Suddenly, light warmed the room from above, bringing into view the towering obstruction. Shelves upon shelves brimming with old books waited lethargically behind a metal grate that stretched floor to ceiling. Each binding's title was desperate for Juno's eyes, as hers were for them. She tried to open the barrier but a fist-sized padlock kept them sealed from her longing desire.

Her heart sank.

She forced herself to forget about the books for a moment and diverted her attention to the rest of the Silver Dollar Supply under its new glow of light. Lining the walls and ceiling was the most captivating woodwork she had ever seen. Handcrafted layers of dark cherry and rich mahogany laid out intricate designs of flowers, curves, and swirls, as if to spin an elegant tale of long-forgotten skill sets. Everything flowed together so seamlessly that it would have been difficult to convince Juno that the trees had not originally grown with those patterns. And below was no different. Shelves, tables, and podiums housing countless antique objects were equally as engrossing as the decorations on the wall. The young girl was taking it all in when she spotted Lexa rotating a large crank behind a long counter made of the same impressive carpentry. *Is that how the lights came on?* Juno wondered, still mystified.

"Hey Lexa," Juno asked. Her voice was absorbed pleasantly by the warm wood.

There was a grunt in Lexa's voice while turning the handle. "What?"

"Why are all of these books behind a cage? Don't people want to read them?"

"Books are more valuable as fuel nowadays," she explained, still cranking. "Not many use them for knowledge." Then, turning the crank a final time, Lexa shouted, "Dakota!"

They waited for an answer, but only heard silence.

There was a stiff feeling inside the Silver Dollar, as if it had been filled with the exact same air since the beginning of time. Lexa came out from behind the extra long counter and told Juno to wait again while she checked upstairs for her friend, Dakota.

Juno wished the book cage was unlocked, but at least she was free to look at all the other interesting trinkets. As she moved from shelf to shelf, she picked up and inspected items with wonder. Everything was so foreign to her, so exotic. She opened a glass casing atop a wooden pedestal and removed an oddly shaped object. It was black, smooth, and had four colorful buttons on one side. She rotated it in her hands until it fit snugly between her palms. Her thumbs gravitated to two jutting sticks that circled around their housings delightfully. With seemingly no practical use in the slightest, Juno relished in the clicks of buttons and triggers the mindless object provided.

After far too much time spent with the handheld gadget, Juno returned the thing to its display and moved on to a rotating rack that caught her eye. It was filled with square pieces of paper, all the exact same size, with a variety of pictures and words on them. Juno twirled the rack, then picked up a postcard with a smile. "Welcome to Leadville," she read. The letters of Leadville were large and hollow with colorful city landmarks presented inside of them. She recognized the tall steeple in the "D" and the Silver Dollar was inside the first "L". The vibrance in which Leadville was displayed gave Juno such a warm feeling that she decided to keep the card. She gave a quick look around before secretly slipping it into her bag. Shortly after, footsteps returned.

"We need to get out of here," Lexa said, booming down the stairs. She immediately rushed back behind the long counter. "Come help. Quickly."

Juno came around and watched Lexa slap a small silver cylinder onto the counter. "Grab more of these from the register. Same size."

Juno picked up the silver battery and asked, "What's a register?"

"The thing at the end of the bar with all the buttons."

Shrugging, Juno floated over to the register while Lexa tore apart the shelves below the counter in search of something. All of the buttons looked daunting. She pressed down a couple and received a *ting!* from each. Nothing else happened. She scratched her head and began reading what was marked on the buttons in worn out handwriting. A row of single letters, a row of numbers, and a row of brief phrases like `No Tax` stared back at her. After attempting a few combinations of each, the result remained the same.

"How do I..." Juno thought aloud.

Lexa, still sifting through the shelves, answered, "Pull the lever."

There it was on the side; a big wooden lever. Amused at how she missed it, Juno reached out and pulled it down. A few ticking noises followed by a more advanced chime sent the drawer flinging open. Revealed was a small fortune of silver objects. From left to right the batteries varied in size and shape, each neatly organized in their own little partitions—flat circles on the left and thick squares all the way on the right. What Juno needed was right in the center so she scooped them all out and closed the drawer.

"Got it!" Lexa praised from below, then bumped her head on the way back up. She cursed while rubbing her scalp. "The batteries?"

Juno handed them over. Lexa removed a covering on the back of a new contraption and inserted four of the cylinders. Then she flipped the device over and quickly twisted a small knob. A harsh noise like a foot dragging through gravel came from inside the object. Seemingly satisfied,

Lexa immediately twisted the knob back the other way and stuffed the device in her bag. "Alright, let's go."

They hurried into the blackened rear of the Silver Dollar and slipped out the back door. The alleyway was tight and filled with piles of plastic garbage bags that they had to maneuver around. Juno was trying to figure out why they were in such a rush when a shift in the wind blew between the two buildings. Lexa stopped them dead in their tracks and tilted her head upwards. "Do you smell that?"

Juno sniffed the air. Not garbage. The new scent was extremely familiar yet completely alien at the same time. Her brain subconsciously wrinkled her face as she guessed, "Smoke?"

"Get behind me."

Lexa and Juno squeezed through the cramped alleyway and the smell grew stronger with each step. At the mouth, Lexa peered around a corner for any signs of life. Empty. Every road was as deserted as when they arrived.

Across the way was a brick building that looked like it had been sliced off diagonally from roof to floor. A slight trace of smoke billowed from one of the glassless windows. Lexa ordered Juno to remain in the alley and scurried over to investigate. She stepped over a pile of bricks leftover from the missing half and immediately covered her mouth in horror. It was now clear why Leadville was barren.

When Lexa turned around she was startled that Juno had followed. Her instincts urged her to cover the young girl's eyes, but there was no use. Juno had seen the devastation before them and there was no erasing it. So, together, they stood and watched with respectful silence.

The charred pit of smoldering bodies emitted a steady glow of red embers. They counted fifteen on the surface and two more skewered mouth-to-tail across the top like a barbarous rotisserie. There was no telling how many innocent victims had already been reduced to ash.

Juno followed the spewing smoke upwards and wept. "Who would do such a thing?"

The incessant crackling stung at their ears like burns of their own. The acrid smell stabbed at their nostrils.

"Men did this," Lexa seethed, spitting the word *men* from her mouth as if she had accidentally swallowed poison. "Come."

They returned to the back entrance of the Silver Dollar Supply and were greeted with forlorn darkness. Whatever juice Lexa had given the lights earlier had now run out. With arms stretched outwards, they felt their way back to the long counter in search of the power-producing crank. Lexa's hand brushed against the cold metal and she began turning it. But before the lights came back on, she heard a faint voice.

"Hey Lexa?"

Juno was at the other end of the bar, closer to the window. Lexa could see the outline of her arm pointing towards the haze of sun coming through. She dropped the crank handle and walked over. "What now—" she started, but was cut off by a cluster of silhouettes on the opposite side of their obstructed view.

Lexa immediately crouched to the ground and pulled Juno down with her. She put a hand against the young girl's mouth, looking her square in the eyes. "Listen to me. This is extremely important. We are about to be attacked and our only chance at survival is to funnel them into this building. You remember your training?"

Juno shook with fear, unable to move. Lexa sighed.

"It'll be okay. Just stay inside and keep out of sight. I'm going out there. When I come back in, don't reveal yourself. They must *not* know you exist. Understand?"

This time a nod broke through Juno's trembling.

"Good."

Lexa stood up and, after Juno slipped behind a large shelf, grabbed the door handle. Before turning the knob she paused for one last message. "Listen, if I don't make it..." She chewed on the words for a second. "Don't let them catch you. No matter what." A whimper of agreeance wafted from the dark, then she exited the Silver Dollar.

Nine men stood around Lexa in the street. They were haggard, ghoul-like creatures, pale with anemia and crooked from osteoporosis. Blue veins crawled up their bleached necks and dried blood dripped down their raggy shirts. The sun chewed on their squamous lips as they licked their chops. Their beady eyes had the black gumption of those who had just tasted meat for the first time.

Lexa had encountered molemen before, but never more than one or two at a time. Leadville had a reputation for keeping them out. These men tended to keep to themselves, thriving in the dark underbelly of what remained of the old world. Sewers, mines, caves, tunnels...any hole dark, damp, and dreary enough to scare away the competition. No, she had never seen anything remotely as organized as this—at least not out in the open—yet here they were. Desperate. Hungry.

"Who ya talkin' to?" the one closest to Lexa asked.

She assumed he was their leader since he was still articulate. And because a menacing pump-action shotgun with a barrel that looked to be snapped off ungracefully at the midpoint rested on his shoulder. The odds of him having actual shells in the chamber were miniscule, but she kept an eye on it anyway. "Where is Dakota?"

"Oh, my! *Another* woman." The leader grinned to his salivating lackeys. "Sorry, we didn't get a chance to ask everyone's names."

Even though he had just answered her question, she asked again. "Where is Dakota?"

"Listen here, sweet cheeks." The leader pulled the shotgun from his shoulder and bounced the forestock in his boney hand a couple of times. "This town's under new management and we ain't answerin' no one's questions. Now who were ya talkin' to?"

The gun did not frighten Lexa. She had been at the other end of this bluff a hundred times before. She knew how easily she could pounce on someone carrying ten pounds of awkward weight, but she needed closure first. "Did you rape her, or eat her?"

The leader bared a brown-toothed smile and stroked a patchy beard. His hand must have clipped an open sore because a streak of fresh red stained his cheek. "Yer a mouthy one, eh? Yer friend was too. Nothin' a strong rope and a tight knot couldn't fix, huh boys?" He ended with a chuckle that the group happily joined in on. "Lucky for her, she accident'ly slipped and hung 'erself last night. Shame. We hadn't planned on killin' her so long as she was still…" His mouth stretched wide. "Functioning."

An acute rage exploded inside Lexa's chest. The Dakota she once knew would never have been so careless. She removed her duster and tossed it to the side. The nine men could now see the outline of her body *and* her weapon. She was glad.

"Woah! You got a nice set on you, woman. Prolly fetch a pretty penny from the Scab King." The leader hoisted the gun barrel up and flicked the tip at Lexa's chest. "Give us that knife and we'll *try* to go gentle on ya."

As her reply, Lexa brandished the sharp kukri from its holster and said, "Take it from me."

Her defiance slapped the jovial demeanor from the leader's face. It was clear he did not like being challenged. "Look, you might not understand this 'cause yer a woman, but this here is a shotgun. It'll blow a hole right through them pretty little tits when I pull the trigger. Now, gimme the knife."

Lexa watched the rest of the men shift their weight ever so slightly. A sign of angst. But she also knew they would not advance until ordered, so she remained rooted like a tree of confidence.

"If you don't hand over that knife I'm gonna blast yer head clean off!" His tongue slid across his chapped lips, then added, "We don't mind. The rest'a you'll still be warm for a couple hours."

Lexa squared her stance and judged the distance between herself, the trigger-happy leader, and the rest of the crazed molemen.

"This is yer last chance, lady."

She was ready.

The leader tucked the stock into his shoulder and aligned his eyes with the iron sights. All for show, Lexa was almost certain. He let out a heavy sigh and pulled the trigger.

Click!

Tension flushed from Lexa's spine like cold water down a drain. She took the lapse in fear to lunge forward and rip the gun from the diseased man's grip. Then she kicked the knees out from under his waist. He buckled, dropping to the ground like a folding chair. Screaming in pain he ordered, "Get that bitch!" but Lexa had already evaporated into the unlit refuge of the Silver Dollar Supply.

Before the men burst in, Lexa caught the shimmer of Juno's eyes in the blackened room. She put her index finger across her lips, then readied herself in the dark. Her kukri knife was held forward and the weight on her feet was spread evenly. She exhaled slowly.

Bam!

The door ripped from the hinges in a shattered mess. The first man came barreling through blindly and Lexa caught his arm. She cut it off at the shoulder, then drove her blade through the side of his neck. One down.

The second arrived crouched low to the ground. With her free hand, Lexa swooped a feeble leg out from underneath the malnourished man. As he flipped boots-up, she assisted his fall to the ground with a forceful stab in the chest. Two down.

Three and Four squeezed in at the same time. Lexa kicked the nearest one away from her to buy a few seconds. The other had his arms reached out so she removed both of his hands and ended his life through the heart. After recovering from the kick, the fourth lunged at her as she spun to meet him. In an instant, Lexa stepped to the side and sliced the knife through his exposed neck with all of her might. His brittle bones snapped loose an expressionless head that rolled into the darkness.

The decapitated skull stopped eyes-up just short of Juno's feet. A deafening screech followed just as the fifth man entered. Hearing the scream, his compass led him directly to the shrill voice in the shadows. Lexa bolted after, kicked number six back out of the door as she passed, then plunged her knife into the spine of number five, snapping his ribs like dried branches. Blood sprayed Juno's shirt as she witnessed the tip of the kukri burst through the man's chest. Lexa tossed him to the side and grabbed the girl by the arm. "Up the stairs!"

They both sprinted over to the staircase at the back of the Silver Dollar while the rest of the men poured through the front door. The last to stumble in was the audacious leader with the broken knee, his leg wobbling as he hobbled. Lexa pushed Juno ahead to start her up the steps first. One of the men tried to grab at the young girl's foot, but Lexa had stopped him by the neck. She slammed his skull into an iron light fixture on the wall and both man and metal clunked to the ground. Three to go.

Now four sets of feet clambered up the old wooden staircase like an ugly drumroll. Juno's heart raced as her eyes tried to maneuver the darkness. At the top was a narrow hallway that led around to the front of the building. When they reached the end, Lexa picked Juno up by the scruff of her jacket and tossed her out an open window. The young girl rolled across the rickety awning. "Hide!" Lexa commanded, but just as the word left her mouth the two men on their tails tackled her to the ground.

Juno heard the *thump!*, but did her best to obey and stay out of view. She sat down where facade and awning met and held her knees to her chest. Then she rocked back and forth while the horrible grunts and shuffles continued to trickle out the window.

Inside Lexa was scraping for her life. She was fatigued from staving off the first six men and needed to catch her breath while taking on two more. One of the men worked his hands towards her neck while the other climbed to his feet. The brief lapse in the attack allowed her to take in a couple lung's full of air and calculate a way out.

What she decided was to drive her left boot right between the standing man's legs, which sent him toppling over. Making it a one-on-one fight, she pulled the other man's arm down and rolled him over with all of her weight. Now she had the top mount advantage, but missed what passed behind her.

While Juno was cradling her legs, a sickly head popped out from the window. Her body released like a spring as she screamed, "Lexa!"

"Ain't no one here to protect you now, little boy," the leader said as he pulled his useless leg out onto the awning with the rest of him.

Juno slid backwards, fumbling for her knife. She felt its profile in her coat pocket, but the handle caught on the fabric inside, just as she had been warned. Now in a panic, she tugged and tugged as the man hopped towards her.

"How old 're you anyway?" He smiled, flashing moldy teeth. His beady eyes were focused on Juno's neck. "You got a body to match that smooth face?"

The knife was stubborn, but she kept yanking on it. Why had she not taken Lexa's advice and strapped the new one to her chest? Tears began to swell in her eyes as the man closed in. There was no more awning to retreat to before falling twenty feet to the ground...

Just one. More. Tug. Got it!

Much to the man's amusement, the boy now held a small folding knife out in front of him with both hands. "Ain't that cute. And just what're you gonna do with that little toothpick, son?"

Terror scrambled its way into Juno's head and pulled her eyelids shut like curtains, shielding her from the unthinkable brutality of the outside world. She stood frozen. All she could do was hope he would trip and fall on her outstretched blade.

Suddenly Juno was pulled upright by her arms pinned to her side. The crisp clang of fallen metal told her she had dropped her only exit. She clenched her eyes tighter, hoping, just hoping, that it was her mom coming back to rescue her. That she was there to carry Juno off to bed and kiss her goodnight. But the stench of squalid breath squandered the faint wisp of hope. She opened an eye.

"Now let's see what we got here," the repugnant man breathed. He set her down and gripped the lower half her face between his thumb and fingers, ensuring she could neither run nor scream. His rough hands scratched her smooth stomach.

"How come you're wearin'..." he muttered to himself as he lifted the boy's shirt to inspect the silky skin. Then, stumbling back as if he had seen a ghost, "Jesus, fuck! You're a—"

The saliva dripping from the man's mouth had drowned out his statement. He immediately glanced back towards the windows he emerged from to listen for the scuffle.

Nothing.

His dogged attention fixated back on Juno. She was squirming in his arms. He breathed in the top of her hair and exhaled. With the same satisfaction of having just smelled cooked meat, he touched his crusted lips to her fragile ear and divulged, "I can't wait to taste your smooth—"

But the sentiment was interrupted by a quiet gasp of pain. Juno pried open both eyes to see the man still standing in front of her, only with mouth wide open as if he were choking. He hung there for a moment. Then he shifted, but not by his own muscle. Gravity eventually claimed his body as he dropped Juno, tumbled off the awning, and slammed onto the ground twenty feet below with a solid, lifeless *thump!* Standing in his place was Lexa, covered with blood and fury.

Juno immediately cried. Not the light whimper of a stubbed toe, but a primal, infant-like sob. She could not control it. The monstrous events that had just unfolded were like nothing she could have imagined over five lifetimes. The raw animosity...the detached emotion...the desperation... Her naiveté could no longer obscure the savage propensity of man. What she experienced was reality, *true* reality, and it was as swift and sharp as an axe into bark.

So, she wept.

Due to the urgency, Lexa was able to coax Juno off the awning and back out in front of the Silver Dollar Supply. There the empty shotgun laid as rigid and lifeless in the dirt as its former owner. She picked the weapon up and inspected it for damage. It looked to still be in working condition so she attached it to a spare strap around her bag and slung it over her shoulder with ease; hoping the added weight would provide more protection than burden.

Back on the road Juno had a cold aura of silence around her. She had seen too much too quickly. Lexa, tracing the scar across her own eye, understood well enough. She had been tormented by hostility for so long that she nearly forgot the effect it can have on someone so fresh. So undeserving. As with herself, the only crime the young girl had ever committed was being born. It was a violent, unforgiving wasteland, and they were both paying for it.

As the two headed west out of Leadville, the sun winked its last gleam over the Rocky Mountain peaks before leaving the world in darkness. Lexa looked over to see if Juno was watching the warm colors of the sky wash over the stunning landscape, but her head was fixed firmly on the ground. She was broken.

In a spark of unity Lexa tapped Juno's shoulder. Without looking up, the young girl reached out and clasped the offered hand. Together, they walked into the night.

Ten days and hundreds of tireless miles later, Bishop and Deacon were nearing their destination. Trekking the highways from Denver to Utah, they survived on little rest, little food, and little water, each a necessary sacrifice to cross such a distance in such a short time. Little was all they needed, however, all they required. It was in their blood.

When the need to replenish did arise, the two acolytes got by on hijacking any poor soul unfortunate enough to cross their path. The way they saw it, they could help themselves to anything they needed without penance. For they were on a mission; a hallowed crusade gifted to them by their Creator.

Deep in the heart of Uinta National Forest, they took a route that had been ingrained in them since they could first form memories. A collection of dried river beds, bypassing caves, and inscribed landmarks carved out the only path to their promised land. And even though the sun had already broken the ridgeline, they could have just as easily found the one mountain they called home in total darkness. A mountain as divine to them as the one who occupied it. A mountain fit for a king. Sanctuary.

They turned down a cliff-lined path that eventually led them into a barren, circular clearing of gravel closed off from the rest of the world. Encompassing them was nothing but grey stone, grey rock, and grey boulders. In front, however, was the glorious entrance to the Grotto.

A smattering of corrugated sheet metal, collected road signs, and steel beams carved into spikes encompassed a colossal drawbridge fashioned out of a CamChem billboard. Ever burning torches lined the fifty-foot front door bearing the faded image of a shielded logo and a man smiling by a car. Stains of old blood spilled from the top and dripped over a single scribbled message at the center: CREATOR OF HEAVEN AND EARTH.

Among the cluster of rusted chaos was a skull dangling from a chain. Bishop walked up to the morbid doorbell and pulled on it. A faint *gong!* squeezed out the sides of the drawbridge. After a short pause, the massive chains slowly lowered the metal door, revealing a black hole carved out of the mountain rock with perfect precision. A cool rush of air sent the torch flames dancing. Then came a rapid pitter-patter, slapping like hard rain, until something emerged from the opening.

A small man on all fours scurried out into the clearing and hissed at the morning sun. Except for the black and red blemishes consuming his emaciated body, his skin was ghostly white. A tattered leather skirt circled his thin hips and a worn leather hood once used for falcon training covered his head and eyes—the top of which splayed a decorative crest of preserved feathers. Locked around his neck was a metal collar with a prominent hook meant for a leash. When he curled to speak, his spine protruded. "What dossst thou ssseek from the massster?"

Bishop rolled his eyes. "You know of the imperative circumstances of our visit, Locust."

"You come empty handed. He will not be pleasssed."

"We have news," Deacon spat. "Now fuck off."

The virulent dog of a man raised his head to Bishop and sniffed the air. Then to Deacon. Then back to Bishop. "Where isss the third?"

"You little cretin!" Deacon made one forward motion and Locust hopped back like an insect, hissing. "Move aside or go get the boss!"

A tense silence filled the opening until Locust felt satisfied with the discomfort he had contrived. "Very well. You will wait here."

The decrepit man scampered back into the cave where the patter of his hands and feet faded.

"Jesus Christ that thing gives me the heebie jeebies," Deacon said, feigning an exaggerated shiver.

"Slaves are plentiful," Bishop sneered in response. "It's beyond myself why He chooses to keep *that* one."

Time crawled as the two acolytes kicked lines in the dirt or looked up at the sky. The sun had drawn a sharp line of protective shade in the clearing that forced them to shuffle forwards every few minutes. When they finally heard the pattering return, Bishop was scratching at a sore on the back of his hand and Deacon had just pulled out a handful of wispy hair.

Locust reappeared and squatted obediently by the side of the Grotto's black entrance. Shortly after, a low plod bled out from the cave and echoed through the clearing. Deacon moved behind Bishop in the way a knight picks up a shield. Bishop noticed, but was focused on the impending reproach growing louder and louder and louder.

Suddenly, the reverberation dissipated. Materializing from the cave were two gigantic men, equally wide as they were tall, that were covered in the same attire and ghoulish skin as the small, squatting Locust. In their hands were two golden posts attached to a platform behind. On the platform was a turquoise-laden chair shrouded by a small awning that draped translucent silk curtains. Further back, two more giants of the same breed emerged sharing the same load.

The entire caravan stopped just short of the shade's cooling border. A voice rattled from behind the curtain. "When I blessed you with the highest honor of Bishop, I anticipated you fulfilling my destiny. Instead you return with no child and one less to my clergy."

Bishop pressed his hands together and bowed. "As always, I am humbled by your—"

"*I* am the humbled one!" The voice boomed as it found sudden strength. "*You* are a gift of *my* grace; a lamb for *my* offering."

Bishop fell to a humiliated silence. "Apologies, Creator."

"And since you have returned with less than you were given, I pray, for your sake, that there is a compelling basis to darken my doorstep."

"We..." Bishop started, then swallowed an uncharacteristic lump of nerves. "We've laid eyes on the child, dear Creator, and returned with proof of her existence."

Disdainful stillness padded the clearing, but curiosity proved to be the victor. "Present your findings."

Deacon scooted hesitantly out from behind Bishop and handed over the two-foot section of hair they had recovered in Denver. Bishop took it in his hands, ran a thumb across the soft brown strands, then started towards the chariot. After only two steps Locust skittered over and snatched the hair from Bishop's hand. "No one approachesss Creator," he hissed.

Stunned, Bishop and Deacon watched as the small man climbed up one of the giants like a ladder and hopped onto the platform. There he knelt, presenting the hair in upturned palms as if it were a holy relic. A smooth, oily arm extended from behind the silk curtains and carefully accepted the offering.

The line of sun burning across the clearing had reached the front of the carriage so the giants reactively took one step backwards into the shade. It was also now bright enough to reveal that the silhouette behind the curtains had the ponytail pressed against its face.

"Tell me," the one they called Creator commanded, "How is it you came to acquire the hair of the child, but not the child herself?"

Bishop slightly raised his shoulders, unsure of the exact words to use. "When we discovered her, your reverence, we assumed she'd be alo—"

Deacon bumped Bishop as he stepped around with newfound bravery in his boots. "That bitch Lexa axed Laity and took the damn girl. We found the hair inside a house while we were trailin' them."

"*Who* was with the girl?" Creator bellowed. They could see the curtained outline slide a hand down his forehead and across his cheek. Anger tempered his voice. "Are you implying that the heathens of the dome are now involved?"

"It appears so, your reverence," Bishop admitted, knowing exactly what was around the corner.

"This would not bear any correlation with the mother you allowed to escape, would it?"

Bishop's head felt heavier on his neck. He remembered that night vividly. It was all routine. He was preparing the mother for the ceremony when—

"This day is met with great disappointment," Creator continued. "Tell me you have returned with more news than this contemptible donation of hair."

Deacon stepped back in. "We found out they took the mountains southwest through Leadville. Most likely to avoid us trailin' em on the highway."

"You knew their heading yet arrived here instead? Explain."

"That land is swarming with molemen," Deacon added. "Their numbers have surged since they took to cookin' humans."

"Answer my question, Bishop," Creator grumbled.

Worried Deacon would get them both crucified if he spoke any longer, Bishop took over the reigns. "The mountains are too dangerous for a woman and a child to venture alone. There is less food and more hostility than ever before. I predict they will resort to established roads in short time. Fortunately for us, there are only two paths that lead to Arcadia. Paths we can choke."

A silence followed that was so extended, the giants had to take another step backwards into the shade. The shamed acolytes could feel the heat from the sun on their necks, but they dared not move.

"No," Creator finally spoke. "I will not allow that transgression to spend another moment with that which belongs to me." Then, after some thought, he addressed his failed trackers more severely. "Bishop.

Deacon. You will re-embark with thirteen of my clergy's strongest. They will answer only to you. Scour the mountains, smoke them out if you have to, so long as you bring them *both* to me. Alive. Anyone who stands in your way will be considered a martyr to my divine crusade. So says I."

The giants shrugged the strain from their shoulders and began turning the chariot around. The two acolytes looked at each other with a grave sense of understandment.

"Oh, and Bishop," Creator mentioned as his back was being turned for him, "If you are unable to complete your mission this time, the hunt will turn to you."

Bishop blinked.

The four giants disappeared back into the Grotto with Creator in hand. After they were out of site, Locust announced, "All hasss been heard! Fear Him and keep His commandmentsss, for thisss isss the whole duty of man!" Then he scampered back into the darkness as well.

Bishop and Deacon both muttered, "Amen."

Shortly after, the two acolytes heard another sound swelling inside the black hole. Not slapping or pounding, something far more shrill. Something that sent eager electricity up their spines. It was their reinforcements, and they were howling with bloodlust.

Entry 34

This is the first time I've been alone with my thoughts since Leadville. I hoped it would be such a nice place to stop on our way to Arcadia, but I was wrong. Nothing in this world is nice.

That day keeps playing inside my head over and over. I don't think Lexa knows, but I heard the whole conversation she had with those evil men. What they did to her friend with the ropes.

Then they ran in through that door and she

just...cut them all to pieces.

I know they deserved it. Of course they did. But that head. I can't get it out of my mind. It stopped at my feet and looked right at me. His eyes were so empty. There was nothing behind them.

The last thing I really remember after that is Lexa throwing me out of a window. That wicked man with the wobbly leg crawled out and asked me how old I was and told me he wanted to taste me. Why?!

Anyway, the last few days have been very quiet between me and Lexa. We hike, we sleep, we eat, and we hike some more. She's even more closed off now. I can't help but feel like she's mad at me. I feel like I let her down. I could have helped if I wasn't so stupid. She warned me my knife would get stuck and that's exactly what happened.

I need to be stronger. Smarter. But I'm too scared.

The ceaseless sun was directly overhead and it was again too hot to move on. At two miles above sea level there was little to no shade, and even less remorse for anything living. Lexa and Juno had to seek cover for the afternoon.

Far below was a cluster of four structures not quite large enough to be considered a town. Juno mumbled that she did not want to go anywhere near another building, but Lexa insisted they might contain useful supplies, so they compromised and started down the mountain.

Three fourths of the cluster consisted of a dried up gas station, a rickety convenience store, and a dusty auto shop brimming with stacks of cracked tires, all underneath a towering red shield that read CamChem in bold white letters. On the opposite side of a buckled interstate was an abandoned restaurant. All four of the units were battered by time and had already been ransacked by scavengers. It was rare to find any sort of former business still stocked with goods and this place was no different. Yet they diligently searched the gas station and worked their way clockwise to the auto parts warehouse. Besides gobs of discarded plastic packaging, each location turned up empty.

When they crossed over to the restaurant, Juno spotted a large plastic decal on the ground near the street. It had fallen from a tall black post that stretched over thirty feet in the air. Out of curiosity, she walked over to look at it. The sign was in the shape of an arch. Inside a white border was some purplish coloring and a large pink bell swinging a yellow hammer. At the bottom were eight letters that were crumpled by the fall. "Come," she heard, then joined Lexa at the door.

Inside was the usual: broken chairs and tables, scattered trash, and no food. Lexa gravitated towards a machine with a bunch of spouts and buttons that said `push` and started taking it apart.

Juno wandered around. She hopped over a sooty counter and kicked a bunch of patterned paper out of the way. On the ground were some shattered black screens, some purple trays, and a plastic container of pamphlets. She slipped out one of the folded sheets and blew off the dust. "Taco Bell Menu," she read aloud, then flipped it open. Her mouth began to water.

Pictures upon pictures of hot, vibrant foods taunted her stomach. Juno recognized rice, beans, and red sauce, but there were so many more colors these delicacies had to offer. Melted strands of yellow, dollops of white, slivers of green, chunks of brown, all wrapped up inside a flat piece of bread. It was not until a drop of saliva landed on a dish named `Crunchwrap Supreme` did she notice her jaw hanging open. She shook herself out of her hunger-fueled stupor and slipped the pamphlet into her backpack. It fit nicely next to the Leadville postcard.

Lexa called Juno over as she finished zipping up her bag. She had gotten a tube loose from the nozzle-filled machine and they topped off their canteens with what water was left.

"Hungry?" Lexa asked when they were finished.

Impossible to describe how hungry the menu had made her, Juno simply said, "Yes."

In the back was a stainless steel kitchen Lexa once again found herself using a portable cooker in. She flipped through the MREs and sighed at how few she had left. If they did not start making better time, they would really have to start scavenging. "Rice and beans again?" she asked.

Knowing the food pack would taste nothing like the rice and beans in the photos, Juno's mouth evaporated. "Sounds good."

"Go clear off a table and set up two chairs. We should be safe, but keep an eye on the road."

Juno left and Lexa dumped the dried food mixture into some warming water. Leaving the food set for a while, she searched around the kitchen, yearning for some much needed luck. The shelves and containers out in the open held nothing. Even if they did, the contents would be so petrified that it would have been impossible to consume as food anyway.

At the edge of the kitchen she spotted a large stainless steel door that was padlocked shut. Lexa stirred the food as she passed by on her way over to it. She inspected the old padlock and hoped age had weakened its inner workings. Then she pulled a small bobby pin from a pocket in her bag and jammed it where the key would have gone. After wiggling it around for a few moments, she heard a click and the lock released.

A horribly stagnant cloud billowed from the door as new air rushed in. Lexa pinched her nose tight as she breathed with her mouth. She entered the dead freezer and predictably found shelves of plastic containers housing food that was rotted and dried beyond recognition. She almost left when she spotted a box on the top shelf that was still sealed. She grabbed it and quickly closed the foul-smelling vault behind her.

Lexa stirred the almost-cooked MRE once more, then slapped the box down on one of the counters. She cut the tape with the unnecessarily large kukri knife and pried back the flaps. Inside was a thick plastic bag filled with hundreds of individually wrapped packets that said FIRE on them.

A sudden mass cracked and fell from the frozen glacier around Lexa's heart and warm sorrow poured out. *It isn't fair!* she screamed inside. *She doesn't deserve this!* The torment that was her entire life struck the back of her eyes like a maelstrom. Tears streamed down her cheeks as she leaned onto her elbows, fists clenched. *She deserves a childhood, Pan. It's not my fault I didn't work. And it's not her fault she does...*

Lexa nearly pounded a dent into the steel countertop when she smelled the slight burning of food. "Shit," she exhaled, then rushed back across the kitchen to remove the pot from the small burner. After rubbing away the escaped tears with the sleeve of her duster, she took a deep breath and left the kitchen with food and Fire Sauce.

Back in the lobby Juno was sitting at an intact booth that she had proudly cleaned off. Set on the table were two purple trays, two black plastic bowls, and two packets of plastic cutlery. She watched as Lexa served the pot of rice and beans evenly between them, then put the pot aside. Her sleeve was damp, but Juno was not about to ask why.

Lexa sat down across from the young girl and watched her take the first mouthful. Juno's face scrunched from the slightly burnt paste she had to force down.

"I found you something," Lexa said before Juno moved on to the second bite.

Juno's eyes widened skeptically as she sat back in her seat. "Really?"

Lexa reached into her backpack and tossed a plastic bag on the table. Juno excitedly picked it up before she saw what was inside. "Fire? What's that?"

Lexa shrugged. "Try it."

Juno thought she detected the slightest grin on her companion's face before ripping the bag open. She took out one of the red packets and inspected it closer. `Hello` was written inside a small white square under the label so she said, "Hello," back. Then she tore a corner off the packet and squeezed its contents onto her meal. Spork in hand, she scooped in another mouthful.

Juno's face immediately turned red as the sauce started aflame on her taste buds. She chewed and swallowed as quickly as possible, all while grasping for her canteen. After she emptied half of the soothing liquid over her tongue, she slammed it back on the table and continued panting frantically through her mouth. "What *is* that stuff?"

This time Lexa was actually laughing. Well, as much as Juno assumed Lexa *could* laugh. A grin with exhaled air through the nose was more than she could have ever expected. And so, despite her pain, she giggled too.

The hot sauce had relieved some of the unspoken tension and they settled back into the regular silence experienced during mealtimes together. Juno looked over at a window. It was hot inside the restaurant, but not as scalding as it was outside. Invisible waves danced on top of the black pavement. She watched the shadows cast by mountains crawl across the ground, slowly extinguishing the radiant heat.

"Why is it called mankind?" Juno asked abruptly, still gazing out the window.

Lexa gave a confused look. "What do you mean?"

"Mankind," Juno said, returning to her food. "Why is it called that?"

"It's just a term. The collective of everyone."

Juno took another bite, careful to avoid the hot sauce. "Well, they should change it."

"And why's that?"

Juno's eyes fell to the ground. "Because I've never met a man that's kind."

The fog between them suddenly cleared. Lexa watched as Juno slowly understood what she herself had been forced to learn long ago. She understood the young girl's confusion, the contradicting feelings bubbling inside. But Juno did not need a lecture from a stranger right now. What she needed was a friend.

"I agree," Lexa confirmed with an amused smile.

Massaged by the unexpected affirmation, Juno released a heavy sigh. "Well, at least I have you on my side."

Lexa's eyes did the smiling this time. "That you do." Then, after glimpsing the shade enter the windows, she added, "Let's finish up and head out."

On semi-full stomachs, Lexa led Juno back up the mountain they had just descended. She could tell that Juno's muscles and lungs were adapting to the terrain because she had, for the first time, not slipped or complained once on the ascent.

When they reached the top, a cooling pink sky chased an orange sun behind the endless vista of mountains. "Wow," Juno gasped as the magnificence of the rose-painted landscape swelled. Despite the bleak desolation of the scorched earth, beauty still found ways of thriving.

Watching the quiet serenity alongside, Lexa spoke. "Juno. It's extremely dangerous out there and it will only get moreso. What you saw the other day was not uncommon. Do you understand?"

"Yes," Juno nodded.

"It's just us girls out here. We need to protect each other." Then Lexa kneeled down so they were at eye level. Equals. "Do you trust me?"

Juno's eyes welled before admitting, "Yes."

"Good. If you can be strong, and listen to what I tell you, then we'll stop somewhere I think you'll enjoy."

A glass door whirred open in the still of the night. A young boy walked barefoot down a cold, sterile hallway lined with other glass doors that led to offices. A faint yellow light spilled out from one such room at the far end of the corridor. The rest of Arcadia was asleep.

The door of the office slid silently and the boy entered. It was a rectangular room with nothing on the white walls but the materials used to build them. To his right was a small cot, large enough for one person, and to his left was a grey sofa with small bookshelves on either side. At the far end sat a woman with short sandy hair wearing an all-white jumpsuit. She was at her desk, working diligently through the night.

The boy sleepily tugged at her shirt. "Mommy?"

The woman nearly jumped out of her seat, then placed a hand on her chest after realizing who it was. "Rodan, you scared me! What are you doing awake?"

"I can't sleep," the boy replied, rubbing his eyes to sell the story.

Setting down her glasses and her pen, the woman spun around her chair and lifted the boy into her arms. "Now Rodan, we've talked about this. You need to call me Pan. Do you understand?"

The boy nestled his head into her shoulders. "Yes."

Pan carried Rodan back down the long hallway and into his room. The glass door whirred shut behind them as she laid him gently on his bed. "So, what is keeping you up tonight?"

Rodan pulled the covers up to his neck. "I'm worried about Lexa," he said.

Pan gave him a comforting smile and smoothed out some of the ruffles in the blankets. "And why would you be worried about Lexa?"

"Well," he started, almost too embarrassed to say now, "it's just that I haven't seen her in a really long time."

"Lexa has been very busy lately, Rodan."

Disappointed with the non-answer, the boy turned his back to Pan in a huff. She knew he was not actually mad at her, but it stung just the same. His only interactions with Lexa as of late had been at night, in secret, and against the strict will of the council. Pan may have been an enabling third party, but the truth about Lexa's permanent hiatus still needed to be saved until he had older ears. Her exile was not something she was willing to expose to the boy quite yet. Not while there was still hope.

Pan stroked the top of Rodan's head until something positive popped into her mind.

"She's on a very special mission, you know."

Rodan uncurled and rolled back towards Pan. "What kind of mission?" he asked, clearly curious.

Pan flashed her comforting smile again. "A super secret mission," she winked.

"Woah!" Rodan half shouted half yawned.

"Woah indeed."

The boy imagined a super secret mission in his head for a while. From his books he pictured far off mountains, a daring hero, a valiant rescue, and, of course, danger. "Do you think she's safe?"

"Of course." There was a sliver of uncertainty in Pan's tone. "I'd expect so."

"Pinky promise?"

Rodan lifted his small hand with his smallest finger extended. She gripped it in the same way and nodded. "Pinky promise."

With the boy now appeased, Pan stood up and lifted the blankets to tuck him in properly. He shuffled around while she watched warmly. There was a short silence in the room before Rodan asked, "Is Shelby in here?"

"Oh, I'm sure she's around somewhere."

After a few more moments of calm, Pan inched towards the door so she could head back down the hall and resume her research. She had nearly made it when she heard, "Hey m...Pan? Is it an important mission?"

"Yes, Rodan. One that could save all of mankind."

"Awesome," he yawned again. "Good night."

Pan flipped the light switch off, sending the boy to sleep. The glass door slid open to reveal a small, dark tortoise inching its way across the hallway floor. Pan gently lifted the animal and set it inside the terrarium on Rodan's desk. She absorbed the welcome tranquility like a thirsty sponge and whispered, "Good night."

Entry 38

Things have been a lot better between me and Lexa. I still have no idea why it's so important I get to Arcadia, but at least she's making sure I get there in one piece. I think maybe I could annoy some answers out of her. I also think she doesn't want to talk about it. I didn't want to say anything at the time, but I noticed her sleeve was wet at the Taco Bell. She's so tough, though. She probably just spilled.

How are the mountains, you ask? Still just as hard to climb as ever. But I'm getting used to it. It still gets super cold up here at night and last night we had to sleep under the same blanket for warmth. I'd never tell her this, but I liked it. It felt like before.

What else is new...

Oh yeah, Lexa has been staying up later and later. Some days I don't know if she sleeps at all. I wonder if she thinks we're being followed. I can't imagine chasing anything up here. You'd either run out of breath or slip and fall down a mountain. That'd be funny to watch!

One last thing. A few days ago Lexa told me we're headed somewhere she thought I'd enjoy and it sounds like we'll be getting there tomorrow. I'm so excited! Most of my time has been spent trying to think of what it could be. A candy store? A notebook store? A regular book store? Probably not up here...

Alength of rope flew in the air and slapped against the rocks as it unraveled. Juno stretched her arm to reach it as she clung to the cliffside. "Do you have it?" a voice called from above, but she could only graze it with her fingertips. "Not yet!"

Actual rock climbing was a first for Juno. Her legs and back had gained an exponential amount of strength from the endless days of hiking, but her arms and shoulders still left much to be desired. She was barely hanging on. Muscles twitched. And a quick scan across the jagged rock wall returned no more footholds. *How did she get up there so fast?*

"I can't reach it!" her voice echoed upwards after a few more tries.

A head poked out over the crest and shouted back, "One second!" The rope swung outwards and grazed against Juno's back. She managed to snag both of her hands around it and clenched tightly. Trusting it would hold, she leaned backwards. "Got it!"

When Juno reached the end of her ride, she saw Lexa had reeled in the entire rope with arms and back only. Her jaw nearly dropped in amazement. Clearly she had work to do.

Lexa let the rope fall to her side, then followed a long stretch with a heavy exhale. Her forehead was dotted with sweat.

While Lexa packed up, Juno timidly took a look around. They were in a flat area of land between conjoining peaks. All she saw was dirt and rock even dryer than below. An arid summit smothered by the sun. "Why did we come all the way up here?" she asked. "There's nothing."

Lexa had finished shoving the rope inside her backpack and slung the bag around her shoulder. The motion had been noticeably less fluid since the added awkwardness of the shotgun. "You'll see."

Juno bit her tongue and followed Lexa down a short slope. Near the nadir, they turned a corner towards an unassuming path. The gravel below their feet was not packed down tightly like an established trail, but something about it still guided them in this direction. They walked a while before finally arriving at two titanous fallen boulders, each as big as a house, wedged between the mountain walls. Between the leaning stones was a gap barely wide enough for one person to slip through.

Lexa did exactly that.

Juno hesitated. Something about two building-sized rocks resting against each other did not sit well in her stomach. The incident in Leadville had shown her primal fear, but being flattened by boulders was sensible fear. "Come on!" she heard from the other side, so she swallowed the lump in her throat and squeezed through the cleft.

Waiting on the other side was something Juno never would have fathomed. Something she could not even dream up to sketch in her notebook. She found herself standing inside a bowl, perfectly scooped out with a spoon, surrounded by smooth mountain cliff on all sides. Other than the small gap Lexa had somehow known about, there was no other way in or out. They were utterly and completely secluded.

After a few steps inward, Juno discovered the mysterious basin concealed more wonderful secrets. The rough gravel under her feet transitioned to sand so fine, so white, that each grain could have been bleached and polished individually. It was soft too. Plush enough that Lexa's footprints created ovoid indentations that held perfectly in place. And no matter how hard she squinted, not a single fragment of trash sullied the ivory blanket.

Juno's eyes followed the impressions down the bowl where she saw the true incentive for their visit. At the center of the basin was a massive pool of water so blue that even the sun was unable to blanch its color. It sat waveless like a panel of glass, beckoning to be disrupted. Juno's heart fluttered. For the first time on their journey they would fill their bottles and stomachs with fresh water not soured by rusty pipes.

But just as quickly as Juno's heart rose, it also sank. Standing just short of the water's flawless edge was Lexa. She was naked.

"Are you coming?" Lexa shouted at Juno's frozen body. Her voice echoed invitingly against the surrounding rock.

Head down, the young girl slowly joined at the edge of the water, her eyes diverting Lexa's body as if they were magnets of the same polarization. She had never seen another person naked before.

"Well, come on. Take off your clothes and hop in," Lexa said with a flick of her head towards the cerulean pool. Then, without hesitation, walked into the water.

As Juno agonizingly removed her own backpack, jacket, shoes, and socks, she found herself sheepishly studying every movement of Lexa's physique. Her strong shoulders led Juno's eyes down a muscle-lined canyon that stopped just short of her curved hips. Her backside was elliptic and robust, and was supported by powerful legs that were amplified by the sunlight. Her amaretto skin glistened in tune with the water's reflection. Juno was so mesmerized that she hardly noticed the slight discoloration of scar tissue spanning her back like a rake through sand.

Lexa turned and saw Juno's face flush with red embarrassment. She looked down at her own exposed frontside and smiled. "Like I said, it's just us girls out here!"

Juno had bashfully removed her sports bra and bottoms, but still covered everything she could with her arms. Their figures were so vastly different that an apologetic remorse for her own body felt like a hundred-pound blanket. Lexa was so strong, so full, while she was flat and twiglike; one undeserving of the presence of the other. She wanted to bury herself in a hole.

"Hey," Lexa said after quickly dipping her head under the surface. Beads of water sparkled on her skin. "Never be ashamed of your body. Someday you'll be twice the woman I ever was."

There was an arduous truth underneath that statement that Juno had yet to understand, but Lexa's reassurance at least removed the red from her face. She took a bashful look around, lowered her arms, and stepped into the water. It was cold! Her body tensed as the frigid water nipped at her toes, then her calves, then her thighs. Once she was waist deep, she paused.

"Now what's wrong?" Lexa asked while casually wading in circles.

Juno had never been inside a body of water larger than a half-filled bathtub. "I—" she cut herself off, embarrassed yet again. "I don't know how to swim."

This revelation did not appear to surprise Lexa. "I suppose not, huh? Come out here as far as you can stand and I'll teach you."

Now acclimated to the refreshing cold water, Juno shimmied inward up to her chest. Lexa came around and instructed her to lean backwards. As her body tilted, one comforting hand lifted her legs and one braced her lower back. Juno floundered for a minute until she realized she was being held in place.

"Be still," Lexa instructed. "Breathe normally and focus on staying flat. I'm going to remove my hands." Juno immediately tensed up at the thought of being on her own so Lexa repeated softly, "Relax."

Juno took a deep breath and closed her eyes. First the hand on her lower back vanished, then the one from her legs. She mentally braced for drowning. A few seconds passed, then half a minute, then a full minute until she realized she would not sink. The cool water cradled her back while the warm sun caressed her front. There, floating naked in the middle of a lake, in the middle of a basin, in the middle of a mountain, was the first time Juno felt truly free.

They spent over an hour practicing the front stroke, backstroke, and doggy-paddle, but, most importantly to Juno, they were smiling. Swimming was strenuous yet immensely rewarding. Traversing the water felt as much like a cleanse to her built up stress as it was to her built up grime. Body and lungs worked harmoniously for the satisfaction of gliding through something other than land. And it made her happy.

Soon after Juno could sustain on her own, Lexa returned to the beach and emptied their bags. She collected all of the clothes and washed them in the clear water. Then she had Juno return to help lay out the articles across sunkissed rocks to dry. Finally, they each filled up their canteens and sat on a blanket Lexa had laid out at the edge of the lake.

Juno quenched her thirst and sprawled out. The sun warmed her bare body as she closed her eyes to listen to the water. It was as quiet as glass once again. She breathed out a heavy smile and absorbed the stillness until, surprisingly, Lexa kindled a conversation.

"You know, this is what girls did all the time back in the old days. Go for a swim, lay out on the beach, read a good book."

Juno rolled her head sideways and squinted one eye open. She caught an intimate glimpse of Lexa's nude profile once again, but the previous shame must have drowned in the water. "That sounds really nice." Then, careful not to spoil the perfect afternoon they were having, she slipped back into the safety of silence.

But Lexa continued on. "So tell me about your favorite animal."

Was this some sort of test? A lesson? Was Juno supposed to describe the defensive behaviors of wildlife and how she could apply them to her daily survival? But since she was forced to leave behind her field guide as a reference she asked, "What do you mean?" just to be sure.

Lexa was gazing at the sky. "You were unreasonably excited when you thought a malformed slave driver was a turtle. And I heard you muttering that power lines in the road looked like snakes. So I figure you're interested in animals."

"Tortoise," Juno chimed almost too eagerly, but it was hard to conceal her elation from the question.

"Huh?"

"He looked like a tortoise. Have you ever seen one?"

"Oh, yes," Lexa said, "legs, not flippers. I have seen one. It's been a while, though."

Juno's right hand clenched the edge of the blanket like a vice grip. "You have! Where?"

After suspending Juno until she was practically shaking, Lexa teased, "If I tell you, you have to keep it a secret. Deal?" She held out her fist and extended her smallest finger. Juno stared at it quizzically. "You wrap yours around mine. It's called a pinky promise."

Juno did the same. It felt unbreakable. "Pinky promise," she repeated.

After another theatrical pause, Lexa continued. "I know someone in Arcadia who has one."

It was all Juno could do not to pack up her bag and sprint to Arcadia that very second. The pressure of excitement built up in her throat like steam until she released it with a high pitched screech. Now relieved, she drew in a new breath and got down to brass tax. "Boy or girl? What's its name? Is it Box or Painted or Spotted?"

"Hm..." It was not the question that surprised Lexa, but the lack of an answer. She had never cared enough to gather details. "I'm not sure. Brownish. Probably Torty or something."

Juno returned to her back and huffed. A lull swelled between them before someone spoke again.

"What would you name it?" raised Lexa.

"Hm…" Juno reciprocated. Truth be told, she only ever knew two people outside herself. "If it was a girl, I would probably name her Lexa."

"I would be honored," Lexa smirked. "And if it was male?"

Juno chewed harder on this one. What was a worthy male name? Dean was kind of a hotshot at the highschool in her ancient teen romance book, but that hardly seemed appropriate for a tortoise. And she had certainly never met a real life man who's name she admired. So she floated back to the only other person she ever loved. "Maia."

"Maia," Lexa repeated. "That's a nice name. Where does it come from?"

"It was my mom's name."

They both turned stiff as corpses. Juno felt the overwhelming guilt she had been suppressing return. How had she forgotten about her mother so quickly?

Lexa rolled over to her side after what felt to her like the appropriate amount of time. "Say, Juno. There's something I need to tell you. About your mother."

Culpability faced Juno to Lexa, but there was something curious about Lexa's eyes. They were in her direction, but not on her. Then she heard it. They both did.

A group of outside rocks tumbled down the inner edge of the basin, leaving a trail of white dust behind. Before the first stone reached the ground, Juno could have sworn she saw something retreat from the crest of the ridge. Something dark. But it disappeared as quickly as she spotted it.

Lexa interrupted Juno's gaze with a shove on the shoulder. "Get dressed. We need to move."

The two of them gathered up their now-dry clothes and slipped them on. They were stiff from the lack of detergent, but at least they were clean. Lexa rolled up the blanket on the beach while Juno topped off the canteens.

Dry and fully clothed, Juno again realized how unforgiving the sun really was. A little bit of movement had her wiping droplets of sweat from her forehead as she longed for the lake one last time. Would she ever step foot in a place as beautiful as this again? Was this a final memento from the way the world used to be? One that somehow managed to seclude itself from man's destructive nature? Could this have all just been a wonderful dream she would wake from at any minute?

She did not know, but they left the same way they had entered: as if they had never been there.

The storm came abruptly and with malice, as if its sole purpose was to harm. Gales of dirt and debris bombarded the sierra. Rocks pelted the cliffside like unwieldy rain, wind shredded what little bark clung to dead trees, and the earth swirled up into towering clouds. An amber atmosphere of soot blotted out the sun, eliminating the shadows of everything below. Nothing exposed to the rabid tempest would escape unscathed.

The man pulled his makeshift cloak tightly around his body while he scrambled down the rockface. As the storm picked up momentum, the growing fragments in the air became increasingly deadly. He needed to find cover. A cave, a house, a hole in the ground. Anything to shield him from the life-taking hail.

When he cornered a jagged, protruding boulder, a gust of wind swept his legs out from underneath. In the air he felt gravity's grasp yank his body downhill. He landed hard on his side, sending sharp pain from his hips to his shoulders, and went tumbling. Nearly four flailing rolls later he caught the side of a fallen tree trunk with his spine. It hurt, but it saved his life.

He shook the pain off and scanned the side of the mountain through what little visibility remained. It all blended together in a greyish brownish paste. Only able to make out the faint outlines of objects, he stayed tight against the bulk of the mountain, and felt his way along with outstretched arms. There had to be something...

There!

Behind a cluster of stumps, and between two jutting rock formations, a dark slit in the mountainside revealed itself. He lowered a pair of protective goggles and sprinted over using everything left in his numbed legs. Debris pelted him, surely creating a matrix of bruises along the way. When he finally reached the crevice he did not immediately enter. Something told him to turn around, to peer once more into the raging sandstorm.

With a gloved hand, the man swiped a layer of quickly accumulating dust from his glass lenses and took one last look. There they were. Below, about a hundred yards or so, were two silhouettes. One his size and one much smaller. Both were struggling against the wind.

The man bit his lower lip, noting how chapped it felt against his smooth teeth. This situation assumed an immense amount of risk, and the reward was not in his favor. The simple facts were either he would be killed on the way towards them, or, if they reached the safety of the cave, killed *by* them.

While he mulled over his options a branch struck the head of the larger silhouette, dropping them heavily to the ground. The smaller silhouette followed.

You have got to be the dumbest man alive, he thought to himself. Then he pulled his cloak taut and made a last-second dash into the all-engulfing storm. The wind pushed and pulled on his balance but he remained planted. Step after stubborn step he crossed the distance.

"Wake up!"

The voice was distorted by the sand. It sounded high-pitched. Youthful.

"Lexa!"

Must be a name.

"Stand up! We need to—"

With one arm the man heaved the screaming child to their feet, then kneeled down to scoop up the larger one, backpack and all. As he lifted the lifeless body the hood of its jacket was ripped down by the wind, revealing a startling truth about the stranger. *A woman? Out here?* Another branch flew by, reminding him to put a cork in his queries.

"Follow me!" he yelled to the child over the storm, then started up the hill. "Keep your head down!"

The added weight did not do his legs any favors, but he managed to get himself and the woman all the way back to the cave's opening without delay. Before entering he waved the child through. This time he would not look back.

Either the howling wind or the crackling fire brought Lexa back to life. She sat up like a stepped-on rake and was immediately aware of her missing baggage. Behind her the storm raged on in the dying light. Before her was a dark tunnel. A faint orange glow flickered on and off the damp walls.

Lexa jumped to her feet and was pulled over to the cave wall like a magnet. She caught herself with an arm and braced her weight. Her head had been split in two and was now swirling. Vaguely, she remembered a branch...

On the ground was a blanket and her duster. They must have fallen off when she stood up. Her hand groped across her chest until it rested comfortably on the handle of her kukri knife. She hefted a sigh of relief and slouched down, forcing her mind to overcome its vertigo. Once the cave stopped spinning, she started down the tunnel.

Voices trickled from around the glowing corner. She pressed her back to the cold cave rock and listened silently. Between fire snaps, Lexa heard at least two; one older and male, and one definitely Juno's. She inched closer to the opening, keeping a tight grip on her knife. The low murmur of the man's voice was interrupted by another crackle of flame, then...laughter?

Lexa's eyes widened. She jumped into the opening with her blade held forward. But before she could rescue Juno from the sadistic kidnapper, he spoke to her.

"Hey there," the man said kindly enough. "You were out for quite a while. How are you feelin'?"

On either side of the warm fire were two people Lexa desperately did not want exposed to each other. To the left was a man about her age, skin dark as freshly tilled dirt and a head of tightly kept black hair. Thick, muscular arms reached out from a sleeveless cloak to poke at a burning log inside the flames. On the right was Juno, looking neither scared nor worried.

"Get up, Juno," Lexa said, flicking the kukri towards the shotgun and two backpacks on the ground nearby. "We're leaving."

"But—" Juno contested.

"Now."

The man smiled a knowing smile. "Now hold on there. Unless you plan on battlin' that sandstorm in the dead of night, I—"

"You," Lexa interrupted while Juno looped the bag over her outstretched hand. "You do not tell us what to do."

Juno's arm was nearly pulled from the socket as Lexa yanked her out of the opening. She was hauled back down the rocky tunnel and all the way up to the cave's entrance. Then she was suddenly released. Juno rubbed her shoulder as Lexa watched the storm rage on from the edge of the mouth.

"Fuck!" Juno thought she heard before it was silent for a long time after. Long enough for her to sit on the cold, rough ground while she waited. Eventually Lexa hung her head and came back inside.

"Juno," she said as she kneeled in front of the girl. "What did you tell that man?"

"What do you mean?" Juno asked genuinely.

"About me. About our destination. About your..." Lexa paused. "What did you say?"

"I didn't say anything!"

"If he finds out what we're doing...how important you are..."

Juno was backed into a corner; trapped on all sides by old fear and uncertainty. It was a feeling that followed her every movement since she had started remembering things. All her life she was only told *that* she was important, but never *why* she was important. Tears welled. She was ready to snap.

"I'm not special!" she barked. "I'm just a kid!"

Juno darted past Lexa and attempted an escape to the outside. She made it through the threshold before her face was immediately assaulted by sand and wind, drying and amplifying her tears simultaneously. When the sting was too much to bear she turned back into the cave. Inside she bumped into Lexa's waiting body, wrapped her arms tightly around her waist, and cried deep tears into her chest.

Two arms pressed against the young girl's back and stayed until she was ready. Once Juno was drained, she stood back and wiped her eyes and nose with her sleeve. "Sorry."

Lexa looked down. She knew how much she was hiding from Juno, how much she still needed to be taught about her purpose. About her body. But the bitter truth would crush the young girl. And against her heart's wishes, Lexa's head told her now was not the time to do any crushing. Now was the time to get Juno across the Rocky Mountains in one piece. No matter what.

"I know this is hard," Lexa said after kneeling eye-to-eye once again. "Do you remember that horrid slave driver? Do you remember Leadville?" Juno nodded for both. "That is how men are. They cannot be trusted even when they wear a smile. They'll use it to lure you in close so they can take what they want. Understand?"

Juno sniffled and nodded again.

"We will spend the night in this cave out of necessity only. At sunrise we part ways." Juno turned to start back down the tunnel but Lexa stopped her with a firm hand on the shoulder. "And under no circumstances can he learn that you're a girl."

Juno flickered a sneaky smile. "Don't worry, I already told Kareem about us."

"Kareem?" Lexa trailed.

When they returned to the opening, the man had just set down another log on the fire. He squatted back on his makeshift seat of one flat stone cushioned by a folded blanket and looked up at them with friendly eyes. "Thought you'd be back."

Lexa said nothing, instead ushering Juno around to the other side of the fire. But before they sat, the man got back up, leaned over, and extended a hand. "Name's Kareem."

Lexa only looked at it with a disdainful glare and sat anyway.

Kareem chuckled and shook the air's hand. Then he returned to his bench and said, "I was just keepin' your son over here entertained while you slept off that nasty bump. You were sweatin' somethin' fierce so I moved you away from the fire."

Son? Lexa glared at the young girl, who pretended not to notice.

"Kareem was telling me how hard you hit the ground after that log smacked you," diverted Juno, unsuccessfully stifling a grin.

Lexa surveyed the cave while keeping one eye on Kareem at all times. It was a circular room of stone and dirt with only one way in or out. Her mind was eased, but only slightly. "Thank you," she intoned, "for bringing us in."

Kareem maintained his polite smile. "Oh, it was no trouble at all. I was comin' down the face when the wind struck. Spotted you two seconds after I spotted this place. Guess we all got lucky."

Lucky indeed, Lexa squinted. It seemed convenient for all three of them to be in the same place at the same time. Then she remembered their interruption at the lake; the rocks sliding down the hill as a figure slipped behind the ridge. Her long suspicion that someone had been on their tails was rapidly coming to form, and it was solidifying just across the fire. "You've been following us."

The accusation stabbed at Kareem's friendly grin, but only briefly. "Beg your pardon?"

"I've had a hunch someone had picked up our trail the past few days. Yesterday we had a close call. Today confirms it."

"I promise you I was unaware of your presence. I'm new to the—"

"Then how do you explain knowing our exact position when the storm hit?"

"I was just comin' down from a water run and spotted you before I ducked in this cave."

Lexa's eyes narrowed even further, if that were possible. "Water run, huh? Big hidden lake?"

"Yeah…" Kareem's smile had disappeared at this point. He switched to the offensive. "Do you own it or somethin'?"

"That's just perfect. Did you like what you saw?"

Juno, dead silent while they bickered back and forth like old enemies, started to assemble the pieces of this puzzle in her mind. If Kareem was getting water from a hidden lake…and that lake was at the top of a mountain…and she and Lexa had just been swimming in a lake at the top of a mountain…then that would mean he had seen…

Juno's eyes shot wide at the thought of someone witnessing her exposed body. Her face burned red with embarrassment but luckily the fire burned hotter. She slouched down, covering her torso with her arms. When the heat flushed from her face she tuned back into the tail end of the argument.

"Listen, lady," Kareem asserted, "I know tensions are high out here, but I was just helpin' out a couple of folks in need. Nothin' more, nothin' less."

When it was clear Lexa had nothing to add, all three of them sat quietly around the glow of the fire. Kareem got up to grab another log while Juno watched. He seemed young. Older than her, but at least as young as Lexa; maybe younger. He had strong, smooth arms that caught the fire's light in just the right places. Juno felt her cheeks growing warm again and looked away.

"Lexa," the woman said, breaking the silence with the smallest hint of shame.

After sitting down, Kareem looked back at her, nodded, and brought out his gentle, almost infectious smile again. "Pleasure to meet you, Lexa and Juno. What brings you two out smack dab in the middle of the Rockies?"

"Our business is our own," Lexa recited as if she had rehearsed it a million times.

Kareem gave a polite nod. "I can respect that. Truth is everyone's business is their own. Ain't no virtue in being nosy." Silence nearly filled the cavern again when he added, "Hear what happened in Leadville? Shame."

Juno's ears perked up and she decided to chime in. "We were in Leadville! There were old buildings and a fire and a bunch of bad men that like to taste people. Lexa took care of them all, tho—"

"That's enough, Juno," Lexa urged.

Kareem glanced at the shotgun strapped to one of the bags, then looked the woman up and down. "I don't doubt she did." Then his gaze turned to her son and he gave a wink. "I know I wouldn't mess with her."

Juno's eyes lit up and she bared a full smile. Lexa, still uneasy about the amount of information being shared, intervened. "It's getting late. I'll take the first watch."

Kareem gave a long stretch and yawned. "Can't argue with that!" He reached into a bag of his own and pulled out a tightly rolled up piece of rubber. After removing a plug he began to fill it with air from his lungs. "Just...pfff...let me know...pfff...when...pfff...you get tired."

Lexa made sure Juno set up behind her and waited for them both to fall asleep. It was not until after that did she realize how much her head really hurt. She combed her fingers through her short hair and felt a sharp pain behind her ears. After wincing, she pulled her hand and saw speckles of dried blood on her fingertips.

The first scar's always the hardest, she smiled, then stayed a diligent eye on their one way out.

Lexa and Juno left before the sun could even peek over the mountains. Yesterday's storm had settled, leaving behind a soft indigo sky, yet most of the valley still hid in darkness while they slunk down from the cave. The morning air was cool so Lexa was able to push Juno into moving quickly.

Once they started up the next mountain, though, the day became hot and dry just like every other. Juno mused that despite their canteen weight diminishing, their bags always seemed to get heavier. Maybe it was sweat. Maybe it was fatigue. Maybe it was heat. One thing was for sure, she was always glad to stop for a break.

"Why'd we have to leave Kareem without saying goodbye?" Juno asked as they hid from the afternoon sun under the shade of a lonely rock.

Lexa poured out a mouthful of dried oats and raisins, then passed the packet. "It's best you forget about him."

Juno eyed the arid grains and reluctantly poured her own. Usually they came soaked in a bit of water first. "It's just that he was really nice, you know."

"Anyone can be nice for a short time. What happens when he gets hungry, or thirsty?" She paused, then waved her hand around her pelvis. "Or curious?"

"What do you mean, curious?"

Lexa took the package back from Juno and dumped what was left into her mouth. "Men don't always think with their heads, Juno. Sometimes what guides them is a little further south." Juno looked down at the ground, not quite understanding the reference. Lexa noticed and added, "Let's just say people like you and me have something they want very much. And it's not our personalities."

Just as confused as before, Juno furrowed her brow. However, when she looked up Lexa was grinning, so she smiled too. "Well, we could have at least said goodbye. My mom always told me it's good to be polite."

Lexa folded the empty packet and returned it to her backpack. When she stood up she saw the late afternoon light painting the peaks to the west orange. "Your mom's a smart lady," she said, starting up the path. "Next time we see Kareem we'll be sure to say goodbye."

Entry 40

Another night, another bumpy sleep in the freezing air. I almost miss the pile of cushions and coats back at the building in Denver. Almost.

Lexa's out scouting while I'm tucked under a boulder with not one, but TWO blankets wrapped around me. I wish we could start a fire, but she says it's too risky. She's still convinced someone is following us.

Instead she's letting me use this thing called a L-E-D flashlight so I can see my journal. It uses two of those silver battery things we took from the Silver Dollar Supply and somehow uses them to create light. She says she doesn't know why I waste my time writing in here. I mean, come on! I always like reading what other people have written down, so maybe someone will want to read this someday.

Lexa also has another gadget in her bag that uses four silver batteries. She called it a two-way radio. When she turned it on all I heard was the sound of sand dumping onto the ground. Or maybe it was closer to a fire being put out. Either way, she said if this radio can reach another radio you can talk to whoever's on the other side. She doesn't try very hard, though, because she turns it off almost immediately every time. I wonder who she's trying to talk to? Maybe a BOYFRIEND! Ha!

It's been a couple of days since we met Kareem. He's this guy that saved us from a storm and brought us into a cave. Lexa DID NOT like him. But she hates every man. Actually, I think she hates everyONE.

Except me. I mean, she brought me to a lake, taught me how to swim, told me about a LIVE tortoise in Arcadia. You don't do that stuff with people you hate. Now that I think about it, she's taught me a lot of cool stuff.

Ok, secret time. I liked Kareem. Like, a lot. Not only was he super nice and funny, but he was really interesting to look at. I'd never seen someone with skin that dark that wasn't because of dirt or scabs. And his arms were so muscly. And he had such an infectious smile. I wonder what he thought of me?

Lexa would say it doesn't matter what he thinks. She's probably right. It's not like I'll ever see him again.

Since they were still trying to make up for the day of travel lost in the storm, the following morning Lexa guided them down the mountain to take advantage of an empty road. A long, winding, craggy highway had caught her attention from the peaks. It sat there, half eroded. Tawny sand and rocks smeared the pavement as if time itself was trying to wash the blackness away. Perilous as a trade route, to be sure, but the harsher a road was for carts and feet, the safer it was for them.

Juno stepped on a slippery patch of loose gravel that twerked her right ankle. She did a double hop on her left foot, then continued lightly as the pain slowly faded to numbness. "I think I prefer the mountains," she snarked.

"Your legs are strong now," Lexa replied from a distance ahead. "This should be a piece of cake."

When Juno's ankle returned to normal she sped back up to her companion's side, careful of her footing. "What's that mean?"

"What's what mean?"

"Piece of cake," Juno reiterated. "What does that mean?" She could not see Lexa roll her eyes, but she could feel it.

"It's a figure of speech. It means that this should be much easier than climbing mountains."

"Oh," Juno said. She thought for a quiet moment, then added, "I've never had cake."

"I guess you'll have to add it to your bucket list," replied Lexa offhandedly, immediately regretting the turn of phrase.

"What's a bucket list?"

The morning miles rolled by quickly with a series of questions and answers about dated expressions to keep them distracted. Juno, curious as ever, and Lexa, annoyed that each explanation opened at least three more doors for inquiries, continued until sweat soaked their clothes. A cloudless sky listened in on their conversation while the barren valley seemed to magnify the heat of the unforgiving sun. Realizing they could not continue safely through the afternoon, Lexa kept an impatient eye out for options.

"There," she said, pointing at a shabby grey structure resting at the base of a mountain. "We'll wait inside until it cools off."

Half an hour later they reached the moldering cabin and circled around. Judging by the crusted planks clinging lifelessly to the skewed frame, it was most likely a remnant forgotten by time. The windows had all been blocked by boards so Lexa had to peer through rifts in the siding created by ages of waned moisture. When all was considered clear, she shouldered in the back door and they entered.

Sunlight carried beams of dust from outside through the same cracks Lexa had used as peepholes. Directly inside was a small table with a single metal chair tucked under it. At the edge was a counter wrapped around an old refrigerator and oven; both missing their doors. Behind them the wooden door creaked and slowly closed, as if it knew itself not to be inside.

Despite the stale heat hovering around them, Juno felt chills raise every hair on her body, a feeling now enhanced due to the short hair on her head. She crossed her arms and followed Lexa into the next room. A wireframe bed sat against the wall and there was a small doorway that led into an attached outhouse. Other than a faint offensive smell, the room was deserted.

The final area was the largest and most unsettling. A long, stained table on top of an equally long rug crossed the center while some odd hooks hung from chains attached to the ceiling. Juno made a face and turned away while Lexa continued her probe.

Juno was now facing the kitchen again and realized there were no stairs leading upwards or downwards inside the small cabin. Just three rooms on one floor. Then she saw something that made her wish she was still out in the sun. "Uh, Lexa..."

"What?" she heard from the other room.

"I think you should see this."

Lexa's boots thumped loudly along the rickety floorboards until they were next to Juno's. "What is it?"

The young girl did not say anything. Instead she pointed at the back wall of the kitchen. Surrounding the door they had entered through were hundreds upon hundreds of knives hanging from rusted nails. There were small ones, big ones, crooked ones, hooked ones, cracked ones, and stained ones, but the one that scared Juno the most was positioned just above the door frame. It was a massive, flat blade, almost like a square, that, unlike the others, reflected sharply in the grim light. It had recently been cleaned.

"Let's go," Lexa said without hesitation.

But then she hesitated.

From somewhere inside, a faint rustling made itself known. The sound was part human and part metallic, and entirely desperate. She closed her eyes, exhaled a painful sigh, and stomped once on the wooden floor again. It was hollow.

Lexa turned back into the room containing the table, rug, and hooks and started thumping her boots along the floorboards. Each time the echo returned more swollen, and each time the rustling was more despondent. Eventually the sound led her right up to the edge of the rug.

"Help me with this."

Together, Lexa and Juno leaned against the table and pushed. It was extremely heavy and neither of them could have moved it by themselves. After grunting for a while they finally managed to slide it just enough to reveal what was below.

A long, singular board, much newer than the rest, greeted them with a black iron handle. Juno's heart sank. She had spent nearly all of her life hiding below such a device.

Wasting no time, Lexa gripped the metal ring and yanked opened the hatch. A floor of precisely-spaced metal bars filled the void of the missing plank. Attached to the bars was a smaller handle. And a lock. This addition was new to Juno.

"Hand me my light," Lexa demanded. The girl reached into her bag, pulled out the palm-sized LED, and handed it over. Lexa clicked a button and shined it downward. What skulked below did not surprise her in the least. She wished it had, but life had numbed her to the core.

Juno, on the other hand, could never have braced herself for what attacked her senses. At least a dozen people cowered against a damp corner of an underground cage. Each had a decrepit burlap bag covering their heads and they were fastened together with chains around their necks. From there down they were completely nude, both men and women, she could now see, all smattered in muck and—

Lexa hovered the flashlight to the other side of the cage, which led right below the bedroom...and the outhouse. Reflected in the light was a massive heap of rotting excrement that assaulted Juno's nose. These dejected souls were imprisoned along with someone else's—

"Hold this," Lexa said, handing over the flashlight. She brandished her kukri knife, got down on her knees, and slipped the flat edge underneath the hinge of the cage door. The hinge flexed under her prying, but did not crack. "Shit."

Not wanting to break her most reliable weapon, she slipped it back into the sheath on her chest and started for the kitchen. Her eyes were set on the cleaver above the doorframe but something about the room had changed. The sunlight outlining the door was now obstructed at the base, the middle of either side, and the top center. Someone had returned.

Lexa immediately shoved Juno behind the partition wall of the room housing the cage of slaves. "Be ready," she barked, and tugged a strap on her backpack. The shotgun landed rhythmically in her hands and she took aim.

The door opened slowly. In stepped a man who was forced to crouch underneath the frame. He was far taller than Lexa and at least twice her weight. His bulging arms hung out of a pair of tattered overalls that did nothing to cover the scabs all over his shoulders. She forced fear down her throat with a swallow.

As soon as the man realized something was amiss, a cold metal ring was making an imprint in his chest. He took a slow glance past the woman and saw the table and rug moved aside. Then he flashed a greasy smile. "Come to join the party?"

Lexa bared her own teeth. "Move one inch and I'll blow a hole through your chest."

The hulking man was unphased by the threat and went to scratch his neck with arms as thick as tree trunks. "Unlikely. Way I see it, you'da already done so if you had any shells."

"Try me," Lexa spurred, pushing the barrel deeper into his crusty skin.

Instead of backing down the man wrapped his inflated fingers around the end of the gun and jerked on it, pulling his assailant closer. He looked her in the eyes long enough to know she was bluffing. "I'm waitin'."

In a flash, Lexa released her grip on the gun and ducked out of her backpack's straps. Within the same motion she removed her large blade from its sheath and came around the side to cut the huge man's achilles. But he was ready. The stock of the gun swung by her face and she only narrowly dodged its hard edge by stumbling backwards onto the kitchen table.

"Feisty one, are we?" He threw the gun and took three thunderous steps in her direction. "Well I like 'em better with a bit of fight!"

Lexa recovered quickly and rolled off the table before the man could break it in half with the weight of his forearms. She slid by him and guarded the door that led into the cage room, knife held in front, ready for an attack. But instead of a full on assault, the man lumbered over to the door he came in from and reached for the polished cleaver. Lexa could not allow the giant to arm himself so she plunged forward and shouldered him with all her might. His lumpish body sent the door and nearly a quarter of the wall splintering outside like an explosion.

Rolling to his back, the man used a huge forearm to block his face from the blistering sun. Lexa slammed one boot onto his chest and heard the door crack further underneath him. As he groaned, something shiny revealed itself from the top of the overalls' chest flap. A key was strung around his neck. And there was only one use for a lock way out here…

When Lexa reached down to snatch up the key, a hand wrapped completely around her arm and threw her effortlessly to the side. Now she was on her own back. Before she knew it a globular mass was straddling her. His fat head and immense shoulders blotted out the sun.

"Ah, ah, ah," the man said, wagging a distended finger above her face like a metronome. "We don't touch what ain't ours."

"Those people in there don't belong to you!" she rebuked.

But instead of being humored, a sledgehammer fist smashed into Lexa's chest, cracking more than a few ribs on its way to thrust every last atom of air from her lungs.

"Yer right about that," he smiled as he pushed on his knees to stand up.

Tears flowed from the corners of Lexa's eyes as she silently gasped for air. Like a closed valve behind a vacuum leak, nothing could enter. The blow had frozen every muscle in her diaphragm, disabling her lungs. Darkness vignetted her vision. She felt both of her legs being raised and her back began to slide. The brightness of the sun was replaced with the darkness of the cabin. She was being dragged.

As Lexa fought violently for air, she faintly heard mumbling. The man was speaking but her ears could not decipher the words. Instead, a brief flash from her past came into her rapidly closing mind. *When the wind is knocked from you in an attack, breathe through your mouth. Push your abdomen out and pull it back in to jumpstart your lungs.* Lexa closed her eyes and focused. She used the muscles surrounding her stomach to pull air in through her gaping mouth, and then again to push it out.

Pull in...

Push out...

Oxygen was returning.

Pull in...

Push out...

Her vision had cleared.

Pull in...

Push out...

Just as the giant was crossing the threshold of the kitchen and into the room with hooks above and a cage below, Lexa's lungs snapped from their paralysis and she wheezed, "Juno! Now!"

"What the?" growled the massive man and he dropped the woman's legs. Juno leapt from hiding with her new knife extended, but was immediately stopped by a hand able to palm the top of her head and toss her back into the wall. "Now this is too perfect. When He finds out I captured the g—"

The entirety of Lexa's kukri blade entered the back of the man between his right shoulder and spine. She pulled down on the handle, causing him to grunt out in pain. Then she pulled harder until his balance and stubbornness gave way simultaneously. He was down again, rocking like a tortoise on its back.

Lexa backed a few steps away and held her hand out. "Your knife, Juno."

Juno slapped the handle in Lexa's palm, then scuttled back to the corner before the fight could resume. Lexa dropped her duster and wiped her forehead with the back of her arm. She took deep, reviving breaths as the man lurched up to his feet. She was ready.

"Everyone's out lookin' for you an' that girl, missy," he said as if he was savoring the pain. "Now be a doll and c'mere." But after he raised his left arm, his face soured. He then looked down at the one hanging limp to his right and seethed. "What'd you do to me, bitch?"

"What's the matter?" she smirked. "Can't get it up?"

"I'll fuckin' kill you!"

The giant charged like a cornered beast but Lexa easily slipped to the side and slashed at his abdomen. He did not seem to notice, or care, because he turned back and swung his tree trunk arm with intent to remove her head. Lexa ducked and jabbed the blade into his right thigh, briefly sending him to his knees. Still the pain could not hold him down for very long. He ascended to his feet and lumbered back in the direction of Lexa, who had already hopped up onto the heavy table and was adjusting one of the hanging hooks.

When the massive man reached her he was in a blind rage. He grabbed the edge of the table with his one working hand and flipped it legs-up as if it weighed nothing. But before it could take Lexa's balance she jumped and swung out of the way by gripping the chain.

I only have one shot at this...

Banking on the giant to continue his charge in an adrenaline-fueled frenzy, Lexa held the chained hook out like a matador's muleta. Sure enough he ran straight towards her with blood in his eyes. Braced for impact, Lexa reached out to accept his arm, spun him around by his own momentum, then let him stumble the entirety of his own weight onto the suspended hook.

At first the giant man was unaware of what truly happened. He felt pain in his spine, but not enough to hold him back. It was only when he tried to step forward did he realize his demise.

Lexa casually walked over to the other end of the chain hooked into the giant's back. A fulcrum in the form of an iron hoop taunted him from the ceiling. She tugged on her end and the man clenched his teeth. "Toss me the key," she said, implying more pain if he refused.

"Yer makin' a big mistake lady. He'll do ten times worse to you than you've done to me."

"Doubt it," she smiled, then yanked on the chain with pleasure. He howled in agony as the hook tore through his skin. It was lodged so tightly now that when she let go the hook stayed in place. "The key?"

The overgrown man did not speak until after a dozen smoldering breaths. "This lot belongs to Creator..." He took another bloodsoaked lungful. "...If they go missing...If He finds out you...Agghhh!"

Lexa yanked the chain downwards, then tied her end to a leg of the massive, upturned table. Once the man hung unconscious, she ripped the key from his neck and unlocked the cage door. The naked, bag-covered slaves whimpered at the sound of the clanging metal and huddled tightly together.

"You're all free," Lexa announced, then dropped the key below. It made a soft *tink* on the damp ground. "You hear that? Pick it up and get the hell out of here!"

Entry 43

I think Lexa's really hurt. When we got away from that psycho house she took off her shirt and had me wrap this roll of white bandages around her chest. "Tighter," she kept saying. Her skin was all purple and red.

She killed a guy by hanging him on a hook! There, I said it. I don't even want to think about it, but I had to say it. It was just as horrible as the chopped off head, but somehow neither of those things are the worst thing I've seen so far.

How could anything be worse than locking

people in an underground cage filled with...well, you know. No food, no sunlight, no clothes, no hope. How could anyone be that evil? What happened to men to make them want to be this way? Maybe Lexa is right about them.

And what did that giant man mean by "everyone's looking for us"? Someone he called Creator is supposedly gonna do something ten times worse to us. Worse than being hung on a hook? It makes my tummy hurt just thinking about it.

Anyway, I took the flashlight out of Lexa's bag so I could write again. She's been asleep since before the sun went down so I don't think she'll mind. She swallowed some brown tablets from an orange container and told me not to go anywhere. I really hope she doesn't die. If I lose her I'll be on my own.

Creator. Where have I seen that word before?

"And just where do you think you're goin'?" Deacon chided as he pulled a gaunt woman to the ground by her thinning hair. "If I didn't know better, I'd say you were on the run."

Bishop loomed over the tortured and tattered soul and lifted up the burlap sack barely covering her bony hips and chest. He frowned. "Or rather from *where* is she running?"

"Please," the woman whimpered, exhausted. She gave a weak attempt at returning to her feet, but failed. It was like her muscles and bones could no longer agree on which controlled the other.

Deacon strutted back over and kicked her in the ribs for no real measure at all. "Please what? You're lucky you made it this far."

"Easy, Deacon." Bishop commented on the violence, but made no motion to stop it.

The woman had been running for days. Her anemic skin was plastered in filth that clung to the outlines of her protruding bones. She was frail from starvation. Emaciated. A tender red ring around her neck still bared indentations in the shape of chain links. She felt less than human. "I swear I don't know where I was. I can't even remember my own name!"

The more eager of the two men wound back a leg for another blow, but Bishop held up his hand. "Take a step back, Deacon. We don't want to mistreat our only witness, do we?"

Kicking a discarded plastic container instead, Deacon walked off in a huff. Bishop reached out a helping hand to the woman and, after some careful consideration, she took it. He leaned her against what was left of a blackened tree and joined her on the ground.

"I apologize for the way my friend over there greeted you. He can get carried away when he's under immense pressure." Bishop brushed away some wispy hair that was dangling in the woman's face, not realizing how easily it would pull from her scalp. He wiped the stragglers on his pant leg and continued. "You see, we are spearheading a crusade for Creator himself. It is of the utmost importance that we find a woman and a young girl that belong to Him. Would you happen to know anything, anything at all, about these two absconders?"

More out of fear than certainty, the woman shook her head no.

Bishop stared at her for a moment, then resolved to a different tactic. He reached into his satchel and pulled out a single-serve plastic cup of chili, label still intact, lid still seductively red. "You must be starving," he smiled, cracking open the plastic seal. After three twists of the lid the woman's nose drifted towards the savory scent. "I'd be willing to wager you have information inside that head of yours worth this entire portion."

"I..." She stopped. This felt unnervingly similar to the situation that got her chained up and stuffed into a cage in the first place. But she was so hungry her stomach felt like a wet knot. She had to eat. "You gotta promise not to hurt 'em."

Bishop made three ticking sounds with his tongue and lamented, "We would never dream of it! These two are holy instruments destined for the hand of Creator himself."

She held out until her stomach churned. Her hesitation was unbearable. She reached over to grab the cup of preserved and processed chili, but Bishop pulled it away. "Information first. Then food."

"Ok," she caved, nearly out of breath from the sudden movement she had just made. "I mighta seen 'em. A woman and a kid. Buzzed hair. Coulda been a girl I guess. Woman made short work of the bastard that caged us. Hung him up good. Then she gave us the key and left. That's all!"

Deacon reapproached the interrogation at the base of the tree so Bishop politely excused himself and rose back to his feet. The woman kept her eyes fixed on the food the entire time.

"She talkin', boss?" Deacon asked.

Bishop recounted her take on the story. "It certainly sounds like our two, but there's a newer, more unfortunate piece to the puzzle."

"What's that?"

"We've lost a Behemoth." Bishop then nodded his head towards the girl. "And an entire shipment of fresh slaves is now on the loose. All news that I would particularly like to avoid delivering."

"Fine by me," Deacon started, a little too casually. "Let's get the info we need and dispose of our witness."

Bishop shrugged in agreement and walked back over to the woman, plastic cup in plain view. "In which direction did our two outlaws venture?"

"I dunno," the woman said.

He shook his head and asked once more.

"I don't know!"

Pulling the cup further away from her grasp, Bishop spoke severely. "It would be most unfortunate starving to death after acquiring your newfound freedom. Out here, all alone, well, a lot of terrible things can happen." He gave her time to look into his eyes instead of at the chili.

"Now, which way did they go?"

The woman was so dried out her mouth could not even water. This was the end of her road if she did not put something in her body. "It was after midday. They went towards the sun."

Bishop rested his hand on top of the starving woman's head and said, "Now that's a good girl." He swung the cup of chili in front of her face and watched her nose follow it as he pulled it away. Then he took a bite of his own and called Deacon over. "Take care of this," he ordered, then turned to rejoin the hunting party of thirteen acolytes waiting patiently in the blackened wood. They were snickering.

Quickly, like a last thought, Deacon gripped a hand around Bishop's arm. "Say, Boss? No sense lettin' her go to waste while she's still kickin', eh?"

Bishop eyed the rest of the acolytes, who were murmuring in approval. This would be another test of his leadership, and of his patience. All part of the prestige Creator had awarded him. After some thought he held up the cup of chili, said, "You have until I finish," then, focused, started west on his own.

"Wait!" the woman cried, too depleted to notice Deacon and the others approaching like shadows around her vision. "You said I could eat!" Her tears were as dry as the desert, her stomach as barren as the earth, her heart as black and still as the tree trunk she rested against. "I'm so, so hungry…"

The woman's pleas trailed off. Mercifully, the gentle hand of fatigue pulled her eyes closed and began shutting down her organs one at a time.

An armful of logs clunked to the ground, startling Juno upright. She had been placing the last few stones around a hole she dug when Lexa returned with the firewood. Her fingers were numb from the cold.

"That should be enough for the night," Lexa said as she staggered over to a nearby fallen tree. She kept one arm wrapped across her ribs while the other braced her squat onto the trunk. She tried not to wince from the agony of sharp movement, but that almost made it worse.

"Why is it so hot during the day and so chilly at night?" Juno asked as she dropped a few of the logs into the pit.

"There's no moisture in the air to hold the heat," Lexa said, shifting to find relief. "And up here there's less air to hold moisture."

Juno did not really understand the science, but she said, "Oh," like she had. After adding a couple more logs to the hole, she sanctioned her work by patting the perimeter of rocks tightly together. She looked over at Lexa who nodded in approval.

"Here." Lexa tossed Juno a small booklet of matches and immediately regretted the sudden movement. She followed up through a clenched jaw. "Know how to use those?"

Of course she did. Back beneath the floorboards lighting candles was one of the few luxuries Juno could afford. Without hesitation she ripped one match from the packet, flipped the lid over, and pinched the red head between the flint strip and the flap. A swift pull later and there was fire between her fingers.

She brought the match over carefully, using a curled hand for protection, and dropped it down into the pit. Seconds later some small twigs curled with orange ambition that spread quickly to the logs. A few more seconds later and the flame began its heat-giving dance on the arid wood.

Juno blew into her cupped hands and splayed them out near the blaze for warmth. She was shivering.

"Put your hands on the stones," Lexa encouraged. "They hold the heat well."

Juno did so, smiled at the toasty revelation, and asked, "How are you feeling?"

"Better," she lied.

"I could have gone out and gotten the wood when I was finished digging."

"No need. My legs still work." Lexa had dismissed the offer out of irritation. She had already been sidelined from injury twice on this errand, costing them days of travel, so it was in their best interest that she kept an unwavering appearance of strength. For Juno. "Besides, you'll want to rest up. I suspect we're halfway there and we need to start picking up the pace."

"Fine," Juno sighed. She did not have to know her escort for very long to know she was headstrong. But despite her frustration at Lexa's constant refusal of offered help, she was quite happy to be sitting around an actual fire again.

After her hands warmed up, Juno took out the notebook from her backpack. She slipped the pen from the binding and began scribbling on a blank page: Entry 44

"What are you writing about tonight?" Lexa asked with vague curiosity.

Juno's tongue curled around the corner of her upper lip until she finished her sentence. "I dunno. Usually I just write about what happened today. Or something new I learned. Or sometimes things that have been bugging me."

Lexa slid down the log onto the ground and leaned her back against it. She caught a bit more of the fire's comfort. "Ever mention me in there?"

"Mmmaaay-beee..." Juno said with some added sass.

Lexa raised an eyebrow. "Oh really? And which category do I fall under?"

Juno tried desperately to hold in her laughter when she said, "Mostly under things that have been bugging me," but erupted as the last words left her mouth.

Lexa admired the delighted amenity Juno had felt towards her lately and relaxed a little. And since she had finally found a more comfortable position, it became easier to continue the conversation. "So how did you get started on this hobby of yours?"

"My mom," Juno said while scribbling down a new trick for warming up cold hands. "She taught me—well, *made* me—learn how to read and write and said that I should use both skills at least once a day."

Nodding silently, Lexa watched as Juno continued to put pen to paper. The young girl seemed to be perfectly content inside her own little world. Impressive, considering what she had been through. To witness emaciated slaves tied together or jammed in a cage. To be attacked by men whose only impulses are for lust and profit. To see limbs dismembered and bodies hoisted on hooks. To suffer the loss of a mother...

"To be honest, she's probably worried sick about us," Juno added thoughtfully.

Us...

It was time, Lexa decided, to confront Juno about the fate of her mother. The young girl deserved to know. Flexing the muscles that were still holding her ribs together, she stood up very slowly. If she was going to be the one to break the news, she would at least have the decency of offering her shoulder.

"Juno," Lexa started as she took slow, careful steps around the fire. "It's important to know that your mom would be very proud of the young woman you're becoming."

Juno nearly dropped her pen as she looked up. "You really think so?"

"I know so," Lexa confirmed, though only knowing the girl's mother by way of a bloodstained piece of paper. A final plea. She knelt down next to Juno. "And I think she would want—"

Crack!

"What was that?" Juno asked. She felt a brush of cool air tickle her spine.

"Not the fire," Lexa hissed. "Get behind that tree!"

Juno crossed the fire and hopped over the fallen trunk Lexa had been resting against. Lexa readied herself, ignoring the twinges pushing and pulling at her ribs simultaneously.

Snap!

The sound came again. Somewhere out in the dead, lurid forest. But from which direction?

Shick!

Behind!

Lexa slipped into the darkness of the woods while Juno peeked her head out from behind the log. All she could see was the orange dome of light given off by the fire and the surrounding blackness trying to consume it. Then she heard a myriad of sticks and branches crunching under more than just one set of boots. Juno watched, waited, with fearful eyes and white knuckles. It was too cold to end up in a cage...

Suddenly, two shadows emerged from the wood, one right behind the other. They were moving succinctly like a march, or a stickup. The one in front was a head taller and an arm's thickness wider than the one in back. And the skin was very dark. Once they were near enough to the fire, the front shadow's knees buckled and fell forward into the light. Juno's eyes widened excitedly. It was Kareem.

"I *knew* you were following us!" Lexa snarled. The tip of her knife was pressed firmly into the man's back, lacking just enough force to draw blood. "Give me one good reason why I should keep you alive."

From his knees, Kareem raised his arms up in an attempt to look as harmless as possible. "I mean you no harm. I just saw the light of the fire and—"

Lexa shoved him face down with her boot and leaned as much weight as she could between his shoulders. "Lies!"

Juno popped up from behind the log and yelled, "Wait!"

Kareem spat out some loose gravel that entered his mouth. "I'm not lyin'! I just wanted to see if you—"

"Silence!" Lexa demanded, blind with rage. "All men are the same. They see a smooth-skinned woman and think they can have her in the dead of night." She was nearly foaming at the mouth. "I know your schemes, I've seen your deceptions, and now you've breathed your last—"

"Lexa, wait!" Juno screamed, now right next to them. She put her small hands on Lexa's arms and guided the knife away.

Lexa shifted her attention to the young girl, but kept her weight firm on the intruder. "Juno, you've seen where this leads. You know what happens next. I cannot let anything happen to you."

Juno looked at her with the strength of young eyes that are only forged in truth. Eyes that glisten kindly in the moonlight. Eyes that can always distinguish right from wrong. "Can't you see he's different?"

The swirl of adrenaline that came from a lifetime of fear and resentment drained from Lexa's head, allowing her to briefly see what Juno was seeing. What she had seen from the beginning. The man below her had rescued them from a storm, kept his distance in the cave, and had not combated Lexa's authority in the slightest; even as his life was now in danger. She exhaled a slow, pensive breath that was devoured by the blackness of night and lifted her foot. She did not believe for a second that he could be trusted. But maybe, just maybe, he was not like the others.

"I just want to thank you for lettin' me enjoy the warmth of your fire tonight," Kareem said with his thick arms extended to the flame. "Looks like now we're even."

Lexa and Juno sat opposite him, against the fallen tree, just as before. One was eying him intently and one was deciding which she hated more: the pain in her over-stressed ribs, or the fact that a man was once again sharing their precious space. Within reach a black shotgun gleamed slightly in the fire's light. It was not there by accident.

"Put your hands on the stones," chimed Juno with a proud smile. "They hold the heat well."

Kareem did just that and nodded. "You're a smart young man."

All three of them sat in silence long enough for the wood to ember. While Lexa brooded, Juno got up and tossed in two more logs. Once she sat back down she nudged Lexa in the arm, careful not to bump her broken bones.

"What?" Lexa sneered.

"Should we see if he's hungry?"

Kareem overheard them and added politely, "I could eat," then, "as long as there's some to spare."

Lexa rolled her eyes and went to her bag for an MRE, a pot, and a canteen of water. When she returned, Juno had scooted closer to the fire and was already brimming with curiosity for their visitor.

"So how come you're out here and not back at your cave?" the young girl asked.

"Heh, well," he flashed that infectious smile Juno so fondly remembered from the first time they met, "It wasn't really *my* cave. I just borrowed it to hide from that doozy of a storm."

"Oh." Juno scrunched her face. "Then where do you live?"

Kareem watched as Lexa turned a mixture inside a small pot that was held over the fire. "Good question. I guess the world is my home and I just kind of sleep wherever the wind takes me. Ya know?"

Juno mouthed, "Wow," at how poetic the response sounded. She was about to launch the next in her list of infinite questions when Lexa scoffed and said, "On the run, then?"

Nodding, Kareem exhaled amusingly through his nose. "Aren't we all? Been so long now I consider it wanderlust."

"Where are you from?" Juno slipped in before her inquiries got sidelined.

"Out East. Place once called West Virginia."

A memory of a map hanging on her bedroom wall popped into Juno's head. All of the bold lines carving out the shapes of former States like a stencil. She knew they were currently smack dab in the center of a continent bordered by endless pools of blue, and recalled West Virginia was near the eastern edge. "Have you ever seen the ocean?"

Kareem looked down and revealed a different kind of smile. Not stretched tight from joy, but close-lipped and soft with reminisce. "Growing up, all the time," he said. "One of my daily chores was descending the Appalachian Mountains to collect as much water as I could, then haul it back up to my family for desalination."

"De-sal-in—" Juno sounded out.

"It means removing the salt from water," Lexa interrupted. She passed the small pot handle-first to Kareem so he could have the first bite. "Ocean water is too salty to drink on its own."

He handed the food back to Lexa. She took a bite, gave it to Juno, then carefully sat back down against the fallen tree, never turning her back to Kareem.

Juno was still detailing the bedroom map in her head. Curious on how he could have walked hundreds of miles each day to gather water, she asked, "I thought the ocean was farther away?"

"It was," Kareem acknowledged. "A long time ago. Now the mountains are the only thing stoppin' it from coming further inland. I barely had to walk halfway down to get my toes wet!"

Lexa made an arduous sound as she shifted the shotgun into her lap. Although it rested harmlessly across her legs, she made sure the barrel still pointed menacingly in their guest's direction. "That still doesn't explain what you were doing out here in the middle of the night."

"That's fair," Kareem said while receiving the pot from Juno this time. "I suppose I'd be spooked too if some stranger came out of the woods after dark!" He laughed a genuine laugh and swallowed another bite. He handed it to Juno, who passed it to Lexa. "Would you like the short version or the long version?"

Lexa studied him carefully. Despite her injuries, he needed to know she was in control. "The version that convinces me not to tie you to a tree and leave you to rot."

The campfire fell quiet with the sounds of crackling and chewing. Unbeknownst to Juno, a silent game of strategy was being played in the flickering light. Finally, Kareem spoke. "I suppose if it's gonna be the last time I get to tell it, I better go with the long one..."

As he trailed, Juno readied herself by pulling her legs crossed and leaning in with open ears. She loved a good story.

"I was lucky enough to be raised by my parents until about, well," he nodded across the fire, "about your age."

Picturing Kareem at thirteen made Juno smile.

"They raised me well. Taught me how to survive, taught me how the world worked. Loved the hell out of me. We didn't bother no one and we helped anyone who asked. The few that stuck around knew us as good people.

"But somethin' else was brewing down in ol' Appalachia. Somethin' dark. A group of religious nuts was growin' in those mountains, spreadin' like a disease. They were sellin' this false promise of salvation that our desperate neighbors bought up in droves. Soon good people were followin' orders with total blindness, carryin' out insane requests that could only be derived from a madman. Everywhere they went they sucked up resources, homes, families…

"Anyways, it didn't take long until, oh, no thanks. You eat up!"

Kareem waved off the pot for Juno to finish, then glanced over at Lexa. Her attention was still on him, but she was mindlessly running a finger down a prominent scar on her face. It gave him a sense that she knew exactly the type of madman he was talking about. When Lexa realized he was staring, she pulled her hand away and gave a conscious nod. He continued.

"It didn't take long 'til these zealots found my home. They came for us in the middle of the night. Took me, mom, dad. We tried to fight back, but their numbers were too great. We were dragged kickin' and screamin' to some unbelievably huge building in a nearby abandoned town. Inside was a towering ceiling, a wide stage, cages filled with prisoners, and an aisle lined with hundreds of wooden benches. Each seat was filled with these crazed followers, all of them either shoutin' or booin' at us. They walked us right up onto that stage, nailed my mom and dad to massive wooden crosses, and hoisted them twenty feet in the air usin' only ropes and hysteria. I can still remember their screams…"

Kareem looked down between his knees and subtly shook his head.

"After forcin' me to watch," he resumed after a brief reflection, "they ripped off all my clothes and held me up for display like some sort of trophy. Then a figure, the Wizard, they called him, appeared in an all white robe and a tall, pointed hat. He spouted off some bullshit about God's wrath, their promised land, and how the fertile were meant to be punished for the sake of mankind. Then, when the mass of crazies was in an all out frenzy, the Wizard pulled out a sharp, crooked knife and castrated me on the spot."

Kareem pretended to stretch something out in the air and cut it off with his hands.

"When the Wizard dropped me to the ground I suspect he thought I'd stay put. He was wrong. While he kept on preachin' his poison, I took one last tearful look at my dyin' parents, slipped out behind the stage, and ran so fast I thought my legs would fall off."

Juno's hands were now cupping her open mouth tightly. She did not know exactly what castration or Wizard or "punishing the fertile" meant, but she had learned enough in the past month to know where things involving knives always ended up. When all was quiet, she turned back to look at Lexa. Her face was as cold as ever in the warm firelight.

"Go on," Lexa instructed.

Kareem took the lack of empathy as gracefully as he could. "Right. How I ended up here. Like I said, my parents had taught me how the world works. Wild as it might sound, they also taught me about its beauty. We'd sit around as a family at night and look at old nature books and magazines until our solar-lights died. My whole life I had always wanted to see what the world still offered, if anythin'. So there I was—naked, bloody, and all alone in the crooked soul of Appalachia—when I looked up to the sky. The moon shared its silver smile from the west, invitin' me to follow. So, like all new life attracted to light, I just started walkin'.

"And despite the unspeakable things those radicals did to me and my family, I knew deep down I would not be as lucky the next time. No second chances. So I figure what better way to honor my folks than by seein' all the things they had shown me from the livin' room? My journey has taken me to the Great Basins up north, the Missouri Canyon, the Dakota Badlands, and now here: the majestic Rocky Mountains.

"And, if I might boldly add, this is by far and away the most beautiful place I've ever stepped foot in. Probably why I've stuck around so long!"

Having witnessed the sun set over the vast mountain range herself, Juno wholeheartedly agreed. Then, while Lexa forced her to clean up and neatly pack away the supplies used for dinner, she continued to bombard Kareem with an onslaught of questions. Where he had been, what he had seen, who he had met, if he spotted any animals. Every detail was catalogued in her mind so she could regurgitate them into her notebook later on.

"You know what?" Kareem asked when there was a welcomed pause in the conversation. He clapped his hands and rubbed them together. "I think tonight calls for dessert!" He reached into his own bag and pulled out a silvery package. He tossed it over the fire and told Juno to open it. She gripped the thin rectangle with her fingers and tore off a corner. When she tilted it, nuts, raisins, and chocolate candies fell into her hand. Her eyes lit up.

"Been savin' it for a special occasion," Kareem smiled. It was the one stretched with joy again. "And it's not every day I get to have dinner in the company of a beautiful woman and a strappin' young man."

Juno was unsure whether to accept his compliment or not, but she blushed all the same. If she had to play the part of a boy at least she was a strapping one. Lexa, on the other hand, was not amused.

"So why right here?" she interjected while Juno's mouth was momentarily occupied with a sweet and salty mixture. "Why tonight?"

Kareem's joyous demeanor faded, but only slightly. He took a handful of the trail mix for himself and tossed it into his mouth before he spoke. "When I woke up alone in that cave, I got to thinkin' there was somethin' about you two. Somethin' special. I can't really explain it, but I felt like bringin' you in from that storm was the most important thing I'd ever done.

"In an hour or so I shrugged it off and did the same as I'd been doin' for years: Collected my things and set off west. But a day's travel or so later I came across a cabin. Popped my head in for a moment of rest and saw somethin' that rattled me to the core. Reminded me too much of back East. A wall full of knives, a giant of a man hoisted dead from a chain, and a cage beneath the floorboards left wide open.

"Now I'd be lyin' if I said I didn't immediately think of you two. About your safety. So I followed your footsteps as far as I could; which wasn't easy since one of you has mastered the art of coverin' up your tails. Eventually it got to point where the only thing I could think to do was head for higher ground and hope I could spot somethin' that said you were still alive. I almost gave up, too. But when I saw the glow of a fire tonight, my heart sang."

Lexa narrowed her eyes and Kareem waved his hands in a harmless manner. "I promise I wasn't gonna approach. My only intent was to get a good look and move on." He laughed and shook his head. "Turns out I'm not as sneaky as I thought."

Juno dumped the rest of the silver package into her mouth and chewed happily. After swallowing, she pointed back at Lexa with her thumb. "Well you have perfect timing! When Lexa fought that big guy she got real banged up—"

"Juno!" Lexa snapped. She gave the young girl a look she herself had received many times during her youth. A look she had resented most her life. One that said, "Your mouth is going to get us killed."

Kareem understood Juno's intent and attempted to smooth over the rocky expression coming from across the fire. "*You* hung up that big guy? He had to be at least three-fifty, four-hundred pounds!"

Still glaring at Juno, Lexa replied. "I prefer not to romanticize life or death decisions."

"Fair enough," Kareem agreed. "Best not to gloat about good fortune."

The final log had disintegrated, leaving a charred pile of orange and grey embers. The firepit was still red hot and radiated enough light to outline facial features. Kareem leaned over and grabbed a good stick to stir the coals with. Juno watched his every movement with an unfamiliar curiosity. The grooves stamped in his arms by flexed muscle, the way his angled jaw caught the moonlight, the radiant smile. Her body temperature began to rise...

Lexa struggled to her feet, removing the gun from her lap as well as Juno's attention from a sudden fascination. The motion reminded her for a third time this evening that she was in no shape to stave off another unwanted attack. Kareem, on the other hand, had the mass of someone who knew how to survive. Someone who could protect. But what was his price? A judgement had to be made. Either she risked going it alone, or risked asking for help.

Lexa pulled a half-empty canteen from her bag and tossed it emphatically to Kareem. "If you keep your hands to yourself," she said, "and carry your own weight, then you can stick with us until we cross the mountains."

Without a word, Kareem reached out a friendly hand and accepted the offering.

A grey, arid sky cast no shadows in any direction, leaving the landscape as dry and colorless as a pencil sketch. The haze graciously blanketed the searing sun which allowed a rare opportunity at an entire day's travel.

Single file they walked through the afternoon. Kareem always at front, Juno always in the middle, and Lexa always at the rear so she could keep an eye on both. Westward was their heading. Down one grueling ridge and then up another was their path.

After a life-threatening encounter involving a cabin, a cage, and a giant, Lexa insisted they avoid any and all roads for the remainder of the expedition. She needed to put that lapse in judgement behind her. Unfortunately, however, each step on the unforgiving terrain served as a constant, painful reminder of her mistakes.

Along with the tepid climate was a frigidity of unease between the bow and stern of the newly formed triad. Lexa's eyes were constantly shifting from Juno's immediate danger to Juno's impending danger. There was no trust lended to the newly accompanying man, and there was always concern about what may lie waiting in the mountains. If Kareem had indeed not been following them, that left their fragile door open for just about any intruder.

In contrast, Juno found it refreshingly easy to keep pace as of late. "A piece of cake," as she liked to broadcast now. Her legs and back grew stronger every day and, at this point, the added weight of her backpack seemed diminutive. Lexa might be proud, she thought, if Lexa felt such things.

Juno also enjoyed her spot at the center of the line. She suddenly had the insurance of Lexa behind her combined with the pleasant display of Kareem's features in front. This was the first time she had seen him in the daylight and there was plenty of time to study him thoroughly. He wore a cloak which, to Juno, was similar to her own duster jacket except it was a worn khaki color and lacked sleeves. His broad shoulders stuck out of the cloak like boulders and continued down to muscular arms that were nicely defined in the overcast. He was tall, too, with long legs that she could only imagine to be as remarkable as his arms.

And then, right below the bottom of his backpack, was a feature Juno found her eyes quite attracted to. She could not explain it. She had seen Lexa's bare as the day she was born, but it had not carried the same magnetism as the one before her. Back and forth she watched it shift, round and carrying enough power to drive all of the blood in her body to her—

"So where did ya'll come from?" Kareem asked, turning his head to look at them.

Juno quickly averted her eyes. Her cheeks splashed red.

"West of here," Lexa replied before Juno could blurt out sensitive information.

Kareem simply followed with a thwarted, "Hm."

Juno shook off her discomfort and asked a question of her own. "Where are you headed next?"

"West of here," he joked. Then, after a chuckle, he continued light-heartedly. "I heard the San Andreas Fault has been turned into a thousand-mile-long waterfall. I'd also like to see the Bonneville Salt Flats, but I'm not sure I could carry enough water to enjoy it properly. Most of all I want to see Zion. The pictures I saw of that place as a child had colors and geological formations that can't even be described with words."

"I've never heard of Zion," Juno said curiously. "Could you try and describe it?"

Kareem tilted his head at the boy's unabating curiosity. "That's a good question," he started. Then, after a moment's thought, "Think of taking a gigantic hammer to one of these mountains, crushin' it into hundreds of goofy shapes and sizes, then buryin' those pieces underground. Now picture wind and water slowly diggin' those pieces out over millions of years. Every hundred or so of those years the wind, rivers, and rain decide to use a new color from the rainbow to paint their progress on the next layer of exposed stone. Finally, when the evenin' sun makes the sky blush..." He stopped suddenly, as if disjointed. "I'm sorry for the bad description. I'm not that good with words."

Juno saw him shake his head from behind. His depiction painted a lovely image in her head just as the elements had painted the formations. "I think it sounds beautiful," she said.

"Place is a tribal warzone," Lexa announced from the back. "But if you're lucky they've killed themselves off by now."

Kareem side-eyed Juno and muttered, "Is she always this delightful?"

Juno had to cover up her laughter with a hand before a strong gaze burned a hole into her back. Despite the few fleeting moments of empathy Juno had glimpsed, Lexa's default setting was astonishingly rigid.

It was quiet again for some time until the three of them were met with an abrupt ridge towering over the end of their trail. To the right was a sheer cliff that dropped straight down to an old highway, and to the left was a rocky pass that would easily add an extra half day to their hike. The most efficient option was to climb.

After discussing the most viable route, Lexa tightened all of the straps on Juno's bag and told her she would be sent up first. The face that led to the summit was craggy enough for the girl to climb safely without ropes, but they were separated by a distance of flat rock face that stretched higher than Juno's reach. To remedy this, Lexa leaned down and locked the fingers of both hands. Juno balanced herself against the flat wall of stone and stepped onto the hoist with both feet.

"Alright. One...two..."

Lexa bobbed Juno up and down with each count. Then, when Lexa said, "three," she lifted with all her might and immediately felt every single fracture stab like a hundred dull knives inside her chest. Juno went tumbling to the ground while she keeled over in pain.

"Woah, easy there," Kareem said as he rushed over to brace Lexa. "Are you alright?"

Lexa, face flushed red with pain and embarrassment, shrugged off his supporting arms. "I'm fine."

"That grunt of yours didn't sound fine to me. Come here Juno."

Before Lexa could protest, Kareem had Juno step up onto his cupped hands. He lifted her effortlessly above his head with the stability of a ladder. Then he inched towards the rock face until Juno could easily grab the edge and pull herself up. "That's it! You got it!" he encouraged. Before he knew it, Juno was climbing away.

"I'll go next," Lexa scoffed when Juno was far enough from Kareem's reach. She approached the same flat wall of stone where she botched Juno's lift and tightened her own straps. When she was ready to jump, a dark shadow loomed closely behind her. Too close.

Lexa spun and went instinctively for her knife. Two strong hands stopped both of her arms in place and pushed her right up against the hard rock. Kareem was holding her firmly, but his attention was focused upwards. She just as soon realized the shove was neither vindictive nor painful, merely a guiding force to remove themselves from Juno's eyeline.

"What the hell's goin' on here?" Kareem was assertive, but careful to remain non-threatening.

Lexa looked deep into his cedar eyes. This was the first time a man had had her up against a wall without nefarious intent. "What do you mean?"

"Don't you think it's a little dangerous for a mother and son to be takin' a road trip out here all alone?" Kareem's eyes narrowed. "Can't say I've seen a family this young since Appalachia and here's one out and about like they're on vacation."

"Our business is our—"

"Yeah, yeah, you said that last time," Kareem interrupted with growing annoyance. "But seein' as your body's broken from head to toe, and you obviously haven't told the kid anything, I'd say it's becomin' *my* business pretty fast."

Lexa frantically searched for lies. What could she say that would not only be believable, but still protect the truth about Juno's identity? If he found out how important she was he would never be able to resist...

"Look. I just want to know what kind of shit I'm gettin' myself into," he coaxed. "Continuin' on with you and the kid."

Lexa's mouth opened, then closed, then opened again. *Something* had to come out. "Remember that group of extremists in Appalachia you told us about? The ones that killed your family?"

The question grated against Kareem's good nature. "Are you tryin' to upset me?"

Shaking her head, Lexa became more poignant. "Think of them with unlimited numbers and unlimited resources. With a leader whose grasp reaches across the entire range. Everyone as far as you can walk fears the Scab King."

Kareem's face stiffened in thought. "Shit." He dropped his grip on Lexa, took half a step back, and scratched his scruffy chin. "Scab King. I've heard that name whispered in these parts. What's his story?"

"He calls himself Creator and he holds a grudge." Lexa rolled her eyes, then tapped a miffed finger against the scar across her face. "We've met before."

Kareem mildly shook his head. "So it's *you* he's after. Sheesh. You and your son are chasin' the sunset, then?"

Lexa's eyes widened. His inference actually worked itself out. As long as he believed that she was the victim, and that Juno was a boy, there could be no consequence.

"More or less," she finally confirmed. Then removed the heavy backpack from around her shoulders and shoved it into Kareem's chest. He noted the still-attached shotgun. "The point is," she continued with a slightly more vulnerable tone, "We need to get Juno to Arcadia in case something happens to me. No matter what." Eventually Kareem felt the gravity in her eyes and nodded. She replied, "Good. Now hoist me up."

Kareem lifted Lexa in the same way he did Juno. When she left his hands and started climbing, he took a moment to scratch his head and think about the life he would be giving up to travel with the woman and the boy. Was it worth risking his own neck for the safety of two strangers if something *that* terrible was truly after them? More importantly, did she say, "*We* need to get Juno to Arcadia"?

He looked down prudently at the bag Lexa left with him. It no doubt was brimming with valuable supplies that could be used to survive alone for quite some time. Food, water, blankets, maybe even some shells for that shotgun. It would be so easy. If he disappeared now, they would never catch him. No one would be hurt. No one would ever have to know...

An hour later a dark, muscular arm stretched over the summit's edge and pulled Kareem up with it. He had two bags wrapped around him, one on his back and one on his chest, and was dripping with sweat.

"What took you so long?" Juno asked spritely. Herself and Lexa had been waiting patiently at the top for a while.

"Heh," Kareem half-laughed-half-grunted as he rolled the rest of his body over the jagged threshold. He climbed to his feet, dropped the two heavy backpacks, and brushed off the caps of his knees. Before replying to Juno, his eyes caught Lexa's cautioning glare. "I guess I'm just too slow for you, little man."

The greyish haze had dissipated entirely, leaving behind a brilliant scene of reds, oranges, and yellows that could only be dreamt of from behind closed eyes. A thin strip of purple traced the caps of distant peaks with the precision of a penknife. Below, deep shades of blue and grey swallowed up the landscape as night hungrily approached.

Kareem stepped forward to join Lexa and Juno. "Wow!" he marveled. "If that ain't the most beautiful thing I've ever seen."

The three admired the vista in agreeable silence as the sun retreated from the moon. At one point Kareem glanced over to Lexa. Her face was elegant, yet powerfully stoic. The mountains themselves could not pry a secret from her expression. Then he turned to Juno. The child's face was so young, so innocent, so filled with wonder that, for a moment, he understood why Lexa kept certain truths hidden. Maintaining a childhood was a rare luxury almost none could afford.

The congenial lull brought a smile to Kareem's face. Not one displayed by stretching muscles and squinting eyes, but one dragged from the bottom of a long-broken heart. Being on the run for over a decade had taken its toll on his soul. But a life of tragedy and solitude was little excuse to surrender the enjoyment of a breathtaking view with two new companions. And so, he began to sing.

> *He was born in the summer of his twenty-seventh year*
> *　　Coming home to a place he'd never been before*
> *He left yesterday behind him, you might say he was born again*
> *　　You might say he found a key for every door*

Juno looked up at Kareem with astonishment, almost smitten. He nodded without pause.

> *When he first came to the mountains his life was far away*
> *　　On the road and hanging by a song*
> *But the string's already broken and he doesn't really care*
> *　　It keeps changing fast and it don't last for long*

"Woah," Juno gasped. "What *is* that?"

Kareem tilted his head. "What, John Denver?"

"Who's...?" Juno was confused. She did not know exactly how to describe what she had just heard. The way his voice went up and down, the way he held onto some vowels, the way the phrases sounded alike. "No. What you were doing with those words."

Kareem released a humble laugh deep from his gut. "You mean singin'?"

"Yeah, that. I've never heard anything like it. It's wonderful!"

"I don't claim to have the best voice," he said once he finished his chuckle, "But I can carry a tune." Then he leaned over to Juno as if he were telling her a secret. "You wanna know somethin' that I bet no one else knows?"

Juno peeked around him at Lexa, as if asking permission, then nodded briskly.

Kareem paused long enough to build some suspense. "John Denver wrote that song about these very mountains."

Juno scrunched her face. "How do *you* know that?" she asked skeptically.

"Look at that view," he cajoled, gesturing outward with a strong arm. Cool shades of mauve and blue replaced the warm tones from earlier. "If that ain't somethin' to write a song about, then I don't know what is."

Juno shrugged. "I guess I don't know. That was the first song I've ever heard."

There was a glint in Kareem's eye, as if he knew the secret remedy for an ailment. "Well then it's high time you learn to sing one, too! Try and mimic exactly what I say to you. Ready?"

But the Colorado rocky mountain high...

After swallowing down some heavy reluctance, Juno opened her mouth and repeated the words. Her pitch and cadence were not very balanced, wrenching both Lexa and Kareem's ears, but she had to admit it felt soothing to sing words instead of speak them. Like a drink of cold water on a hot day.

I've seen it rainin' fire in the sky...

She repeated again. Much to Juno's delight, her voice matched his a lot closer this time.

The shadow from the starlight is softer than a lulla—

"Down here!" Lexa called out, diffusing their rhythm.

Following the voice to the edge of the peak, Kareem and Juno saw that Lexa had left during their singing lesson. She was now standing inside a small alcove just below the summit. It was surrounded by rock on three sides that would serve as a shield from the chilled, late-night breezes. Lexa flapped out a rolled blanket and laid it on a smooth section of ground. The three of them would share a camp, a meal, and a fire together for a second night in a row.

Entry 45

Music! Songs! Rhymes! I think I'm in love!

Kareem taught me a song called Rocky Mountain High (which is where we are right now) by John Denver (which is where we started)! I've been singing it over and over and over and over again inside my head so I don't forget it. Can you believe there were millions of songs a long time ago! Why'd everyone stop singing them?

You shoulda seen last night when Lexa caught Kareem sneaking around in the woods. I thought her head was gonna pop! I don't know why, though. He was nice the first time we met him and just as nice the second time. I know she's been telling me since day one that men can't be trusted, and I've seen my fair share of it already, but he's obviously different than all the other ones we've run into. Right?

I don't really know who to believe now. Kareem told an awful story about his childhood, even worse than mine, and he's not out there eating people or tying them together or throwing them in cages.

Either way, he must've said something that convinced Lexa to let him stay. My guess is she's more hurt than she's admitting and doesn't think I can tell. She could just ask him for help instead of being like, "Oh, I guess I'll let you live for now." Sheesh!

I for one am happy Kareem's with us. He makes me smile. He taught me to sing. He doesn't mind answering my questions. Pretty much the opposite of Lexa.

Don't tell anyone I said this, but when I look at Kareem I get a funny feeling down...uh, you know. Down there. I can't really describe it. It kind of feels like I have to pee even though I don't and my face gets all hot. I want to ask Lexa about it, but I know she'd just say, "Focus Juno," or, "Keep moving."

Maybe I'm being too harsh. It seemed like she was really starting to warm up until we went into that house with the knives on the wall. That terrible, terrible house. (I just shivered!)

Alright, time to write down the Rocky Mountain High words before I forget them in my sleep!

Lexa cringed as Juno began singing yet again. For the entire morning it was as if someone had left the young girl on repeat and disabled the off switch. Every time the words *born in the summer* flicked Lexa in the back of the head like a tossed pebble, her shoulders tensed and her face tweaked. If she had to listen to the onslaught of prepubescent pitch squeaks one more time, she told herself she would not be responsible for her actions.

"*And the Colorado rocky mountain high!*"

"Juno!" Lexa snapped. "We are trying *not* to draw attention to ourselves."

Abrupt silence followed. Then Juno curteously waited for Lexa to turn back around before inflicting unspeakable revenge with her eyes.

"At least she's not getting worse," a quieter voice chuckled from Lexa's side. It was Kareem, no longer forced to walk a safe distance ahead of the two.

"Did you have to encourage the one thing that would make me want to strangle—"

The tune revitalized as a hum from behind. Lexa's face squinched once again, but at least the overall output was softer. Kareem was all smiles.

"When a young man gets a song stuck in his soul..." Kareem explained. Then he paused for a moment with a reflective look on his face. "...Besides, what's catchier than Rocky Mountain High?"

Lexa mumbled, "I would have taken you for a Country Roads guy," then clammed up as if the banter slipped out by mistake.

Kareem's handsome smile stretched farther. "I'll be damned! Do I see a crack in that rock-hard exterior?"

If Lexa had produced a smile, he had missed it.

The three of them caught a natural trail leading to a ridge and followed it upwards for the better part of the early morning. They had finally traversed the last of the perilous pinnacles that made up the bulk of the Rocky Mountains and were tapering down into rounder, more infrequent peaks. From atop the highest summits these had looked like mere moguls. However, on foot, they soon realized a mountain was still a mountain.

As always, temperature became an unwelcome guest on their journey. Though the sun had barely reached its hands over the horizon, the heat of the day had awoken even earlier to get a head start. Nagging beads of sweat dripped from their foreheads and were instantly swallowed whole by the thirsty terrain.

Once they reached the summit, Lexa quickly sat against a large rock in an attempt to reel in some of the pain escaping her ribs. Kareem produced a clear plastic water bottle from his bag, took a large pull, then offered it to Lexa.

"No," she said without looking. "Mine."

Quietly questioning her for a moment, Kareem shrugged. He returned the bottle to his own bag and pulled an aluminum flask from hers. After tossing it over compliantly, he sat down across from Lexa, taking advantage of a sliver of shade produced by the remains of a barkless tree. "It's gonna be a hot one today," he sighed after wiping his forehead.

Between them Juno drank from her own canteen while eyeing a distinct, perfectly rounded stone on the ground. After putting back the bottle, she looked at Lexa, who was resting near a gap in two large rock formations, then over to Kareem, who was against one of two trees separated by a bit of distance. An idea began taking form in the young girl's head.

Naturally, Juno walked over and kicked the round rock. It slid across the loose dirt and grinded satisfyingly to a halt. She followed to where it stopped and kicked it again, this time aiming between the two post-like trees Kareem was now lying under. The rock went skipping through the gap, scoring Juno her first point in the new game she had just created.

"Woah, careful now!" Kareem advised with a yawn. "Don't wanna wake up you-know-who."

Juno turned and saw Lexa's head tilted back, her mouth half open, and her eyes sealed shut. Not sleepy in the slightest, the inventive girl chuckled, then trotted back to the stone she had scored with.

Back and forth, over and over again, Juno scored point after point on the mountaintop playing field. Each time the stone either slid or skipped, depending on how hard she booted it. Unexpectedly, after her best kick yet, the stone clipped the inner side of the rock-formation-goal near Lexa and ricocheted into the air. She ran after, only to watch it roll out of reach down the cliffside.

The tumbling stone bounced and bounded like a pinball until finally smacking a massive boulder barely clinging to the mountain's face. Juno froze solid as the *claps!* of rock-on-rock echoed throughout the range. *Clap!...ap!...ap!* Then all fell silent. But just as her shoulders began to relax, another noise followed. The huge boulder shifted and grated against the loose gravel beneath; setting free aeons of trapped pebbles.

Before she knew it a trail of sediment was hissing down the mountain like a bone-dry waterfall. Juno covered her mouth, eyes following the unintentional rockslide for what felt like an eternity; following it all the way down until the stones settled and the white dust dissipated. The breath she had been holding for the last full minute was almost allowed to escape until it was trapped again by a distant group of objects clustered near a gaping black hole. A black hole of which one of the peculiar objects had just entered.

"Hey, guys," she projected at whoever was listening. "What's that over there?"

Like a reflex, Lexa snapped to attention, used her knees to prop herself up, and walked over to see whatever it was that Juno was pointing at. "Where?"

Juno pointed harder. "Right there!"

In view was the same desolate landscape of mountains, rocks, and dirt they had been fully engulfed in for nearly a month. There were various shelters, trails, and roads carved into the terrain, but nothing out of the ordinary. It was not until Lexa raised a hand to her brow that she saw what Juno was referring to. What appeared to be another weathered highway leading into the mountains was actually a weathered highway leading into *a* mountain. It was a tunnel. And scattered before it were over a dozen moving dots.

"Hand me my binoculars," Lexa ordered.

"Your what?" Juno asked.

"I'll get 'em," Kareem offered, awake now and climbing to his feet. He reached into Lexa's bag and sifted around. There were clothes, a few tools or knives, a handful of remaining MRE's, a two-way radio, binoculars, and zero shotgun shells. His head bobbed slightly. At least he knew for sure now.

"What's the hold up?"

Kareem yanked out the binoculars and trotted over. "Sorry 'bout that. I didn't want to dump everything out to find them."

Lexa snatched the binoculars from Kareem's hand without consideration and held them up to her eyes. She turned the focusing dial with a finger. The clear zoom of the lenses brought to life the little dots in front of the tunnel. "Shit."

Juno and Kareem both gave each other a confused look. It was not the fact that the dots were actually people that got to Lexa, it was the fact that every single one of them was an acolyte.

"What's goin' on? What do you see?" Kareem asked. Lexa handed him the binoculars and he focused in. He looked for quite a long time before saying, "That's them, then?"

Juno squinted. "Is that who?"

"Yes," confirmed Lexa, mindlessly tracing her scar with a finger. A heavy sigh fell from her mouth. "But they usually only travel in threes. Sometimes fours."

"Who usually travels in threes?" Juno followed up.

Kareem took the binoculars from his eyes and held them at his waist. "That ain't a big deal. They're miles away and headed in the opposite direction. No way they could find you two out here."

Juno now recognized the thing called binoculars as the device Lexa had put up to her face back in Denver. Curiously, she pried them from Kareem's hand. He did not seem to notice since all of his attention was on the conversation with Lexa, who was now walking in a slow circle.

"I recognize one of them," Lexa scowled with a hair's width of worry in her voice. "The fact that they're even in the same area makes me think…"

The conversation faded into the background as Juno held the lensed device up to her eyes. Her head retracted immediately at what binoculars were capable of. How far away she could see!

When the wonder wore off, Juno looked through the lenses again.

Disoriented, she scanned the base of the mountains until she landed on the length of road that led to the big black hole. She understood why Lexa was worried. The small dots were enlarged into fourteen different people—one less since entering the tunnel—all wearing tattered shades of browns; save for two that donned strangely dark trench coats.

The men were all about the same size, but something was off about each of the ones wearing rags. Juno had to blink her eyes just to make sure. A few had arms too long or arms too short, a couple leaned on stubby legs, some had limbs much wider than the opposing ones, and one even looked to have had his neck put on sideways. The entire company looked unnatural to her.

Juno followed the road slightly further up to the mouth of the tunnel and spotted something equally as striking. Aside from the crumbling arch mysteriously holding up the weight of an entire mountain, a sign still stubbornly clung to the rock, looming over the entrance. It was large and rectangular, not unlike the billboards she had seen back in Denver. On it was a face and a name she could not seem to escape. First the office nameplate, the magazine cover, the Denver billboard, Silver Plume, and now here.

Cameron Friedrich's headshot was displayed in full view alongside a familiar shielded logo. But this one was more curiously vandalized. Over his head was a painted gold ring, like a halo, and to the right were scribbled words from the same spray can: SO HE CREATED MANKIND IN HIS OWN IMAGE. She remembered the man Lexa had slain outside her door in the Genesys skyscraper. His scabbed body, his disproportionate arm. Was this strange message written out of admiration or malevolence?

"Let's go, Juno."

Lexa's voice. She had heard that same phrase a thousand times. "Alright."

Juno pulled the binoculars from her eyes and rejoined her two companions. Lexa was pulling on the strap that held the shotgun firmly to her bag while Kareem took one last sip of water. He held Juno's backpack in the air and she slipped into it as if a gentleman was holding a jacket for her. Then she followed them down the western slope of the mountain, the mysterious face of Cameron Friedrich burning hotter in her mind than the midday sun.

After days of spreading out their search across the Rockies, Bishop and Deacon returned to the rendezvous as empty-handed as the rest of the acolytes. All thirteen waited impatiently while their dark-coated superiors approached from the melting highway. The carnal desire that had briefly given them energy had faded, and talks of mutiny hovered between their ears.

"I'm startin' to think he don't know which ways is up," one disgruntled acolyte spat just loud enough to cut through the air.

"Who said that?" Deacon fired, scanning the scabbed heads of his brethren. All of the men looked at the ground as he paced back and forth before them like a ranking official.

Bishop had stepped off to the side in deep thought. The hot breeze lifted the flaps of his dark trench coat while he stood unmoving. His hands were clasped firmly behind his back. "Where could they have gone," he muttered. The flowing premonition he was so gifted with seemed to be tapped dry. He had no heading. All he could do was impatiently await an answer to present itself. "There must be a sign."

Despite the heavy weight of the sun and the lamentable circumstance of their convergence, a third factor was stirring the nerves of the acolytes. It came in the form of a looming black hole that had been carved from the mountain behind them ages ago. A pitch-black fissure that swallowed things whole and spat nothing back out. To escalate their unease, a line of shade provided by the ridge above was slowly betraying them, pushing the group of fifteen ever closer towards the obsidian mouth.

Minutes passed until Bishop left his chamber of thought. He gazed out openly onto the group, who were exchanging their own deceitful looks between themselves, the ground, and over their shoulders. "Has anyone arrived bearing fruit?" he asked half-heartedly.

The eyes continued to shift.

"We have followed Creator's bounties this far," Bishop continued, "but unfortunately their scent has escaped us."

Silence between the numbers remained steady as the temperature continued to climb. Before Bishop proceeded, Deacon approached to bend his ear. "There's a whole lotta land out there to cover—dangerous land, too—and we're tryin' to find two tiny people. Odds are not in our favor. Hell, chances bein' what they are, it'd be more likely that they slipped and fell dead in a ditch by now."

Bishop raised a flinty eyebrow. "You would not be proposing an act of weakness during our time of need, would you?"

Deacon understood Bishop's words to be a fair warning and shook his head. "No, sir."

"Good. Because I trust I will need your assistance momentarily." Bishop dismissed Deacon by moving him to the side with the back of his forearm, then addressed the glowering group once again. "If anyone has acquired any information, speak now or be held in contempt."

They all faced the hopeless probe with silence. They were weary and wished to be anywhere besides where they currently were.

Fed up with the weeks-long scour under the sun, an especially grizzled acolyte wiped a layer of sweat from his forehead, crossing a few loose scabs in the process. The salt stung like pins in the freshly opened skin, amplifying his irritance just enough for him to limp forward on a stubby leg. "We ain't got nothin' but dry mouths and burnt skin!"

Bishop narrowed his eyes, and dismissed the matter. "An unworthy protest," he said. "Were we not created to ascend such ailments?"

The grizzled man took the reminder in stride and gestured back to his similarly miserable brethren instead. "Why are we out here tryin' to fix your mistakes anyways? The way we see it, Creator never shoulda gave you a second chance!"

Unmoved as a steel beam, Bishop nodded at the affront. "And do you all share this grievance?"

A slight rumble of agreement vibrated between the acolytes, boosting the confidence of the grizzled man to dangerous levels. He lifted a brave finger and jabbed it in his superior's direction. "There ain't no way we're gonna find no one that don't wanna be found in these mountains. And you know what I think? I think you've lost your touch."

Bishop's eyes scanned across the men like a spiteful spotlight. Regardless of his recent fall from Creator's best graces, he still outranked each of these men tenfold, and he had never failed at acquiring that which he seeked. So it was no surprise to him that instead of speaking up, the rest kept their opinions glued to their lips. Still, Bishop knew, that despite their hesitance to speak out, the slight waver in confidence meant an example had to be made.

"Deacon," Bishop ordered, then nodded towards the defier.

Without delay his partner strolled over to the grizzled acolyte and kicked backwards the knee on his longest leg. The man cried out in agony and crumpled to the hot pavement at the edge of the shaded line. The cement hissed at his skin. The rest of the acolytes gasped and shuffled backwards, careful to keep a reasonable distance from the light-consuming blackness behind.

"Perhaps a sacrifice," Bishop smirked. His attention was now on the tunnel as well. "An offering in exchange for a sign from our Creator!"

Murmurs blew through the acolytes like a light breeze. It was an air of curiosity and excitement.

"You broke my fuckin' leg!" the grizzled man spat. He was on his back, rocking side-to-side while clutching his knee in a half-fetal position.

Bishop raised a steady hand. "Silence!" he commanded, then sauntered over to the injured man and squatted down, examining him without pity. "What is your name?"

The man looked up at him with all the hatred and desperation prey feels towards a predator. "Ch...Ch...Chaplain."

"Well, Chaplain, you will make a glorious contribution."

"What the hell do you mean..." He trailed off in anguish from the throbbing, hyperextended tendons.

Bishop returned to his feet and flicked his head from Deacon to

Chaplain. Recognizing it as an order, Deacon locked his hands in Chaplain's armpits and hoisted him up without warning. Chaplain grunted at even the slightest weight placed back onto his knee.

Bishop then walked through the cluster of still-standing acolytes and they separated around him like oil through water. Deacon followed him towards the tunnel, guiding Chaplain with his arms as if he were a puppet on strings. The rest watched in deadly anticipation. Their mouths would have been drooling with elation if they were not so desiccated.

"We are in desperate need of a sign," Bishop announced in a preach-like manner, loud with a flowing cadence. There was a slight echo against the nearby mountain rock. "Something to guide us towards our shared objects of desire." He paused as the acolytes huddled behind him. "But what is the price of such a sign? And how are we to pay it?"

When they reached the entrance of the tunnel, Deacon released his support, leaving Chaplain to hobble awkwardly on his short, stubby leg.

"Behold," Bishop continued with his arms outstretched to the billboard above. It featured a charming man with dark features enhanced by sacred, golden graffiti. "Our precursor, Friedrich! Without whom our Creator would not exist. Without whom our lives would not be possible. You, Chaplain, will enter under his eyes; offering your life in exchange for a blessed sign!"

Chaplain gazed up at the oversized advertisement, then into the unholy darkness. The heaviness of fate settled on his shoulder like molten lead. He turned to the man now in sole control of his life. "Y...you can't send me in there with those...those...molemen! They ain't human!"

"Molemen?" Bishop jested. "But they are just like you and I, brother. Survivors of old. Only they journey on without our Creator's blessing." There was a chuckle from behind, enticing Bishop's theatrics. He was regaining favor. "Tell us what you know of the so-called molemen, Deacon."

"Besides the fact that they're a degenerate lot of cannibals?" Deacon scoffed. "Only that they stick to the darkest, dampest holes known to man until they get too hungry. Then," he continued with arms above his head, fingers wiggling like a ghoul, "when desperation sets in, those albino freaks slink out in the night and set fire to any poor soul that has meat enough on their bones to eat. Hell, a cluster of 'em somehow took Leadville!" He ended his rant there, but not after tacking on one last insult. "Buncha cretins."

"Primitive, yes," Bishop nodded. "But men just the same."

Deacon spat on the ground. "*Hungry* men."

Chaplain continued to stare into the gaping blackness. He considered for a moment that it, along with their threats, could be empty; that they were only tormenting him for speaking out. "You're just gonna send me in there empty-handed? Then what?"

Wrapping his hands around Chaplain's hunched shoulders one finger at a time, Bishop replied gently. "Do not for a moment think I would send you into total darkness without light, my brother."

Bishop snapped towards the side of the road where a few dead trees were lying on their sides. Deacon, understanding the intent, followed its direction. He jogged over, broke off a thick branch, and returned to place it in Bishop's empty grasp. Then he retrieved a plastic lighter from his pocket and lit the top. A slow fire turned the tip of the log even blacker.

"Enter, Chaplain!" Bishop announced, resuming his sing-songy cadence. He shoved the torch into Chaplain's hand, then shoved him in the back. "For whoever wants to save their life will lose it. And whoever loses their life for Him will save it!"

Chaplain hopped on his good leg, oddly energized by the chaotic sermon. "And if I survive?"

"Then we will feast together in Sanctuary!" Bishop sang with a smile.

Chaplain stepped forward, careful not to put weight on his throbbing knee. The acolytes behind him watched with savagely eager eyes.

"Enter," one of them said.

"Enter," three of them said.

"Enter," they all said in a mindless, unifying chant. "Enter...Enter... Enter..."

Warily, Chaplain continued. Each hobbled step was a nail driven into his coffin. But he carried with him a newfound desire. A hope that he would become the linchpin to Creator's search for the young girl and her defiant escort. That it could only be accomplished by his sacrifice.

"Enter...Enter...Enter..."

When Chaplain had finally reached the mouth, nothing looked back at him but a totality of blackness. How could anyone, or anything, survive inside? How long would he need to—

"Enter! Enter! Enter!"

Holding the torch as far out in front as his arm would allow, Chaplain crossed the threshold of darkness. How the acolytes cheered! One step, two steps, three steps. He was soon devoured by the absence of light with only a small torch to guide him.

Bishop, Deacon, and the rest of the acolytes watched the glow of the torch gradually shrink. Even the extreme heat from a fresh flame could not combat the tunnel's obscurity. It was not long before all they could make out was a faint, flickering orange surrounding Chaplain's torso.

But suddenly there were reflections. Pairs of pale dots blinking curiously in the blackness. Eyes. Deeper the flame traversed and the things surrounding the floating dots began to take shape. Little by little, the figures made their outlines known to their approaching meal...

A sharp yell and a swung torch followed the new reflections. Back and forth the fire flitted like a brush of orange paint on a black canvas. More shapes and more eyes sprung from every swipe of the light's flailing radius, multiplying in droves, crawling over one another in a starved, shambolic struggle. What the acolytes were witnessing could only be described as a hive.

Hundreds of eyes now followed the flame until the torch suddenly extinguished to the ground, succumbing to the power of total darkness. The final thing to exit the tunnel was a scream that scratched all the way down to Deacon's bones.

Suddenly, an echo ricocheted off the looming billboard above. The acolytes all jumped at the sound and spun to locate its source. To Deacon's surprise, one of the acolytes was already staring at a lonely mountain many miles away, his arm outstretched to a trembling point. Deacon lifted his hand to shade his eyes and squinted the distance into focus. All he could see was the white dust left behind by a recent rockslide.

"Bishop," Deacon called out. "What the hell is that?"

"*That*, my fellow acolyte..." Bishop began as he stepped around his partner's side, unbothered by the event that unfolded inside the tunnel. Deacon turned his head to a rare smile stretched across his leader's face. "...is our sign."

"Juno, quick!"

Kareem was kneeling over an old ice machine that was deteriorating next to an even older CamChem convenience store. Lexa was inside sifting through expired food that might still be edible while he was supposed to be checking the outside pipes for water. Juno, as instructed, was relieving herself far from anyone's line of sight.

"Hurry!"

Juno pulled up her pants and turned the corner of the building to find Kareem waving her over with a frantic arm. It worked, too, because she ended up in a full jog just to see what all the fuss was about.

"You ready?" Kareem asked. He had one hand gripping the once-silver handle of the ice machine's weathered door. Its sheen had long since withered to brown rust. Juno nodded, then quietly leaned over with her hands on her knees. "One..."

Kareem started pulling the door open, careful not to let too much light in all at once. The squeaks of corroded hinges trailed behind. Juno peeked through the newly created gap, but could not see anything in the dark, barren container. It was early morning and the sun still needed time to share its full glow.

"Two..."

Juno squinted, trying to adapt her eyes to the dim box.

"Three!"

A sliver of warm light painted the far corner of the interior orange.

Then it spread inwards like a triangular spotlight as Kareem kept pulling the door steadily. Highlighted first were a few clumps of dried dirt; nothing unusual. Following were a couple of small twigs. Larger and larger the section of light became until a circular formation came into view. It was a round clump of sticks and dirt and leftover fragments of discarded plastic containers with a small hole poked into the top. It was brazenly clear to Juno that the object inside was not created by years of accumulated trash. It had been constructed.

Once the door was propped completely open, Kareem stepped back. Juno pried her gaze from the lackluster reveal and turned to him. "What is it?"

"Just watch," he said, flashing that infectious smile that she was quickly developing an addiction to.

She returned her attention to the rusted box and leaned in closer. A few moments passed while she narrowed her eyes into adjustment. Something moved! A slight gasp left her mouth but she captured it with her palm.

"Keep watching," Kareem encouraged.

The entirety of Juno's attention was now fixed on the tiny constructed mound with its hollow center. She leaned her forearms on the edge of the ice machine's mouth and dipped her head farther inside. Something rustled again, but this time she did not flinch. All fell quiet. Unable to restrain her curiosity any longer, she stuck out a cautious finger to see what the little mound might be hiding. Slowly she moved it towards the heap of dirt and sticks and scrap. Right before touching the clumped object of her desire, she took a deep swallow, then made contact.

Out popped the head of a creature that startled Juno so abruptly, she screamed and fell backwards onto her rear. However, childlike excitement rebounded her body near immediately. She sat back up with persistent eyes as focused as a laser.

From the side of the eroding steel container that once condensed water into cubes of ice, a tan reptile with patterned black spots emerged and froze solid; and Juno along with it. She locked eyes with the lizard and witnessed it tilting its head with speeds that would break a human's neck. A moment of silent anxiety filled the space between the two, then the reptile flicked a forked tongue into the air and skittered back underneath the machine.

Kareem erupted in deep laughter while Juno sat dumbfounded in the dirt. A tide of euphoria had swelled up inside of her and she did not want to exhale for fear of ebbing it away. This was the first living animal she had ever seen in her entire life. But when her lungs could hold no longer, she exhaled and joined in on Kareem's merriment.

Suddenly, Lexa burst from the CamChem entrance with scorn. A large kukri knife was brandished in her hand, sending the two into a fit of laughter like guiltless children caught in the act. When she realized what was happening her shoulders slumped. "Is everyone okay? I heard a scream."

"Lexa!" Juno yelped, rushing back over to the lizard's fortress. "Come look at this!"

Unamused, Lexa slipped her kinked knife back into the sheath fastened to her chest and walked over to join Juno at the ice machine. She gave Kareem a look as she passed. "What is it?"

Juno was pointing at a clump of dirt and debris with a hole poked in the top. "There's a lizard in there!"

Lexa leaned over the opening and peered in. There was no hesitation in her action. "Is that so?"

"Kareem found it. I've never seen one before!"

The mound sat motionless in the yellowing light. It only took a few moments for the scraping sound to return from within. Lexa eyed it carefully, briefly, then plunged a hand into the hole with the precision of a needle. A mixture of noises followed—squealing, grunting, shuffling, clattering—while Juno watched idly with a new representation of horror. Then, just as abruptly as the bizarre action began, Lexa's arm recoiled with a flailing creature in hand.

"No!" Juno cried, tears already wetting her ducts. "Don't hurt it!"

Lexa wrestled with the animal until she got one hand firmly around its tail and the other around its neck. Every muscle in Juno's body pulled inward in disgust. Even Kareem spoke up. "Now just hold on a min—"

But Lexa ignored their pleas. Instead, she continued wrangling the sprightly creature while it wriggled furiously. The lizard broke the grip of one of her hands, forcing her to twist to catch it between her arm and torso. Then it attempted to squeeze forward like a greased ball. Lexa was ready with her free hand. Over and over they battled until one came out the victor, and the other fell limp.

Juno saw the animal lying motionless in Lexa's arms and reactively began to sob. "You killed it!" she sniffled. Then, more faintly, "How could you?"

"That *was* pretty cold," Kareem trailed.

Lexa turned to Juno with the reptile gripped firmly and kneeled on the ground next to her. "It's okay. She's only stunned."

Through soaked eyes, Juno examined the scaly creature as it laid congealed in Lexa's hands. It was not until after she wiped away the tears could she see rapid breaths raising and lowering its abdomen.

"Do you want to hold her?"

Juno looked up at Lexa. All of the hatred she had briefly felt had vanished like water dousing a small fire. She nodded.

"Be careful," Lexa instructed, holding out the slender animal as if it were made of glass. Juno reached her arms out gently to receive it. Before releasing control of the lizard, she continued. "Now hold it like this. Keep a firm grip but don't squeeze. There you go. Nice and easy, like she's your friend."

And just like that Juno was holding her first living animal. Not preserved with chemicals, not stuffed with cotton, but living, breathing flesh like her own. The lizard's scales were surprisingly cool and dry, not at all like what she expected from the slimy-looking photographs inside her field guide. It's heart beat rapidly, much quicker than her own, yet it stayed completely placid in her hands. She used her thumb to stroke the top of its head while admiring the beautiful creature up close. Most noticeably was the pleasing tan color, similar to the ground she stood on, and the pattern of dark spots peppered along its back. It almost resembled a—

"She's called a leopard lizard," Lexa said, interrupting Juno's deep concentration. She ran a finger along the animal's midriff. "See these reddish markings? That means she's carrying eggs. Probably why she built her nest inside that old ice machine."

Juno's eyes and ears absorbed every detail. "How do you know this?"

Lexa sat backwards onto the ground and leaned against the metal box. She briefly noted that her chest emitted more of a dull throb as opposed to a sharp pang. Progress. After a forced sigh she said, "They used to be all over. But, sadly, when people get desperate they'll eat anything that moves. Then, instead of solving problems they create others. I now see maybe one leopard lizard a year if I'm lucky..."

Lexa's words trickled off as if she had tightened a leaky faucet. A few steady drops of subtext and then nothing. Frustrated, she tilted her head back and noticed the soft light of the morning growing harsher. "We better make up some ground before it gets too hot."

Reluctant to let the most fulfilling moment of her entire life slip from her hands, Juno momentarily considered keeping the leopard lizard. But the red splotches brought her back to her senses. This animal was a soon-to-be mother. And what kind of cold-blooded reptile would remove a beating heart from the safety of their own home?

Juno shook her head before her thoughts got any heavier. She brought the lizard back to the decrepit ice machine and set it gently inside next to the mound of dirt. When she released the leopard lizard it remained still for a while, as if still in shock, then finally tasted the air with a slender tongue. It flicked its head once again at breakneck speed so that Juno could see her own tiny reflection in the creature's eye. "Goodbye," she whispered, and watched it scurry back into its hole.

"And here I thought I had you figured out," Juno heard Kareem say as she rejoined the group. He chuckled, shook his head, then added, "I was dead certain you were wranglin' up some breakfast."

"No need," Lexa replied impassively. "I found some food inside still worth eating."

The three of them returned their efforts to scavenging the Cam-Chem convenience store. Kareem staved in a bathroom door at the back of the building and filled up their containers with water from the sink pipes. And though the shelves inside were picked clean, the other two pillaged a storage room that Lexa had picked the lock on before rushing out to Juno's scream. Seven cans, two boxes of dried pasta, one sack of pinto beans, and a handful of salt packets for flavor.

They all met out front and distributed the load. Then, with bags strapped firmly to their backs, the trio set off to chase a shadow as it circled a westward mountain.

A sharp beam of sunlight stabbed at Pan's eye, reminding her she had yet again been up all night. A shaky hand removed a pair of thick-rimmed glasses while the other pressed firmly against her temple, failing to knead away the wrinkles created by time and stress. The sigh that followed was long and slow, as if her lungs had been pricked with a small pin. She blinked over the redness glazing her eyes before returning them to the microscope below.

Underneath the lens were three circular dishes attached to an oscillating tray. Pan ticked the knob that brought the next dish into view and inspected it closer. Magnified was a small group of cells trapped inside a streak of deep red. She adjusted the focus and watched for a moment. Thousands of globular flecks lay nearly stagnant. They were all uniform in size, pinkish in color, and translucent.

Pan's eyes tracked the entire petri dish until they were snagged by something on the bottom left of her view. It was rigid and lighter in color; almost yellow against the bright backlight provided by the microscope. Then, after spotting the first anomaly, the rest of them stuck out like stars in a night sky. The entire sample was littered with them.

Sighing once again, Pan pried her head from the eyepieces and returned the glasses to her nose. She swiveled her chair over to an adjacent desk that contained the bulk of her research. On the sides were stacks of medical textbooks and periodicals and mixed in were journals filled with the work of herself and her colleagues. In between the stacks was a notebook lying flat. Scribbles of her current theories filled every available line. Shaking her head, Pan turned to a fresh page, lifted a pen, and wrote:

Sample: V342
Subject: Male, Middle-Aged
Cell Type: Blood, Red
Location Recovered: Utah, Salt Lake City
Phthalate(P)/BPA: Positive

The next petri dish contained a different type of cell. One from deeper inside the body. Pan had to quadruple the magnification to make out the structures clearly. Amorphous blobs began to take shape as she dialed in the focus. Unlike the red cells from the smear of blood, these were more distinct. More unique. More important.

After a slow turn of the weighted knob, Pan could clearly make out a membrane, a patchy cytoplasm, and a dense nucleus at the center. Although just a bunch of splotches and dots to her naked eye, Pan knew the nucleus contained the building blocks to life. The parts that molded mankind as she knew it.

Pan flipped to the longest lens, setting the magnification to a thousand times normal, and studied the center of the cell. Like a blurred jumble of coiled ropes, the genetic material lay in a knot of stasis. Dark worms curving this way and that hinted at a code she feared could never be cracked.

Though a clear visual of the process was impossible at this magnification, Pan understood how strands of DNA had written an ancient formula, how proteins carried the information, and how chromosomes held it all safely together. But then she spotted an intruder. Just as with the blood cells, a small bead of yellow made itself known among the darkness, winking at her with a sinister sparkle.

Pan retracted her head from the microscope and uttered something foul underneath her breath. Then she grabbed her glasses, rolled back over to her notepad, and picked up her pen.

Sample: V869
Subject: Male, Mid-Twenties
Cell Type: Eukaryotic, Prostate
Location Recovered: Colorado, Boulder
Phthalate(P)/BPA: Positive

As Pan's pen stroked the final letter, something gently nudged against the side of her shoe. She slid her chair backwards and dipped her head to see if she had accidentally elbowed something off the desk. Nothing of hers was on the ground, but carefully tucked in a shadow cast by the warm morning light was a hemispheric creature.

"And what might you be doing in here, Rodan?" she asked.

"It's after eight," said a young voice from behind. "You weren't at my birthday breakfast."

"Oh no!" Pan reacted, still watching the tortoise. Slowly, four legs and a head emerged from the shell with newfound curiosity. "Was that today?"

Rodan took a step inwards to the lab and sighed, "Yes."

Shelby extended her neck as far as it could reach and nipped at Pan's shoelace.

"And how old does that make you today?" she asked with an enticing glimmer in her tone.

"Officially thirteen!"

Pan reached down to pick up Shelby, careful to remove her grip from the shoelace gently. The tortoise's limbs sucked back into its shell like a vacuum while Pan returned it to Rodan. "Thirteen? Wow! You know what that means?"

Rodan's head nodded with buoyancy. "I get to start my training?"

"That's right," Pan said, placing a hand on his shoulder and turning the young boy back towards the door. "But today you should celebrate. Let me finish up here and I will join you for lunch."

Without realizing it, Rodan was already in the brightness of the hallway. He looked up at Pan's comforting smile and relaxed. "Promise?"

"If I'm late, you can send Shelby back in to retrieve me."

"Deal," Rodan agreed, then rushed down the empty hall.

The dense weight of responsibility slumped Pan back into her chair. She rubbed her forehead again. The technology required for her research had been lost in the shadows of the past and was still decades away from being reengineered. But as she placed a hand on her lower abdomen she felt humanity's precious time running out. How could she explain to Rodan his importance while still maintaining the boy's youthful optimism? He was their absolute final chance at survival. He and the girl Lexa was sent to—

An idea spread across Pan's mind as severely as a streak of lighting. She rolled back to the table containing the microscope and collections of samples. She sifted frantically through the stack of petri dishes until she found the one she was looking for, then replaced it under the lens. After turning the knobs quickly and precisely, she brought the red blood into focus.

Up and down, side to side, her eyes flitted across the sample. Thousands and thousands of identical pink cells laid under the lens without a single bright interloper. She held her breath and swapped in some ovarian cells from the same subject. Not a single flake of yellowish reflection.

Her head flung back in awe. A million theories suddenly coursed through her brain. The answer was inside these samples. Something in their code had made them resistant. Immune.

Pan shook her head and laughed. How had she not thought of looking deeper into this subject before? Then, after briefly scolding herself, she went back to the desk holding her journal. It was filled with so many entries marked Positive that she nearly abandoned the research altogether. She picked up the pen knowing that if this information did not provide a backup plan, then at least it would provide hope. Perhaps even a future. Finally, hands shaky with a rare excitement, she pressed the ink to the paper.

> Sample: R264
> Subject: Female, Late-Twenties
> Cell Types: All
> Location Recovered: Utah, Arcadia, East Gate
> Phthalate(P)/BPA: Negative

That night Juno sat on a crest gazing out into the distance. The sky was cloudy or dusty or whatever flavor of haze she had come to expect so she diverted her attention down to her hands. She held them out as if they still contained the first live animal she had ever seen. She wondered if the leopard lizard would continue to survive in this environment. She wondered how many babies might hatch from her eggs. And she wondered how soon until someone killed them for food.

Behind her a loud clunk disrupted her daydream. Kareem had returned with the firewood. She spun around like a top, hopped down from the rock, and jaunted over to the small encampment.

Lexa was preparing a ration of food for their nightly meal while Kareem had kneeled over the hole Juno had already been told to dig out. He loaded the pit with dry tinder, sticks, and logs, patted the stones surrounding them tightly together, then tossed in a match. The fire sprang to life.

"Don't you worry about them seeing us?" Juno asked as she sat down within the radius of the new glow.

"Who?" Lexa asked. She was pouring just enough water over some dried noodles so they could be chewed.

"The people we saw on the road."

Lexa came around to Juno's side of the fire and placed two long branches across the top of the pit, like a makeshift bridge for the pot. "Not anymore. They are very far away."

Having adapted to the typical Lexa response mechanism, Juno knew the way to get more answers: by prying. "But won't they see the light from our fire?"

"Unlikely," Lexa said. When she sat down she gathered a frustrated look on the young girl's face and rolled her eyes. It astounded her how little people knew about survival, yet somehow still survived. "Are you familiar with rise?"

Expectedly, Juno shook her head.

"When you look up one side of a mountain you cannot see the other, correct?"

Juno nodded.

"That's how rise works. As long as someone is below the peak, anything on the opposite side is invisible to them. To enhance the effect, we only rest in areas that dip lower than their own immediate surroundings. Kind of like sleeping in a bowl, I suppose."

"But what about the light above the fire?"

Kareem chimed in while Lexa tried to focus on stirring the noodles. "Same concept. That's why she has you dig a pit. It keeps any unwanted light even lower still."

"And the smoke?"

"Extremely dry wood is about the only advantage of this eternal drought," Lexa continued. She removed the pot from the fire, took a small bite of gluey pasta, then passed it on. "The more dehydrated the wood, the less smoke it emits. Plus," she gestured out into the distance, "the sky pretty much resembles smoke most of the time anyways."

Juno thought she had outsmarted them with the smoke question. Maybe she was still too young to understand all the workings of the natural world. Thirteen was such a small number and her companions had at least twice that amount of experience. Temporarily appeased on the topic of fire, she chewed on a mouthful of stodgy food until another nagging thought popped into her head. One that had followed her all the way from Denver. "Who's Cameron Freed-rick?"

Lexa coughed suddenly, then spasmed, trying to stop the pain between her ribs while keeping the food inside her mouth at the same time. As she clutched her chest and lips, Kareem cleared his throat and, in an attempt to distract from the situations on both sides of the fire, began searching quietly for his water. It was apparent that neither of them had expected to hear those three words this evening.

Kareem eventually found his plastic bottle hiding underneath his bag and took an obligatory drink before lightly asking, "Where'd you hear that name?"

Juno was just as surprised that they were surprised. "I've been seeing his name and face all over. He was on the big sign above those people on the road yesterday. There was a poster of him in Silver Plume. And I saw him a bunch of times back in Denver."

"Hm," Kareem nodded. "His name still pops up like a stubborn pimple from time to time. He was a big shot back in the day, you know. I've heard everything from tycoon to savior to—"

"Exterminator."

Lexa. She had recovered in time to silence Kareem's enthusiasm with both a sharp glance and a single, malign word. When all fell quiet around the campfire, she refocused on Juno. "It's pronounced Fried-Rich and he's the reason we're eating expired pasta on top of a cold mountain right now."

The fire crackled on while Lexa's brash statement settled into Juno's mind. *An exterminator?*

"Oh, come on," Kareem decided to argue, "Friedrich was the only one even close to comin' up with a cure."

Lexa scoffed. "A cure for what? His greed?"

Kareem took another drink from his plastic water bottle. "You know..." He hunched and curled two fingers twice in the air. "...the plague?"

After rolling her eyes again, Lexa boasted, "Nature didn't do this to us. Man did."

"Seriously?" Kareem gestured to the open landscape. "You can't possibly believe one guy caused all of this."

"No. I'm saying one guy *created* all of this."

The two exchanged squints of skepticism while Juno gawked at the alien argument. It was as if they were speaking an entirely different language. In that time, noodles passed from Lexa to Kareem to Juno and they each took one last bitter bite. Silence closed in on the smokeless fire like an incoming choke.

Juno, flipping a log over with a stick, asked a bit more timidly, "So who was he?"

Lexa smirked, then told Kareem to go ahead and tell his version as if the effort alone would be meaningless.

Now it was Kareem's turn to roll his eyes. He turned to Juno and mustered up the smile she had become so fond of. His mouth opened and closed a few times before settling on where to begin.

"Way back...back before all of this..." he twirled a finger in the air to signify everything, "...people were everywhere. Moms, dads, young women, and young men, just like yourself," he pointed at Juno, "made up the fabric of society."

Juno's hand went through her short hair at "just like yourself", briefly wondering if she would ever be allowed to grow it out again.

"Prosperity was at an all-time high," Kareem continued, "and the world was becomin' more connected and more complex. Cities filled up with sky-scraping towers," he held an arm up high, "people were talkin' and workin' wirelessly with other people halfway around the world," his fingers began to type on an imaginary keyboard, "everyone had vehicles to get where they were goin'..." He gripped an invisible circle and finished his thought with a disappointed chuckle. "Humanity was headed in the direction it was meant to be goin'. Advancements around every turn, food in every belly, water in every pipe, and a roof over every head. But just as the world was gearin' up for its next big thing, the plague hit—"

"Plague?" Juno asked curiously. Something about the word felt inherently treacherous.

Kareem tapped his chin in thought. "It's sort of like a disease, but worldwide, and nobody knew where it came from. Still don't." Then he pulled the collar of his shirt down and pointed to his smooth, shadowed neck. "You know the people with all the scabs and the weird lookin' body parts?"

Juno nodded.

"That's plague."

A faint, yet sharp, puff of air exited Lexa's nose from across the fire. Kareem chose to ignore it.

"Anywho... The scabs didn't actually come in 'til much later on. The first thing people noticed was they were no longer reproducin', er, havin' babies. Every decade or so the number of fertile people on the entire planet shrunk by half." He saw a look begin to form on Juno's face and added, "About every ten years."

"I know," Juno lied. "Was Cameron Friedrich one of those people?"

Kareem chuckled. "Very astute! I was just getin' to that part. The way I understand it, Friedrich was one of those rich and powerful men that took notice of what was goin' on. He had tons of money—" He stopped himself after seeing the same look crawling up Juno's face. "Do you know what the old concept of money is? Dollars, cash, wealth?"

The question caught Juno by surprise. Not because she had no idea what money was, but because she thought she already knew without it ever being explained to her. It just made sense to trade something for something else. "I think it has something to do with those batteries Lexa gave to the tortoise man in exchange for water."

"Tortoise man?" Kareem asked, though Lexa did not confirm.

"Yeah! He was this creepy looking guy with goggles and scales and a big body like a tortoise. We saw him on the road with a cart full of junk. A bunch of people behind him were tied up..." Her voice and eyes trailed to the side when she remembered how that same reptilian man had tried to purchase her.

"Ah," Kareem nodded, "a slaver. You're right, though. But instead of useful silver batteries they spent useless silver coins. Kind of silly now that I say it out loud. Now, where was I?"

"Friedrich," Lexa spat from the flickering shadows. "You were going to tell us all about him."

After Juno's face relaxed from thoughts of the tortoise man, Kareem kept going. "Well Friedrich was especially good at makin' money. In fact, I think he was the richest man on Earth at one point or another; not that it hardly matters now. But people looked to him like a lantern in a cave. He realized that the global population was depressed, helpless, unable to procreate, and decided to put his money where his mouth was."

Another scoff squeezed its way through a gap in the conversation.

"So he was a kind man that people loved?" Juno asked.

Kareem scrunched his face. "I think most did. When it came down to it, there was him and there was God. Some preferred the God explanation, but, in general, Friedrich was the one runnin' the show." He watched Juno mouth the single syllable of "God" and jumped in. "God was somethin', or someone, that many people believed in as the answer to unanswerable questions. If you didn't know where people came from, God created people. If you didn't know why the sky was blue, God painted it blue. If you didn't know why your body was covered in scabs and one of your legs was longer than the other, well, God had a reason for that, too."

"Interesting," said Juno, drawing a shape in the dirt with a stick she had picked up. The idea of higher powers had never occurred to her. "Does that mean God has a reason for locking starved people in cages?"

A grimace plastered itself on Kareem's face. "Eh, mostly he was used under positive circumstances."

"Oh, so God's a *he* now?" Lexa challenged. Her smile bared venomous teeth.

Juno looked at Lexa, then back at Kareem with intense speculation. Kareem waved his hands as if they were a barricade to the rapid fire he was receiving. "Look, I'm not gonna sit here and try to explain the ins and outs of his...or hers...higher power. Can I please just get back to the story?" When there were no more opinions, he said, "Thank you...

"Now, when the bodies started mutatin', suddenly God wasn't quite good enough anymore. People wanted answers. They wanted a *cure*. So

Friedrich, with his unlimited piles of money and resources, founded a company called Genesys with the sole purpose of developin' and mass producin' an antidote for the plague." Before Juno furrowed her brow again, he clarified, "An antidote is like a cure, or a prevention of a disease."

Juno, who was enthralled with all the new information, found herself eager to skip to the conclusion. "So did he find it? Did he make the ant-ee-dote?"

"That's the kicker!" Kareem laughed with little exaggeration. "Not even all the money in the world will keep you alive forever. Friedrich died before he could find the cure. The plague got to him, then Genesys shut its doors for good."

The sound of Juno's shoulders slumping was almost audible. It was not the climactic ending she was expecting. "Oh."

The fire crackled on. Juno made a shape in the dirt with her stick while Kareem swallowed another drink of water from his plastic bottle. A slow breeze pushed by them, separating the flames like a comb through hair, shadowing Lexa's grim expression. When the flames returned upright a smile was spotlighted on Lexa's face. Soon after, a sound Juno thought she would never hear in a million years emerged from the light. Lexa was laughing.

"What?" Kareem sighed, more than a little annoyed now. "That's the story. Things didn't end up this way because of your so-called exterminator. They ended up this way because of—"

"Man's hubris," Lexa affirmed with abrupt absolution. Her laughter had subsided and her tone was now grave. She focused on Juno until their eyes met. "Write that down in your notebook and don't forget it."

The focal point around the fire shifted to Lexa as she stood up with deliberate intent. Kareem eyed her, but before he could object to her brazenness, she spoke again. "Juno, grab a handful of that dirt you're playing with and tell me what you see."

Confused, Juno glanced over to Kareem for a second opinion. He shrugged earnestly, also unsure of what the strange request could possibly represent. She looked back down at the trapezoid she had scraped in the earth and cupped a large handful of loose soil. After a brief second of inspection she said, "It's just dirt."

Lexa told her to look harder with a glare instead of words.

With a heavy swallow, Juno shimmied closer to the fire's light and brought the dirt up to her face. At first it seemed another simple clump of dust and soil, but, when the flames flickered just so, it was clear something else lay among the cupped mound. Juno wiggled her fingers, allowing some of the smaller particles to sift through them, then inspected the remnants even closer. There *was* something else! Something she had seen littered across the empty floors of the Genesys building, sprinkled throughout the barren riverbed in Silver Plume, stacked in the alleys of Leadville, and, most recently, built right into the leopard lizard's homemade mound. Poking out of this worthless handful of earth was something mirrored in every heap of trash she had ever encountered: Sand, pebbles, and, "Plastic."

When Juno finally looked up, there was tremendous weight behind Lexa's nod. "There's your plague," she said.

"Now just hold on a second!" Kareem blurted. He was shaking his head and holding spread fingers out in front of his chest like two stop signs. "Plastic? Don't you think the old scientists would have figured that out right away? I mean, damn near everythin's made of the stuff. Hell, most of it's *still* around today!"

While Kareem rambled on, Juno was still sifting through the pile of dirt in her hand until only a few pebbles and a few shards of white plastic remained. She picked up one of the shards and inspected it against the fire. It was rather unimpressive to her. It was not shiny. It was not warm, nor cold. It was not sharp. Not heavy. It was just hard. "What's so dangerous about this stuff?"

Juno's simple question cut through Kareem's rhetoric like an axe. He fell into silence and looked up at Lexa, seemingly with the exact same question.

Lexa took the subdued moment to walk around the fire and kneel down next to Juno. "What do you notice about that piece you're holding right now."

"Um," Juno thought with her tongue pressed between her lips. "It's small. But it looks broken. Like it came from a larger piece."

"That's right," Lexa continued. "And what happens when you break your piece into two pieces?"

Pinching the two ends of the plastic shard with both hands, Juno spent little energy before it snapped in half. A tiny trail of white dust was left behind on her fingertips. She rubbed off the powder and said, "It breaks again."

"What's this got to do with anything?" Kareem interjected. "Plastic is *supposed* to be replaceable. That doesn't explain how a plague wiped out humanity."

Lexa glared at him. "The fact that you are even calling it a plague is proof that the lies prevailed. The narrative of your hero, Friedrich, is one that people are still living and dying by today."

"I never said he was my hero..." Kareem added quietly as Lexa sat on the ground between himself and Juno. He saw only a slight twinge in her face from the slow movement.

"It's time you learned the truth about mankind," Lexa said. Then she shifted her head from Juno to Kareem. "Both of you."

Lexa allowed the fire's crackle to fill the space for a few moments. "Cameron Friedrich was no visionary," she began after absorbing a lungful of crisp air. "Was no genius. No philanthropist. He was a corporate mogul that took advantage of the weak and confused. A multi-trillion-dollar false prophet that deceived the people into believing he would be their savior. But it wasn't humanity's belief in him that caused their near-extinction. Man's greed was at the beginning, and man's greed was at the end." Then, without missing a beat, "Greed, Juno, is if I had more batteries than anyone else in the entire world, more than I would ever be able to spend, and still wanted all of your batteries, too. It is a deadly plague of its own."

Juno processed the idea blankly.

"But greed alone was not why people no longer had children," Lexa continued. "Scientists knew from day one what was actually causing infertility, but a rich and powerful man like Friedrich could make sure those facts remained hidden."

"What do you mean by 'hidden'," asked Kareem.

Lexa picked up the stick Juno had been dragging through the dirt earlier and stabbed at the fire. A log flipped over and tiny embers escaped into the sky. "Did you ever wonder *how* Friedrich became the richest man in the world?"

Kareem's lips separated, but the lack of words created a vacuum that pulled them back shut.

"Friedrich didn't make money from his pet project, Genesys. He made his money from CamChem; the world's largest supplier of oil, gas, and chemicals; like the resin and polymers that make up plastic. In other words, the planet's primary poison provider. I won't pretend to know how the old governments used to operate, but it was shockingly easy for the world's largest plastic manufacturer to buy their undivided silence.

"At first it was just general misinformation. Words like 'BPA-free' and 'ninety percent recycled' put everyone's minds at ease. But as soon as the population shrank and the scabs covered their skin, well, let's just say 'plague' makes a much better headline than 'It's too late because plastic has already poisoned everyone who will ever live'."

Kareem held up a small blue fragment that he himself found nearby on the ground and said, "How can this be the cause? I've never eaten plastic. And even if I swallowed this piece right now it would pass through my body in a couple of days."

Lexa jerked as if his remarks offended her. "As Juno demonstrated, plastic is very easy to break down. Even though it takes over a thousand years to decompose, it will never fully be reduced to nothing. As it breaks smaller and smaller, it contaminates the earth in a form called microplastic. But it doesn't just poison the ground we walk upon, it poisons everything that walks upon it as well. Once microplastics make their way into our bodies it does terrible things."

"How so?" asked Juno. She was filled with so many questions they were nearly pouring out her ears.

Lexa hesitated briefly before proceeding. "Juno, do you know how babies are made?"

Juno looked at the ground with a red face. She always had in the back of her mind what she assumed was the answer, but her body had been telling her otherwise as of late. In the end, she went with what she had read in her field guide. "I had a book that said males put their seeds inside the females so her eggs can grow babies."

Lexa silenced a snicker from Kareem and told Juno her version was accurate enough for the story. Then she took the stick and started drawing shapes in the ground. "When microplastics get into the various systems inside your body," she started, drawing the outline of a human and long lines running away from its heart, "they can change the way information travels from one organ to another."

The body filled in with various shapes. One of which was an upside triangle with two stalks stretching from the top like weird eyes. When Lexa drew two legs underneath the unusual shape, Juno's eyes widened. "They can also block vital chemicals from developing what they should be developing." A line slashed through the middle of one of the stalks. "At first, in the case of humans, that meant half as many seeds and half as many eggs for each new generation of children."

To the side of the human model, Lexa drew rudimentary outlines of a river, a flower, a bee, a bird, and a cat. One by one she crossed them out as she explained. "What followed was even worse for all living things. The longer plastic became synonymous with humanity, the more microplastics made their way into entire ecosystems. Every form of packaging, every drop of water, every bite of our food, our food's food, and their food's food had traces of these relentless chemicals."

Lexa shoved the stick back into the fire until the end charred. Then she tapped the black ash all over the human she had drawn. Finally, she used the tip to exaggerate one of the shoulders and made an arm twice as long. "Once we ingested enough microplastic, our very DNA had been altered. Cancers, mutations, and, as you've seen, horrible scabbing formed. The poison that is plastic literally broke down the human race from the inside out."

Off to the side, Kareem took a dire look at his clear bottle lying on the ground next to his bag. How many times had he drank from it? How much shrink-wrapped food had he scavenged? How much plastic had his entire family tree ingested?

"But Kareem said Friedrich was working on a cure," Juno said. "So maybe he wasn't so bad?"

A single, dangerous laugh escaped from Lexa's lungs. "No, he was even worse. Friedrich was never working on a cure in the first place. Genesys had been a corporation in disguise. A lie. Something much darker was going on behind those walls. But once his scabs started showing to the public, it was too late. He disappeared, Genesys closed its doors, and humanity was abandoned. In the end it was their faith in *his* greed that doomed them all."

Chagrin crawled under Kareem's skin. His body and face exceeded the warmth of the fire. This was not a brief spell of embarrassment, but a deep shame that came from a whole life of believing fiction to be fact. He shook his head and said, "This is unbelievable. How do you explain how I was born? Or you? Or your son? Our skin is smooth; our bodies are the right shape!"

Lexa's eyes flickered from side to side, but were luckily hidden by the shadow of night. Now was not the time to reveal her own truths. "That part is a little more...complicated. What I know is that some human bodies can naturally reject plastic from the system and pass it unwittingly. But the number of humans left that can still do this is at best microscopic, and at worst non-existent. My guess is all three of us share some version of this trait."

Kareem's eyes narrowed at *version*. All of this new information was too much; too overwhelming. He felt attacked in a way he had never been attacked before.

"So why aren't you back in the safety of your home pumpin' out babies?" he blurted out of frustration, then immediately stopped his tongue.

Lexa's eyes caught ablaze with an unmistakable rage. A rage that every woman felt deep down when being told what their purpose was. A rage that could never be understood or controlled by man. Even one as seemingly harmless as Kareem.

"Sorry," he conceded, choosing his next words extremely carefully. "What I meant to say was shouldn't we be doing all that we can to preserve the human race?"

"Shouldn't *you*?" Lexa sneered.

Kareem looked away, afraid of what else he might see behind Lexa's eyes. Suddenly he was back in Appalachia, stretched out on that stage, bleeding. Trying to make sense of it all. The fear, the lies, and the truth. Plastic was an immense staple in his life despite its final units rolling off the line well before he was born. Humanity could never have forfeited a product that was so abundant, so useful, and so cheap to produce. He was not even sure if he could. "I deserved that."

Juno had been silent for quite some time. She kept scooping up piles of dirt and collecting the pieces of plastic from each handful. It was astounding how commonplace the man-made material was now that she knew to look. Why had her mom never told her about this invisible killer? Did she even know? Eventually Juno mused, "Maybe he did find a cure."

Lexa casually shrugged. "He didn't. That's the one part of Kareem's story he got right."

"Well," Juno said with a slight curve in her voice. "When I was in his office back in Denver, I found a small bottle called Fertimol...or Fertilima...or something like that. It was orange and it was inside his desk. Maybe that's something?" Then, suddenly rising to her feet, "What if we went back to get it? Maybe it could fix everyone who's sick!"

"Out of the question," dismissed Lexa immediately.

Kareem's head snapped back at what had just been said. "Hold up. *You* were in Friedrich's office? What else did you find?"

Juno thought for a second. "Nothing special. Papers, pencils, oh, and a big bag of candy!"

"Any other information about the medicine? What it did? Were they pills? Shots? Serums?" Kareem was chomping at the bit.

"Um—"

"It doesn't matter," Lexa interjected. "We're not going back."

"Why not?" Kareem's attention was turned to Lexa now. "And where were you while your son was rummagin' through arguably the most important office in existence?"

"Enough with the questions," Lexa groaned.

Juno chimed back in, "What if it really was a cure?"

"I'm certain it wasn't."

"How would you know?" Kareem challenged. "It sounds like you were nowhere to be seen."

"I... I was probably asleep."

"If we just went back, we could maybe help a lot of people!"

"I agree with Juno. We have to at least—"

Before another word could be spoken, Lexa was at Kareem's neck with the angled blade of her kukri knife. Despite the residual pain in her abdomen, she still had a job to do, and nothing could be allowed to stop her. "Juno," she snarled. "Get behind me."

"But—"

"Now!"

Juno sank behind Lexa as quietly as a dropped cloth.

"You listen to me, Kareem. I have one purpose, and one purpose only, and that's getting Juno to Arcadia. No matter what. If I need to add your head to the pile, then be my guest."

Kareem began to stand, but the edge of the knife kissed his neck, holding him in place. He swallowed around the blade and spoke. "You don't even care, do you? There could be a cure sitting a few miles away and there's nothing I could say to convince you to try?"

Lexa's nose was now almost touching Kareem's. "There. Is. No. Cure. Friedrich lived a life of deception. You're welcome to head back and collect that bottle of lies, but you will not include myself or Juno."

Hoping that because Lexa had not killed him yet that she would not now, Kareem mustered the bravery to speak again. "But how would I know where to look?"

"You tell me," Lexa spat. "You're the one who's been following us this entire time."

"I—"

"Enough!" Lexa removed the blade from Kareem's neck, but not without flashing its sharpness in the light of the dying fire. "The truth is now yours. You will either be here in the morning or you will not." Then, "Juno, bed."

The only sounds for the rest of the cold night were the drowsy snaps of escaping air as the fire settled onto a bed of coals.

Entry 49

Hubris.

Lexa told me to write that down and remember it, though I don't quite know what it means yet. "Things ended up this way because of man's hubris". Is that the same as the greed thing she was talking about? Or is it about lying? Maybe it doesn't have a clear definition. Maybe it's something I just have to figure out.

Right now we're stopped for the night on something between a hill and a mountain. A hilltain? There are a lot of trees here. Well, the skeletons of trees. So many of them still have their branches even though they're all dead. Their skin is all black and crusty like the men who keep trying to kill us. But I know trees were different than men. They were nice. All of them. They were here for a long time to help us, and I can tell they are sorry they had to go.

Today we walked for a long time. No one said anything. I know Kareem wants to go back for the medicine I found. Every time we stop to rest he looks to where we've been while Lexa only looks to where we're going. I never should have said anything.

Speaking of Kareem, he said he went out to get firewood a while ago, but I don't think he's coming back. He was so excited about finding a way to help people and now he's gone. I really liked having him around, too. I should have told him while I had the chance. He made me smile. He liked to have fun. He saw the prettier side of the world. He's also really pretty himself... (Remind me to maybe erase that later!)

And I know Lexa would never let anything happen to me. But lately she's been so much colder. She is like the mountains we keep climbing (powerful and secure) while Kareem is like the old trees (warm and helpful). Not to say me and Lexa didn't almost have fun a couple of times, but I know deep down it was always disguised as a lesson. All things are with her. I just wish she could have seen Kareem the same way I saw him.

Well, that's all. Kareem left, Lexa's silent, and for some reason I feel more alone than ever.

The full moon's silver light poked through a break in the atmosphere and glazed the forest in a hazy glow. Juno could clearly see the crooked frames of long-dead trees and their equally jagged shadows cast below.

Gusts of wind pulled and twisted on petrified branches, sending ethereal howls and moans echoing into the night. Though the breeze was not as crisp as it was way up on the highest peaks, it was twice as frightening.

After she tucked her notebook away, Juno pulled her duster's hood over her head and crossed her arms tightly with the hope of blocking out both the wretched sounds and the heat-sapping wind. Longer hair, she reckoned, would have been a nice buffer too. A shiver went up her spine as she looked down at the empty firepit she had already dug. Small rocks at the bottom were casting small shadows of their own. It seemed to her that the unusual brightness tonight felt less like dusk, and more like daytime in the shade.

A pot clanged against a fallen log, causing Juno to jump in her seat. On the other side of the pit Lexa was gripping the part of her rib cage underneath her chest. The pot lay face-down on the ground below.

"Are you alright?" Juno asked.

Not realizing the young girl could see her clear as day, Lexa removed her hand and bent over to retrieve the cookware. "I'm fine."

"Whatever," Juno muttered, then continued focusing on warm thoughts. A sharp cramp pulled on her stomach and she slouched into herself heavily. She did not remember being very hungry, though it was already nightfall.

From no discernable direction, another gust blew the painful groans from tree branches and settled back down. Juno shivered again. "Will Kareem be back with the wood soon?"

"No idea," Lexa said insipidly. She was trying to read a label on a package under the moonlight.

A few more minutes of wind and silence followed with no words in between. Juno thought harder on the story Lexa had told the night before. She had said Juno possessed some sort of trait that kept the plastic out of her body. Was this trait the reason she was so valuable to Lexa? Was this trait the reason her mom abandoned her and sent this woman in her stead? As per usual there were too many questions she wanted to ask, but it never seemed to be the right time…

Something in the nearby woods snapped and Juno spun around. *Kareem is back!* But all that was under the silver light of the moon were the black trees and their blacker shadows. Her eyes scanned the forest warily for movement, but everything was as still and dark as a stained painting.

A loud shriek came from elsewhere.

Juno spun back around, this time to her greatest fear. Across from her, Lexa stood utterly still. There was a dark arm around her mouth and a knife was sticking out from her right thigh. A black splotch was growing around the handle.

If it were not for the unnatural brightness in the sky tonight, and the unnecessary hours she spent studying his body, Juno might have thought Kareem had come back to prove he was everything Lexa had thought he was. But this interloper was too small. Too frail. Too malformed.

"Now let me tell you how this is gon' go," said the interloper confidently.

Male, Juno confirmed. She watched Lexa's leg give out briefly as the interloper wrestled her back up.

"The girl comes with me," he continued, "and yer gon' crawl in that hole she so kindly dug."

How does he know I'm a—

Lexa flopped face first into the ground. She immediately tried to snap over to fight back, but a boot came down that held her in place. The interloper leaned over and disappeared his hand under Lexa's breast. She struggled for a moment until he pulled out something long, sharp, and angled.

"This here's a purdy knife," the interloper said as he held it against the moonlight. His finger traced one of the slanted edges. "Almost as purdy as two nekkid girls layin' out in the sun."

Realization struck Juno like a falling boulder. This was the man Lexa had actually seen while they were sunbathing, not Kareem. He must have been tracking them since the beginning. Watching quietly; waiting patiently for the perfect moment to strike. *But how?*

A beam of moonlight highlighted the interloper like a streak of chalk and Juno's gut wrenched more than before. One of his gaunt arms reached nearly to the ground while the one holding the knife was thick and short. His gap-toothed grin was surrounded by a lifetime of scabbing so abused that even in the sun it would have been impossible to tell what color his skin was.

The interloper drove a kick into Lexa's side and he told her to start crawling towards the firepit. The utter humiliation of the scene pulled Juno back from her dumbstruck gaze. The young girl stood from the log she was sitting on and drew the knife Lexa had given her, now always strapped firmly to her leg.

The interloper only chuckled. "You see that?" he directed to the woman on all fours. "I like a girl with some spunk." Then he focused on Juno. "Now unless you want yer friend here to die a lot sooner, I suggest you put that toy away."

Juno sheathed her knife and watched helplessly as Lexa was forced to drop into the hole she had dug for a fire, now turned into a grave. Powerless emotions swirled throughout her entire body; rage, fear, sadness. All she could think to do was cry.

"No sudden movements," the interloper warned as he made his way over to the young girl.

The wind picked up again, sending the trees into a dance of cracks and creaks like stiff bones stretching after a day of stillness. The young girl's body hardened like ice. Droplets of sweat beaded on her cold skin as the interloper reached his pole-like arm out and ran scarred fingers through her short hair, then down to her cheek. Soon the gust dissipated and the only sound remaining in the dark wood was Juno's frantic breath. Her eyes looked up and away, watching the observant moon retreat behind the haze, leaving her in utter darkness.

Then there was a crunch on the ground.

Then another.

And another.

A hulking arm appeared out of nowhere and staved in the interloper's chest. Juno had not seen it completely, but she heard multiple ribs pop like snapped branches, and felt a body fling into the brush multiple feet away.

"Who the fuck..." the interloper wheezed. He climbed awkwardly to his feet, brandishing Lexa's knife in his lopsided arms. "Someone else come to die?"

What followed happened unseen in the blackness of the forest. Juno could only make out two shadows, one much larger than the other, fighting for control of the dark. She took advantage of her moment of safety by helping Lexa out of the hole. Then, while she leaned her protector against a fallen log, the moon made itself known again, revealing the severity of the knife wound.

"Grab my bag," Lexa exhaled.

Juno turned to retrieve the backpack and was stricken with the spectacle the moon now decided to spotlight. The larger shadow lifted the interloper from the ground and raised him high above its head. Uneven arms dangled lifelessly against the landscape. Then the large shadow took three steps away and heaved the interloper over the cliff's edge as if he were a bag half-filled with sand.

With that the evening fell calm. Placid. A slight breeze turned the trees once again. The large shadow started towards the camp. Juno panicked again until the moon's intensity fully returned, highlighting a deep blue in the shadow's skin. When he reached them he said, "Sorry I took so long," in a warm, helpful voice.

"Kareem!" Juno screeched as she ran over to give him the biggest hug she had ever given. But, when she got close enough, she saw the side of his coat was split with precision. There was blood.

"Careful now," he smiled, hugging Juno with the opposite side. After the embrace, he moved over to Lexa, who was struggling to find her bandages tucked away in her bag. He kneeled down beside her. "You dropped this."

Lexa's glazed eyes looked up at something reflective in Kareem's hands. Her kukri knife. With a brief smile, she reached out for the familiar safety of her weapon's handle, then fell into blackness.

The glass door of the lab whirred open unnoticed. A handful of adults in white jackets were shuffling around with various pieces of equipment that all looked foreign to a young girl. A quick scan of the room made it clear an experiment was in progress, but the hour was late and she had been promised an answer. So, casually, she shuffled her way through the hustle and bustle until she found who she was looking for leaning back in a chair with her legs raised.

"Hey mom?"

"Shit!" the woman cursed, nearly dropping a glass of fluid, then turned towards the interruption. "You know you're not supposed to be in the lab, Lexa. And don't call me mom."

Lexa rolled her eyes and took a bite from a bright red apple in her hand. "Fine, Pan. You said you were having birthday dinner with me tonight."

A man came over with a clipboard and a vial that Pan glanced over quickly, then waved him away. "I'm sorry, Lexa, but the timing of this procedure is extremely sensitive. Can we try again in a couple of days?"

"But my birthday won't *be* in a couple of days," Lexa said smugly with a full mouth. "It's today."

"I know. And I prom—can you please dispose of that apple? This is a sterile environment."

Lexa took another bite. "Relax. I won't touch anything."

Another woman approached Pan with a tray of syringes and she told them to give her a couple of minutes. She then lifted her legs from the chair's stirrups and released a heavy sigh. "What is it you really want, Lexa?"

Proud of her earned moment of attention, Lexa dove right in. "As you may have forgotten, I am officially sixteen today. I'm ready to have my first baby."

Pan's face sank to the floor. She opened her mouth but no words made their way out.

"What?" Lexa casually continued. "Just put me in the chair after you're done."

"Lexa..." Pan managed to start.

During another bite of apple, Lexa said, "We can even do it tonight. I'm ready!"

Someone nearby cleared their throat, causing Pan and Lexa to both look up at them. They were tapping their watch and holding up a glass tube filled with some translucent liquid. Pan nodded, hopped from her chair, and ushered Lexa towards the exit with a hand on her shoulder.

"Why are you acting weird?" Lexa blurted, still working on her snack.

"Lexa," Pan was attempting eye contact with the budding sixteen-year-old and only continued when she received it. "I'm afraid that's impossible."

"What's impossible? If you can do it, I can do it. I want to help."

A severe expression consumed Pan's face. "How to put this... Although you are *from* me, you are not *of* me. Some time before you, we recovered a technology that has allowed us to fertilize an egg in this lab and then insert it into my body. In vitro, they call it, and it's an extremely fragile, extremely temperamental process. And while we have had our share of successes, they were, unfortunately, not *complete* successes."

Lexa narrowed her eyes at Pan. Though she understood all the terminology from her studies, she was not quite following.

"You're sixteen now, yes?"

"That's why I'm here," Lexa retaliated.

"Your body has filled out the shape of a woman, but have you ever experienced menstruation?"

"No," Lexa said after a swallow, "But I thought—"

"We need to hurry, Pan," an irritated woman in a white coat barked. "This is our last shot at this."

"I'll be there in a second," Pan replied, then put a delicate hand on the sixteen-year-old's shoulder. "You have no eggs, Lexa. You will never bear children. I'm terribly sorry."

Pan removed herself from the conversation and hustled back over to the chair. As she was lifting her legs back into the stirrups, Lexa glared with unprecedented disdain. What she had always felt she was born to do was just taken from her in the span of one sentence. *You will never bear children...*

A man carrying a metal tray scuttled nearby and Lexa slammed her half-eaten apple on top of it, sending silver utensils scattering across the floor. Pan turned to see what caused the commotion, but all that remained was a lab coat on all fours picking up tools. When her eyes flicked towards the glass door, a tuft of long dark hair floated away before it sealed shut.

A few hours later, Lexa awoke to warm flames kissing her face and something tugging gently at her leg. Her eyes slowly came into focus on two dark hands working some thread near her thigh. Her pants were torn around a wound and the area was cleaned of dried blood.

Kareem knotted the last stitch and leaned over to bite off the end of the string. When he finished, Lexa sat up straight and saw Juno also watching intently.

"Just in time," Kareem said as he poured a bit of water over the wound and dabbed it with a clean cloth. "Juno was gettin' worried."

Lexa allowed a few breaths to take stock of the situation. Juno first. She was alright, safe. Kareem next. He had returned and disposed of the man who took...Lexa's hand reactively went for her chest and found the worn-in handle of her kukri knife securely awaiting her touch. She relaxed and said, "Thank you."

Juno was giddy with excitement. "You shoulda seen it, Lexa! I was about to get that guy but Kareem came in and threw him off the mountain!"

"I'm sure you were," Lexa winced, nearly expending a laugh.

Kareem caught Lexa trying to stand up and put both hands on her arms to hold her in place. "Easy now. You lost a lot of blood. Best to just eat and rest tonight."

Dizziness swirled in her head like draining water. She hated being this weak, this vulnerable, but there was nothing she could do. When she relaxed back into the fallen log, she focused on steadying her mind. "Are you alright?"

Juno watched Kareem sit on top of the log Lexa was resting against and remove his coat. The pale moonlight traced the deep muscles in his arm with a sharp contrast. He looked down at his side and inspected the slit that had been made by Lexa's own knife in the hands of the interloper. The surrounding fabric was stained a deep black. "He nicked me, but I seem to be in one piece," he smiled.

Then Kareem's hand gripped the base of the torn shirt and pulled it up over his head. Juno's attention shot straight to his exposed skin like a high-powered magnet. Between the red light of the fire and the silver light of the moon, she could trace every muscle coiled under his skin like thick knotted rope. The roundness of his shoulders, the broadness of his chest, the endless ripples in his abdomen...

Why was Juno so unequivocally attracted? She could not explain it. Her heart began beating suddenly, erratically, and foreign things began fluttering around between her lungs. She was so absorbed that all self-awareness left her mind, abandoning her to feast on the nooks and crannies of his body with hungry, feverish eyes.

When Kareem twisted his torso to dab at the cut with a wet rag, Juno's face grew red hot from more than just the fire's blaze. The heat expanded through her neck, then across her chest, where things began to swell. She felt a sudden need to cross her arms while the sultriness continued its relentless journey downwards. The ache in her stomach suddenly soothed over and was replaced with a more congenial feeling. One that spread down between her legs like gentle fingers through coarse hair. She closed her eyes.

But at the height of her pleasure a new cramp below Juno's stomach struck with a passionate vengeance, pulling her attention downwards. Instantly the panic of shame went from lukewarm to boiling. Her eyes started to well. The crotch of her pants was quickly darkening with the same intensity as Lexa's knife wound, and there was nothing she could do to stop it.

"Hey little man, you feelin' alright?" Kareem asked when he looked up to see Juno squirming in her seat.

Instead of acknowledging the question, Juno shot up and tried to scurry over to Lexa without displaying the obvious. But the effort was futile. As soon as she took one stride, anyone within twenty feet would have been able to spot the pitch-black blemish between her legs.

Kareem's eyes followed her awkward movement curiously for a second, then popped wide open. "What the—" he exclaimed, falling backwards off the log. "You're a...a...a..."

Lexa's passive awareness snapped back into existence and she immediately saw what was on everyone's mind. "Come here, Juno!"

Kareem was on his feet now, pacing back and forth. "No, no, no, no, no..."

Streaming tears, Juno dove next to Lexa and nestled in close. "I'm sorry!" she cried. "I'm so sorry!"

More than a little shocked herself, Lexa placed one hand on the young girl's head while clutching her tightly with the other. "It's ok, Juno. You've done nothing wrong."

"When were you gonna tell me?" Kareem demanded as he stepped back over the log. "When we were strung up by our necks by every fuckin' psycho in this wasteland?"

Lexa instinctively covered Juno's ears and looked up at him. Scorn was in her eyes.

Kareem was still shaking his head as if trying to reason with himself. "Do you know what this'll mean if word gets out? How much more danger we'll be in? That *she'll* be in?"

While Lexa held her silence he kept rambling. "It's nothin' short of a miracle you two made it this far. But another two hundred miles? In your condition? Impossible."

Kareem left the fire to pace around some more. His hands went from flailing, to resting on his hips, to clasped behind the back of his neck as he looked up at the silver moon. He let out all the air in his lungs and dipped his head.

"Are you finished?" Lexa asked.

"Sorry," Kareem said finally. "This is a lot to absorb right now. I just wish you would have told me, that's all."

"Do you understand why I couldn't?"

He looked over at the young girl, now a young woman, sobbing into Lexa's shoulder. For reasons unknown, his heart swelled to twice its normal size. There was no insatiable lust, no sense of possession. He knew the rarity of a child in the wastes was not entirely unheard of. That there was always the possibility. But a young girl that had miraculously experienced her first period...

"I understand."

"Good," Lexa confirmed. "Because you're needed now more than ever." Then she nodded her head towards Juno, who had receded into a whimper. "*She* needs you."

After a few tense moments of silence, Kareem adjusted his shoulders to the new weight that had been placed on them. He looked up at the moon, suddenly back in Appalachia once again. When he escaped as a boy he was given a second chance. An opportunity to do some good with his life. And that fateful night this same pale moon looked back at him, beckoning him to head west. Maybe it was never calling for his own adventure...

Kareem's gaze returned to the dwindling campfire. Before him was mankind's last hurrah, its unlikely conclusion, and she still had nearly two hundred miles to go.

He quietly watched Lexa rub Juno's back until they both eventually drifted off to sleep. Once they were out he circled around, pulled a blanket from one of the bags, and draped it over both of them. Then, before he turned in himself, Kareem kneeled next to the young woman.

He placed his hand softly on top of her precious head and whispered, "I won't let you down."

The next day was as dreary as it was dragging. Sunbeams tirelessly shimmied their way between blackened tree branches in an effort to carve slices of gold out of a grey sky. Heat was there as well. The more the haze and dust shaded the sun's intensity, the more intensity they seemed to trap inside.

Lexa's fresh stab to the leg did not benefit the trio's progress either. When she was not limping she was sitting. Frequently cleaning the wound and refreshing bandages became a top priority. No matter how short or long the breaks were, her wraps continued to turn red while her wound remained tender and moist. She would also be lying if she said she was not at constant war with fatigue and dizziness. They were formidable opponents.

Juno was still recuperating from the previous night's embarrassment as well. She was hesitant to give any acknowledgment to the supposed miracle between her legs. In truth it felt more like a curse. Eyes were now on her in a way they had never been before; watching, studying, hovering. It was as if Lexa and Kareem discovered she had been lying about something this entire time.

"Look, we need to get you somewhere for a few days so you can recover," Kareem said. He was standing over Lexa with arms on his hips as she tended her wound. "It's only gonna get worse if we keep pressin' on."

Lexa poked gently at the stitchwork, impressed with Kareem's quality despite the circumstances. "And where do you suggest we go? If one man was tracking us, certainly others are, too."

"He was lucky to catch you off guard," Kareem encouraged. "I doubt others will be as patient." Then he squatted down to meet her eyes. "Let me run ahead and see if I can find somewhere safe to lay low. We'll never get Juno to Arcadia if you become dead weight."

Dead weight? Lexa was irate by the insult. But then he poured a bit of alcohol over her gash that shocked her back to Earth. A wave of dizziness pulled on her brain like a suction cup. It took longer than she would ever admit to recover. "Fine," she eventually conceded. "Three days, max."

Kareem flashed his smile and nodded. Juno caught a glimpse of his white teeth and felt slightly less crushed by shame. But before she could say bye, he had already slung his backpack over his shoulder and disappeared to the west. It was her and Lexa again.

After sliding back up against the trunk of a nearby tree, Lexa called over to the young woman. "Come here for a minute."

Juno joined her at the tree and they sat shoulder to shoulder.

"What happened to you last night was completely natural. What's happened to the world is completely *un*natural."

"Then why do I feel so bad about it?" asked Juno, her eyes dodging the reminder on her pants.

Lexa smirked. "Probably because you're the only one left in this world that still wields that power. Hell, I didn't believe you had it in you until I saw it with my own eyes."

Juno mulled on the word *power* for a long moment. What had happened last night did not *feel* powerful. It felt more obscure, like a shape she could not describe with words. Her abdomen had new pains, an unfamiliar substance was discharging from her body, and her emotions all seemed heightened in some complex tangle of ropes.

"Did you feel this way the first time it happened to you?" she eventually asked.

Lexa's face fell heavy as stone and she turned it away before being noticed. Juno felt the dark silence push its way between them like a greased wedge, only to slip back out when Lexa decided to return to the conversation. After a deep breath she admitted, "I never had mine."

"Why not?" Juno said, perhaps too blatantly. "You said we have the same traits."

Lexa shifted to find a comfortable position. If her leg was not throbbing, her ribs were. "That's a bit harder to explain."

"Don't we have time?"

Maybe Lexa was surprised at how grown up Juno sounded now that she was officially a woman, or maybe it was the dangerous lack of blood in her system. Either way, a frustrated laugh exited her nose. "I guess we do."

Then, in the span of a few breaths, she continued. "Although we both have biological mothers, I wasn't brought into this world the same way as you were. How do I explain this? While your mother's egg was seeded *inside* of her body, my mother's was fertilized *outside* during a controlled experiment in a lab."

Juno's eyes grew wide as she fought back a chuckle. "You mean like you were made in a tube?"

"Sort of. Arcadia's survey teams once recovered a limited amount of healthy eggs and sperm from an old research facility in Salt Lake City. With an advanced form of technology, the scientists were able to fertilize these healthy eggs and grow them inside my mother.

"However, the results never came out as they had hoped. Although each of us carried the resistance to microplastics and disease, the conditions were never quite met to make us fertile. Just a bunch of healthy, barren babies."

Despite the large truth laid upon her, Juno was piqued by only one detail. "So you have brothers and sisters? How many?"

"Not in the way you're thinking, but there were thirteen of us."

Juno stared at the hazy forest for a while. The trees were always next to other trees. She thought of the image of the perfect kitchen from the TIME magazine back in Denver. "Wow. You must feel so lucky to have a home and an entire family."

"I'm not so sure," Lexa yawned. Fatigue was closing the distance on her stubbornness to remain in control. "I haven't been back there in a long time."

The two sat in complacent silence. Juno was still unsure about the burden she was born with, but she had never known another body but her own. She had never been *told* she could not have children. She spent time wondering if Lexa was affected by this, or if she even cared. Lexa seemed to know exactly how to achieve a goal at any given moment. Maybe a child of her own was never the objective. Or maybe she was too hurt to admit otherwise.

"You can go to sleep," Juno said after spotting Lexa's head dip. "I'll keep watch."

An obscure shape blocked the light of the sun from entirely entering the room. It took a step forward as the glass doorway whirred shut, slowly balancing out the brightness. Lexa rolled over in her bed and squinted at the figure.

"Who's there?" she asked with sleep still lodged in her throat. "M... Pan?"

"Good morning, Lexa. May I sit by you?"

Lexa nodded and slid over as far as she could in her narrow bed. She yawned, "What time is it?" as her visitor sat down. She could now see that Pan had something oblong in a shawl slung securely around her shoulder.

"It's just after sunrise. Do you know what day it is?"

Scratching her bed-frazzled hair, Lexa made a scrunched face in thought. Then her eyes opened wide. "It's my birthday!"

Suddenly, the bundle Pan was cradling made a tiny squeal and shuffled in her arms. Pan rocked and shushed it back into calm stillness. "I brought you a surprise, but we'll need to whisper."

With liquid grace, Pan pulled the shawl over her head and slid the strap from her shoulder. In the same motion she rotated slightly, held the bundle outwards, and said, "Arms ready."

Lexa's hands went palms up and she engaged her biceps, stronger than ever due to her daily survival and combat training. The bundle had some heft to it, but was also soft and warm and delicate at the same time.

"Support the head," Pan assured, beginning to unfold the cloth now in Lexa's arms.

Inside the shawl was a three-month-old infant, pink and fragile like rose-colored glass. Lexa's heart fluttered as she looked into its deep brown eyes. It made light grunts as it looked up aimlessly. What shapes caught its gaze? What was it thinking? What could it smell? What did it feel?

"Meet Rodan. Your brother."

Lexa gasped as quietly as she could and met eyes with Pan. She did not need to use words to convey her question.

"Our final egg also came from the same woman as yours. You two are of blood. Possibly the last true siblings in existence."

A smile stretched Lexa's trembling lips. Her gaze moved back down to the baby and her long hair cascaded off her shoulder. Rodan squirmed slightly, straining to grasp a clump of the dark amber strands in his tiny fingers. Lexa leaned in to make it easier for her brother, then asked, "Is he...?"

"Yes," Pan claimed proudly. "He was born with healthy sperm cells and no signs of phthalates in his system. A true marvel."

The infant pulled on Lexa's hair a little too hard so she was forced to pry it away. As she delicately separated Rodan's hand, he gained a new interest and clasped onto her index finger. An unrivaled sense of duty birthed in her chest and spread outwards through her body like a warm summer breeze. Not only was this child directly related to her—part of her—but he was healthy in a way that no other human rivaled.

Lexa's eyes hardened with purpose, but then Rodan laughed and she melted all over again. She wiggled her finger and cooed, "We're gonna have to find you a little girlfriend! Yes we are!"

Pan smiled gravely along with them. "Only time and great sacrifice will determine that."

The three remained on Lexa's bed until Rodan grew restless or hungry or tired and began to cry. Pan returned the shawl around her shoulder, neatly tucked the baby back inside, and gave it a breast to feed on. When the newborn finally lost interest in his surroundings, Pan returned to her feet and headed towards the door.

"If mankind is to survive," she said before exiting, "he'll need all of the help we can give."

After Pan left, a dark shadow slowly enveloped the room. Resentment. Despite being under the blankets, Lexa felt oddly cold. Not towards Rodan—it would never be his fault—but towards Pan, herself, and the world around. Why had he been blessed with fertility while she was born as fruitless as the desert? If they were of the same mother, and under the same circumstances, then why were they not equal? Did she not deserve the ability to create life? To be a mother?

Cold and alone, Lexa's thoughts began to sour. The fact that she and her brother shared the same blood only added salt to her wounds. Since she was broken from day one, had Pan ever loved her? It was as if Mother Nature herself thought of Lexa as a cruel experiment; a mistake. And why did men get to cause all of the suffering, yet receive all of the fortune? Nothing was fair.

The poison in Lexa's mind dripped down into her heart, into her soul, and began to harden. A charred blackness formed that she would never be able to chip away at on her own. *Some birthday*, she thought, then buried her head between the sheets and cried the morning away.

"No peeking!" said Kareem as he ushered a blinded Juno forward. His fingers were interlaced in front of her eyes.

Juno nodded excitedly. "I'm not!" she claimed with a wide grin. She would be lying if the smile had not also been a product of the firm abdomen pressed against her back.

"Promise?"

"I promise!"

"Alright," Kareem chuckled. "Ready? 1...2..."

"Just show her already," Lexa huffed, fatigue glazing her throat.

Kareem shot her a glance, said, "Alright, three!" and removed his hands.

A few silent seconds later Juno frowned. "What is it?"

In front of them, tucked deep inside the lifeless forest, a large structure sat dormant. It did not resemble any of the other buildings Juno had seen on her journey, or in her lifetime. Big places like shops or corporations were tall, rectangular, and covered with windows. Smaller cabins and houses were almost always a cube with a triangle on top. This place was different. For one, nearly a third of it was tucked away *inside* the mountain it was built up against. It was also made of an unusual combination of wood, glass, and metal that supported a gradually sloped roof covered with decades of debris. A row of large glass panes stretched across and around the entire face of the structure, similar to the top floors of the Genesys building, but Juno could not see through them. At all.

"It's our new home!" Kareem urged, trying to stoke the dwindling excitement.

Juno's face squinched. The building looked more like a metallic bowtie or a capital "M" than a livable dwelling. "It's a house?"

"Even better," affirmed Kareem. He took a few steps forward, turned, and stretched his arms out wide. "It's a Zeiss Home! We've hit the jackpot!"

On closer inspection, Juno noticed that the building oddly blended in with its surroundings. If they had not been standing twenty yards away in the daylight, she doubted she would have ever noticed it. "What's a Zeiss Home?"

Kareem had already picked up Lexa's bag and slung her arm around his shoulder for support. While the three of them walked towards the front door he explained. "Some people had the good sense, and the good money, to build homes that could fully automate themselves on renewable energy. Power, plumbing, security, lighting...the house does it all on its own. This is only the third one I've ever encountered. And," he said after a satisfying click of the door handle, "the only one I've ever gotten to be inside."

"Why's that?" Juno asked as she stepped through the massive doorway. It was part metal and part opaque glass.

"No power, no security," he winked. They all dropped their bags in the darkened entryway and moved to a large, albeit nearly pitch-black, open area. "Watch the stairs," Kareem added as the floor to the right sank via a pair of steps. "I scoured the entire house. No one has been here for a long, long time."

Lexa felt around for a chair and braced herself into the first one she found. Her thigh began to catch her up on the pain she had been ignoring all day. Her teeth clenched with every throb.

"Now I think I saw the sun pokin' through. If you help me clear off the roof, Juno, we might get a bit of power for tonight."

The idea of *power* was as foreign, yet familiar, to Juno as the idea of money. Still, getting on the roof sounded like an exciting change of scenery and it would give Lexa a chance to rest. "Okay!"

Outside the two climbed up the rockface the Zeiss Home was built into and hopped over to the roof. The slant of it was highest near the mountain, lowest at the center, then roughly half its highest point at the front. Kareem kicked aside a film of dirt that revealed a long black panel housing a grid of black squares. Juno inched to get closer, slipped on some loose dust, fell on her back, and slid down the roof.

"That's one way to do it!" Kareem shouted with his hands circled around his mouth. He burst out laughing when Juno stood up, half-caked with grime. "Come back up here and try again!"

Juno's face was red as she patted the dust from her clothes. "It's not funny!" she yelled back, but when she looked over at the strip she had accidentally cleared, she could see that there were thousands and thousands of little black squares comprising the roof. "Why are we doing this anyway?"

Kareem kept kicking dirt aside as he worked his way down towards Juno. "They're solar panels," he said. "These little black squares absorb the heat of the sun, turn it into electricity, and store the power inside a battery somewhere inside this house."

Juno was now kicking aside dirt as well. "Batteries like the ones used as money?"

"Yep, except these are bigger. A *lot* bigger. Like the size of an entire wall bigger."

"Woah," Juno breathed. "And you think they still work?"

Kareem bobbed his head. "They should. Might not hold a charge as well as new, but you should be able to take a hot bath tonight."

Juno's jaw dropped and her feet suddenly began to dust a little faster. It was not long before she even removed her duster, laid it flat across the panels, and ran it across the roof like a squeegee. Kareem smiled the entire time.

Around an hour later Juno and Kareem had finished and found Lexa passed out in the chair they left her in. A slight gurgling noise came from her throat. Juno could not help but giggle.

"Well, what do we do now?" Juno asked quietly.

"I suppose we wait," Kareem said while feeling around the vast room for a seat of his own. Once he found a long couch he kicked off his shoes, noticing the stench as they dropped, and stretched out sideways. "Good time to catch up on some sleep."

Juno shrugged and found a leather couch of her own in the same massive area, only tripping twice during her search. When she sat down she also removed her once-new boots and held them for a while. They were a stark reminder of how far they had come, and made her wonder how far they still had to go.

When she was down to just her shirt and pants, she curled up against the plush leather and welcomed its cooling kiss on her skin. She was comfortable for the first time in months. Heavier and heavier her eyes grew with each passing second spent staring blankly at the pitch black panels that lined the walls. Then, soon after, everything became pitch black.

Some time later a noise jump-started Juno's heart and pulled her from the afternoon slumber. She looked around frantically in the dark, trying to recall where she was.

"Lexa?" She whispered.

No answer. And no wind. *I'm inside*, she thought, shaking the deep sleep from her head. *Oh yeah! We found a house...I was on the roof...now I'm inside...*

The noise came again and Juno's spine stretched a little straighter. The sound was not the loud clang of something being dropped, or the sharp snap of something being broken. It was more of a mechanical thud that continued to whir and whine.

Juno's voice was now more urgent. "Lexa? Kareem?"

Still no reply.

The humming continued all around her as she reached for her shoes. She slipped them on quietly, then crawled over to where Lexa sat. Lightly nudging on her arm, she asked, "Lexa?"

Lexa grunted and began stirring to life. Juno slipped over to Kareem next and did the same.

Suddenly, the thrum stopped and was followed by countless clicks and clacks. The metallic sounds moved in a way that Juno could follow closely with her ears. They started at the back of the house, then sprinted down the sides until leading right to the front door. *Shhhh-click. Shhhh-clack.*

A blinding light came on above them, showing briefly the vastness of the room they were in, then automatically dimmed to a comfortable glow.

"Welcome home," an omnipresent, yet calming female voice declared. "It is eight forty five pee-em and the temperature is set to seventy two. Conditions are clear. Would you like to watch the sunset?"

Lexa and Kareem were both fully upright now. Juno was as tense as a bowstring, her head on a constant swivel.

Kareem flashed a rakish smile and commanded, "Yes, please!"

The lights dipped back to darkness, sending Juno into a panic. A large pair of hands cupped Juno's shoulders and spun her around. "Check this out," Kareem whispered in her ear.

Juno's eyes grew wide as the black-paneled glass went from opaque to translucent to absolutely, stunningly clear. It was almost as if the entire wall had disappeared completely and the only thing remaining was the impossible orange, pink, and violet of a Colorado sunset.

. . .

Entry 50 (A big one!)

Get this, I am writing and taking a hot bath at the SAME TIME. Not cold, not warm, but actually hot! And not by candlelight either. By REAL light. Did people actually used to live like this?!?!

I should back up. But where to start? There's so much!

Two days ago Kareem found this amazing place called a Zise(?) Home. Apparently this house uses the sun to make its own power and somehow everything still works like magic.

It took a while, though. Yesterday we only had a little bit of sun so we couldn't do much. Everything turned on at sunset (8:45 pee-em according to the voice, which I'll get to) and then turned off before it got fully dark.

It was really cool, though. Lights came on, doors automatically locked themselves, and these black windows seemed to disappear. Kareem explained that these special Zise(?) windows adjust themselves all day so the sun is never too bright. He also said he set them up so we can see out of them at night, but no one outside can see in, no matter how bright our lights are. How amazing is that?

And yet this place has so much more than just cool windows!

Ok, I'll make a list.

1) It's beautiful inside. When you enter there is a gigantic living room to the right with a couch that goes all the way around this sunken area. From there you have a view of the window wall,

or a fireplace at one end.

2.) If we're sitting at the couch looking out the windows, behind us is a fully functional kitchen basically in the same open area. And then a couple of hallways branch off into the main hallway (That goes all the way from the front door to the back of the house) where there are doors to bathrooms and bedrooms and closets and offices. I bet twenty people used to live here!

3) The Zise(?) Home also has what Kareem called "reactive lighting". It means anywhere you go the house knows it and automatically lights the way. The coolest lights are in the main hallway. There are hundreds of little hexagons cut out of the walls and they glow blue as you pass them. And they always keep up no matter how fast you run!

4) Laundry! There's these machines that wash AND dry every single thing we can fit inside. There was even some soap left over that smelled like a flower called lavender. I've decided it's my favorite smell ever. Also, no more crotch stain!

5) The voice. I guess people enjoyed talking to their houses instead of pressing buttons or getting up to make things work. I could say, "Hey house, the water in my tub is getting cold," and the house would know how to heat it up. Actually, I think I will tell it to do that right now!

6) Running water. Ok, this should probably be number one as Lexa says water is the most important thing out there, but I forgot, Ok? Kareem guessed that there is some water or a lake way underground and this house is pumping

it up to us. I don't care how it works, I just know that I'm taking twenty million more baths.

Let's see...what else?

Today was all sun and Kareem expects the batteries, if they're still good, to be fully charged. That means power all night and tomorrow even if there is no sun!

Once the power came back late this morning, Lexa bathed and then slept the whole day. I only saw her once when she gave me these things called tampons and taught me how to use them. If I could describe the process in one word it would be YUCK!

Before I left her room she looked at me and said, "Don't get too comfortable here," but I couldn't help but laugh at seeing her in a white robe and slippers.

Other than that things have been quiet. Kareem's been busy going through the rooms and inspecting every gadget in the whole house. I think he really likes to know how things work. I've just been soaking in the tub, writing, and relaxing.

I don't ever want to leave this place.

The sun had set again before Juno exited the bathroom with squeaky clean skin. While inside, she had seen in the mirror that her hair no longer stood straight up and was just long enough to lay flat on its own. She also noticed that her freshly washed clothes were a little more form fitting than before. Her smile now had three reasons behind it.

Every time she entered the long hallway of hexagonal lights, she tried to outsmart them by switching up her pace. At first she would walk as slow as she could without falling, then she would break out into a sprint, and finally finish at a speed in between. The blue hue matched her every step without fail.

When she reached the kitchen she smelled something strange. The scent filled her nose like a warm gust of wind carrying...carrying...*food?*

She turned the corner to find Kareem standing in the kitchen with a small rag tossed over his broad left shoulder. Whistling, he leaned over to crack open the door of the oven, nod his head, then close it. The aroma came swirling back to Juno's senses.

"What are you doing?" Juno asked as she lifted herself onto a stool at the kitchen's island.

"The good luck keeps comin', Juno!" He clapped his hands and rubbed them together. "I found an air-sealed pantry in the basement that's never been touched. My guess is no one was able to get inside this place until enough dirt covered the roof to kill the power. And by then, everyone in the know was probably dead."

Juno tilted her head at all the new concepts around power, automatic locks, and air-sealing. "What did you find?"

"Damn near everythin' besides produce!" He leaned his elbows on the white marble counter and started counting fingers on a raised hand. "Sugar, salt, flour, corn meal, pasta, rice, spices, canned you-name-it, bottled water..." he paused with a frown, "...in plastic, of course. Point is, I'm cookin' somethin' special tonight!"

"What's on the menu?"

Both of them spun around to find Lexa standing in the mouth of the hallway between a stack of white cupboards and a fridge that mimicked the same cabinetry. She was still wearing the white robe, though the hexagonal lights bathed it and her copper skin in a faint blue. She limped a step forward and Kareem rushed to help her over to the stool next to Juno.

"Easy does it," Kareem smiled. He knew Lexa was embarrassed enough being injured so he tried to make his assistance seem like it was not needed. Once she was seated, he rushed back around the marbled island to check on his meal.

Juno filled Lexa in on the air-sealed treasure while keeping an eye on Kareem while he worked. Something about a strong, kind male making food for them made Juno feel warm inside. Not the type of warmth from when he removed his shirt a few nights ago. This warmth felt comfortable. Safe. Stable.

With some high pitched cooing, Kareem removed the dish from the oven and breathed it in. "You gals are in for a treat!"

He brought the steaming glass pan over to the island and set it on a small knitted cloth. Then he went and grabbed three pristine white plates, bright silver forks, and an equally silver spatula. He gently dealt the plates out like playing cards and scooped a hot, colorful, gooey cylinder of something onto each one. Finally, he poured some fresh water that had already been chilled in the refrigerator over some ice inside three tumblers. Juno marveled at how the crystal clear glass fogged up.

"So," Lexa said after picking up a fork. "What do we have the pleasure of choking down this evening?"

Across from them, Kareem proudly held up his own plate like a trophy. "I never thought I'd get to say this again, but we're havin' homemade burritos!"

"Bur-ee-toes," Juno sounded out, then nodded in approval of the word. "How do you make them?"

Kareem leaned in and winked. "If I told you, I'd have to kill you."

Juno's face went bone white.

"I'm kidding!" he laughed. "That's just an old joke." Then, once the color in Juno's face returned, he continued. "You mix up cooked rice, black beans, yellow corn, and some spices from Mexico in a big bowl. Then you fill up these white things called tortillas—which I made from scratch, by the way—with the mixture and roll them up. Finally you dump red chili sauce all over the top and bake it in the oven until it gets all bubbly. Go ahead, dig in!"

Juno lifted her fork and held it over the burrito with careful precision. Individually she had had a few of these ingredients in the past and never particularly liked them. But maybe now that they were mixed...

She cut through the soft tortilla and all of the rice and beans and corn and sauce stuck to the fork as if they were soldered on. Kareem nodded at her to try it so she lifted the hot food to her mouth, closed her eyes, and bit down. Instantly a swarm of unbelievable flavors and textures erupted. Chewy, melty, salty, savory, tangy, spicy; all words she had known the definitions of but never the taste. She was in culinary heaven.

"So?" Kareem asked impatiently.

"It's the most amazing thing I have ever eaten in my entire life!" Juno blurted. A little rice escaped from her mouth and fell in her lap.

He turned to Lexa, who was already half done. "And?"

"It's good," Lexa said without pause from eating. She must have been starving, he thought.

When the meal was finished, and not a drop of red sauce remained in the glass pan, Kareem collected the dishes and brought them over to the sink to wash. He told them a story about how it was his responsibility as a child to gather the water and wash the dishes every day. How his dad had always told him that routines built good character and strong work ethic. How he should always do a job once and do it right. Eventually he became lost in the work and started whistling Rocky Mountain High.

While Kareem was busy at his chores, Juno watched Lexa empty her backpack onto the pristine countertop to begin assessing its contents. She was marvelously meticulous in her ways as well. The kukri knife was sharpened and polished, silver batteries were stacked in neat piles by size and shape, the binoculars had their lenses dusted, and the radio clicked through static from every frequency. Going untouched, however, was the mysterious orange-capped cylinder that was meant for emergencies only. But if broken ribs or a stab to the leg did not call for such an emergency, then Juno feared to imagine what would. In fact, Juno decided not to even ask when Lexa picked up the shotgun and separated the shortened barrel from the receiver.

Now hypnotized by Lexa's scrupulous inspection, Juno was pulled into a daydream. She was sitting at a white table in a white-tiled kitchen; stainless appliances all around. Every surface was spotless and the hot meal was vibrant with greens and oranges and reds. She looked up to find a tan mother and a dark father standing over her. Their faces were gone but their smiles were as spotless and white as the kitchen. Two hands rested gently on her shoulders, squeezing the tension from her body.

Then her attention turned back to the plate. There was only one portion despite there being three of them. Had they already eaten? No. It was family time. They would have waited for her to get there before starting. So why was there only one? After shaking her head, eight words appeared in Juno's mind: `The secret to feeding your family with less.`

Juno snapped out of her fantasy to find Kareem still at the sink drying a plate. Lexa now had the shotgun fully disassembled and was wiping down a section with a cloth. The three of them could not be further from the normal family depicted in the magazine, except now they were the only normal ones left. The only normal ones anywhere.

"Where did all the people go?" Juno asked, interrupting the comfortable silence in the kitchen.

Lexa lifted another section of the gun and squinted into it. "I told you already. Plastic and greed happened."

"No," Juno shook her head. "I mean now. It's like they completely disappeared."

Kareem, spinning a cloth inside a glass, turned and leaned back against the counter. He looked at Lexa and she looked back at him. "You better take this one," he chuckled. "I know better than to speak first anymore."

Lexa somberly set down the barrel she was cleaning, carefully edged off her stool, and hobbled towards the living room. Kareem rushed around the kitchen island to assist, but she shrugged him off. He looked over to Juno and shrugged as well.

The house's light strips trailed all three of them into the wide-open living room and left the immaculate kitchen in an energy-saving afterglow. When they stepped down into the seating area, Lexa fell heavily into one of the long couches that framed the room. She lifted her injured leg onto a nearby ottoman to relieve some of the throb and closed her eyes.

Juno and Kareem joined close by. Juno still found it amusing to see her draped over a couch donning a soft robe instead of on top of a mountain in combat gear. But the humor faded quickly into silence. This time an uncomfortable silence.

The young woman was just about to open her mouth when Lexa said, "Juno, not everyone's house used to operate like this one. Hardly any did. Men like Friedrich made sure of it."

Juno glanced at Kareem first and he nodded. "What do you mean?"

There was a heavy sigh, then, "The old way of making power was to dig something up and burn it. In this case it was called oil. It was black and crude and sent filth into the air. Houses, buildings, cars, all the way down to the clothes on your back. If you can name it, it probably burned oil at one point in its life."

"I don't understand," Juno returned. "You said Friedrich was bad for making plastic."

Lexa's eyes were now fixed on the translucent wall of glass, deep in thought. "That is only half of the CamChem equation. To put it simply, oil is taken from the ground and turned into two things. One is a fuel called gas, and the other is the chemicals used to make plastic. Fortunately for Friedrich, and many others, this double product was extremely profitable, and extremely easy for people to consume.

"And consume they did. So much that it was mindlessly sewn into the very fabric of their daily lives. A plastic water bottle here, a drive in a car there, and soon there was enough filth put into the air to heat up an entire planet."

Juno was scratching her short hair. "How does that work?"

"The way my parents explained it to me," Kareem interposed, "is that some called it global warmin', and some called it climate change." He lifted his arms in the air and traced a large orb around himself. "Basically the filth in the air created a big bubble that trapped in the sun's heat. Over time it melted ice caps, dried out lakes and rivers, and created those wild, unpredictable storms like the one we met in."

"Woah," Juno said with curious shock instead of excitement. "Then why didn't more of them start living in houses like this?"

Kareem and Lexa exchanged looks and Lexa continued. "The thing is, you either had to be extremely wealthy—or extremely educated—to escape the oil-burning system that had been deviously designed by powerful men like Friedrich. Too few were ever that lucky, and even fewer cared enough to live in something like a Zeiss Home. It's a shame, really. All people had to do was stop giving CamChem their money, but, from what I can tell, convenience always beats conservation."

The crash course in global economics was falling hard on Juno's brain so she decided to revisit her initial question. "So where did they all go? Every place we've gone has been completely empty."

"As you've seen," Lexa sighed, "humans are very resilient. Above all else they want to survive. The ones that were left migrated north, hoping to find cooler weather, lush forests, and brimming lakes, but they were only met with more of the same. Mankind had doomed itself to live out the rest of its days inside a hot bubble of its own creation. All that remains now is a planet as scabbed and barren as themselves."

Kareem noticed the harsh weight of knowledge beginning to press down on Juno's shoulders so he tried to switch gears. "But we're all here, right? That's proof that not everyone has given up quite yet."

No one responded. The room swelled to an infinite size. For a moment each of them felt utterly alone.

"When we part ways, Juno," Lexa began again, "you will be taught the full truth of the past, and the reason things could not continue as they were. And you will see how powerful you really are."

Part ways? Juno had never considered such a reality. She had grown so accustomed to her new life with Lexa and Kareem that she considered them unceasing companions. Friends. Perhaps even a…

"Or," Juno half-teased. "We could just stay here forever! This amazing house has everything we could ever want. We'd be like one of those families from the magazines!"

Lexa's face hardened. "You know that's not an option. As soon as I'm able, we must push forward."

The overwhelming blanket of helplessness once again smothered Juno's spark. No one really knew what to say. Lexa had told her from the beginning that they had one goal and one goal only; to reach their destination. No matter what. But that did not take away from the fact that something about being here, inside this house, on this couch, together, just felt right.

"The atmosphere is unobstructed tonight. Would you like to see the stars?" The room suddenly announced.

Kareem beamed and looked up at the ceiling. At this point he would do anything to put some slack in the tension. "Yes, please!"

Silently, they all slumped deeper into the long couch while the light strips gently dimmed until turning off completely. The front wall gracefully transitioned from filtered darkness to the pureness of a clear night sky sprinkled with white dots, like tiny reflections on an undisturbed lake. A fire sprang to life in the corner, alarming Juno, then simmered into a soothing orange glow. The entire transition felt as if the room had sensed the friction between the three and remotely ushered them into relaxation.

"You know," Kareem exhaled, interlacing his fingers behind his head and leaning into the appendaged basket. "I *could* get used to this."

Lexa sulked quietly, squirming for the right angle that disturbed neither her injured leg nor her healing ribs.

"This is just like the night sky I watched on my birthday," said Juno after a while.

"Birthday?" Kareem leaned forward. "When the heck was your birthday? Do you know how old you are?"

"I turned thirteen the day I met Lexa."

"Thirteen?" Kareem exclaimed again. He scratched his stubbled chin in thought. "Well that explains the— Wow! Thirteen..." He reminisced with the stars for a moment before proposing, "Juno, tomorrow night we're gonna celebrate. That cool with you, Lexa?"

After no response, Kareem tore his eyes from the twinkling night sky to look over. Lexa had passed out with her mouth wide open. Juno started giggling.

The following day was filled with a haze that the sun could not break through until late afternoon. Kareem estimated, given the sun's modern intensity, and the thoroughly cleared-off solar panels, that the batteries should have charged completely anyway. The only thing he could not estimate, or measure, was if the power supply could even still reach full capacity after all these years of dormancy. Either way, they had thoroughly enjoyed warm lights, hot water, and cold air conditioning through the entire night and morning.

Lexa slept off and on into early afternoon, only waking for water, food, and bandage replacement. Her hobble had digressed into a faint limp and she mentioned to Kareem that her ribs now felt only slightly bruised. Other than her brief appearances, she took advantage of the rest allowed by a comfortable bed in a dark room so she could get back to completing her mission.

Juno spent most of the day bathing, playing with various buttons and panels throughout the house, and filling her journal with notes of her technological discoveries. She found an illuminated panel she could slide her finger across to change the air temperature from hot to cold. Kareem had asked her to stop playing with it right away. There was also a room filled with metal bars, thick iron plates, and black machines with mounted picture frames she learned were called high definition touchscreens.

Her favorite exercise machine was the one she could sit on and pedal because her effort somehow powered the attached screen. After cycling the pedals for a few moments, a video appeared with another person doing the exact same thing. This person kept telling her to "go harder!" then said she was, "doing great!" Juno was also thankful for the built up sweat because it meant she could take another hot bath.

With the clocks in the house now working and automatically adjusted, Kareem told Juno and Lexa to convene in the kitchen at seven o'clock sharp. Juno, after learning what a clock was, reveled in the formality of it all. She was informed that it was officially her special day and she could barely contain her excitement for the upcoming surprise that evening.

But then, alone in her room around six, she thought of her mom. Of Maia. Her birthdays were never surprises, but they were always her favorite day of the year. Candy, a new journal, and a few games of slapjack filled their tiny haven with much-needed laughter. It was the only day Juno had not had to wait in the darkness below, alone, wondering if she would ever return.

Traveling with Lexa had given Juno perspective on what her mom had gone through to keep her safe and smiling. That the reason her mom had been gone for days, sometimes weeks, at a time was to provide a better life for Juno. She now understood the sacrifice ultimately made to bring her this far. No, Lexa did not have to say the words; would never have to explain. Deep down Juno knew they would never be reunited. And it was no one's fault but the world's.

But isn't this exactly what she would have wanted? Juno thought, flopping back onto the plush down comforter wrapping her memory foam bed. *For me to be in this house...the safest place in the world...with two people that can protect me?*

She wiped a warm tear sliding down her cheek. Seven was fast approaching and she wanted to be happy. Guiltless. She wanted to have fun. "That's what birthdays are for," her mom had told her, "to celebrate life." Juno glanced at the tattered, half-filled notebook on the dresser. An early present given to her the day before they parted ways for the very last time. She whispered, "Thank you," then, just like her mother, slipped from the room like a shadow and went down the long, lighted hall to celebrate.

"Juno!" Kareem blurted when she turned the corner. He and Lexa were waiting at the kitchen island with something tucked away behind them on the counter. "Are you ready?"

When she nodded, Kareem hopped up from his seat and rushed over to cover Juno's eyes. Before they were completely shrouded she caught Lexa shifting the hidden object. At first she smelled the sour twinge of smoke, but then it got sweeter as she was pushed forward. If this was anything as good as the burritos, it would be the best birthday ever.

"Aaaand," Kareem sang, "open!"

His hands disappeared to reveal an object on the island glowing in the dimmed kitchen. Juno heard them both begin singing a tune with the words "happy birthday" in it, but it soon faded into the background. What she was focused on was the food in front of her and, more importantly, what was burning on top. Stacked over a foot high were these flat, tan, plate-sized circles containing brown speckles throughout. Oozing down the side of the stack was a thick amber liquid, almost like dark blood, that pooled onto the plate itself. And at the very top was not one, but thirteen little sticks with a tiny flame flickering on each.

When the song finished, Kareem said, "Make a wish and blow 'em out!"

Juno tilted her head. "Wish for what?"

"Anything you want!" he chuckled. "That's how birthday's work. You make a wish, blow out the candles, and never tell anyone or it won't come true!"

She looked over to Lexa, who surprisingly had upturned lips. Lexa nodded and said, "Make it a good one because we leave at first light."

Juno sighed at the thought of leaving, then returned all her focus to the candles. She considered her wish for a long time. Instincts told her to wish her mother could walk through the front door to celebrate with them, but her mind knew it could never be. Then she wanted to wish to live in this house forever, but Lexa already nixed that one. Finally she had it. Nodding to herself, she closed her eyes and blew out all thirteen candles with one swift breath.

"What are these?" Juno asked before she loaded up a fork with the mystery sweetness in front of her.

"They're called pancakes," Kareem explained, "and I made 'em as close as I could to the real thing. Normally I would need... Ah, nevermind. The stuff on top is called maple syrup and it lasts damn-near forever in a glass container." He winked at Lexa for his packaging awareness. "We also found a sealed bag of chocolate chips and mixed those in as well."

Juno eyed the moist, chocolatey, syrupy pastry. "You helped, too?"

"Of course," Lexa nodded. "It's your birthday, isn't it?"

"Was it a piece of cake?" she asked wittingly.

Lexa's eyes widened, then her face rested into a light smile. "Yes, literally."

Juno had eaten more syrup-doused chocolate chip pancakes than her stomach could hold when her fork dropped to her plate with a clang. It was only yesterday when the burrito was the most delicious thing she had ever eaten in her life. Now it was definitely pancakes. She chased it all down with an ice cold glass of water before slumping into her stool with the beginnings of her first ever food coma.

"Don't hit the sack just yet," Kareem said, nudging her arm. "I've got one more surprise for you after we clean up."

"We?" Juno yawned.

"Yep! You're officially an adult now so you get to share in the adult activities!" Kareem could not help but heckle at his own joke.

All three of them lined up at the sink. Lexa washed the dishes, Kareem dried them, and Juno rushed back and forth returning them to their homes in various cupboards and cabinets. Something about the assembly line caused Juno's heart to fall in place like a square peg into a square hole. Everything fit. *Is this what it used to be like?* Juno wondered. *What it's* supposed *to be like?*

When the kitchen was clean, the automatic lights followed them into the wide open living area once again. Lexa and Juno both cupped steaming mugs of warm tea with honey mixed in—another new delicacy preserved by the Zeiss Home—and were asked to take a seat on the long couch. Kareem then directed the overhead light to dim and for the fire to ignite as he went over to an inconspicuous black shelf near the fireplace that could easily have been mistaken for a polished bench.

"I stumbled across this earlier today," Kareem teased. After pressing on a glossy touchscreen, white letters and numbers magically appeared and the shelf began to shift. Two large panels on the side slid inwards, revealing two non-reflective black cubes, and the top panel split in half and tucked neatly inside of itself. Then he opened a hidden door by pushing it with his hand and pulled out a flat, square object.

Juno squinted in the adjusted light, but only caught a quick glimpse of the thing Kareem was holding. It was some sort of artwork. At the bottom right corner was a red circle, to the left of that was a yellowish hexagon with a smiling face inside of it, and at the top were big red and white words. She could only catch DON'T PLAY THAT SONG before Kareem pulled out a black disk and set the colorful container aside.

Next Kareem tapped on the illuminated screen and gently rested the disc on top of the peculiar glossy obelisk. Juno desperately craned her neck to see what exactly he was doing, but the couch area was two steps down from where the action was happening. She recalled the lesson on rise she had been taught a few nights earlier.

Kareem made one last motion with his hand and a sudden crackle filled the stillness of the room. Juno instinctively looked at the fire, but it was as silent tonight as it had been since they arrived; something else she could not yet explain. Then a deep *bum bum bum* sound, followed by a *shhhck*, and another *bum* enchanted the drums of her virgin ears.

Bum bum bum, shhhck, bum.
Bum bum bum, shhhck, bum.

"Don't play it no more!" sang Kareem as he shuffled to the center of the open area, paused, and held out an inviting, upturned hand. "Come here, Juno!"

The song continued and Kareem kept singing. Juno's entire face slackened as if she had been hypnotized. Protruding from the glossy black box were the most elegant, most beautiful, most unusual sounds she had ever heard. The deep thumps of the bass, the high chants of rhythm, and swimming through it all like a blade through water was this voice! It was nothing like when she or Kareem sang Rocky Mountain High. This voice was raspy, haunting; in pain, yet overflowing with grace.

"Are you comin'?"

Juno snapped from her trance. "What is this?"

"This," Kareem cooed, stepping side to side with the beat, "is the single greatest thing to have ever happened to the human race: Ben E. King."

"It's the most wonderful thing I've ever heard," gawked Juno. She just now realized her head was swaying.

"Of course it is! And would you believe he sang this all the way back in the sixties?"

Unsure of what year it truly was, Juno had to assume right now was much later than that. "The twenty-sixties?"

"What?" Kareem asked, then flung his head back in laughter. "No, the *nineteen*-sixties! Now are you comin' or what?"

Juno and her full belly slid off the couch and approached Kareem's outstretched arms. When she reached them, a large hand pulled her in closer by the small of her back, and another clasped her own, lifting up her arm. She nearly melted in the sudden embrace. Their feet were pointed directly at each other. "W...what are you doing?"

Kareem looked deep into her eyes and shared a wide smile as sweet as the syrup from dinner. "Givin' a young woman her first dance."

It was then that all of Juno's curious, carnal, and complex feelings toward the beautiful man dissipated like grime in a hot bath, leaving only the purity of clean realization in her heart. He was not some fleeting crush, or some object to gawk at. True he was large, muscular, and attractive, but he was also tender, compassionate, and caring; unlike any male figure she had ever crossed paths with. Kareem was someone that would protect and revere her no matter what. Almost like a—

"Ready?"

Juno nodded warily.

"Alright, follow my lead."

Kareem showed her how to step side to side, back and forth, and twirl underneath his arm, always counting the beats along with the music. "One, two, three, four. One, two, three, four. One, two..."

Juno, to her surprise, caught on rather quickly. Dancing was strikingly similar to what Lexa had taught her about knife wielding in combat. Stand at a slight angle. Spread your weight out evenly. Step towards your opponent. Follow their momentum. Every single motion carried from one art form to the other, or was it the other way around?

After a spin, Juno glanced at Lexa curled up on the couch in her robe and smiled. "Do you want to try? I think you'd be good at it!"

Lexa only pointed at her leg and sipped her tea.

Each song on the album provided a new tempo as well as a new challenge. As they adjusted for the next, Kareem shared something with Juno.

"I have a confession," he mused aloud. "I'm bein' a little bit selfish tonight."

Juno looked up and nearly stepped on his toes. After she corrected her footing, she asked, "How so?"

"Earlier I told Lexa that this is how I grew up. My whole family would pitch in and work hard every day. We made meals together, cleaned up together, read stories together, laughed together. But every few days, when our solar-powered record player we had rigged up fully charged, our little community gathered and danced all night until the batteries died. Boy, if only we had found a place like this!"

Juno pretended to look down at her feet. "I'm sorry you lost them."

"Nothin' to be sorry about!" he chirped, keeping the mood light. "I'm just thankful I got the time that I did. If they could see me...us... right now, I think they'd all be proud of my choices."

She saw a gleam in his eyes, but he blinked it away before it developed.

"Anyway," he continued. "Thank you for lettin' me relive a little bit of my own childhood on your special day." Then, flicking his head in Lexa's direction, he added, "Might be the last time either of us has any fun for quite a while."

They fell into a steady rhythm for the next couple of tunes, but, at the end of the sixth song, Kareem suddenly beamed with anticipation. "Double the volume!" he shouted at the ceiling. A couple of crackles filled the gap between tracks, then a deep bassline saturated the vastness of the room. "Best song ever written!" he declared, then lifted Juno effortlessly into midair and began singing.

When the night, has come,
 And the land is dark,
And the moon is the only,
 Light we'll see...

They twirled their way over to Lexa, who rolled her eyes when they arrived. Kareem saw her expression, dipped Juno backwards, and sang the next part to both of them.

No I won't, be afraid,
 Oh I won't, be afraid,
Just as long, as you stand,
 Stand by me!

Juno witnessed a wry smile cut through Lexa's lips as sharply as the blade she normally kept strapped to her chest. Kareem had spotted the grin as well so he inhaled a lungful of air to belt out the chorus. But just as his vocal chords started vibrating, the music dropped, and the fire went out.

"What the heck?" chided Kareem. He let go of Juno and rushed over to the fireplace. The overhead lights suddenly illuminated to full brightness before dimming back down normally. Then the fireplace ignited. Then the music picked up where it left off. "Must be on the fritz," he shrugged.

"Switching to reserve power," the Zeiss Home announced. "Would you like me to restore your previous settings?"

"Yes, please! And restart the song!"

The music hummed again and Kareem took Juno back into his arms. They danced the night away with Stand By Me on repeat until Juno memorized every last word. Midway through her third cup of tea, Lexa nestled into the couch and humored them with a smile until she eventually dozed off. All three were completely unaware of the eyes watching them through the crystalline wall of windows.

A blood-stained rag lay rigid between Bishop's fingers. It was as stiff and crusted as his dying trail. They had all followed the rockslide for days and came up with nothing but a smothered firepit and a single besmirched bandage.

"Could be anyone's," Deacon growled. "We're damn near to Utah and still ain't found 'em."

"It would appear so," Bishop affirmed as cold and emotionless as the clear night air.

A member of the scouting acolytes bumped shoulders with their appointed leader. "It's not lookin' good for you, Bishop. Can't help but think that heads're gonna roll."

Deacon rushed to the protester, grabbed the base of his throat, and pulled out a haggard knife. "You better show some respect, plebeian. Unless another visit with the molemen is in order?"

Knees now in the dirt, the acolyte bared a deadly grimace. "Yer head rolls same as mine."

"Enough," Bishop commanded. He waved his hand in the starlight and the scuffle separated as an autonomous reaction. Despite their ever waning confidence in him, they were still mandated by a higher power to obey his rank. "We shall keep moving. If their destination is Arcadia, then our paths will cross in time."

The group continued west through the blackened forest, doing their best to avoid tripping on fallen branches that blended into the floor like dark waves on a darker ocean. Deacon accidentally put his boot through one log, which disintegrated into fine mulch, then stumbled into another that was harder than stone.

Eventually they came across a smaller peak. Determined to close the gap in distance instead of searching the landscape thoroughly, Bishop recommended they go around instead of up. But the lack of elevation did not prove to make their path any easier. It was hard enough to traverse the abundance of tree limbs during the day. At night they became grueling, camouflaged obstacles not suited for those with oblong appendages.

When the final acolyte cleared a particularly rough section of the underbrush, he nearly bumped into the one standing in front of him. "What's goin' on," he asked, nearly out of breath. "Why'd we all stop?"

The man in front of him turned his crooked neck. "Dunno. Bishop's been standin' there for a while."

At the front of the pack, Bishop conspired with Deacon. "Do you notice something about the ground we're upon?"

Squinting in the starlight, Deacon shrugged. "We're 'bout a mile further than we were?"

"Anything else?"

Deacon rolled his eyes in the dark and squinted harder. The mountain sat before him, the dark sky was above, and on either side was an endless forest scattered with the crooked remains of trees. Then it struck him. "It's flat."

Bishop nodded slowly. "Precisely. But why is there a path that seemingly begins here and stops at the base of that mountain. It leads to nothing."

"I dunno. Maybe one of those storms flattened it out."

Bishop stared unmovingly at the end of the trail. The picture was not painted well by the shrouded light of the waning moon. Then, after a gust of wind finished blowing a haunted song through the ravine, he said, "Perhaps," and moved along.

The group of men in the night continued for a handful of steps when a bright light suddenly shadowed them against the backdrop. Some crouched, others froze. But as soon as the illumination came, it disappeared, leaving behind a glowing waypoint of answers.

Bishop's lips curled upwards at the sudden intrusion. Before them, at the end of the trail that led nowhere, sat a squat, angled house built into the rock itself. And it was occupied. "Ask and you shall receive," he avowed with pleasure.

Twelve men plus Bishop and Deacon snuck over to the night-shrouded dwelling. It was strangely dark and rigid, as if it were designed to absorb light rather than reflect it. In fact, they would have missed the house entirely if the lights had not so abruptly beckoned them to its location.

Through an entire wall of crystal clear glass, Bishop could see his prizes. Months of thirstful searching now salivated his mouth. He counted two of them. Lexa, clear as day, casually sat on the couch. She was wearing an unusual white garment while drinking from a small mug. His scabbed skin crawled at how much of an annoyance she would certainly turn out to be.

Standing, no, swaying in the middle of the room, facing away, was a large, dark man. Judging by his size, Bishop considered him to be a threat to the mission as well, though previously unaccounted for.

Now where is the girl?

His eyes scanned every corner of the massive room yet the child was nowhere to be found. *She must be with them*, he thought unbendingly as the swaying man began to pivot. But just as the dark man turned, the glass of the house went pitch black, resealing the acolytes in darkness. *Damn!*

A desperate plan needed to be hatched, and this was Bishop's last chance to lay one out. *Wherever Lexa goes, the girl must follow*, he mused. *Perhaps I can use that to my advantage...* Then he glanced briefly at his team of faltering acolytes and shrugged passively. *At least there will be fewer mouths to feed—*

"Is that...music?" Deacon interrupted from the shadows nearby.

Bishop heard it now, too. A low thrum of bass kicked quietly against their surroundings. It must have been extremely loud to protrude the impressive construction of the house.

"I saw 'em!" one acolyte screeched. "Let's take 'em out!"

"No!" Bishop commanded. He held his hand out to stop any motion from advancing. "This structure runs on battery power. Its burst of guiding light must have been a malfunction while transferring to a backup resource. If my plan is to work, we will first wait for the occupants to run it dry."

The hand that covered Juno's mouth was neither Lexa's nor Kareems. It was rough, like sandpaper, and had a faint smell of rot. She immediately awoke with an impulsive writhing. But her squirms were subdued as her head was smashed deeper into the thick pillow she had been sleeping on. Another hand tugged at her waistband.

"Best to keep quiet," a wheezing voice in the darkness warned.

A snap of cool air nipped at her pelvis as her skin became exposed. Adrenaline surged through her veins, allowing her surroundings to halt for an instant. The thick pillow obstructed her peripheral vision so, with all her might, she managed to slip her head to the side. She could see the room now. More importantly she could see the nightstand, on top of which was her notebook...and a pen.

Since the assailant was busy with her mouth and her pants, Juno was able to slip an arm free and reach for her only chance at escape. She stretched her fingers like elastic until the tips felt the smooth casing of the writing utensil. Confident of its location, she flicked the pen towards her palm, gripped it tight, then jammed it into the stranger's neck.

"Lexa!" Juno screamed from her freed mouth, curdling the blood of anyone within earshot.

The stranger recoiled backwards and stumbled off the bed. "Goddammit!"

Juno hopped off the bed as well. Her adrenaline rush had adjusted her eyes to the dark room and she could now see the intruder's features. He was a spindly man, with abnormally long arms and legs, and was covered neck to feet in some sort of shabby outfit that was all the same faded material. His face was dark. Not like Kareem's, but textured, as if covered in scabs.

The stranger yanked the pen from his neck and locked eyes with Juno. A black blob on the collar of his shirt was growing. "C'mere you little bitch."

Juno took a step to the left, never breaking eye contact. On the floor between her and the door was her backpack. The knife Lexa had given her was inside. She would need to make a jump for it if she wanted any chance of leaving the room alive.

Juno's gaze flicked from the stranger, to the backpack, then back to the stranger. He noticed. When she made her lunge, he lunged too. They met in the middle and both grabbed onto a strap. The stranger flashed his crooked yellow teeth. "Fool me once, heh, heh, heh."

He yanked on the bag with his spidery arms, pulling Juno in closer. She felt her feet slide, but she refused to let go. It was her only escape...

Then the bedroom door flung squarely into the stranger's right side, dislodging every bone it came into contact with. Another dark looming figure entered.

"Christ sake, I was just comin' out!" the stranger cried, trying to push his right arm back into its socket.

The new figure shrouded Juno's view of the stranger like an eclipse. All she heard next were a few grunts, some meticulously cracked bones, and a thump to the floor. The spider had been squashed. But by then, the looming figure turned around.

Juno's arm was already deep inside the bag, gripping the handle of her knife, when she heard, "Are you hurt?"

Kareem kneeled down and placed his smooth hands on her cheeks. She wanted to cry. "I'm okay."

"Good," he confirmed, wiping a tear from her cheek with his thumb. "I don't know what I'd do if we lost you."

More scuffling echoed through the open door, along with voices. There were lots of them.

"Get dressed," Kareem whispered, closing the door quietly. "And pack your stuff. We need to grab Lexa and go."

Kareem waited by the door with his back turned while Juno changed. Through the terror, she nervously slipped on her bra, pants, shirt, socks, boots and duster jacket, then filled her backpack with the few things readily within sight. When she was ready, she tucked herself behind Kareem's legs. He cracked an opening to the long hallway that stretched from the front entrance to the back of the house.

"Stay close," he instructed. "I don't know how many there are."

After a silent countdown from three, Kareem and Juno flung out into the hall. They were met with the dim blue glow of hexagonal lights that detected motion. A warm breeze brushed past them. They craned their necks to the right and saw a cold darkness in the entryway. The front door was wide open.

Then a guttural cry pulled their heads to the left. At the other end of the hall, basked in a blue haze, was Lexa. She was pulling her kukri knife from the chest of a limp body. A streak of blood stained her white robe.

"Where's Juno?" Lexa called with dangerous poignancy.

"I got her!" Kareem called back.

They started towards Lexa, but she barked, "No! Get Juno to safety. I'll find you."

"You got it," he replied, then pulled Juno in the opposite direction like she was a weightless doll. She saw Lexa retreat into her room.

Their boots, big and small, clunked down the tiled hallway as they strained their legs to reach the front door. The entryway was in complete darkness, save for the cerulean haze trailing them, and nothing was known on the other side. When Kareem and Juno reached the end they stopped just short and waited for the blue light to fade back into obscurity.

"Stay here," he muttered, but just as he took a step out into the open landing, five sillhouettes stormed through the front door and headed right for him.

Kareem immediately lifted Juno and threw her into the living room.

As she bounced off the back of the couch and onto the floor, he was tackled by the intruders. All six of them slid back into the hallway. "Get to Lexa!" he snapped before falling from sight.

Juno sprang back up and searched the vastness of the open room. It seemed endless in the dark. She could not remember the windows being this clear earlier in the night and was spooked by the hazy moonlight coming in. As she krept backwards towards the kitchen, she spotted two figures standing just outside. Their clothes seemed different—black, more put together—and their bodies were proportional. Their postures were straight and calm. For some reason they frightened her far more than the crooked men inside.

When she made it to the rear of the kitchen, Juno ducked back into an entrance at the other end of the long hallway she had just been thrown from. She peered down the shadowed tunnel and saw no blue glow, no bodies, and no sign of Kareem. After taking a heavy breath, she darted across, and slipped into Lexa's room.

Lexa was seated on the bed tightening a bandage around her thigh. On the ground next to her was another limp body in the same ragged clothing.

"What are you still doing here?" Lexa snapped.

"F...f...five more," Juno trembled.

Lexa stood stiffly from the bed as if a hundred extra pounds had been strapped to her back. Her face winced and, as she leaned down to pull up her pants, a dark strip began to draw itself on the white bandage. There was no time for Juno to comment on either Lexa's ribs or leg before the loud slam of splintered wood interrupted.

"Get behind me," Lexa ordered. She slipped her angled knife into the holster on her chest, threw on her coat and backpack, and unclipped the empty shotgun she had been keeping close by. As she lifted the stock up to her shoulder, she flicked open the door with the barrell, and stepped out.

Three haggard men were waiting for them. They all carried knives and smiles that reflected blue in the hexagonal glow. Lexa raised the gun to eye level, but none of the men so much as flinched.

"You ain't got no shells for that thing," one jeered.

"Try me," Lexa dared.

The three exchanged hesitant glances until one finally shrugged and stepped forward. Lexa held her ground and, when it was clear she would not back away, the man froze and waited to see who would make the next move. It seemed that the man carried a pin of bravery, but not the whole grenade.

But the standoff was short lived. Juno peeked her head around the door and the men immediately responded.

"There she is!" the one in front yelped. "Git 'er!"

All at once they rushed forward, carefree of the gun still aimed at their faces. Lexa immediately spun the gun stock-forward and checked the first man's jaw straight into the wall. He hit the sheetrock with a *thwack!* and keeled over, mouth dangling by a thread.

The next two rushed at the same time. They both went for the blunderbuss-turned-bludgeon in Lexa's grasp. To their surprise she let them have it, and, now that their hands were occupied, an angled blade revealed itself from her chest. It was her turn at offense.

Lexa watched patiently as the man on the right released his hold on the gun and sprung forward. But before he could reach her, or react, the knife had already caught his outstretched hand through the center of his palm and plunged deep into his heart. A trail of black escaped and splattered against the hexagonal glow. Then, with a quick twist, a pull, and a shove, he was released to collapse next to his jawless counterpart.

Meanwhile, the other man had regained control of the shotgun. Lexa turned to the weapon pointed directly at her chest and followed the barrel up to a toothy grin. His body was trembling with excitement. "Hand over the girl or I'll shoot!"

Lexa's rage-fueled gaze burned deep into the scabbed man's soul, daring him to try. Sweat dripped from his balding scalp into his bloodshot eyes. Still he held the gun steady. It was only when she lowered her knife did he pull the trigger.

Click!

Lexa smirked at his bemusement. "You were right. No shells."

Juno covered her eyes before she could watch what her protector did to the man. She heard the squeals and cracks that came from a life of pain, suffering, and fear. She wanted to think that it was not his fault, that men could be good if given the chance, but then she remembered the cool air on her hips only moments ago.

"Come on!" Lexa barked, grabbing Juno's arm and pulling her through the kitchen. They had been fortunate enough to grab most of what they needed to survive, but they were still missing one thing.

"Where's Kareem?" pled Juno.

"He'll be fine."

When they reached the living room, Lexa shoved Juno down behind a chair. The house was quiet, but the room was vast and dark, and there were many shadows to hide inside. Lexa stayed low and started skimming all of the potential entries and exits. The atmosphere was still too eerie for a safe jaunt out the front door.

Juno peeked over the arm of the chair and saw that the two men from earlier were no longer standing there. She felt it necessary to notify Lexa, but just as she began the word, "Hey," someone had picked her up. She screamed instead.

Lexa turned from near the fireplace when a sweeping fist colliding with her left ear staggered her to a knee. The room went much darker for a moment, then returned in the form of spinning vertigo. An incessant ringing filled her head as the rest of her senses rebooted. It felt like an eternity before she was able to climb to her feet and re-orient herself in the blackness of the massive house.

"Juno!" she called while searching for the hand that had grounded her.

Another strike came from behind that caved in the back of Lexa's legs. She went down again, this time feeling the pain. The only upside was she now knew there were multiple assailants around her. Ones she could adjust for. Lexa stood up for a second time, spun around sharply, and backed against the wall. She would not be caught from behind again.

On the other end of the room, Juno writhed until she was dropped inside a shadowed corner hidden from the view of the living room. She came back swinging her fists, but a large hand stopped their momentum with ease. A large, yet soft, hand.

"Do you remember how we got up on the roof?" Kareem whispered.

Juno realized they were by a door she had never seen before. *Where am I?* she started to wonder, but two hands shook her shoulders back into focus. She nodded, "Yes."

"Good. This door leads out the back. Climb up there and stay hidden." He could see the terror on her face and added with his signature smile, "I'll be right behind you. No matter what. Now go!"

As Juno slipped out into the still forest, she saw Kareem disappear into the darkened house. *No matter what...*

Lexa was now dealing with three men. She had one of their legs barred in one arm while she swung her blade to keep the other two from advancing with the other. When there was a second to breathe, she twisted the leg she had captured until she felt a tendon snap. The man lost balance and she used his momentum to toss him to the ground, but not before she felt a hard fist emphasize the bruising on her ribs. She lurched over in crippling pain.

Then, as if vanishing into thin air, the man who had just struck Lexa was no longer beside her. Instead, he had been lifted and thrown headfirst into the stonework of the fireplace where his neck snapped on impact. He was dead before he even hit the ground.

"No time to take a nap!" Kareem teased as he helped Lexa to her feet.

She leaned her weight against him, felt around her ribs for fractures, and grunted, "Took you long enough."

But then, like the instant a rock hits a window, something shattered in the chaos that ushered in a primal, yet venerable force of calm. Suddenly the room was as silent as a stolen breath, as unbroken as a windless lake, as patient as an elder mountain. Kareem looked down at the tiny silver point of a mysterious knife quietly protruding from his abdomen, and exhaled a puff of amusement. How had he missed a third man?

For the first time in her life, Lexa froze. Her entire body seized up as she watched Kareem slide forward off the blade and crumble to the ground. Until this moment she had never witnessed the mortality of someone she truly cared about. Someone she could call...a friend.

Fury snapped her gaze back to the scabbed man still flaunting the life-stealing weapon with pride. He was ready for the next round. So was Lexa. But before the mangled man could even think about a next move, his throat was split wide open by the sharp edge of a kukri. Both life and torment poured out of the fissure and stained the carpet black.

With the midnight siege at its close, Lexa breathlessly dropped to the floor and lifted Kareem's head into her lap. Then she held her hand in front of his nose: still breathing.

"Stay with me," she said calmly, trying to ignore her own injuries. She saw his soaked shirt and shook the image from her head. "We still have a long way to go."

Kareem took a hard breath inwards. Lexa could hear the blood gargling in his lungs. There was no saving him. Not here. Not even with the incredible resources this house provided. And he would never make it to Arcadia...

"She's," Kareem wheezed. He slowly brought a quivering hand to Lexa's and gripped it tightly. "She's..."

A cold tingle pushed against the back of Lexa's eyes. Her mind knew the truth, but her heart pulled every ounce of rationale into disbelief. "Don't be so dramatic. We still need you. *I* still need you."

Kareem coughed a blood-steeped chuckle, his sense of humor immortal. "She's...on the roof. Safe."

"Thank you. For everything. Now let's—"

Her words sputtered out. They could do nothing.

"Don't ever let her go, Lexa." Then, with whatever strength was still left inside, he gazed deep into her eyes and smiled his infectious smile. "No matter what."

When the final breath exited Kareem's body, and his grip on Lexa's hand went slack, she gently set his head down. Somberly, she stood up and tried to allow her heart to return to ice. Feelings would only add an extra weight she could no longer carry. She collected her knife, bag, and unloaded shotgun, and ran over to the house's side door.

Moments later Juno saw a familiar arm reach over the edge of the Zeiss Home. She had been hiding in the center groove of the roof, waiting desperately for her family to return.

Lexa heaved herself up and rolled onto her back, gazing up at the starless night. Juno crawled over.

"Where's Kareem?" Juno asked with a trembling voice.

Lexa said nothing.

"Where's Kareem?" she asked again, a bit stronger. When she received no answer the second time she shoved Lexa's shoulder with anger. "Where. Is. Kareem!"

Lexa eventually turned her head to look at the girl. All Juno could make out was the glimmer of tears on a face made of stone.

The first light of the morning brought with it a tempestuous aura. Everything felt absolutely still, as if the wind had blown in a mauve cloud that smothered the previous night's memoires. Had there been music? Was there an attack? Did they escape?

Juno awoke from two hours of sleep with a stiff back and an even stiffer recollection. She looked around her surroundings as far as her aching neck would allow without having to move her body. Her bag was lying next to her on the left, and to the right was some peculiar scenery. The trees, the rocks, the floor beneath her, even in the haze, felt vaguely familiar. Everything save for Lexa, who was nowhere to be seen.

After sitting up, a throbbing headache pulled Juno's hand to her head like a dull magnet. *Why does my whole body hurt?* She twisted her spine from left to right until the compressed tension dissipated in the form of cracks and pops. Finally, once her body felt usable again, she got to her feet.

The ground was at an unusually steep angle and was smooth as glass. And the trees seemed half as tall as they usually did. Then it hit her.

When did I get up on the roof?

She scratched her matted hair and her fingernails collected a bit of dried blood. The events from the night before were still hazy and the dark red flakes seemed odd. She did remember pancakes; their sweet and savory flavors. She also remembered dancing. Oh, and music! Such an elegant pairing. Moving along with those dazzling sounds of instruments and voices would stay with her forever.

Then she recalled waking in the middle of the night. A hand was on her mouth. Another tugged at her pants. She stabbed him with a pen. How many of them came into the house? Eight? Nine? Lexa had saved her, made quick work of the attackers. They all looked the same, yet crooked. She was jumped in the living room next. No, wait, another figure had carried her to safety. There was a blue glow. Men screaming. Blood splattering. Only two left the house...

Kareem!

Suddenly Juno felt dizzy. She stumbled around on rubber legs. The roof's angle may as well have been a cliffside this morning because she fell hard and slid to the center.

Just like when we got here...

Cold water splashed Juno's face back into consciousness. Still disoriented from the tumble, she sat up like she was spring-loaded. A hand cupped her mouth as she gasped for air.

"Keep quiet," a voice directed. "We're not alone."

Lexa was crouched next to Juno and only released her hand when the young woman nodded in return.

"Alright," Lexa continued. "They don't know we're up here, but it's only a matter of time before they find us. Take these."

Juno fumbled the binoculars shoved into her chest and they fell into her lap. "What for?"

"Follow me. Keep low."

Lexa crawled to the northwestern edge of the roof, where the Zeiss

Home met the mountain, and leaned against the rock. Juno followed, though much slower. She was still collecting the scattered pieces of the night before.

"Look," Lexa said, pointing a ways down the paved path that led west from the house. "Over there."

Juno held the binoculars up to her eyes. Two men were standing on the pavement in the dawn-lit haze. She knew their dark clothing and rigid postures from the night before. But how, exactly?

"See them?"

Still attached to the lenses, Juno nodded. They stood in a haunting manner, like two dark spectres trapped in place by the light.

"Those are the men from Genesys. They've been hunting you," Lexa confided, then her voice turned more severe. "Their leader will do anything to make sure you are brought to him."

Juno slowly lowered the binoculars and looked up at Lexa. "But... why?"

"You have something he wants. A power no other human possesses. Understand?"

That word. *Power*. It was starting to frighten Juno. She nodded.

"I'm not going to let anything happen to you," Lexa continued. "This is obviously a trap; they want to draw me out. But I don't see a way around. Only through."

A heavy sigh came before Lexa admitted something further. "Juno, I can't confront them *and* protect you at the same time anymore. Not in my condition. If one of them was able to distract me, even for a second, the other could grab you and that would be the end of it. So we're going to split up."

Panic swirled inside Juno's stomach and shot up her throat. Before she knew it she had painted a few solar panels in a thick, mahogany paste; syrup and chocolate chips. Cold sweat beaded her skin. Then, as she wiped her mouth, she noticed the bandage around Lexa's leg had bled through her pants.

"I can't go alone!" Juno paused, anticipating another wave of vomit, but it flushed away. "I'll never survive out here. I'll get lost or killed or put in a cage—"

Two hands rested on her shoulder like a warm, comforting blanket on a freezing cold night. Lexa had kneeled down to her height. "It's okay. I have a plan. I'm going to go down there and...take care of our obstacle... and you're going to climb up this mountain. When you get to the top, look back down at the road with my binoculars. I'll be waving at you. Got it?"

Wiping a terrified tear from her cheek, Juno shook her head. "I don't wanna..."

"You have to be strong, Juno. It's our only way out of this. Do it for me. Do it for—" Lexa had to stop to clear her throat. "Do it for Kareem."

Juno sniffled. "Is he really gone?"

Lexa searched back and forth in Juno's eyes for the right answer. She did not know what to say in a situation like this. Or how to grieve in general. Up until a few weeks ago, her interactions with other humans only ever consisted of hard cynicism, pragmatism, or violence.

"Only out here," Lexa finally said. She pressed two fingers firmly to Juno's chest. "But never in here."

A delicate calm cradled Juno's racing heart. She swallowed down her anxiety, then nodded once she felt she understood the gravity of their situation. "You promise you'll be waving?"

"No matter what," Lexa winked.

With the sleeve of her duster, Juno wiped her nose. "Then I'll do my best."

The two parted ways for the first time since they had met. One scurried up the rockface while the other cringed in pain during her climb down. Neither looked back.

Lexa emerged from the dead forest at the same time the sun peeked over the eastern ridge. The sudden reflection off the smooth pavement skewed her view so much she had to lift a hand to block it. The motion itself, however, was a persistent reminder that her entire torso was one massive bruise.

I hope this works, she thought as she sauntered down the driveway of the Zeiss Home. The road was long and narrow. It headed west between the mountain Juno was climbing and an endless sea of petrified trees. She heard a sudden breeze brushing the trees to her right. Then, out of the corner of her eye, a stone tumbled down the rockface to her left. However, instead of hearing the light clatter she would normally expect, it now felt like someone was squeezing that half of her skull. *What the hell?*

"Well, well, well, what do we have here?" One of the two men before her jeered in the haze. The sun had provided a spotlight that obscured their misty silhouettes.

Lexa acknowledged them both venomously. "I didn't think you scabs were allowed this much slack in your leashes."

"S'matter Lexa?" the first one taunted again. "Miss your big black boyfriend?"

Her hand gripped the kukri knife's handle and flashed its flawless bolster. Her antagonizer reached for his own blade. Instantly they became two predators in a deadlock over the same meal.

"Enough, Deacon," the other man finally said. He stepped forward with an extended hand. "I'm sure we can resolve this amicably."

Lexa held onto her blade firmly. "You want me to shake that, or cut it off?"

A haunting chuckle came from the one who seemed to be in charge. "You're a difficult fox to hound, Lexa. But not impossible. I remember fondly our last confrontation. How is your eye, by the way?"

His words made the long scar across Lexa's brow and cheek bite at her skin. It was more than just a wound on her face, it was a singed mark on her soul. Something she touched every day to remind her of the past.

"Not one for conversation this fine morning?" the man goaded. "Do you not remember our introduction?"

"I remember you ran for your life."

That bought a few seconds of hesitation. But she needed more.

"Fine, we'll cut to the purpose of our intrusion. Where is the girl?"

"What girl?" Lexa snorted.

The man crossed his arms behind his back and leaned in slightly. "You know very well who we are referring to. We saw you leave with her at the Precursor's fortress. Clever escape, I might add; using the elevator."

"Oh, *that* girl," Lexa feigned. "She died. Couldn't take the heat."

"Is that so? Then am I to believe that you and your dark companion were just enjoying a quiet night in together? You do know that windows work both ways, do you not?"

Sounds like he still hasn't laid eyes on Juno, Lexa deduced, then tilted her chin in pretend thought. "No idea what you're talking about."

"Will you listen to this bitch, Bishop?" The other man snarled. "I say we teach her some respect."

He made it two steps forward before his partner stopped him with an outstretched hand. *That's right,* Lexa thought, *Just a little bit closer...*

"As much as we both enjoy your company," Bishop continued, "my patience has worn very thin over the weeks. We've eliminated the male, we've scoured the house, and we've smoked you from your hole. Now hand over the girl and we'll be on our way."

Lexa was nearly foaming at the mouth from resisting the urge to attack, but they were both still standing too far out of reach. She needed to taunt them more. "Why don't you just ask all the dogs you sicked on me last night? But wait, you're the only two left."

Bishop stepped forward again, his expression still one of optimism. "The acolytes were an unfortunate sacrifice, yes, but a necessary one; for they executed my plan without flaw. See, I knew you would hide the girl, so the only intent was for your feet to stand before me at this precise moment."

"Wow. You really will do *anything* to climb farther up the Scab King's ass, won't you?"

Swooping over to Lexa with scorn, Bishop drew a small, hooked blade. "Do *not* call Him by that name," he warned.

The tiny words and the tiny knife hardly worried Lexa because she now had Bishop at arm's length. Now for the other. She flicked her head towards the ill-tempered partner. "You there. Did your lips get that scabbed from kissing two asses?"

The man lunged forward as if a nail had just gone through his foot. His eyes were spirals of violent fervor. But when he was a step away from his target, Bishop halted his progress yet again.

They're both close enough, she confirmed. Subtly, she tightened her grip on the handle of her knife and waited for them to drop their guard. All she needed was for one to turn ever so slightly to the other and they would be hers for the picking. She ground her foot into the dirt.

"Do not waste your energy on her futile derision, Deacon." Bishop then leaned to his partner to add, "We have *other* ways of handling her."

Now!

Lexa shifted her weight, pivoted her back foot, and slammed face first into the ground. Her knife skittered across the pavement to Bishop's feet as her head whipped back from the impact. Immediately, she spun around to find three acolytes looming over her like a bad dream. Then, in a mixed effort of gratification, those same three men got in their shots on her ribs before hoisting her body back up by the arms.

How had she missed them? She had looked everywhere in the hazy forest and found no traces; saw no stragglers. And everyone inside was dead. Which meant they had been planning this.

Impossible. I would have heard them!

Lexa lowered her head in disbelief. While she tried to sort out the pieces of deception, she heard the men talking around her, but, strangely, only from her right side.

Oh no! The blow from last night must have ruptured my eardrum!

Betrayed by the sudden and complete deafness inside her left ear, Lexa closed her eyes. After all the distance, all of the narrow escapes, and all of the unexpected affection grown towards the young girl, she had failed.

I'm so sorry, Juno.

Once Lexa was well restrained, Bishop approached her with a sinister smile. "We will have the girl," he said, then ran a coarse finger across the length of the scar on her face. "And you're going to lead her right to us."

"No, no, no, no, no!" Juno cried from behind fogged up binoculars. She had reached the top of the mountain just in time to find her only remaining connection to the world lying face down on the road.

Three mysterious, misshapen men hovered over Lexa that had not been there before she started her ascent. They were reminiscent of the intruders from last night, except somehow still breathing, still standing, still kicking. Using their oblong arms, two restrained Lexa after a brief, one-sided assault while a third tied her hands behind her back.

The recognizable two in darkened, more complete outfits were still there as well. They were the ones that had somehow tracked them. Tracked Juno. One had Lexa's shotgun slung around his shoulder and was digging through her bag. The other stood with his arms behind his back, appearing to be giving a speech.

"C'mon Lexa. You can take 'em!" Juno whispered.

But as much as she pleaded with herself, it was not meant to be. Lexa was lifted to her feet and shoved forward. She stumbled from the force and went back to her knees. One of the men kicked her in her side twice, then yelled at her until she stood back up.

Juno watched helplessly as her companion, her protector, limped down the road. When she could not bear the sight any longer, she dropped the binoculars, curled into a helpless ball, and wept until her body surrendered to an eclipsing lassitude.

You must wait here, a voice entered from the void. *No matter what.*
Juno looked around, only to find herself inside a room without walls, a floor, or a ceiling. Just her and the darkness. "Mom?"

I can't take care of you anymore. Someone will come for you. I promise.

A floor shored up beneath her. It was hard and moist and cold.

"Mom? Where are you?"

One at a time, barred walls stretched around, welding themselves together at each corner.

"Mom! Who will come for me this time? I'm all alone!"

This is goodbye, Juno. You have to let me go.

The voice fluttered by Juno's ears as a hatch of thick floorboards slammed down onto the finished walls. Claustrophobia took her breath as the enclosure shrank around her. Where was the exit? *There!* A handle etched itself into the wooden planks as if it were drawn by an invisible hand. She reached for it.

"Don't leave me again! I need you!" she cried as the hatch came nearer.

Once she reached the handle, the floor raised slightly, allowing a dark breeze to enter the gap. On the other side the voice withered to nothingness. *Just wait here. No matter what.*

The cage continued to shrink. Juno leaned her shoulder into the hatch, but it would not budge any farther. Suddenly, a dust-ridden rug stifled the incoming breeze, followed by a loud scrape. It sounded like wooden legs; the type that were attached to a massive table resting beneath a ceiling of chained hooks. Then the door slammed shut, throwing Juno down onto the cold, damp floor. Finally, with the click of a lock, her fate was sealed inside a hollow cage that would never be opened again...

Juno suddenly woke to the sound of sweat sizzling on her face. The sun had broken through the morning haze and would soon be too dangerous for bare skin. Thinking quickly, she threw up her hood, grabbed her bag, and slid over to a jutting rock casting some diminishing shade.

No matter what.

The phrase echoed in her mind over and over and over again. Every time she heard those three words she lost someone dear to her. First her mom, then Kareem, now, "Lexa!"

She scooped up the binoculars and peered over the mountain's edge to the west. She followed the path from the house until it merged with a larger road in the distance below. Then she traced its dark line as far as the lenses would focus. *How long was I asleep?*

She kept scanning the landscape until she came across a group of boulders at the foot of a small mountain that created a healthy shaded area. There they were, waiting out the sun. Juno counted five nefarious bodies and could only imagine how they were torturing the sixth. Helplessness returned like a sudden nightfall.

Juno leaned back into the shade-providing rock, slid down onto her bottom, and tucked her head between her knees. Tears would have surged through her eyes if the sun had not already stolen the moisture from her body.

What could I possibly do? There's five of them and only one of me. But I can't just sit here. I'll die. I could stay at the house...No. Like Lexa said, it's not safe here anymore. This is the first place they'd look for me. Think, Juno, think!

Her sleeved hands covered her mouth and she screamed every drop of energy she had left into her palms. She was sick of being weak. Sick of relying on others. Sick of waiting around. Sick of being powerless to decide her own destiny. And for what? Because she was scared? Lexa was never scared. Lexa taught her how to fight. How to find water. How to travel unseen. How to survive. How to swim—

Before she realized it was there, Juno felt a small prick in her clenched fist. She turned her palm upwards and opened her fingers. A tiny sliver of blue plastic was lodged inside her skin. She looked at it with disdain. How could something so insignificant, so wasteful, so small that she had not even noticed it beneath her be the sole reason this world she had been born into existed?

Juno plucked the small shard from her palm and flicked it over the edge of the mountain. A small bead of blood was left in its wake and she watched as it slithered across her open hand.

You told me I had power, she recalled as the red streak formed a droplet that fell to the earth. *A power no one else in the entire world has.* She squeezed a fist. *And I'm going to use it to save you.*

No matter what.

Juno rose to her feet, picked up her backpack, and took one last quick glance through her binoculars. After confirming Lexa's position had not changed, she climbed back down the shady side of the mountain as fast as she could.

When she reached the bottom, Juno entered the Zeiss Home expecting the worst. Due to the late-morning sun the power had been restored. But even with its sophisticated air filtration system the house still reeked of death. Around every corner was a gnarled, lifeless body.

Her first stop was the bedroom she had called her own for a few days. Juno emptied her bag onto the bed and lined up only the necessities. She would have to travel smart, and she would have to travel light. Only one extra set of clothes, her knife, a single blanket, a box of matches, a small first-aid kit, and, of course, her journal made the cut. The rest would have to be food and water.

Inside the air-sealed pantry was the largest amount of edible food she had ever seen in one place. There was an endless supply of canned and boxed meals, jars of honey and syrup and fruit preserves, condiments galore, and unopened boxes of MRE packets. Of course, cans were too heavy, and boxed food took up precious real estate, so she stuffed her mouth with every ounce of sweet, sugary goodness she could stomach, then bitterly loaded only MRE's into her bag.

Her final stop was in the kitchen. She lined up every aluminum canteen left behind and filled up as many as she could shove into the backpack's dwindling space. Before she left the kitchen of her dreams for the final time, she downed the entire pitcher of iced water Kareem had kept filled inside the fridge.

Kareem...

Juno heaved her now fifty-pound bag over her shoulders and dropped down into the living room. Kareem lay there on his back, still and peaceful as a fallen tree. It hurt to look at him. *You should be here with me*, she sniffled, fighting back an onslaught of tears. The only thing keeping her upright was the joy he had been able to provide during their too short of time together. The jokes, the music, the infectious smile. She cherished everything.

When she could not bear to look at his breathless body anymore, Juno moved across the living room to the cabinet near the automatic fireplace. Once she found the panel that had turned it on, she readied the Ben E. King record, and carefully placed the needle on the edge. After a few soft crackles, the first song sprouted.

Don't play that song for me
   It brings back memories
Of days that I once knew
   The days that I spent with you

As the music found its stride, Juno made her way over to the exit, but froze solid before crossing the threshold. The rest of her life was waiting for her outside that door. The rocks, the wind, the dust, the heat, the men...she would have to face all of it alone. But she would not have to finish her life alone. Not if she was strong.

"You rest here, Kareem," she said without looking back into the room; without looking back into the past. Then she flipped up the hood of her duster and took her first step out into the unknown. "I'm going to rescue Lexa."

Entry 54

It's day three of following Lexa's trail and I'm starting to regret my decision. It's so much more miserable out here when you have no one to talk to. When you're all alone. I don't know how she made it all the way to me in Denver without going crazy. Then again, it was probably me making her go crazy.

Luckily (I guess?) the evil men who took her are really easy to follow. They just stay on the big 70 road. And I can see why because it's SO MUCH faster than climbing mountains, which I still have to do by the way. It's not as hard as it used to be and it keeps me from being seen. I can thank Lexa for that. In fact, I almost never get sore anymore except for my shoulders. My bag is really heavy.

When I get to a good spot that's high up, I watch them through Lexa's binoculars. I get the feeling that the men don't need to stop, but have to because they keep hurting Lexa. They push her around a lot and they don't give her much water or food. Sometimes she falls and they drag her until she gets up. It makes me so sick I cry.

I want to just run down there and free her, but she taught me better than that. I would just get us both killed...or worse. I still haven't come up with a plan. If I only knew where they were going it might not be so hard.

In other news, I'm super close to a state called Utah now. (Oo-taw or You-taw?) I saw it on a sign after we all passed through a town called Grand Junction. I was able to sneak into a house and refill my water thanks to Lexa's little toilet trick. I also found an unopened box of crunchy oat bars. They're tasty, but I'm afraid I'll break a tooth on one!

From where I'm standing Utah looks a lot like

Colorado, but different at the same time. The mountains are a bit smaller and way more spread out. It already feels like I have to walk about twice as far as them just to stay out of sight.

But I suppose it's for the best because the 70 road is full of spooky people. Sometimes I watch them walk around from my binoculars and pretend they're new animals. It still blows my mind that little bits of plastic twisted their bodies into...into...whatever they are. One had a huge arm that dragged on the ground. One was connected to another person by the hip. There was even one I saw that walked flipped over on all fours like a crab!

It's also crazy to look back at the Colorado mountains and see where I came from. They're huge and purply and rocky. Then I turn around and these new ones look like they're made of colorful layers. It reminds me of how Kareem described that magical Zion place he wanted to go to.

Wow. I really miss him. He'd probably still be alive if he had never met us. He'd be going on all kinds of adventures and seeing all those beautiful places he talked about.

I really wish I wasn't special. Then none of this would have ever happened. I don't even want a baby anyways. What are they gonna do when I get to this Arcadia place? Force me to have kids? No thanks. I'd rather be like Lexa. Someone strong and beautiful who makes their own rules.

Maybe even someday me and Lexa will sneak away and go to Zion together. We'll take Kareem's

> memory with us and then we'll tell him all about how pretty it is in our dreams. And no one at stupid Arcadia will be able to stop us because we're so fast and deadly and hot.
>
> But my dreams don't matter anymore. Kareem is gone, Lexa was taken, and I'm just sitting around and writing in my stupid journal.
>
> It's not fair and I hate myself for it.

After Grand Junction, the caravan of Lexa's captors turned north on a road that was marked by a shield housing the number 139. And a couple days after that Juno found herself face to face with the most peculiar named town she had ever seen.

"Dinosaur?" she felt she had to say out loud just to make it real. But sure enough the sign read `Welcome To Dinosaur, Colorado` with a Stegosaurus proudly standing between `Welcome` and `To`.

A mild delight came over Juno as she was reminded of the early pages in the reptile section of her abandoned field guide. Along with prehistoric creatures such as alligators and tortoises, the greatest reptiles of all once wandered the Earth, and here was an entire settlement named after them!

Early on it was clear that Dinosaur was a ghost town, sure, but one with the most magnificent ghosts. Every corner contained a new showcase of wonderful and decrepit imagery and sculptures. If entering the town on Stegosaurus Freeway was not enough, then walking by Dinosaur City Hall, past Triceratops Terrace, and onto Dinosaur Library definitely was. Juno's favorite specimen was a green, round-headed, upright dinosaur standing inside a tiny wooden cage with the words **Keep Out** scribbled across its once-white chest. It even managed to pull out a smile she had so cautiously tucked away since the Zeiss Home.

Though she wanted to spend the entire day scouring the library for every remaining book on dinosaurs, Juno knew that time was a luxury she could not afford. Especially on her own. Instead, she broke into the nearest still-standing house and found some pipes containing precious water. Without the use of Lexa's wrench, however, she had to get clever—three or four kicks to a rusty coupling clever, to be specific. But she was proud of her ingenuity and, if anything, it kept her out of the scorching sun for a little while longer.

Juno left the house with full canteens and a song stuck in her head. She repeated what words she remembered of "Rocky Mountain High" over and over again as she strolled to the northern part of the town. And although she was careful to stay out of sight, she had not anticipated someone overhearing her tune.

"Who there?" a burdened, wheezing voice asked from an alley between two houses. "I hear ya!"

Before her entire body seized in the middle of the street, Juno quickly dove onto a weathered wooden porch attached to a nearby home. She crouched underneath a busted window and focused on quieting her breaths.

"I know yer out there," the voice called again.

When it was quiet for enough time, Juno mustered up the courage to stretch her eyes up to the window ledge. The house was small and square, with the back porch window looking straight through to the front window. No glass remained in either so Juno got a clear view of the man's bulbous midriff as he floated by the front. She ducked back down as swiftly as she could.

"C'mon out now, y'here? Ol' Grubby don' bite."

Grubby?

"I don' git many visitors," he continued, now on the side of the house.

It was too late for Juno to run so she clutched the handle of the black knife strapped to her leg and remained completely still. The man emerged from the corner carrying with him a distinguishing smell. Her face curdled as the scent crawled up her nose, but she managed to keep it in her lungs without coughing.

She could now see that the man had dark skin, like Kareem's, wrapped around a long, skeletal frame. He was over twice as tall as herself with rangy arms and legs that would have looked more at home on a tree. Layers of wrinkles replaced what would have been scabs on most of the people she had encountered over the past two months.

"It's so lonely out here all alone. Be nice to have someone to talk to..."

To Juno's surprise, the man kept on walking until he was in the middle of the road she had just been singing on. He had not so much as glanced in her direction.

She watched patiently as he paced around and sniffed at the air. At one point he tripped over an old tire and stumbled into a rotted fence on the opposite side of the street. The man seemed harmless. Clumsy, but harmless. And his sentiment about being all alone resonated deeply. Maybe he was just trapped in Dinosaur; nowhere to go and too afraid of what was beyond. Juno understood those feelings all too well.

Slowly, she rose to her feet, heedful to keep both eyes on the man at all times. Her bag brushed against the peeling paint of the porch.

The old man's head contorted at an angle. "What's that? You say somethin'?"

Juno swallowed down the disturbing movement and held up a hand to shield the sun. "Are you alright?"

"Ah, there ya'are," confirmed the old man by twisting towards Juno's direction. She could only compare his jittery actions to that of a lizard. "Yes, yes, Grubby's good as new! Not a day old'r'an yesterday, heh, heh, heh!" His laugh sounded like rocks sliding from his mouth.

A warm breeze blew between the two before Juno spoke again. She was thankful it pushed the smell of the old man away from her. "Do you need anything?"

Grubby's long fingers scratched at the ring of grey hair still clinging to his head. "Now that ya mention it, a drop 'r two of water'd be mighty kind."

Juno looked beyond her hand to squint at the sky. Not a cloud was in sight and this man stood out in the open as if the sun was missing. Curiously, she said, "Okay," pulled a canteen from her bag, and unscrewed the lid. When she took a step forward so did Grubby.

Like a standoff in reverse, Juno and the old man approached each other one pace at a time. He understood every time she took a step without ever looking directly at her. It was unsettling at best, but she had already committed.

When Juno was three or four of her own arms'-length's away, she cautiously held out the metal container. Grubby stopped and waited. He alternated twitching his ears and nose in the air before asking, "Where'd ya go?"

Is he serious? I'm right here...

Another hot breeze swept the sour stench back into Juno's nose, forcing her to lower her sun-blocking hand to plug it shut. It was then that she saw the grisly cause for Grubby's abnormal behavior. His reason for not looking *at* her, but *around* her. His eyes contained no color, no pupils at the center, just a grey haze as if they had been filled with smoke. He was completely blind.

"Come now. Ol' Grubby's thirsty."

But there was more reason for concern below his clouded sockets. Pink scars in the shapes of fingernail scratches led down his cheeks and onto his neck. And resting comfortably on his shoulders was the source of the smell. Like a pendant of death, countless severed fingers and toes hung from a loose piece of rope, skin still rotting from the bones.

Struck from horror, Juno let the bottle slip from her hand and plunk to the ground. Water escaped, making a dark stream towards Grubby's crooked bare feet. As soon as the life-giving liquid touched his calloused toes, he splayed a rakish mouth half-filled with cracked teeth, and said, "I told ya I don' bite."

Grubby lunged.

Juno screamed and high-tailed it back towards the moldering porch she had been hiding on moments ago. He chased her like some reanimated corpse with half of its original muscles. She tried the door, but the handle was stuck, so she jumped through the window and backed into a corner.

"I'ma git ya!" he hollered, fumbling around with something that jingled.

Taking a moment to control her fear, Juno breathed in deeply, then gagged. The same putrid smell was inside the house!

But the door soon clicked and the knob turned. Juno rushed from the room and into a kitchen. She immediately had to cover her mouth to keep from hurling. Blood stained every single surface, the sink was filled with half-chewed bones, and what was left of someone's leg lay on a rickety table. A large bite was taken from the calf.

The house fell eerily quiet. Tears streamed down Juno's cheeks, but she dared not make another sound, or breath. Then a creak. "Ol' Grubby's willin' to share. Just come on out!"

Juno now heard him skulking at the opposite end of the house. Her eyes darted towards the front window, it was her only chance. She took two silent steps towards it. The third one hit a loose floorboard.

Rrreak!

Unseen bare feet thumped across the rooms towards Juno. She took a running start and dove out the glassless opening. But just as her backpack cleared the gap, a bony hand snagged her leg.

"Get off me!" Juno screamed, high-centered and flailing on the windowsill.

"Y'ain't stayin' for dinner?" Grubby wheezed maniacally.

She kicked and squirmed until her foot caught his chin and sent him stumbling away. Her body wriggled out the window, dropped onto the front porch, then jumped to its feet. Grubby was back on his, too.

Instead of running, she turned back to the window. The old man was feeling for the opening. When he found it, he stuck his head through just as Juno was grabbing the top of the open sash. It creaked. In an instant Grubby's arm burst out, clutching Juno's leg and pulling it in. A word then tried to exit his mouth, but was flushed away by two greater forces: Juno's scream, and the impact of the window frame crushing his neck.

The arm attached to Juno's leg fell limp and slapped lifelessly against the wood siding of the house. Grubby was dead.

Instantly, Juno leaned over the porch railing and vomited everything inside of her stomach. Then, after wiping her mouth, she threw up everything else.

What have I done?

When her stomach recovered, she slunk back around the house and retrieved the bottle of offered water that had slipped from her hands. Both sun and ground had swallowed every last drop. The arid dirt showed Juno just how quickly kindness could be taken from this world, and the empty container showed her how it could be used against her. *Lexa was right this whole time...*

Juno had just killed her first man. It was something she would never be able to forget. Witnessing Lexa and Kareem do the dirty work no longer offered a small barrier to the devastating reality of ending a life. Yet despite almost being eaten by a crazed blind man, the murder still felt unjustified to her. It felt wrong. As if it were never in her blood to take life, only to give it.

How could I have been so stupid? Juno scolded. *So careless. She taught me better than this.*

On her way out of the town with the prehistoric namesake, Juno came across another whimsical sign. `Welcome To Utah` it said in big bold letters. Underneath was a faded Tyrannosaurus Rex romping across the desert. Just a few short hours ago it would have brought joy to Juno's heart. Now she never wanted to see another dinosaur again.

W*here...*
Where am I?
Underneath me...something loose. Sand and stone. I'm outside.
Can't see. Can't hear.
Head throbbing.
Behind me is something hard. Jagged and cool. Must be a boulder.

The air is hot and unmoving. But I don't feel singed. Somewhere in the shade, maybe evening.
What if I try...
No, that hurts. Nearly all of my ribs are cracked. My shoulders hurt, too. Can't move my hands. Ah, that explains it. My wrists are tied behind my back.
Tongue feels like dust. Stomach is cramped with hunger. How long have I...
... I hear something; right side only. Left feels compressed. Deaf.
"Looks like our little princess is awake. Should we take her for a ride?"
Who is that?
"Touch her and the boss'll have your neck. She needs to be *alive* for Bishop's plan to work."
I recognize that voice, and that name.
"Heed Deacon's caution. She needs to survive our expedition. If she does not, my report will reflect poorly on the three of you."
Five total. Bishop, Deacon, three more. They all sound the same.
Vision is still hazy. Light is coming in, though. It's bright. Like a needle in my eye.
So hungry...
Deep breaths. Nose hurts, too. So does my thigh. It's as if a razor is cutting away at my skin one layer at a time. Best to sit still. Conserve energy...
"Better get her some food and water before she kicks the bucket on her own."
Food.
I remember!
There was a house. We were inside. But who's we? Three of us, I think. I remember food; sweet, savory. A warm drink, tea with honey, a soft couch, and music. They were dancing.
Who were they?
One was large, powerful, gentle. Not like the rest. The other was young, bright, and—

I can focus now. Not clear, but there are unsharpened shapes. Dull. A shadow is panning in from my left. Something's grabbing my jaw.

"Now hold still! I'm just tryin' to feed ya."

It enters my mouth. A thick paste of some sort. Doesn't taste like food. I don't want to swallow, but my stomach requires it.

"You should be grateful."

Six spoonfuls of bland batter and a mouthful of tainted water. The shadow leaves. I'm so empty that my body has already absorbed whatever passed as nutrients. At least the nagging cramp has subsided.

Now what was I thinking of earlier? I can't remember. It feels like heat, thirst, and hunger have erased my memory completely. Who are these men? How did I end up here? Should I even be alive?

My sight has returned. I see them now. All five. They're standing around a small shelter. Two are shaped like men, the rest are only jagged tracings of men.

Bishop...

Deacon...

Those names! I've heard them before. They tricked me on the road. I'm so foolish. How could I fall for such a simple scheme?

Thought we had killed them all. Mistake. Left ear is worthless. Injuries beyond repair. Judgement clouded.

Stop! No excuses. You are better than this. Better than them.

There's a road nearby. It's a long highway. Mountains too, but not as many as before. Must be headed West. But to where?

I feel like I used to be sharper than this. Maybe not anymore...

I see ridges nearby. If I look up I can barely see the top. If I could only get up there to hide, they'd never be able to find me. Maybe if I try this...

Ouch!

Everything hurts. What remains of my bones is strapped firmly to this rock. I'm not escaping or outrunning anything ever again. My body has fought its last fight. She'd laugh if she saw me now...

Who is she?

I can't recall her name, but I remember pretension. I was only an experiment to her. Once she knew that I was barren, my purpose shifted. Instead of giving life, I was trained to take it. I became a sharpened tool. Commissioned to please her whims. All of us were...

Yes, I remember.

Pan left me to die. Ran like a coward to save her own skin. That's why I left.

But she always managed to suck me back in. Hunt me down. Corner me. How was I so easily persuaded? It wasn't like I needed money, food, water. I was never short on resources. Yet I remained in her palm. Funny how far desire for parental approval can stretch.

"This one is different," she'd say. Or, "Do it for Rodan."

Ah, yes. The golden child. That kid doesn't know how good he has it. He's lucky he's cute, or I wouldn't be out here trying to track down his little girlfrie—

Juno!

No, no, no! I failed her! That young woman trusted me with her life and I failed her. I'm such an idiot. She doesn't deserve what the world will do to her.

Ow. I flicked my head backwards into the rock I'm tied to. It stings, but not as bad as my defeat.

Juno. So many things I should have taught you. So many things I should have said to you. Why did I remain so distant? Too many years of bathing in my own neglect and it washed over to her. If only I could go back—

Wait, what is that? The five men don't seem to notice it, but I do. It came from up there. No, higher. Higher still. There, at the crest of the ridge. What is that?

It's moving. Careful not to be seen. It's staying tight to the edge, using the rise on this side to its advantage, just like I would...

No.

No, it can't be.

You idiot! Do you know what they'll do to you if you get caught? Run as far away from here as you possibly can! Disappear forever. Forget about me. I've brought you nothing but suffering.

I'm the worst thing that has ever happened to you—
Footsteps are coming.
"What the hell are you lookin' at?"
Pretend to be delusional. Roll your head over with a blank stare. Drop your jaw a little. Hold it.
"Gah! Fellas, she don't look the greatest..."
Hold it.
"Let me see."
Hold it...
"She'll be fine. Probably just exhausted from Deacon kickin' her around so much."
"Heh, you're probably right. Get her some more water, then tie her up in the shack so she don't go missin' in the night."
It worked.
Need to get my head straight. Stay focused. Rest when I can. I must borrow whatever strength my broken body will still lend to me. Knowing her, I'll need it.

Entry 56

I've been seeing a lot of signs with words I don't know lately: Utah, HWY 40, Uinta, Wasatch, Provo.

It's like a completely different language was mixed in with our own. A beautiful language. I want to learn about it someday.

Tonight is pretty cold. It seems like there is a lot more wind on this side (west) of the mountains than the Denver side (east). I really hope another sandstorm isn't coming. We've been caught in two already and both have knocked one of us out. There's even a dumb scar on my forehead to prove it. Plus if I lost sight of Lexa I might never find her again.

    Speaking of Lexa, those men are directly below me tonight. They just pulled her into some shack off the road. I hope there's not a cage of people inside.

    On the bright(ish) side, I think they must be really dumb because they have no idea that I've been following them for over a week. I could literally wave down and they'd have no idea I was up here. Turns out keeping to the opposite side of a peak and digging a hole for a fire really works. What did Lexa and Kareem call it again? Rise?

    What else is new...

    Oh, yeah. I killed a man.

    I didn't want to! But he was going to eat me. EAT me! Can you believe that? Disgusting!

    I seriously promise it was an accident. I was just trying to stop him from grabbing me so I could run away. But when the window came down it was already over.

    Grubby was his name. He was old and blind and didn't have any of those scabs most people do. He could have just been trapped, hungry, and alone in that dinosaur town. But now that I think about it, he couldn't have been alone if he had all those fingers and toes around his neck... Ew! Makes me want to throw up again.

    I guess what I'm getting at is that it's a lot harder out here than I thought. Not the finding water and food and shelter part, which is tough, but the making decisions that keep you alive part. Lexa always made it look so easy, so effortless,

> but even SHE got captured by those men...
> Ugh, I hate them!
> I need to rescue her soon. Tomorrow, in fact. There are no more houses or towns for days. Only this new set of mountains. If I don't do something, I'm scared she'll die by the time we get to the other side. I just need to figure out a way to get to her. She'll know what to do next. She always does.
> So, for anyone that happens to find this journal in the future, I probably got caught or died a horrible death. Or both. The paragraph below is what I know about my location:
> Five men are currently dragging Lexa through these mountains called Wasatch. According to some signs I read, they are part of the Uinta National Forest in the state named Utah. The men are following a weird set of pathways that I think only they know about. It's been easy to keep up, but hard to guess their next turn. Maybe this really tall mountain nearby has something to do with all of this. Provo Peak.
> Never, ever, go there.

Late in the day, a group of five men and one woman entered a circular area of grey gravel flattened between a cluster of cliffs. The sun cast a peak-shaped shadow in the clearing that pointed directly at a drawbridge made of a decrepit billboard surrounded by scrap metal. Burning torches climbed its sides. The men kept to the shadow, but threw the woman out into the sun. She felt the small rocks sting her tied-up arms when she hit the ground.

"Better get her inside before she drops dead," Deacon said as the five lined up along the protective edge of shade.

It took the remainder of Bishop's hunting party a little more than a week to arrive at Sanctuary, pushing the woman to her limit. It was the crowning achievement of his crusade, considering last time he returned empty-handed. "Patience, Deacon. She has survived thus far. I expect her duty to the child will prevent her from surrendering to the sun so easily."

Bishop went over to the shrapnel wall and pulled on a skull hanging from a chain with confidence. After a short time, the drawbridge shifted, juddering the torches that lined its edge so that drips of crude oil pattered against the dirt, and lowered mechanically. A pale, contorted man scurried out of the opening on all fours. The small man with a leather hood over his eyes smelled Lexa immediately and skittered towards her, paying no attention to the line of acolytes.

"Not so fast, Locust" Deacon sneered after stepping on a short length of chain attached to the small man's shackled neck. "Go get the boss."

The small man hissed. "I mussst inssspect the woman."

Deacon gripped the small man by the collar and threw him back toward Sanctuary's black mouth. "You don't need to do a goddamn thing," he warned. "Except get the boss."

Uninjured, but lightly vexxed, the small man scanned the group of six with his nose to the air as if he were breathing their aggravation. "He will not be pleasssed with your insssolencssse."

Deacon readied the back of his hand to strike. Locust yelped and scurried back into the cave without another word. The selection of acolytes all laughed at the bumbling creature. All except Bishop.

"You should be wary of taunting Creator's servant," he warned. "Its loyalty is only to Him."

"Calm down Bishop. I was only havin' some fun."

Bishop turned to Deacon and closed the gap between their bodies. "And I believe you've been having a little *too* much fun for the duration of our journey. It would be wise to—"

The loud thrum of approaching footsteps interrupted the discussion. The acolytes reactively fell back in line and straightened up their spines. Moments later, four giants emerged carrying an opulent stretcher. On top was a turquoise chair shrouded in silk shades. Inside was Lexa's greatest fear.

"I trust your presence is not another test of my patience, Bishop," boomed a voice from behind the curtains.

"No, your reverence," Bishop submitted, "quite the opposite." He bowed and stepped to the side, revealing a tied-up woman on the ground. She was hunched over on her knees. "I come bearing gifts."

"Is that?" Creator asked, nearly at a loss for words. Nearly.

"It is."

The platform upon which the chair sat shifted as the silhouette inside rose to its feet. Two oily arms emerged from the silk curtains and pulled them aside. The two giants in front kneeled to the ground, lowering their handles carefully. Out stepped Creator himself. He ran a pale, scabless hand through his thick head of dark hair as he stepped onto the earth below. His long black robe flickered in the breeze.

Creator, taking no further steps into the open, commanded, "Bring her to me."

Deacon shoved his hands under Lexa's armpits and jerked her upright. "You're not gonna like what happens next," he whispered salaciously in her ear as he walked her forward.

Suddenly, Lexa's body stiffened and she slammed the back of her head into Deacon's nose. It broke instantly, cracking inwards through his skull. She spun around, looped her tied hands around the back of his neck, and, using what remained of her weight, pulled his head straight into the dirt. He retched satisfyingly.

"That's for my big black boyfriend," Lexa spat.

Immediately, three acolytes swarmed her, but not before she got her own shot in on Deacon's ribs with a knee. They celebrated their amusement of Deacon's folly with maniacal laughter while they dragged the woman off him.

"Impressive display of futility, Lexa," the one that called himself Creator jeered as she was dropped at his feet. She shrugged the restraining hands away with repulsion and stood up to face him. "Welcome back," he smiled.

Lexa spat a blend of saliva and blood at the dirt. "Been a while."

"Too long. I trust my acolytes treated you amicably?"

"They were too scared to rape me, if that's what you mean."

Creator narrowed his gaze. "Indeed." He studied her body next. His eyes traced her legs up to her hips, across her stomach and around her breasts, climbed her neck, and finally stopped at her dark eyes with disgust. One in particular claimed the bulk of his attention. "Our analogous scars appear to adhere us in some spiritual manner. I believe you and I were meant to collide again; meant to stand here in this moment. Perhaps we can begin our relationship anew."

"Save your pious bullshit for the next prisoner," Lexa exasperated. "I'm not as hungry for lies as your toadies."

Creator allowed a moment to absorb the insult, then said, "Subdue her."

The two acolytes came back up behind Lexa, hooked her arms in their own, and kicked the backs of her knees forward. Dropping directly onto loose, jagged rocks, she cringed as the searing pain shot up from her knees to her thighs. A fist was added to her already re-bruised ribs for good measure.

Creator leaned over and lifted her chin with a hooked finger. "Enough of your effrontery. Where is the girl?"

Lexa breathed in the numbing pain for a second before exhaling, "What girl?"

"My acolytes have witnessed you chaperoning a ripened child. Her fruit belongs to me. Now, where is she?"

"Never," she inhaled, "heard," then exhaled, "of her."

With a flick of his head, Creator had his acolytes lift the broken woman to her exhausted feet. She refused to stand under her own weight, but they had no qualms about dragging her. "Take her to my quarters," he ordered as her boots spelled lines of defeat in the sand. "And give her a little something for that temper."

Once Lexa was pulled into the cave, Creator stepped back onto the chair-resting platform. The two kneeled giants effortlessly rose back to their feet. "Approach me, Bishop."

While the others dismissed themselves, Bishop walked over to the suspended dais. He had to step around a bitter Locust who refused to move. Normally he would brace himself for Creator's scalding disapproval, but the only heat he feared this day was that of the sun.

"You fail me again Bishop," Creator announced expectedly. His voice echoed mildly in the unoccupied clearing. "You return with only half my recompense. I'm beginning to doubt my own judgement in your abilities as a bloodhound."

Bishop bowed. "I understand, your reverence."

Creator leaned forward and raised an eyebrow split in half by a long scar. "Though your serenity says otherwise. Advise on why your head should not be our next doorbell."

"Because," Bishop began, then paused. He overemphasized a flick of his eyes towards the surrounding ridgeline. "The child has already arrived."

Creator craned his neck around the curtains toward Bishop's cue. A solitary stone trickled down the rockface and rolled out into the clearing until it stopped at one of the giants' feet. His highest ranked acolyte reached down, picked up the rock, and held it up to him with pride. A wider smile could not have been painted with a brush.

A fter recovering from a hundred-foot roll down a sheet of loose rock, Juno inspected the damages. Her elbows and knees were all scraped, her left shoulder felt bruised, and she could stick her finger through multiple new holes torn from her clothes.

"Dang it!" she said out loud. *I'm in real trouble if anyone saw that.*

Juno shook the pebbles from her coat pockets, hood, and boots, then stood up to scan her surroundings. At first she considered climbing back to the top, but decided against after witnessing Lexa hauled into the only visible entrance. It would be impossible to maintain the element of surprise by simply walking through the front door.

A warm breeze brushed against her sweat-stained back and she realized her shoulders felt much lighter. Her bag was missing. A twinge of panic pulled down her stomach until she saw a dark hump resting even farther down the back side of the mountain. Cursing her clumsiness, she began shimmying downwards, careful not to create miniature rock slides with each step.

What am I gonna do? She mused, trying to work out something that resembled a plan. *How many of them are there? I counted the five who took Lexa. Then there was that little guy walking on his hands and feet; he made my skin crawl. And there were four huge guys carrying that thing with a chair on it. I feel like I've seen them before, but how? And where? And who was the last one? He seemed different from all the rest. Yet at the same time most familiar...*

Ten minutes later Juno reached the foot of the mountain where her bag lay. She blew a sigh of relief when she picked it up and found the top flap still fastened. Everything had stayed secure inside the immensely durable backpack Lexa had given her.

Now a little more relaxed, Juno set the bag on the ground and sat down next to it. In truth, she was exhausted. Physically and mentally. She had traveled in the scorching heat, survived an encounter with a scrappy cannibal, and raked together all of the skills that Lexa had taught her just to reach this moment. And where was she? Lost. Without so much as an inkling of how to rescue the only person alive that still cared about her.

Juno slammed her fist into the loose ground below and fell off balance. Her hand had sunk much deeper than expected. She looked down and saw that not only was she seated on an unusually soft pile of pebbles, but that they were all rounded smooth. She scooped up a handful and liked how they felt in her palm. They fell through her fingers like thick drops of water.

A few colorful pieces of plastic also made their way into the collection. Juno pinched a red one and held it up to the sun. It was just as burnished as the pebbles except it allowed some evening light to pass through its chemical makeup.

Interesting, Juno thought. *How did these all get here?*

Shrugging, she took a drink from her last half-empty canteen. The light swishing inside of the metal canister tickled her ears. But, curiously, the trickling continued long after she had capped the lid and put the container away. It was a sound she had only heard once before in her life, and it was close by. Extremely close.

Juno heaved her backpack over her shoulders and followed her ears towards the sound. At the base of the pebble-lined mountain was a circular ridge that, as far as she could tell, was shrouding the source of the trickle. The closer she got, the more a feeling of reminiscence softened her long week of agony. *To be floating once again...*

When she eventually reached the edge of the overhanging ridge, her lungs gasped at what she discovered. The same loose pebbles that had led her to this peculiar cliff poured over and down into a massive sinkhole like a stagnant waterfall flash-frozen in time. Then there was what sat at the bottom. Quiet and deep, with no end in sight, was possibly the most valuable remnant left in the entire world. Without a second thought, Juno leapt into the air and slid on her rear a hundred feet below ground.

At the base of the rockslide, Juno hopped up and dusted herself off. She stretched her neck back up to the ceiling. On all sides of her were overhanging sheets of brown sandstone that created a bubble so secure, the only entering light was from the small slit she had just slid down through. Then she walked forwards to her grand discovery. Barely glistening in the dim cavern, a colossal, crystal-black lake hovered peacefully inside the depths of a gargantuan crater.

Juno felt the coolness of the water's presence, how it brushed the heat away from her face with a single stroke. The gentle reach of the ebb and flow was more than equal to music in her ears. Not far out in front was a tender shimmer spotlighted by a single dying sunbeam. It dared her to jump in.

"Tortoise!" she crooned with hands cupped around her mouth. The echo bounced throughout the slated sphere and pulsed back into her ears. Nothing else followed. *It couldn't hurt to take a small break...*

Juno flipped off her shoes, dropped her bag—both making satisfying crunches against the rounded pebbles that made up the beach—and rolled up the legs of her pants. Then she tip-toed her sweat-stained feet to the edge of the lake and welcomed the cold water brushing over them. The chill was shocking, at first, but as each section of skin tempered, she inched one more step inward. A lost smile returned to her face.

Up to her knees now, she felt the water soak into her pants. It was an unpleasant feeling despite the refreshing coolness.

"Well, no one's around," she shrugged to herself.

Juno sloshed back to shore and undid her waistband. But just as she had her pants around her knees, a mechanical thrum scared her flat onto her back. The sound echoed off the walls in the same way as her voice had. It was an uneasy noise, so deep that it shook her insides. In turn, she yanked her pants back up and slipped behind a nearby boulder.

The humming continued without cease while Juno's heart raced towards an invisible finish line. She inhaled deep breaths to slow it back down to idle before she dared look around.

Nothing in the cavern had changed, save for the slight ripple on the surface of the blackened lake. Juno crept back out into the opening. She was still alone. Her bag and shoes remained untouched.

Where is that sound coming from?

The thrum was too large for humans to make. It almost reminded her of the electric power inside the Zeiss Home, but amplified beyond compare. Her eyes scanned the edges of the vastness, slowly adjusting to the unswallowed light in the cave.

Over there!

On the opposite end from where she stood, a faint circle of illuminance beckoned her. The glow came from what appeared to be a tunnel leading deeper into the mountain above. There were other objects highlighted as well, ones that protruded from beneath the water. Despite the larger-than-life atmosphere of the cavern, everything felt so artificial. So...man-made. If this did not represent a beacon leading to Lexa, she thought, *Then I don't know what would.*

Juno shoved her shoes and socks inside her backpack and zipped up all the zippers, buckled all the buckles, snapped all the snaps, and slung it around her shoulders, hoping it would be sealed enough to keep out the wetness.

"Right," she nodded while fastening the final straps around her waist and chest. "Let's see if I remember how to swim."

"I still don't understand why we had to shave our heads," moaned Lexa as she and Dakota trailed Pan into an abandoned library. The entryway was small and uninviting, consisting mostly of ill-funded furniture and windows abused by time. Dust blanketed everything. Hazy sunbeams streaked inwards toward an old receptionist's desk bookended by two hallway openings. "A bun would have worked fine."

"We went over this, Lexa. The purpose is to minimize distractions and to conceal identities. Now focus."

Lexa was beginning to notice how Pan always said her name with a certain air of exhaustion. She stopped walking to stick her tongue out at the back of Pan's head, then turned to Dakota, whose hand was stifling a chuckle.

"Well I think it looks badass," Dakota added, playfully nudging Lexa with her elbow as she passed by.

Scratching at the rigid fuzz left behind by her long waves, Lexa could not help but smile back. Her and Dakota always had an exclusive bond. Not because they both exited the woman leading them down a dark hallway, but because they were unique to the others that shared that same point of origin. They were outcasts.

"Besides," Dakota resumed once Pan was too far ahead to overhear, "the new 'do will help me blend in once I ditch Arcadia."

Lexa barely saw a fallen bench in the middle of the unlit corridor and tripped right over it. Dakota caught her by the arm before her head went straight into a wall. Once she recovered, she dusted off her pant leg and asked, "You're really thinking of leaving, aren't you?"

"Hell yes!" Dakota yawped. Pan shushed them from ahead. "As soon as we find this girl, I'm outta here."

A few silent steps later Lexa released a dispirited, "Oh."

Dakota reached an arm around Lexa's back and squeezed her shoulder. "Look, I know this is your first time out on a mission. It *feels* exciting, I get it, but it's always the same old shit. We go out on a whim, we come back scarred and empty handed. We go out on another whim, we come back more scarred and still empty handed. Truth is, there ain't a woman alive that's any more fertile than the dirt outside."

"But Pan says—"

"Screw Pan," Dakota interrupted boldly, but leaned in with a softer voice before continuing. "She's delusional, Lex. She did the best she could with what she had, but she failed. Twelve daughters and not a single egg between us." Then she used her free arm to gesture between them. "Just look at me and you. My skin's like deep copper and yours is like glowing topaz. Pan's white as marble. I'd say we're mommy's little defects, but she won't even let us call her that! Hell, we might as well be total strangers."

"Thirteen," Lexa corrected timidly. "Rodan is fertile."

"Yeah, and ain't that a bitch? The only one of us brought into this world with a working reproductive system and it went to the male. It's no wonder she risks *our* lives trying to find *him* a girlfriend."

A contemplative quiet followed until they heard, "Please try and keep up!" from ahead.

They separated from their embrace and Lexa shuffled on, now more careful of her footing. "I guess I never thought of it like that."

"Hey," Dakota injected with some lift. Lexa squinted at her in the shadowed hall. "I'm sorry. Maybe I'm just bitter because I'm your older sister."

Laughter came from Lexa's nose. "By *five* years!"

An arm swung out of nowhere and hooked around Lexa's neck. Dakota's rough knuckles oscillated firmly into her scalp. "And don't you forget it!"

Lexa struggled until her face went red. "Stop it!"

The release felt like a rush of cool air. Lexa gently massaged the top of her head while giving her sister the stink eye.

Dakota sighed. "There's always hope, y'know?"

Lexa was desperate to change the subject. "Where will you go?"

"Good question." As they passed an adjacent room, a glimmer of window light highlighted Dakota rubbing her chin. "I think it'd be fun to own my own shop. Sell booze and gear to travelers. Get filthy, stinkin' rich. I've heard Leadville is ripe with that sort of thing. Safe, too."

"Rich? You can't eat or drink old batteries, Dakota."

Lexa received a glare, but she did not see it in the dim hallway, though light was pouring in from a room up ahead.

"You're starting to sound a lot like Pan," Dakota chided. "Don't buy into everything she teaches you, Lex. Sustainability is great, but people *respect* money. They crave it. It comes in handy when you need something out in the real world."

"I guess. It's just that—"

The two gabbing sisters nearly bumped into the back of Pan, who was standing like a statue in the mouth of a massive rotunda. Their jaws dropped. Encircling them were towering bookshelves, each over two stories tall, arranged like desolate dominos. There were no books anywhere, save for a few scrapped covers and pages littered across the tiled floor. A stained glass dome above allowed the sun to squeeze through and simmer it all into a sepia soup.

"Why'd you stop?" Lexa asked.

"She was supposed to meet us right here," Pan replied with a fretful tone. "But something feels...off."

Dakota tapped the handle of the new kukri knife strapped to Lexa's chest, then drew out her own. "Tits up," she cautioned lightly, knowing her younger counterpart hated the substitute phrasing.

Lexa shook away her smirk while both girls moved around Pan as if she were a stone in a stream. They began sweeping the room with rigor. Almost mechanically, they checked behind every bookshelf, every doorway, and every nook and cranny. Pan remained still and observant.

"Over here!" Dakota called out after a second sweep. Pan and Lexa met her crouched down in the doorway to a room of archives. Where the door had once been latched now remained splinters, and there were black drops speckled into the decrepit carpet. "Blood."

All six eyes followed the dark droplets along the floor, then all six legs entered the archives. The room was littered with rusted file cabinets, drawers left half open with nothing inside. The air was hushed.

Dakota yanked on a curtain and light flooded the room. The dust in the stale atmosphere scattered as if it had been caught at the scene of a crime. Lexa coughed after inhaling a plume. Pan pulled her robe tightly to cover her face.

"What's that smell?" croaked Dakota, but they had all spotted the source at the same time.

The black trail scribbled a line across the room until it reached a lone, paint-peeled wall. At the center, sprawled as wide as the bones would allow, was a single woman. She was without clothes, mangled, and tied tightly around the wrists and ankles so she could be hoisted to her body's limits. Scrawled between the condemned soul's legs, using her own blood as ink, was a single word: BARREN.

Everything—chairs, cabinets, tables—had been shoved to either side like some macabre frame to a malicious portrait. This was no mere murder of vengeance or lust. This was a statement. A warning.

Tormented tears from each eye slid painfully down Lexa's innocent cheeks. She covered her mouth to hold in her despair.

"We need to leave," Pan urged. "Now."

Dakota stepped in front of Pan to block her from exiting the archives. "You're not seriously going to leave that poor woman up there?"

"Step aside, Dakota. There's nothing more we can do for her."

Pan sidestepped, but Dakota mirrored. "How can you just walk away? We can at least give her some dignity!"

Lowering the section of robe covering her face, Pan glared at Dakota with shattered eyes. "This is not the time to question my authority. We are all in significant danger. Now move!"

Despite her formidable strength, Dakota was jarred off balance as Pan shouldered her to get by. She stood frozen. Once again she allowed herself to be unquestionably walked on top of. And in front of her younger sister, too. It was then she decided she would no longer lie down as Pan's personal dust mat. Not ever again.

Lexa, avoiding eye contact with the noticeable shock on Dakota's face, slipped by more carefully. Once she joined Pan back in the domed library, a hand reached out and covered her mouth.

"Hush. We are not alone."

In the massive circular room capped by a stained glass dome, there were many doors leading in and many doors leading out. These paths branched out into the rest of the library like sturdy roots of lost knowledge, and merged at the center in the trunk-like rotunda. And inside this rotunda, backing away very slowly, were Pan and Lexa.

At first it was the footsteps that worried them. Then it was the sinister laughter. One by one, in no particular order, crooked acolytes emerged from between the bookshelves, all scabbed and grinning.

Lexa's knife was held steady at her side, but her heart did all it could to disrupt her stillness. Pan inched behind her bodyguard and pulled the robe's hood back over her head to cover her face. They were now surrounded.

"No need to hide behind that veil," a voice confidently resonated from somewhere in the room. "We all know it's you."

Lexa forced a thick lump down her throat and adjusted her grip. *Where is Dakota?* she worried.

Three men materialized from a shadow cast by the enormous bookcases and moved towards them. Unlike the rest, their bodies were proportional. The two on either side were dressed in stained rags and their faces were skewed by sores. The one at the center was smooth, almost oily, and donned more suitable attire for shading the sun; a black robe.

Must be the asshole in charge.

The smooth-skinned middle man snapped his fingers and Pan and Lexa each found their arms suddenly restrained by four others, then wrestled down to their knees.

"Is this your latest pet, Pan?" the one in charge jested. He gradually approached Lexa until he was so close their noses nearly touched. He placed a hand on top of her head to control its position. "She's beautiful...golden..."

Lexa recoiled at the drool seeping from his lips.

"...And lively."

"What do you want, Scab King?" Pan prodded.

The man's face scrunched up in distaste. Then he breathed out slowly while running his fingers through his greased-back hair, still inches from Lexa. "Do not utter that name to me, woman. *I* am Creator."

"The only thing you've created is these scabbed abominations."

That was enough to pull Creator's attention away from the younger woman. He paused for a moment, then smiled. "Are they really so different from your own failed experiments? Or is this little one a miracle?"

Lexa turned to Pan with uncertainty. *Failed? Miracle?* she asked with her eyes.

Pan, whose pale face now wore a thin mask of red, addressed their captor. "You know nothing of our research. What I've sacrificed to preserve—"

Laughter filled the room before Pan's point could escape her mouth. Lexa watched in astoundment as the one that called himself Creator so effortlessly regained control of the entire room. She had never witnessed Pan in a state of submission.

"Excellent work tracking these two down, Abbot." Creator was addressing the man to his left, though he never abandoned Lexa's eyes. "You may yet earn the honor of Bishop."

The man on the left bowed. "I am humbled, your reverence."

"Now what has Pan named you, young one? Something hopelessly metaphorical, no doubt."

Despite the rise in danger, the reins of Lexa's training began to rear in her heart rate. She was steadily beginning to focus, as if recapturing the time she had lost. "Lexa," she scorned, using the forfeit of her name as a stalling technique.

Alright. There are two holding my arms. Two holding Pan. Three directly in front. About ten between the bookshelves. I can feel the hilt of my knife brushing against my right leg. Pan could assist, but what happened to Dakota?

"Lexa," Creator salivated. "A worthy name if you are indeed a bearer of fruit."

With reclaimed control of her senses, Lexa started thinking clearly. Her years of mandatory combat training had prepared her to operate efficiently against multiple opponents in unfamiliar surroundings. Something she begrudgingly excelled at. And she knew the first step was always to suck the superior in closer. *Cut off the head*, came next. "How would you like to find out?"

That worked. A baleful glimmer crossed Creator's eye like a shooting star. He flashed a noxious smile and leaned forward.

Bingo!

In one fell swoop, Lexa yanked her left arm free, gripped the handle of the fallen kukri knife, cut the achilles of the restrainer to her right, then pulled the blade upwards like a ripcord. The sharpened edge met Creator's left cheek and drew a red line all the way up to his greased hairline.

Screaming, Creator turned away clutching his face. The pause of shock in the rotunda gave Lexa enough time to drive her knife into the chest of the man on her left, then finish off the one to her right. She had taken her next steps towards Pan when she heard, "Restrain her, you fools!"

The men to either side of Creator were on Lexa immediately. She swung her knife to keep them at bay, but the immediate success of her attack had altered her nerves. Arrogance settled in, her focus broadened, and her footing was unstable. She challenged them all to come forth, but before they accepted, one of Pan's captor's kicked in the backs of her knees.

Lexa was swarmed straightaway. The one named Abbot ripped the knife from her hand while the other looped an arm around her neck. Rendered helpless, she was returned forcibly to her knees. She would not be as lucky a second time.

While Lexa struggled in place, Abbot kicked her knife over to their sacred leader. Creator turned around and removed his hand from his torn face; half painted red with dripping blood, the other half with wrath. He leaned over to pick up the large, angled knife, inspected it thoughtfully, then hovered it in front of his assailant's face.

"That attempted stunt will cost you dearly," he snarled, cupping the back of the girl's head with his free hand. "Fortunately for you I am a man of fairness. An eye for an eye, as it were?"

Without hesitation, the tip of the blade entered Lexa's forehead and clawed downwards at a glacial pace. Her teeth clenched. Her nerves erupted. Her mind buried itself behind the agony...

She flinched, causing the knife to hop over her right eye, but it continued to dig a trench in her soft cheek. Holding perfectly still, she turned only her gaze to Pan to silently apologize for her failure. She was hoping for a nod of assurement. A guise that said everything would be alright, that there was still a plan. But Pan only faced straight ahead with a rock-hard expression.

Suddenly, the same sound that a great tree creaking in the wind makes echoed throughout the rotunda. The noise moved slowly, old and deep, and it was followed by an immense *clunk*! Then...silence.

"Hnngh!" a voice stressed from nearby. A female voice.

Creator halted his torture to scan the circular room. "Who dares interrupt the Creat—"

Clunk!

Clunk!

Clunk!

One by one the gargantuan bookshelves leaned into each other and lurched their descent to the tiled floor. The boom they created shook decrepit frames and light fixtures from the walls. Glass from the dome began to crack. The ground shook.

Creator dropped the knife. He looked upwards at the crumbling skylight when a piece of glass fell and shattered nearby. He ordered Abbot to assist in his escape, shouting, "Our paths *will* cross again," before disappearing through an empty doorway.

Other men were not so fortunate. Most scattered, but Lexa watched and shuddered as three were flattened between cascading bookshelves, their screams too faint to overcome the chaos. One in particular saw the moment of panic as an opportunity to reach for Lexa's waist.

"You just gonna stand there?" Dakota barked from across the room. She had just dropped one of the scabbed men dead in his tracks.

Snapping out of her awe, Lexa snagged the approaching arm like a viper and twisted. Her boot slammed into the assailant's kneecap and sent his tendons cracking backwards. As he howled, she rolled over to where Creator had dropped her kukri knife and scooped it up before a pane of fallen glass could slice her in half. The handle felt natural in her hand, perfectly balanced, an extension of herself.

When she turned, the man she had disabled was clawing across the floor at a frenetic pace. At first she assumed he was attempting a futile escape from herself, but, when the final titanic bookshelf swallowed him whole, she smirked at her oversight.

The hole left in the dome sent a pillar of sun blazing into the center of the rotunda. Stagnant dust hung in the air, slowly pulled up and out by a blinding tractor beam. During that time Lexa joined Dakota in the room where they had found the scourged woman and waited for the outside air to clear. The first thing she noticed was the empty wall above the blood-scrawled word.

"Where'd she go?" Lexa asked.

"I couldn't just leave her up there," Dakota sighed. "Hung up naked without dignity." Then she moved over to a cluster of cabinets and slid one to the side. "Help me with this, will ya?"

Still under the veil of shock, Lexa sauntered over. They moved a filing cabinet out of the way to reveal a body-shaped object wrapped in the same rags the scabbed men had been wearing. "Where did..."

"Got 'em off a couple of those men while they were searching the building. I decided to thin the herd a bit while I came up with a solid rescue plan. Worked out pretty well, if I do say so myself." Then, noticing her companion was not expressing the same level of satisfaction, she added, "How's your eye?"

"Fine," Lexa lied. It hurt a lot. She watched as Dakota hefted the body up and over her shoulder with ease.

"Yeah, the first scar's always the hardest," she cajoled, but when she saw the look on Lexa's face she knew the knife had cut more than just her skin. "I'm sorry I couldn't get there sooner. I had to wait for the proper opening. Besides, it's not like Pan was attempting any heroics."

Oh no, Pan! "Where is she? We need to find her!"

Shaking her head, Dakota started towards the door, unconcerned with Lexa's plight.

"Where are you going? What if they took her?"

Dakota stopped. "Look, Lex, there are some hard truths you're going to learn about this world. One of them is that Pan doesn't give a shit about your safety, or mine. Only her own. She fled as soon as there was an opening. Probably halfway back to Arcadia by now."

Lexa tried to protest, but the words jumbled up in her throat. Instead, a swirl of dust circled quietly between them.

Forcing a smile from the dejection, Dakota proposed, "Why don't you come with me?"

A tear drew a line down Lexa's bloodstained face. As the salt entered her new wound she winced. "You can't just leave! What about home? What about me?"

Dakota gently set the woman's wrapped body on the ground and went back over to her younger sister. She wrapped her arms around

Lexa tightly. "I just can't do this anymore. The neglect, the terror, the hopelessness. Arcadia's taken its toll on me. I'm sorry, Lex, but this is goodbye."

"But..." Lexa whimpered, trying not to cry into her tender cut, "...I need you."

Dakota released from the hug and jabbed a finger into Lexa's chest. "Girl, you don't *need* anyone. You're strong, probably stronger than me, and a hell of a lot stronger than those fools back at Arcadia. So from here on out, all you need to do is keep on being strong. For yourself. Understand?"

Sniffling, Lexa nodded.

"Good," Dakota said with some finality. She heaved the body back over her shoulder and drifted once again to the door, pausing before she left. "If you're ever in Leadville, look me up, alright?"

And with that, Lexa found herself all alone. The sweeping silence of abandonment started to engulf her. What would she do now? Should she run away? Could she even go back to Arcadia? Would she ever be able to look Pan in the eyes again? Her whole life she had followed unquestionably, and now, abruptly, everything came into question.

Keep on being strong, she tried to convince herself, but a looming message had forcibly dug itself into her entire existence and nested. Everyone she had ever believed in was gone now. She could no longer embody who she thought to be Lexa. She was an empty shell. Her life, her heart, her loin, all of it...

BARREN.

K*eep on being strong...*
Snap! Snap!
For myself...
Snap! Snap!
"Is she deaf?"
For Juno...

"Perhapsss the other ear, Massster."

Snap! Snap!

Lexa flinched at the sharp noise stabbing at her brain like needles to a pincushion and groggily awoke. Harsh artificial light assaulted her unadjusted pupils. "What's...huh?"

"Finally," a voice entered. "We should have reduced the dosage given the state of her body."

Her mouth was dry as a desert. Her vocal cords cracked. "Where... who are you?"

A brazen chuckle and a snickering hiss pulled her slightly further into the consciousness.

"Have you already forgotten my voice? I'm insulted, Lexa."

The inflection on her name sparked a long dormant pilot light flickering under her gut for over a decade. The rotunda. The body. Her own knife's edge scraping down her face. The abandonment. Each painful scene from her past added more fuel to the inner flame.

"Imposssible, Massster," the other voice goaded. "No one forgetsss Hisss holinesss."

A wet, smacking sound followed.

Lexa flailed. As she attempted to stand, something cold and rough wrapped tightly around her bare skin prohibited her movement. It clinked as it impeded her stiffened body from extending. It was then that she realized she had been stripped down to her underwear and tied up with chains. "What have you done to me?" she slurred.

Her captor's silhouette floated into view. He spun a chair out in front of her, sat down, and leaned his elbows casually onto his knees. His shirtless torso had a sheen. "You've been relieved of anything that could potentially be used against me. Standard precautions, I assure you."

Lexa shivered. Partly from the cold metal nipping at her exposed skin, and partly because the strange, almost rhythmic, smacking sound would not leave her ear. "Let. Me. Go."

"I'm afraid I can't do that. Last time we were in close proximity we both nearly lost an eye. I will not underestimate you again. Besides, you're in no position to negotiate."

"The oilsss are mixsssed," the other voice hissed from nearby. "Presssent the holy ssskin."

While Lexa's stomach churned at the sound of the sloshing, she attempted to assess the room. It was a habitual process she had practiced countless times before, but never through the fog of a strong sedative. Was there a large, windowed overlook at the far end? Were there highly sophisticated machines and computing units along the walls? Did she see lockers to the right? Had there been a small, rawboned man kneading Creator's skin like wet dough? She could not yet be sure.

"Very good, Locust. You know the spots."

"Of courssse, Massster."

During the nauseating kneading, Creator stretched out a finger and stroked Lexa's scar. She recoiled from the oily digit before he could trace the entire length.

"You disgust me!" Lexa sneered, or at least gave it her best attempt. "Sending your monstrosities to hunt down an innocent little gi—"

As soon as that word escaped her mouth she spilled over with regret. There was a fleeting attempt to reshape *girl* into something else, but her mind was lagging three steps behind.

A delighted eyebrow raised from across. "I thought there was no girl?"

"There isn't."

"Ssshe liesss!" Locust whispered into Creator's ear as his hands wriggled around his pale neck.

Creator held up a patient hand to silence the impatient associate. "A welcome side effect of our sedative is an unfiltered fountain of truth from its host." As he spoke, he leaned over to pick something up from the ground, then returned with a tray cradling a plate of food, a cup of water with a straw, and a spoon. All plastic, Lexa noted. "Another is hunger."

Lexa abhorred not being in full control of her mind, but, to be fair, it had not been razor sharp for months. Other feelings had unwittingly been allowed to seep in ever since meeting Juno, massaging her hardened judgement. Compassion, empathy, fear...maybe even love...all ultimately led to her capture. She had gone soft, as they used to tease when she showed the same affections for Rodan, dangerously so.

Despite it all, she could no longer ignore the cramps pulling at the pit of her empty stomach. So, despondently, she decided to play along and separated her lips.

A smile crafted by a lifetime of superciliousness stretched its way across Creator's mouth. He spooned a portion of brown slop and inserted it into Lexa's.

Refried beans, cold, she grimaced, slowly working the thick paste with her arid tongue. After she forced it down her throat she was allowed a sip of water from the plastic straw.

"Now," Creator began as two bony hands glided over his shoulders and down his chest. "Here's how we'll proceed. I will ask you a question and you will give me an answer. If the answer is to my liking, you'll receive more food. Understood?"

Skeptically, Lexa nodded.

"Excellent. Tell me, does the girl bear fruit?"

Lexa stared back with ice in her eyes. She would die of hunger before selling that answer.

"Of course your foolish pride would conceal that information. Fine. How old is she?"

More silence, except for the hands slopping oil and smacking onto skin.

"No? Surely you must be starving." Creator paused, proving his patience. "Alas, we'll try a different route. Where is the girl's mother?"

Considering the circumstance Lexa figured, "Dead," was a safe enough answer.

"Hm." Creator held out another spoonful of brown paste and watched Lexa chew. "So her escape was unavailing after all. Not that it hardly matters. We had already extracted the information we needed from her. In the end she only postponed the inevitable."

Every word from Creator's mouth nearly made Lexa spit out her food, but the hunger begged her to keep it down. "Was that a question?"

"No," he mused, stroking his chin. "No, of course not. Try this. Do you know what it is we do with the fruitful?"

The word BARREN flashed across Lexa's mind in blood-red letters. "You torture them."

Creator had the straw ready for her lips, but set the cup back on the tray instead. "Quite the contrary. I release them of their Earthly burdens. Through my grace they are transcended. Why would anyone want to abscond salvation?"

Lexa's mind was solidifying by the second. The nutrients in the food poked holes in the waning drug inside her veins. "Could be she desired freedom. Or could be she, you know, liked living."

"Freedom? Bah!" Creator dismissed with a hint of revulsion.

Locust's head emerged from behind Creator, fingertips making small circles in his master's temples. The leather hood had been removed and his eyes were the color of his skin. "Sss, sss, sss," he snickered.

The disturbing massage calmed Creator and he continued. "It was because she, like all of you, failed to comprehend the intelligent design that only I can constrive." He sighed heavily, then asked, "Did she flee to Arcadia?"

Lexa, more responsive now, tested the path of strategy. "Yes"

Enticed, Creator brought the straw to Lexa's mouth so she could drink. "Why?"

"To deliver a message."

A bite of refried paste.

"And that message was?"

"No idea. She delivered it to someone else."

The spoon dropped to the tray and Creator leaned forward. Locust's massage followed without a hitch. "And you just *happened* to foil my men at every turn for the last two months? I'm no fool, Lexa. Elaborate."

"I was paid to find some kid in Denver. Your band of idiots just got in the way."

"Pan," he cursed, more to himself than to Lexa. "Why must she always meddle in things she does not understand?"

Lexa smirked, surprising herself. "You can say that again."

Beguiled, Creator fed her another bite out of sheer agreeance. Locust's kneading continued under his armpits and down his side. The air between them constricted while she averted her eyes and chewed quietly.

"Did you know," Creator began again, "that once the girl is in my clutches it will only be a matter of time before Arcadia falls?"

Lexa coughed on her swallow. Arcadia was a near impenetrable fortress. "And exactly how are you planning to accomplish that?"

"Now now, it is I who asks the questions here. Unless you're full?"

She submitted, shook her head, and was allowed another bite. While chewing, Lexa retreated into her own mind, trying to traverse old escape training scenarios of the past, but a chemical roadblock was still in place.

"Open her eyesss," Locust advised as he applied more oil.

Creator ran a hand through his slick black hair and considered quietly for a moment. "I suppose a morsel of truth won't slow down our advancement."

"Precsssisssely."

I can't wait to hear this...

After adjusting in his seat so that Locust could reach his lower back, Creator began again towards Lexa.

"Pan has run out of time. Her scientists are aging. In a couple of decades they will die. And lost along with their lives will be their pathetic research. Even if they opened their doors today, no one alive would be able to operate their machines or even read what they have written.

"Then there's you and the other lab rats. Once formidable, yes, but you will all lose your tenacious allegiance to Pan's delusions when you realize how misguided she is. The senseless woman placed the entirety of her stock in reviving the world the natural way, the *old* way, and what does she have to show for it after all these years? Twelve barren bitches and an oversized garden.

"The simple truth is that Arcadia is a crestfallen monument to centuries of wasted effort. And without the girl that dome will be on the brink of collapse. Pan will have nothing left. Neither will you. So how does it feel to be so completely, utterly worthless?"

Fighting the chains around her body and brain, Lexa lashed out. "What makes you think *your* way is the right way? All you've done inside this forsaken mountain is churn out abominations!"

Creator sprung to his feet, face red with fury towards defiance. Locust tumbled off the back of the chair and hit the ground. "Because *my* way is the future! No one would admit that man needed to adapt, *needed* to evolve, yet now I, and I alone, have the power to create life, to give birth to a *new* mankind. An enduring mankind. One without such wretched weaknesses to sun and starvation and plast—" He cut himself short to exhale.

Locust's cadaverous white arms reached up and helped Creator back into his chair. "Sssit, Massster."

"Tell me, Lexa," Creator sighed when his face returned to its normal pale color. "Do you know why you are still breathing?"

The change in direction caught Lexa off guard. She could not think of a reason. "No."

"An acceptable answer," said the man holding her fate in his palm. He lifted the cup, then watched fervently as she took a sip of water. "By now you are familiar with my right hand, Bishop. As his Creator, I have ingrained in him a unique talent for tracking, and an even greater affinity for watching. He *sees* things my other acolytes cannot: desires...mistakes... weaknesses. You see, it was only a matter of time before he dismantled your little enterprise and delivered the scattered pieces to me. *All* of them."

Lexa matched his malevolent gaze with her own.

"Truth be told, I cannot wait to dispose of you. You have been nothing but a thorn in my side since the day you mangled my perfect face. But the circumstances still require you as my lure. For reasons beyond my understanding, the girl seems to be attracted to you like a lost magnet. Bishop informed me that she has been following your trail for weeks..." A crocodile smile split his face in two. "...In fact, she's so close I can nearly taste it."

Rendered inert by the extreme tension of her bindings, Lexa blinked a hopeless tear down her scarred cheek. She had to find a way to escape the cold chains squeezing her skin or all would be lost. And if anything happened to Juno...

"Now," Creator resolved, holding up a different utensil. Locust had handed him the kukri knife stolen from Lexa's harness. "One last question: What is the girl's name?"

Lexa grunted as she began pulling on the chains attaching her to the pillar. Every muscle and bone in her body screamed. Every vein protruded.

Creator only smiled. He stood up, leaving the tray of food on his chair, and grabbed Lexa's cheeks with a firmly cupped hand. She spat in his face, which only ignited laughter. Then he tightened his grip to keep her head steady and brought the knife's edge up to her eye. "Time to finish what you start—"

Kshhht. Come in! Kshhht. We've located...

Locust scampered abruptly over to a black panel hanging on the wall near the door and pressed a button. "Yesss. Presssent your newsss."

Ugh. Get the boss, shit-for-brains!

Creator paused his torment with annoyance. "Looks like you will be taking a few more breaths," he said, discarding her face like a piece of trash. Then he walked over to the door and talked into the intercom.

"You're absolutely certain?" Lexa heard between waves of blackness. Fatigue and leftover anesthesia had returned to reclaim her after the wasted effort to break free. "Very good," then, "Locust, fetch my robe."

When Lexa came to, the room was deserted. She was alone again, starved and chained up like a sickly animal. Directly in front of her, still on the chair that was inches from her grasp, was the tray teasing food and a half-full cup of water. Or was it half empty?

. . .

Juno unbuckled her sopping backpack, unstuck herself from her soaked jacket, and marveled once again at her surroundings. She had made it all the way to the beckoning light; half by swimming and half by pulling herself along by some large pipes that jutted out unseen from the obsidian lake. She emerged into a darkened corridor. Above her were tubes and shrouded wires racing in parallel lines deeper into the base of the mountain. Water dripped from her clothes onto the polished cement floor beneath her boots.

"What is this place?" she whispered to herself.

The tunnel was extremely long and seemed to split into a "T" at the source of the light. Exhausted, squeaky footsteps carried her forward. *Swimming takes a lot more out of you than floating,* she realized.

The large pipes from the lake also accompanied her in the hallway and were still thrumming steadily. She considered that they may be carrying the water she had just swam through, but was not sure how such a mechanism could possibly be powerful enough to do so. Especially down here.

When she was just about to the fork, a sudden blast of warm air thrusted the beads of water from her soaked duster, followed by a rattling noise. To her right was a large circular vent cut into the wall. The metal grate seemed to be loose. Laughing at how jostled she had just become from a little wind, she turned the corner without a second thought.

Met with another agonizingly long hallway, Juno's jaw dropped along with her bag. Strange metal cabinets displayed intricate screens and buttons while levers and crank pulleys rested under wires that lined the walls like colorful veins. Innumerable doorways branched off to the left and right in perfectly equal intervals. Artificially-white light strips above cast not a single shadow. This intensity was far beyond the spectacle of the Zeiss Home.

Just then, two scabbed men donning white lab coats turned a corner. Juno snapped from her awe, scooped up her backpack, and dashed back into the darker hall she had just exited from. Another gust of air poignantly reminded her of a convenient hiding place. She pulled at the base of the grate, which came loose, and slipped inside undetected.

"Sounds like Containment Three is almost finished," Juno overheard one of the men say. "Need to initiate a new Chaplain in Containment Twenty-Seven."

"At this rate we'll be pulling out ten a day! We're already running at capacity and it won't be long before—Humpf!"

"Woah! Are you alright?"

"Yeah, just slipped on a puddle. How many times do we have to keep reminding those Laities to mop down here?"

The voices trailed away along with Juno's franticly beating heart. More warm exhaust air came down, helping to ease her over. It was soothing. She decided to use the gift provided by her hiding spot to dry off. She stripped down and spread out the contents of her backpack. Fortunately the bag had kept most of the water out so she was able to replace her cold, damp clothes quickly.

Once she was dry and repacked, Juno's nerves had calmed enough for her mind to focus. *Was there something familiar about those men?* She had only caught a glimpse before ducking, but there was definitely something odd about the two.

Eventually the area had been quiet for long enough so she slipped out from under the grate and carefully re-entered the bright white hallway. The coast was clear. Just as Lexa had taught her, she kept to the sides of the hall and stuck tightly to each corner and crevice she could hide inside. When she reached the closest doorway, she studied a sign plate on the wall next to it: `Containment 14`

Juno pulled on the handle. *Locked.* A voice yelped from around a nearby corner so she darted across the hall and, luckily, found an unlocked door. She entered.

Inside the mysterious room was not at all what she had expected, if she had expected anything. There were rows upon rows of shelves filled to the brim with colorful plastic containers. Each of them had a tiny white strip on the front that highlighted bold black letters. Juno read each of the labels aloud as she cautiously explored.

"Batteries-AA. Batteries-AAA. Batteries-C."

The lights above abruptly flickered as she advanced to the next row. She took a moment to freeze until the strobing stopped.

"Capacitors. Circuits. Conductors."

Suddenly, the door handle clicked and two men rushed in. Juno gasped, skipped a few rows, turned a corner, and sat down covering her mouth. She could hear her heart beating between her ears.

"What'd I tell ya? If we blow another damn fuse we're gonna have to send out another damn scouting party! And Creator won't be too happy if he has to wait another month for his new pet..."

Juno's heart picked up speed. *Fuses*, she exclaimed internally, then searched the containers directly across from her. *Shells - 12 Gauge. Whew!*

Only irritated footsteps were heard for a while. Then the sliding of plastic containers. Then, "Here we go, fuses. Was it thirty or sixty amps?"

"Sixty. Now hurry up, I can already smell smoke."

"Alright, alright. Hold on." The footsteps moved away, paused, then abruptly advanced towards Juno. "Say, should I grab a new servo just in case?"

Servo? Her eyes rapidly scanned the nearby containers. *Solenoids. Servo-Motors!* She held her breath. There was only one door in and out of this room that she had seen. *Get ready to run...*

"Nah. Servo should be fine. Now let's get this fixed before it drowns."

Juno exhaled ten lungfuls after the two men had slammed the door. *These men, too! Their voices were just like the ones that broke into the Zeiss Home*, she thought. *But I watched Lexa kill them...*

Baffled, she finally stood up to measure her escape. It turned out that rescuing someone was a lot harder than kicking in a door and jumping down an elevator shaft. Juno envied Lexa's resolve and wondered if she had ever been afraid, too. It did not seem likely.

When Juno's hand reached the knob of the shelved room's door, something tugged at her. A voice. Two voices. A single phrase she had overheard multiple times: "You ain't got no shells for that thing."

Shells - 12 Gauge!

Juno rushed back over to the bin with the familiar sounding label. She popped open the lid and was greeted by hundreds of red, gold-tipped cylinders. Delighted, she scooped as many as she could into the main pouch of her backpack and muttered, "Hope these come in handy," triumphantly.

Once back in the hallway, Juno slipped by the corridor with the broken fuse and bumbling men. She caught a whiff of the electronic smoke they had mentioned as she slipped by. Then, trying to gain as much ground as she could while the workers in white coats were distracted, she ventured deeper into the mountain.

Time moved slowly as door after door passed by in the endless bright hallway under the mountain, and the monotony became dizzying.

"Containment Eight." She read under her breath as she walked by. "Containment Six. Containment Five. Containment Four...Wait a minute!"

Directly across from the door labeled Containment Four was the number 3 she had overheard the two men complaining about when she had arrived. She stepped over and saw a strange saturation of green trying to escape from the gap between this metal door and its frame. *Almost finished,* she recalled, drawn towards the mysterious light like an insect. *But what's almost finished?*

Without apprehension, Juno turned the handle until it returned a satisfying click. The door opened smoothly, silently, and allowed the emerald glow to bask her.

Inside was lined with the same metal cabinets littered with screens and buttons, but they were not the focal point of this space. At the center was the true marvel. An enormous spherical tank suspended between two vertical columns—one extending from the ceiling, the other from the floor—appeared to be levitating with the assistance of thick black cabling snaking all around. Inside, the clear glass orb was filled to the brim with some type of green liquid and, floating at the center, was a darkened mass.

Juno inched closer. Her mind was perturbed, her body was shaking, her skin was crawling. Hovering above, the curled mass began to take form. It was huge, a giant compared to her, with bulging arms like knotted branches and fists like sledgehammers. It floated unconsciously, bobbing up and down with the filtering fluid. One of the snaking cables entered the body through the stomach and another was suctioned to the mouth. Despite the disfiguring liquid and tubing, she felt this monstrosity held some familiarity as well. As if she had met this being in the past. Where or when escaped her, but a residual fear of it still lingered deep inside.

Now directly beneath the tank, Juno reached a weary hand up to the glass. It was warm on her palm. She could see clear bubbles escaping the swirling green bath, feel the vibrations of connected tubes, and hear the—

"Quite impressive, isn't he?"

Juno's heart froze solid and plunked into the acid of her stomach; fizzing wildly. Her hand fell from the glass.

That voice...

Juno had never heard it, but somehow she knew exactly who it belonged to.

Costively, she turned around. The first thing that struck her was his face. The slick black hair, the crocodile grin, the steadfast eyes. It was a face she had not been able to escape since her abandonment at the Genesys building.

Standing across the room from Juno was Cameron Friedrich.

Except it was not Cameron Friedrich. Not really. It was more of a representation, like he had been drawn from the memory of a memory. As if his features were implanted on someone else's scabless, oily body.

"I have waited an eternity for this moment," Friedrich beamed. Due to his long black robe, it looked as if he hovered over to an illuminated panel. "And at last I have you; the final bearer of fruit!"

Juno suddenly felt shrink-wrapped. Unable to move, unable to breathe. Stuck in place until she was cut free. Speaking to her, as clearly as the glass tank behind, was a ghost. A dead man deteriorated to dust for dozens of lifetimes. Yet he was right there. Standing. Moving. Breathing. Talking.

Friedrich pressed some buttons and pulled on a lever. The green fluid in the tank began to swirl faster. "It has taken centuries to perfect the process, but I can now replace a fallen Behemoth within a month. Others even sooner."

Despite the harmless pleasantries coming from the ghost of Friedrich, his unnatural appearance was still constricting Juno like an invisible forcefield. She had to remind herself to inhale and exhale. To blink and think. What alternate reality had she just stumbled into? One where people no longer die? Was Kareem also hiding around the corner?

The emerald fluid spiraled downward, sloshing as it emptied through the base column. Clean air sucked in from the top. The monstrosity inside stirred as it took its first true breath.

This was enough to snap Juno free of her stupor. Ice thawed around the cogs in her brain and they began to turn once again. "You're...you're Cameron Friedrich."

After turning a dial and tapping more buttons, Friedrich looked up. "No," he said, amusement across his face. "*I* am Creator. Friedrich is a forgotten relic. A mere vessel for my reincarnations. A precursor to my all-encompassing glory."

Juno stepped backwards.

"You do not appear moved by my title. Perhaps you've overheard plebeian utterings of the phrase 'Scab King' on your ventures?"

She had heard it once. The men from Leadville said it to Lexa.

"A despicable label, really. The envious always develop such scornful names to dehumanize the superior," he deliberated while stroking a facial scar Juno noticed was similar to Lexa's. Then, with rigor, added, "Myself and my acolytes have transcended the human form; each generation a more indomitable duplicate of the former."

What is he talking about? Creator? Reincarnations? Duplicates?

The flushing liquid behind gulped as the last of it left the enclosure. Already a tightly-wound ball of nerves, Juno jumped and spun around. The giant was on its hands and knees, pulling at the tubes inserted into its body. It was groaning in desperation.

Shlunk! went the tube from its stomach and *shplop!* went the tube from its mouth. Creamy liquid spurted out from their ends. Then, frantically, the colossal being gasped for its first breaths of air and fell head-first into the glass. *Thoomp!* It remained still until the being's lungs were forced to learn the steady rhythm of self-automation. Finally, face still pressed against the enclosure, it opened one eye, followed by the other. Juno, directly below, was gawking in terror.

Their eyes met.

"You recognize him, don't you?" Friedrich interrupted. The thing he called a Behemoth had not yet learned to use its muscles so it focused its strength on breathing and seeing. "Crossed paths in the wastes? I'm postulating a shack of many knives. Perhaps an iron cage filled with a shipment of merchandise?"

Creator paused to study Juno's reaction, but she remained as placid as his Behemoth, staring back and forth at each other like familiar strangers.

"How is this possible?" she finally asked, not retracting her glued gaze. "How are *you* possible?"

Friedrich worked the computer a little more, then floated over to Juno at the containment structure. "My creations are the future of mankind. Its final evolution. Only through constant improvements to man's woeful DNA can we continue to thrive."

Attention still on the massive creature attempting to use its limbs for the first time, Juno said, "But you were supposed to cure all the existing people. Not make new ones!"

An unsettling laugh bounced up and down in Friedrich's throat. "It was never my intent to save the human race. They were pathetically fragile, unable to cope with the intrusion of a few novel chemicals. They could not even accept that their mutations were an evolutionary gift at the fractional expense of fertility. But *I* found the solution. It was written long ago in sacred texts. Long before Cameron.

"So, armed with blessed knowledge and boundless resources, I invited top geneticists and engineers here to Sanctuary and gave them the tools needed to solve the last bastion of human advancement: Creationism."

Juno looked confused. Or maybe she was still processing the bombardment of new words to her vocabulary. "Creationism?"

Creator nodded. "Clones. Replicants. Rapid Evolutionary Change. Whatever you can wrap your young mind around. But to the world it means that I, and I alone, have the sole power to create life."

Juno's stomach retched. The sharp pain reminded her of the cramp she had gotten around the campfire. The mysterious blood flowing out from between her legs. Lexa told her that she was the only one left with that power. That she, too, was able to create life.

A scabbed man in a white coat entered, startling Juno, and began speaking to Friedrich, well, Creator, in private. She was unnerved by seeing so-called copies of the same men that Lexa had continually cut down throughout their journey. Was there an unlimited supply of these mutated beings?

Juno still felt queasy. She was assembling the onslaught of puzzle pieces disguised as large words and peculiar phrasings in her mind. It was dizzying. To breathe for a moment, she looked back at the man behind the glass. He was now standing upright on his tree-trunk legs, stretching his neck.

After the lab coat left, Creator noticed the girl's curiosity. "The beauty of my creations is that they are already born with cognizance. Almost instantaneously they begin to think, speak, recall vague memories of their former, inferior selves, and, most crucially, obey orders. This recipe makes them disposable while maintaining their indispensability."

More words Juno could barely calculate. "So what do you want with me?"

"A very incisive question," Freidrich complimented, his black robe carrying him back to the panel that controlled the cloning array. "God cannot compare to anyone or anything, for He is utterly unique. If there are two of us, then the world's devotion to either will never be absolute."

Juno was addled. *So he knows about me and just doesn't care? Then why was he hunting me in the first place?* "So...you're *not* forcing me to make babies for you?"

Friedrich flipped a switch and turned some dials until he had to shout over a deafening, vacuumed hiss spewing into the air. "Heavens no! Your body will be sacrificed as a final testament to the old world. Your fertile blood will drip down the face of Sanctuary for all to know, once and for all, that I am the one true Creator."

And with that, Juno finally understood what Lexa had meant by hubris. Creator was poisoned by the unyielding belief that he was mankind's only way forward. He desired nothing but uncontested power over all who still walked the Earth. And anything that got in his way, even unknowingly, would become a martyr. And today that martyr was Juno.

Abruptly, a startling blast came from behind her. The large clunk of a freed latch and the popped suction of a separated gasket followed. Juno jumped for the thousandth time that evening and watched as the newly evolved man looked around in befuddlement.

Another mechanism clunked and the giant began to lower into the metal column holding up the glass sphere. It appeared he had not yet had enough time with his own muscles to resist, so he dropped silently. When he was completely out of sight, the column whirred around, revealing an integrated door that swished open. A Behemoth stepped out into the light.

Juno stretched her neck upwards in horror at the fresh creation. He was at least twice her height with arms and legs as thick as her own body; a stark similarity to their last encounter in the shack of slaves. However, this latest iteration had charred skin like soldering wood, and parts of ivory spine protruded from his back. Pink flesh slithered between the cracks in his scabbed body like angry veins. It was barely human.

The increased tempo of her heart warned Juno that her safety net was about to snap. *Be aware of my surroundings*, Lexa had taught, but over the course of the conversation she had already assessed that escaping this room could never be an option. Somehow Creator had already known exactly where she was inside his massive compound. And even if she managed to cut him down by surprise, there would always be another Creator a few steps behind. The remainder of her life would be spent running from the same deranged man.

However...

If hubris was the same type of poison that blinded someone from reality, maybe there was a way to use it to Juno's advantage. If she submitted, if Creator truly believed he was victorious, then there was a possibility he would turn a blind eye to a final request.

Juno slumped her shoulders in false defeat. "Alright, you win."

Creator nodded complacently. "I am humbled by your devotion."

"But I want to say goodbye to Lexa first." Then, betting every single shotgun shell stuffed away inside her backpack, Juno added, "Alone."

The rest of the complex varied wildly from the methodical sterility of the underground laboratory. As Creator's—once known as Cameron Friedrich—new creation chaperoned Juno above ground and towards what he called the Grotto, the surroundings quickly lost their luster. Walls were carved instead of constructed, floors were patted down instead of paved, and the occasional dim lightbulb flickered from a string above. It was essentially a network of natural caves.

The freshly manufactured Behemoth lumbered along through the caverns as if he had lived there all his life. Technically, Juno thought, he had.

They turned a corner and two nearly identical acolytes approached them.

"Woah!" one with a tiny left arm gasped. "Get a load of this, Jacob. Must be the new model the boss was talkin' about."

"Move," growled the Behemoth.

The second man, with a tiny right arm, was a mirror image of the first. Twins, perhaps. He spotted the young girl at the giant's side. "Not so fast, big guy. Whatcha got there?"

"Move," warned the Behemoth again.

But the men did not heed. Instead, the man with the stunted left arm leaned over to talk to the young girl. "You must be the tasty treat the Boss's been lookin' for. I can't wait 'til me and—"

Before Juno could blink, the man had been flattened against the wall like a blood-soaked rag. Then the Behemoth nudged her to keep walking before she even had a chance to think about throwing up.

"Holy shit! Esau! What'd that freak do to you!"

The pleas faded as the giant and Juno turned a corner at another dimly lit tunnel that led down a haggard staircase of stone. They emerged inside a substantial chamber. The open area was vast and mostly barren. Above was a domed ceiling so smooth it looked like it had been scooped out with an enormous spoon. *What kind of machine could have done this?*

Littered across the cavern floor were dozens of scabbed men, four old Behemoths just like the one from the shack, and a strange little man scurrying around like a lizard. They were all in various states of regression. Some were fast asleep wherever they had fallen, some were picking at scabs on their skin, and three were wrestling over what looked like a bottle of brown liquid. The four Behemoths stayed in their pack, unmoving. Two were guarding a strange platform with a turquoise chair on top, even though no one was sitting in it. The other two were standing by massive cranks on either side of the cave's perfectly etched out exit. Juno could not figure out what the small man was doing, though he seemed to be an annoyance to everyone he approached, always shooed away with a kick or spit.

As Juno was shoved along the interior edge of the cavern, far out of reach from the men in the middle, she looked up again at the smooth ceiling. Something was jutting out from the cave wall directly above. It looked like a rounded platform surrounded by curved glass on all sides. Anyone standing inside would be able to survey the entire cave from that vantage. If she were to guess, that is exactly the type of room someone like Creator would call his own.

Maybe Lexa's up there...

After being dismissed from all the other cliques, it was not long before the small man took notice of the girl and the giant. He skittered over excitedly on all fours and Juno shuddered at how quickly he reached them. The pale quadruped wore a leather skirt and a strange hat that shrouded his eyes. While tilting his head, he removed the hood to inspect Juno with pale, glass-like eyes. He sniffed at the air, then circled around to her backpack. His bony fingers extended and uninvitingly pulled on the buckles and straps. Junos heart accelerated.

"Move." The first warning shot was fired.

The small man was unclipping the top flap of Juno's backpack when he retorted, "I only take ordersss from Masssster."

Then came the second warning. "Move."

Juno clenched every muscle in her body tightly. If this creature discovered what she had stolen from the lab below, her bargained time with Lexa would be terminated. Her moonshot grounded. He would notify Creator and she would find herself hanging from the front door in no time. Alone.

Fortunately the Behemoth did not care about the small man's sense of entitlement. He had been ordered to do one job: escort the girl to Creator's quarters. So he took a clumsy swing at the gaunt creature.

The small man scurried under the Behemoth's massive arm with ease, then hissed, "You ssshould learn your placssse."

As one monster lumbered and the other one skittered, Juno took a step backwards. She did not want to become a victim in this bizarre altercation. A darkened entry in the cave wall, just below the viewing platform, made itself known. It called to her, insisting it contained what she seeked. She looked back at the two abominations. The small one was on the big one's shoulders, covering the Behemoth's eyes while its huge arms flailed in the air. She had plenty of time.

One step backwards. Two steps backwards. Three steps backwards.

Run! Juno had made her escape.

Deep inside the safety of shadowlit halls, Juno crept through the inky tunnels unseen. One led this way, another led that, but she gradually worked her way upward in what she thought was the correct direction. She hoped all of the traveling she had done with Lexa and Kareem increased the perception of her internal map enough to find Creator's overlook.

Sprinkled in with the bewildering formations of natural caves was the added dread of being caught at any second. All it would take is for one pair of eyes to spot her and this would all be for naught. What was left of mankind would die along with her. She had already scooped from the bottom of her reservoir of luck and was afraid only fumes remained. Fumes that were evaporating quickly.

And if disorientation, terror, and existential duty were not enough to fill her swirling mind, weariness was. An unexpected yawn reminded Juno how late into the night she was. She had not slept in over a day, and had not slept well in the days before that. But she needed to press on. Juno rubbed the sleep from her tired eyes, hoping it would not come back.

"I wonder when the boss'll turn Lexa over to us," said a voice from around a corner. "I need to return the favor she did on my nose."

Juno caught a gasp leaving her mouth with a quick palm. *Lexa's alive!* She pushed her back up against an unlit section of cave wall, determined to blend in, and stretched her ear for any clues.

"Soon enough, Deacon. Soon enough. Creator is deeply gratified by our service. His reward will be bountiful."

They must be the ones that captured her. The ones in dark clothes. But where is she now?

"Well the longer we stand out here with our thumbs up our asses," the first voice continued, "the higher chance she'll drop dead on her own. I like 'em *alive*, Bishop."

"Patience. Securing this door is our final favor to Him. Let us stand proudly."

"Yeah, yeah..."

All the while Juno had been inching closer to the conversation. Before the corner rounded, there was a convenient cutaway in the wall that she was able to slip into. *Lexa must be behind the door they're talking about*, she resolved, *so how do I get them to leave?*

Just then the reptilian pitter-patter of a creature walking on all fours stopped directly out in front of her nook. It sniffed the air. Juno held her breath. Even in the limited light of the cavern she knew it was the pale, slithering man from earlier. But where was the Behemoth?

Abruptly, the small man stopped his inhales, and peered into Juno's hole. His eyes were milky dots inside his ghastly skull. All of his fingers gripped the jagged edges of the rock as he leaned inwards. Then—

"The fuck're you doin' here, freak?"

The small man hissed, then scampered away towards the voice. A horrible stench of putrid breath slunk into Juno's nose. Her eyes teared.

"There'sss an emergensssy!"

"Then why are you skulkin' around like a lizard?"

Juno overheard some muttering, a guttural gasp, a shuffling of feet, and what sounded like flesh contacting stone. Hard.

"Start talkin'!"

"The girl!" the small man coughed. "Ssshe hasss essscaped. Mussst—*ackh! ackh!*—find her!"

Arguing followed. Blame was passed around. The small man was not released.

"If we do not locate the girl immediately, liability will lie on our shoulders. Come, Deacon, we must resolve this."

Only when all four sets of limbs stomped and pittered away did Juno exhale. *Whew! Sounds like I'm safe for a second.* She waited a few more moments until all was truly quiet, slipped out of her nook, and turned the corner.

A solid plate of metal was perfectly etched into the uneven wall of stone. It was smooth and flat, with no discernable handles, but something told her it was the door she was searching for. When she pushed on it, nothing happened. Footsteps clomped down an unknown hallway in the distance. Frantically, she began tracing the border of the frame with her finger.

Something beeped.

The door whooshed open, sending Juno stumbling inside. Immediately it whooshed back closed.

Turning her head to the left, she saw the glass wall overlooking the wide open cavern housing the exit. *Bingo!* To her right, however, was a chained up woman. She was in her underwear, flat on her face next to a tipped over chair and a scattered mess of brownish paste. Her hair was short and unkempt.

"Lexa!" Juno cried, rushing over to help. A feeble groan came from Lexa's throat as she was heaved up to a seated position. "It's me!"

"Juno...?"

Yes! I'm here!"

As Juno shifted Lexa's body to find a release for the chains, it became profoundly clear what Lexa had endured to get them this far. Her shoulders were swollen, her face was beaten, her shattered rib cage pressed gravely against her famished torso. The entirety of her visible skin blended into horrible shades of blue and purple and yellow. From a distance it would have looked like she was wearing a gruesomely dyed shirt.

"Juno..."

"I'm getting you out of here," Juno assured, leaning Lexa against the pillar she was attached to. She followed the chains around some piping and eventually found a crude padlock clamping the ends together. An image flashed before her. Darkness, moaning, floorboards. It was the same type of lock as the cage.

Reaching for the sheath around her leg, Juno retrieved the knife Lexa had given her. She inserted the tip into the keyhole and pried. Nothing happened, at first, but then she leaned her full weight into the makeshift lever. Juno huffed and pushed and grunted...

Plink!

The blade of her knife snapped right off and went clanging into the distance. The padlock flew in the other. But then a force grabbed Juno by the chest and threw her up against a nearby wall. She coughed a lungful of air and shrouded her face with her arms. "Don't kill me!"

There was a pause.

"Silly girl," she finally heard, readily braced for impact. "If anyone's going to kill you, it'll be me."

Juno opened one eye. It did not matter that she had been starved. It did not matter that she had been beaten half to death. And it did not matter that her skin had been tarnished by a lifetime's worth of scars and bruises. Standing underneath the bleaching white light was the unmistakable silhouette of the most powerful, most beautiful, most resilient woman she had ever known. "Lexa!"

As if removing a dress that was far too tight, Lexa slid the chains down over her waist and stepped over them. Then she reached upwards to elongate her stiffened body as far as it would stretch. Finally, she kneeled down in front of Juno and wrapped her arms around the young girl.

"You're so stupid for coming here," Lexa scorned, then gently added in Juno's ear, "Thank you."

Juno returned the hug as tightly as she could.

The moment between them only lasted seconds before Lexa was already back on her feet. "Well, I'm naked, and you just broke your only weapon. What now?"

Juno stood up, too, and scratched her head. "I guess I haven't really thought much farther than this."

"I'm teasing," smiled Lexa. The expression was alarming, but most welcome. "I'm assuming they already know you're here?"

Juno watched Lexa's battered body contour against the harsh light as she started searching the room and wondered how they could possibly survive what was on its way. "Yes. I saw Friedrich..." she swallowed, "... alive. He grew a whole man in a big green tank."

An acknowledging noise came from Lexa's throat as she opened and closed some drawers.

"Lexa, what goes on in this place? I'm really scared."

"It's called cloning," she said bluntly, continuing her probe throughout the room. "An old technology he thinks he's perfected. Friedrich's been meddling with an unnatural power for centuries. But he's not even Friedrich anymore; just a copy of a copy of a copy. With each iteration his mind deteriorates deeper into madness. He truly believes he is God now. Or, as he calls himself, Creator."

Juno had set down her backpack and started looking around as well. For what, she did not know. "Like the God Kareem told us about?"

"Similar," Lexa scoffed. She was pulling on the stubborn door of an upright locker. "Probably even more full of himself, to be honest. He thinks that he's handbuilt the next evolution of humans. Ones that don't need water or food or love. In his mind, people like you are no longer worthy of existence. That's why he…got it!"

The locker door flung open and sent Lexa to the floor. Her legs were still rubbery from being chained up for so long. Concerned, Juno dashed over to assist.

As if a drop of luck still laid unevaporated inside Juno's reservoir, the locker miraculously housed all of Lexa's belongings. Clothes, jacket, boots, backpack. Even the shotgun was leaning upright against the back.

Lexa dug out her shirt and pants and yanked everything over her limbs. Socks and boots were next. Then she strapped the sheathing apparatus tightly around her torso. She cringed as she pulled the slack from the leather bands, but at least they would hold her bones together. Finally, she leaned over and pulled three items from her backpack: a two-way radio, her flawless kukri knife, and a thin cylinder with an orange cap.

"What about your bag? Or your coat? Or the gun?"

"Dead weight," Lexa dismissed. She turned a knob on the radio and asked if anyone was on the other side. Nothing but static returned. Then she tossed it to Juno. "Keep it on and put it in your bag. We're not far from our destination."

Juno caught the hand-held radio and walked it back over to her own backpack. She kneeled down, unzipped the top, and was proudly reminded of the bounty stolen from Creator's lab. "Uh, Lexa. Will these help at all?"

"Will what hel—" Lexa saw the two bright red canisters resting in Juno's palm and her mouth froze open. "Where in the hell did you get those?"

The gaping expression on her companion's face was one Juno would take with her forever. "I found 'em in a storage room."

"How many do you have?"

Juno dumped dozens of shotgun shells out of her bag. They clinked triumphantly onto the cement floor.

Lexa was in awe. "Well," she shrugged, "our odds of getting out of here alive just grew exponentially."

Just then the door whooshed open and in slunk Locust. His hands and feet slapped coldly on the floor. He had not seen Lexa because she ducked behind the locker and missed Juno because she slipped under a counter. The door whooshed shut. The room lulled.

"Where isss ssshe?" the small man hissed to himself, slithering in Juno's direction. The pitter patter filled the silent room until he came across a surprising pile of shotgun shells lying on the floor. "What!"

The small man jumped and scrambled back to the door he had just come in from. He climbed on top of the nearby desk and reached for a black box on the wall housing an intercom. But just as his pale thumb pressed a green button, it was cut clean off by the tip of an angled knife.

Sparks spewed from the box as the small man howled in pain. Lexa stepped out from the shadows, picked up a handful of shells, and began inserting them one at a time into the shotgun's magazine; six total.

"Hethen! Witch! Sssuccubusss!"

"Save it," Lexa underlined with the mechanical pump of the gun; *Chick-chuck!* She leveled the shortened barrel right at his face and advanced.

Locust clawed himself backwards toward the glass wall overlooking the large chamber, leaving a smudgy red streak along the way. "Massster will never allow your esssscape! He will sssave me. He will sssever the headsss of whoresss!"

Choom!

In an instant, fragments of the small man's head joined the millions of shards of glass splitting from the wall of windows. The sound was impulsive, immediate, indescribable, but left behind nothing more than a whisper. A scratching noise came next. It was the limp body of the pale creature sliding over the edge under its own weight. It, too, disappeared below, leaving nothing more than a whisper.

Lexa pumped the shotgun again. Juno watched a single casing flip through the air as smoke trickled from the barrel's end. What exciting and terrible power this weapon was capable of. When her eyes returned, Lexa was smiling. "They're on their way. Want to try the elevator trick again?"

Juno was ordered to fill up her pockets with as many shells as possible and leave the rest behind. She did so, then slipped her backpack over her shoulders, making sure to buckle the buckles and strap the straps tightly.

Lexa grabbed a length of rope from the locker, pulled her knife out of the intercom, and replaced the spent shell in her gun. When she returned to the once-windowed overlook, she kicked the remaining glass away and slung the rope around an overhead pipe. After tying some form of knot, Juno joined her at her side.

"Grab my waist," Lexa said.

Without hesitation, Juno hugged tightly. She could feel the rapid rise and fall of Lexa's lungs; the frantic beat of her overclocked heart. "Are you sure you're alright?"

Lexa yanked the thin cylinder out of her pocket and removed the orange cap with her teeth. There was a needle underneath. "I'll be fine," she said, then jammed the point into her thigh. A surge of adrenaline raced through her body as if she had fallen into an ice-cold lake. After a few deep breaths she picked up the shotgun and asked, "Are you holding on?"

Frenzied cries of war echoed outside the room. The thrum of footsteps shook the tunnels. Juno swallowed, looked frighteningly into Lexa's dilated pupils, and nodded.

"Then here we go."

Freedom was only a few hundred steps away. A dead sprint could have cleared it in less than a minute. But escape was not so simple as that. It never was. As soon as Lexa landed on the ground with Juno in tow, every straggling acolyte in the cavern was at full alert.

The overhead light in the smooth dome abruptly faded and was replaced with a menacing red glow. It was as if a switch tinted the atmosphere with fresh blood. Deafening sirens followed and screamed intermittently. A voice boomed out of thin air. Friedrich's voice. The acolytes craned their necks obediently to receive the word of their creator.

"Attention my faithful clergy. It is time once and for all to demonstrate our evolved dominance over mankind. To show them the way of Creation!" The scabbed monstrosities cheered with wicked pride. "Our two prisoners have escaped to the Grotto. Do as you please with the woman..." There was a short pause, then, with finality, "...Kill the girl."

One by one the acolytes turned their heads towards their two open targets. They lumbered forward, eyes insatiable with primal desire. Tonight there would be no regard for any lost lives.

Instinctually, Lexa's arm pulled Juno inwards before levelling the barrel of the loaded shotgun at the impending swarm. "Stay close," she instructed. "There are six shells in this gun. You have the rest. Keep count and be ready."

Juno blinked away her paralyzing fear with the comfort of Lexa's confidence. "Got it."

Then, together, she and Juno stepped over the remains of the small man and entered the storm.

The siren squawked. The blood-red glow flickered. The acolytes advanced.

Lexa and Juno took another step.

The acolytes responded.

The siren squawked.

Another step.

Acolytes matched.

Juno gulped.

Red light smoldered.

Choom! Chick-chuck!

Two malformed arms went flying into the strobing darkness, both from different bodies. Their owners screeched and flailed to the ground.

Choom! Chick-chuck! Choom! Chick-chuck!

A head disappeared, then a torso. The siren squawked. Reacting with hysteria, the swarm tripped over each other trying to clutch at their prey. The red glow flickered.

Choom! Chick-chuck!

The slug of spread pellets ripped through a clump of scabbed men, creating a small gap that framed the exit.

"Run!" Lexa yelled.

They both picked up their feet and darted head-first into the chaos. Frantic hands and mouths grasped for the two women, forcing them to writhe as they raced. Lexa's blade flashed in the red light, removed a crusted forearm, and returned to its sheathe before Juno could blink. When they finally made it through the cluster, a man lept out in front of them.

Choom! Chick-chuck!

Half a man.

The siren squawked.

"One left!" Juno cried, handing over five more shells from her pocket. Lexa inserted them methodically as they outran the thinned herd of pursuers.

But every second more and more men entered from tunnels invisible under the red glow. The mass of danger was growing. Lexa spun and continued to shuffle backwards. Howls blended in with demented laughter as the unhinged horde hounded them; each enjoying every gnarled advantage of their unleashing.

Choom! Chick-chuck! Choom! Chick-chuck!

Both flanks were staggered, but only briefly.

"Uh, Lexa!" Juno yelled.

"What?"

But the warning was too late. Before Lexa could spin around she slammed back-first into the hulking mass that was a Behemoth. She was stopped dead in her tracks. Tree-trunk like arms wrapped around her and swallowed her whole.

The red glow flickered.

Crying in pain as the arms mashed her already broken chest, Lexa was lifted off the ground. Her legs kicked and squirmed. Juno was screaming from below. But as Lexa's peripherals rapidly darkened from the outside, she remembered the cabin. The first time her ribs were destroyed. How she overcame. She inhaled deeply using her abdomen. Her vision began to return. Then, stretching her neck to the right, she brought the tip of the shotgun barrel up to her deafened ear on the left.

Choom!

Lexa fell to her feet and gasped for air. The hulking mass thumped to the ground beside. But there was no time to rest because three Behemoths still stood, and one was chasing Juno.

Chick-chuck! Choom! Chick-chuck! Choom! Chick-chuck! Choom! Chick-chuck! Click!

Two received holes where their hearts had once been, but the third narrowly escaped to lumber after the girl.

The siren squawked.

"Juno, shell!" Lexa ordered.

Juno, who was running in a zigzag pattern, making herself as slippery as possible, reached into her pocket. "Catch!"

The red light flickered.

A single gold-capped cylinder hurdled in the air towards Lexa. She snatched the blood-red casing, shoved it into the magazine, and pumped the shotgun.

Choom!

Juno's entire body squinched as hot blood sprayed across the back of her neck. The Behemoth froze. The siren squawked. She turned around and saw Lexa running towards her through what had once been the giant's chest.

The red light flickered.

An eager arm grabbed Juno and pulled her towards the cave's entrance. "Almost there!" Lexa yelled as they came upon a haggard spool of tightly-wound chain. She kicked a rusted lever and the metal links clanged as they slackened. The left side of the massive drawbridge shifted and flexed outwards, letting in a cool gust of freedom. Juno could hear the sound of thick liquid splattering to the ground just before the siren squawked.

"One more!" Lexa yanked Juno to the other side and kicked an identical chained spool.

Like the blast from a landslide, the hoisted billboard came crashing to the ground, sending dust and firelight into the air. More of the hot liquid splashed across the surface of the drawbridge and Juno could now see it was oil from the torches. While the continued assault on their senses was disorienting at best, there was one thing known for certain: they were almost free.

Lexa and Juno rushed from the entrance, but as soon as they emerged Juno was thrown to the opposite side of the mouth. Her boots slid on the slippery black oil, only managing to stay upright by flapping her arms. When she firmly found her footing, she looked over to ask Lexa why she had been tossed. Then she saw it.

Behind the rippling air of the torches' heat stood the final, hours-old Behemoth. The cracks between his scorched, tectonic scabbing glowed orange in the firelight. His eyes red with rage. He lurched forward onto the drawbridge.

"Grab the torches!" Lexa ordered, slipping slightly as the great mass of the blackened Behemoth wobbled the platform. "Throw them on the bridge!"

Juno stood on her tiptoes to reach the torch nearest her. When she lifted it free of its metal enclosure, some oil dripped down her hands. It smelled acrid, like the bodies in Leadville. She tossed it onto the blood-and-oil-stained billboard and the surface immediately ignited. Heat from the wild flame slapped her face as she ran for the next one.

The drawbridge rocked again, throwing Juno off balance and causing her to drop the second torch she had just freed. She spun around to find the charcoal giant heading straight for Lexa, who was standing firm with a torch of her own.

"Move!" the Behemoth barked.

Lexa only smirked. "If you say so," she goaded. Then, stepping gracefully to the side, she hurled the blazing torch at the scabbed colossus. It clipped the top of his massive head, sending flames snaking down his skin as the thick oil oozed.

Soon his entire body was ignited. The Behemoth went berserk and ran blazing across the drawbridge. The metal flopped and rattled under his weight until he reached its end and kept racing into the vast clearing like a dazzling meteor on a starless night. Finally, there was a deep howl at the empty sky before Creator's creation, as well as the fire, extinguished into nothing.

Lexa doused the rest of the drawbridge in raging flames, temporarily keeping the onslaught from the Grotto at bay, then led Juno to the side of the mountain.

"That bought us some time," she exhaled. "Now toss me some shells"

Juno followed orders and emptied two of her pockets. *Not many left*, she counted, then was startled by the blaring siren and howling madness still protruding from the flames. To ease her mind she focused on the immediate confidence only Lexa could provide. One step away, protecting her since the day they had met, was a battleborn woman thriving in the only conditions she had ever known: Chaos.

Who knew how many lives her crooked blade was forced to claim. Who knew the amount of weight trauma added to her thoughts every day. Who knew if she had ever been loved by a mother in the way Juno had been. Who knew if she had ever loved?

Still, with the shotgun now reloaded and strapped to her back, Lexa pointed a finger upwards. There was an eerie calmness in her voice.

"Start climbing. It's going to be a long night."

Whereas the Grotto was a surging cluster of tumultuous violence, the skeletal forest on the western slope of the mountain was utterly silent. The heavy smoke from the dying fire below billowed upwards and hung close to the ground like a wandering ghost, stifling any sight beyond an arm's-length. It was only the hurried breaths of Lexa and Juno that produced any discernible noise inside the thickened atmosphere. But silence did not equal peacefulness. The hunt was still on.

Their brief moments of cover would only last as long as the fire burned across the drawbridge. After that, whatever time it took Creator and his acolytes to scale the mountain would be the fuse to their fate. During that time Lexa hurried Juno deeper into the woods to stretch their distance from danger as far as possible. However, the moon found it difficult to pierce through the hovering haze, making every step a guess to them, and they eventually guessed wrong.

Tripping over a crumbled black branch, both Lexa and Juno tumbled head over heels before slamming into a wayward log. Lexa's spine bounced squarely against the petrified wood and she spun to the side. Juno went one way and her backpack went another.

In pain, but not paralyzed, Lexa crawled back to her feet. "Juno!"

Juno spat out a mouthful of dirt. When she overheard Lexa's incoming echo, she had also laid eyes on her missing bag. "Over here!" she coughed back, her voice echoing in the emptiness as well.

Rapid footsteps snapped ancient twigs until Lexa's face emerged from the dense smoke. "Are you alright?"

"Yes," Juno started, holding up her backpack. A section of the front was torn wide open. "But I lost all the shells."

Lexa muttered something under her breath, then asked, "What

about your pockets?"

As if she had lost a set of important keys, Juno patted down every inch of fabric she was wearing. "None," she frowned, then, "Wait! One left."

Lexa watched the single red casing appear from Juno's coat pocket and sighed. "Alright. Six in the gun, one in the pocket. How do you like those odds?"

Even in the pitch darkness of the forest, Juno could still make out a smirk on Lexa's face. "Like you said, we're almost there—"

"Laaadies!" a sudden voice sang in the unrelenting night. "Come out and plaaay!"

Juno was yanked behind a tree before she could even think to move. The tops of her shoulders were pressed down until she squatted low enough to the ground. Her heart picked up speed. Panic had returned.

"Just breathe," whispered Lexa, resting a hand on the back of Juno's neck. She gave it a light squeeze. "The only power they have is fear. They have nothing if you're not scared of them."

Trembling, Juno replied, "But I *am* scared."

"Don't be. As long as we're together..."

A small beam of light ignited in the distance.

Followed by another.

And another.

Soon, an entire section of the smoky forest illuminated like a starlit, swirling galaxy. Nearly fifty sticks of white light, each about a foot in length, bobbed up and down as stomping footsteps came within earshot. The kaleidoscopic scene chilled Juno to the bone.

"Oh little giiirl!" echoed another identical voice.

The hypnotizing dance of lights swayed back and forth...back and forth...back and forth...approaching ever nearer. Before Creator's hunting party was a stone's throw away, Lexa picked up a large stick and tossed it up and down in her hand, testing its solidity. "Ready?

Juno exhaled a lungful of self-calming air. "Yes."

"Good. Turn off the lights."

"Wha—"

In an instant, an invisible branch soared through the haze and clunked between a group of trees twenty yards downhill. All at once the lights halted, paused, and changed direction. Lexa jumped out from hiding and whooshed silently towards the back of the herd. Juno followed as closely behind as she could.

The first ten men were eliminated effortlessly, their throats cut to prevent any cries for help. But it was not until the third or fourth that Juno understood what Lexa had wanted her to do. She realized it as she stepped over a fallen light bar and saw the color of her clothes as clear as day. *Turn off the lights! I get it!* Then, with sweeping efficiency, she lunged from light to light and returned each one to darkness.

But the suffocation of reliable lambency would only work for so long. By the twentieth man one was bound to shriek, and did.

"They're over he—" the brave soul warned before being cut short of breath and life. The white lights all spun in unison and sliced through the grey smoke.

With a few dozen men still remaining, it was time for Lexa to adjust her tactics. She pulled Juno behind another tree and kept tightly against it.

"Run from trunk to trunk," she told Juno. "I'll be right behind you."

And with that, Juno was shoved away. She froze solid until she heard, "Over there!" then darted for the next tree about twenty feet away. Three men zipped by Lexa in their pursuit and she caught them all from behind with her kukri knife.

Unlike the light snuffing, Juno understood this strategy right away and bolted to another tree, trying to make as much noise as possible in the process.

Four more men passed by Lexa. Four more fell.

Both Lexa and Juno kept zig-zagging their way through the forest, leaving a trail of bodies and stagnant strips of light in their wake, dwindling the herd down to twenty or less. Lexa's cunning proficiency never ceased to amaze the young woman.

They were positioned for their next pass when Juno's foot caught on something and she smacked face first into the ground. Before she could recover, she found herself being pulled away by the ankles.

"Think you're clever, little girl?" a rickety voice snarled. "Now you're all mine!"

Choom!

The man was gone as soon as he appeared in a deafening flash of sound and light. It was almost like a dream. No. A nightmare.

Juno rolled face-forward to get her bearings. Her ears were ringing and the flash distorted her vision. Once she sat up she saw the back of Lexa's silhouette. Bright lights were swarming all around. The shotgun pumped—*Chick-chuck!*—and a shell casing escaped into the darkness.

The horde of lights halted and a voice spoke out. "Enough with this ineffectual charade, Lexa. I have an infinite amount of lives to spend on ending your own."

It was Friedrich. Juno would never forget that conceited camber. *But where is he?*

Unphased as always, Lexa raised the shotgun to eye level. "Then why don't you come out and end it, Scab King?"

Silence followed. The men waited eagerly for orders, but were left waiting. *Lexa must have really gotten underneath his oily skin,* Juno thought.

Then, as simply as an exhale, Creator made his unalloyed command. "Finish her."

What followed, Juno could hardly focus her eyes on.

Choom! Chick-chuck! Choom! Chick-chuck! Choom! Chick-chuck! Choom! Chick-chuck!

Blinding flashes of light. Brain-rattling blasts of gunfire. Colorless silhouettes. Screaming, howling, groaning, laughing. Juno watched one man strobe through the air in one direction, and black blood splatter in another. She heard the crackling of shattered electronic light sticks. She felt the smoke of gunpowder assault her nose. She—

Choom! Chick-chuck! Click!

In a disturbing moment of disruption, darkness swallowed everyone whole.

Shink!

Lexa had drawn her kukri knife to finish the job.

Still on her rear, Juno wriggled backwards using her elbows as stabilizers. She made it until she bumped into what she believed was the trunk of another tree...until it moved.

"You're comin' with us," a voice sneered.

Before Juno could scream, she was lifted off the ground with a hand cupped around her mouth. She kicked and squirmed, but the man had whipped her around so violently her weight meant nothing.

"Not this time," the voice warned.

But Juno was scrappy. She gripped onto the scabbed hand covering her face and bit down on the thumb as hard as she could. Her teeth snapped through a lot easier than she expected. Warm liquid poured into her mouth. The man shrieked something about losing a finger and dropped Juno to the ground, who immediately spit out the putrid digit and cried, "Lexa! Help!"

Then something hard slammed into the side of her head, plunging everything into total darkness.

"Juno!" Lexa called back, unaware she could no longer be heard by the girl. She drove her knife clean through the chest of the final acolyte, watched him drop to his knees, then kicked his lifeless body off the angled blade. Her eyes immediately scanned the trees, straining for a glimpse of movement, but saw nothing. The smoke was still too dense. The air was too still.

A twig snapped, breaking the silence.

"Juno?" Lexa called out. She took a few steps forward and stopped again. "Ju—"

From the shadows, a foreign object slammed into Lexa's torso and followed her to the ground. She flipped over to her back, but the weight of the thing hung on, refusing to let go. Something hard cracked against the side of her head. Then straight down onto her nose. She was being punched!

Like a sixth-sense, Lexa's combat training kicked in to guide her. She grabbed the inner elbow of one of the arms attacking her, shoved a palm into the opposite shoulder, then, using the assailant's own momentum, spun the body over. She was now on top, reaching for a throat with venomous hands. Her victim choked as they tried to take in air, but that only invited her to constrict harder. She wanted them to suffer. She wanted them to feel the razor sharp—

Something abruptly snuck between two of her ribs. Something hard. Something ice-cold. Something that felt no pain, no guilt, and no remorse. The life she had been choking squirmed out from underneath her and she made no effort to stop it. She just slumped down on her knees.

"Pity," Creator jeered victoriously from the shrouded atmosphere. His hand was rubbing his neck. "All of those theatrics and yet you still bow down to the Almighty."

Nothing came to Lexa's mind. No quips. No insults. All she felt was the blade's tip scratch against her lung. She could only wheeze out an incomprehensible, "Juno…"

"You should have submitted when you were given the chance. I could have numbed your final moments."

Her mouth tasted of bitter iron. The life in her veins had found an exit.

"And now, with the girl in hand, I can finally conclude the fated bloodline of mankind."

"No…Juno…"

Friedrich kneeled down in front of Lexa and palmed her head, forcing her to look him in the eyes. "Juno," he sampled on his tongue. "So *that's* the girl's name."

Lexa's head was released and it bobbed limply. There she saw it; the blade that was sucking away her life from the inside like a parasite. "No…"

"How unfortunate that you two were unable to say goodbye."

Slowly, still consciously, her hands wrapped around the black handle and tugged. The immediate twinge was unbearable, but at the same time it jump-started her brain into overdrive.

"I think I will tell the girl you fled. That you abandoned her when—"

"No!" Lexa screamed, ripping the knife fully from her flesh.

She launched to her feet, grabbed Friedrich by the collar, and drove the same blade furiously into his abdomen. With all of her weight, she pushed his stunned body backwards into a solid tree. His head snapped against the bark and his legs gave out beneath him.

"No," Lexa proclaimed. "*Your* kind ends here."

Creator attempted a protest, but Lexa had unslung the shotgun from her shoulder and pressed the barrel's tip firmly to his mouth. He shook his head to the side and laughed. "Foolish woman. You think I fear this masquerade? You're out of bullets!"

Overhead, the thick smoke began to separate. A single moonbeam shined down onto Lexa. She was holding up the seventh shell from Juno's pocket.

"You won't be rid of me!" Friedrich seethed with maddened eyes. "I'm immortal. There will *always* be another Creator!"

Poignantly, Lexa slid the final shell into the shotgun's magazine and pumped it, maintaining pressure on Creator's frightened face the entire time. The mechanical clicks and clacks of the weapon were fulfilling in their finality. The man once known as Cameron Friedrich begged silently for his life, but Lexa only looked into his inhuman eyes and smiled.

Choom!

T he expanding moonlight had turned the thinning haze into a glowing soup. The smoke absorbed the light and reflected it back with a milky whiteness nearly impossible to see through. The ghostly blanket laid the mayhem on the mountain to rest.

Lexa dropped the shotgun next to Creator's lifeless body. Finished with both's volatile nature once and for all, she went looking for the unwavering stability that was her knife. Luckily it was sticking up from the earth near where she had been tackled. She wiped the dirt off both sides using her pant leg, then clicked the kukri back into its sheath. The movement amplified a throb between two of her ribs. She chose to ignore it. There was no time to feel any pain right now. She had to find Juno before the shot of adrenaline wore completely off.

Tilting her chin to the sky, Lexa closed her eyes and listened. Her heart was throbbing inside of her head, beating her brain like a drum. Deep breath in, deep breath out.

Bum, bum, bum, bum, bum.

Deep breath in, deep breath out.

Bum...bum...bum...

Deep breath in, deep breath out.

Bum...

Bum...

Snap!

"Got her."

The noise came from not so far away. She started forward, but slowly. Running would tear apart her insides. As long as she walked, she would remain upright.

Almost invisible in the haze, Lexa lurched through the haunted forest. She used the assistance of an occasional tree trunk to steady herself during her pursuit. Something dire was trying to escape her body, and she was determined to keep it inside. So she would lean for a moment, take a few breaths, listen, then move on.

Soon she heard voices. Two of them, to be exact. She would say she recognized them, but they all sounded the same; rigid and spiteful. Judging by the occasional grunt, Lexa knew they were carrying something.

A sudden breeze flittered between the trees. Their blackened bones twisted and moaned and came into view. Then another came, wiping away the rest of the milky haze like dust on an old window. The forest was now clear as glass. And there they stood, betrayed by the sky's silver spotlight.

"Put her down," Lexa demanded, her knife drawn, reflecting the moon.

The two men froze. One shifted the weight of the body they were carrying while the other turned around.

"Ah, Lexa." It was the one titled Bishop. "Your futile attempt at saving the girl has culminated. Any moment now, Creator…"

Not another word entered Lexa's ears. She stormed right up to Bishop mid-sentence, kicked his legs out from underneath, and thrust her blade into his eye socket. In an instant she flipped her grip and used the handle to accelerate his descent to the dirt below. No longer would he torment innocent lives under the assent of a deranged deity.

"Don't move," the other warned; probably Deacon. He steadied the young girl in front of himself like a coward's shield. A shaky knife floated in front of her throat. He was missing a thumb. "I'll do it."

Holding Bishop's chest down with her boot, Lexa yanked the blade from his skull. She turned to her final target. "It's over. There's no one left. Release her."

"Impossible. *He'll* always create more life. Our reach is infinite!"

Lexa could hear the subtle trembling in his voice. He was terrified of the truth. "The Scab King is dead. The mountain is littered with corpses. You have no future beyond tonight."

"Lies!"

A careful eye would have seen Juno stir in the moonlight. A careful eye would have noticed her digging inside the pocket of her duster. And a careful eye would have acknowledged the unfolding of a small knife given to Juno by her mother. Lexa had a careful eye. Deacon did not.

Juno swiftly jammed the knife into the acolyte's leg and was immediately dropped to the ground.

"Goddammit!" he cried, falling to a knee. He raged at the blade sticking out from his thigh and gripped it with both hands. "You little bitch!"

But before he could remove the intrusion, a shadow was upon him. His gaze suddenly went from looking down at his leg to looking up at his entire body. There was the moon. There was nothing.

It was finally over.

High up on the edge of an impenetrable wall sat a boy and his pet turtle. Once again he had trouble sleeping so he snuck outside to his favorite hideaway. Usually he came out here to watch Shelby stretch her short legs, but tonight something on the horizon held his attention instead.

"Rodan!" a disappointed voice snapped from behind. "Do you know how late it is?"

He turned to see Pan's bust staring at him from the top of a ladder. "I couldn't sleep."

Sighing heavily, Pan finished climbing up onto the platform. "I've been looking everywhere for you. How did you get up here?"

Not wanting to oust his older sister's secret spot, he just shrugged.

Of course Pan already knew the answer, but she walked over to Rodan and sat down next to him just the same. Both of their legs dangled over the edge. "So what's keeping you awake at three in the morning this time?"

"I dunno," Rodan shrugged again. "Something just didn't feel right."

"Can you explain the feeling?"

"Um," he started, then quickly redirected Shelby's course before she went tumbling off the wall. "It's like...it's like something bad is happening, but I can't see it or hear it or smell it. I just *feel* it, somehow."

Pan nodded. "Interesting. And what did you hope to find up here?"

"I'm not sure. I came out here to think about it, but then—There, listen!"

Choom-oom-oom-oom!

Pan heard it. Her head jerked towards a great mountain in the near distance. There was an unusual haze lifting from its peak. Her eyes narrowed.

"But then I kept hearing those noises."

The vastness of the night immediately swallowed the echoing blast. All fell still again.

"Do you know what it is?" Rodan asked innocently.

But Pan only sat there, stoic as ancient stone. Her gaze studied the moonlit horizon patiently. The sound never returned.

"Do you think Lexa's alright?"

The question shook Pan from her contemplation and she climbed back to her feet. "I'm sure she's fine. Grab your pet. You both need some rest."

Rodan agreed with a wide yawn. He picked up Shelby and followed Pan over to the ladder. But before descending, he took one final look into the distance and said, "Good night, Lex."

Lexa scooped the unconscious Juno up into her arms and carried her to a clearing at the edge of the black forest. The moon shined down, sketching the vista with hard silver lines and filling them in with deep shades of blue. Lonely stars twinkled behind the dissipating smoke. A cooling breeze sang a perfect lullaby for the sleeping city below. Under different circumstances, the view would have taken her breath away.

But something else was taking Lexa's breath away. She leaned back into a resilient tree and slid down to the ground, careful not to wake the young girl. The shot of adrenaline had now abandoned her and pain was returning to make up for lost time. It started by claiming the wound on her thigh, which never fully healed, then crawled upwards like a hungry system of roots after a fresh rain. None of the bones in her spine were where they originated. Her ribs had been smashed to powder. And, judging by the wheeze she had just noticed in her throat, one of her lungs had collapsed.

Then there was the matter of the black stain spreading across her shirt. She pressed a finger into the fresh wound and her entire abdomen cinched up like a drawstring. Warm blood oozed out around her knuckle, ushering in a cold understandment.

In dire need of a distraction, Lexa shifted her focus to Juno. The poor thing. Half of her face was cut up and raw, and a thick leather strap was tightly gagging her mouth. "What have they done to you?"

Lexa immediately untied the knot and threw the awful thing into the woods. Next, she gently slipped the backpack out from around Juno's shoulders and dug inside for a clean shirt and some water. She dipped the shirt to get it moist, then gently wiped away the blood on the girl's cheek. It looked like another scar would soon be joining the one that she had received from the storm in Denver. *The first one always hurts the most...*

Juno stirred. Her eyes were open, but not fully awake. They met Lexa's. "M...Mommy?"

"No, Juno, it's—"

Two arms flung around Lexa's torso and squeezed as hard as they could. She flinched. The pressure had shifted her shattered bones, yet pain no longer followed.

"Oh, mommy! I didn't mean to kill him, but he was chasing me. He wanted to eat me. I tried to run first. I promise I did!"

Eat you? Lexa had not the faintest idea what Juno was rambling on about. She started to say, "It's alright," when Juno curled her whole body up into her lap.

"I'm so scared, mommy," Juno continued, her voice waning. "I want this all to end...I just want to go home...I'm not ready to grow up..."

The young girl was in shock. Delusional. Heartbroken. Traumatized for life. Lexa knew the feeling; forced to pick up another's mantle because of the way she was born. It was not fair. It never was. It never would be.

Then came the sniffling. Lexa's shoulder suddenly became a comforting rag for the warm tears of a trembling girl. Reactively, she ran her fingers through Juno's inch-long hair. It surprised her how natural the impulse felt. Something deep was taking over. A forgotten desire ingrained into the very essence of her being was now gushing from her tempered heart.

She wanted nothing more than to tell Juno that it would all be okay, that it would all work out. That they were almost home. That she would be taken care of, kept safe by good people. The *right* people. That they still had a lot of work to do on her combat training. That there was still much to learn about the world; old and new. That she was right about

Kareem from the very start, that it's okay to trust. That if she could have had a daughter of her own...

Lexa's right arm went limp and fell to her side. She could no longer lift it. Looking down, the black stain had engulfed her shirt and was wetting the ground. She now saw with clarity that no combination of words would ever stitch up the young girl's wounds. Only tears. Only time. It would be of no use burdening Juno's mind any further. So Lexa took a deep breath, looked up at the moon, and started to sing.

If the sky, that we look upon
  Should tumble and fall
And the mountains
  should crumble
    to the sea
I won't—

Juno shifted and nuzzled deeper into Lexa's bosom. With her one good arm she pulled the young girl in, kissed the top of her head, and settled into the tree. Staying awake was becoming more difficult by the breath. She looked out into the distance. Down below, at the center of the city, was a domed utopia surrounded by ten thousand tons of concrete wall. Inside that dome waited a young boy with all the kindness in the world inside his heart.

She'll make it, Lexa thought, welcoming the much needed rest about to take her away. *She'll be alright.*

But a soft voice broke through the calming night air. "Keep going."

It was just the right pitch to pull Lexa back from the solace of darkness. "What's that, Juno?"

"Keep going. I love that song."

"Me too," Lexa wheezed. Then, with every breath remaining, she continued.

I won't cry, I won't cry

No I won't shed a tear
Just as long
   as you stand
      Stand by me...

"Ok, stand by me," a familiar voice cutting through the static instructed. A song was skipping in the background.

Huh?

"I have a surprise for you!"

Where am—?

"Do you remember what day it is?"

Juno felt her body ushered forward. Her vision was blocked by something.

"Almost there. Come on. Just a bit farther."

A lattice of fingers separated before her eyes, revealing a table, a plate, and a Twinkie. There was a single candle stuck down in the center of the enduring yellow pastry. It was the only light in the room.

Where am I? The flame flickered. Its light slightly bloomed.

"Thirteen years old! Can you believe it? Almost a woman!"

Juno tried to respond, but nothing came out of her mouth. No air, no vibrations, no voice.

"Oh, and I got you something."

An arm came into view. It was holding a rectangular object wrapped loosely inside of a plastic shopping bag. Juno could see its familiar outline through the semi-transparent sack.

"Don't just sit there. Open it!"

Hesitantly, Juno untied the bag's handles and pulled the object out. It was a new notebook, just like she received every year.

Thanks, she tried to say, though the words stopped right at her brain.

"There's more!"

What? Fluttering again, the tiny flame shined a little brighter.

Certain she had pulled out the sack's only contents, Juno looked back to find there was indeed something else. Something large. Something heavy. Something kinked. Her hand slipped in and gripped a handle that was not there ten seconds ago. She froze.

"What are you afraid of? Go on!"

With enough coaxing, Juno slipped the object out of the bag and held it up. The hard edge of the blade gleamed in the shallow candlelight. She eyed it closely as she rotated it in her hand.

Where did you get this? The flame danced and gained strength once again.

Juno tried to turn her head but some invisible force held it in place. She was stuck.

"Well," the agonizingly familiar voice urged on. The owner of it finally sat down opposite Juno at the table. The increasing glow of the birthday candle stopped just short of her neck. "Make a wish and blow it out!"

A wish? What is this place? Who are you? The small flame grew brighter and brighter with every question Juno wanted to ask but could not. Her mind and body were trapped in the uncertainty of this static-filled room. *A candle? A notebook? A birthday?* Brighter and brighter still until the face of the woman across from her nearly came to light.

The song skipped again.

Lexa leaned forward and blew out the candle.

Bum *bum bum, shhhck, bum.*
Bum bum bum, shhhck, bum.
Bum bum bum, shhhck...
Shhhck...
Shhhck...

The needle on the record playing inside Juno's head kept on skipping. The intermittent scratching grated against her ears, thrusting her back into existence. She gasped for air as she awoke with immense confusion.

Eventually, Juno rolled off of Lexa's lap. The events of the night before were still hazy in her head, and the sharp morning sun was distorting her senses. She was also in a state of unidentifiable pain. One clue, however, was the excruciating soreness jabbing at every muscle inside her body. *Did I fall down? And why does my mouth taste like blood?*

She stretched her arms to the sky and back down to her toes, then spread her legs shoulder-width apart, twisted, and listened in delight as her spine popped back into single file. After her body relaxed, another reminder of the previous night came in the form of a throbbing headache. The flash of a thick tree branch blinked into her mind before abruptly cutting out. She brought a hand up to the side of her face, just below her right eye, and winced at the sting. An open wound had split the skin on her cheek. Mysteriously, though, no blood transferred to her fingers, so she shrugged it off and gazed out into the distance.

"I had the weirdest dream last night!"

Now immune to Lexa's absent replies, she brought her hand up to her brow to shade the view. There was an old, run-down town below them. It was much larger than Leadville, but much smaller than Denver, though it seemed to retain the former's charm. It began at the foot of the mountains and stretched outwards until stopping abruptly at an expansive emptiness. A few paltry mountains jutted from the landscape beyond, but it seemed they had finally reached the end of the Rockies.

"Woah, there's a huge dome thing down there! What do you think it is?"

A warm breeze gently swayed the surrounding trees, leaving behind the typical creaks and whistles, but it brought with it an additional sound that did not feel right; silence.

"Lexa?"

Juno pulled her eyes from the squalid city below to check on her companion still sleeping soundly against a tree. She marched over smugly, ready to rag on Lexa's newfound laziness. "Get up sleepyhead! You can't just sit there all—"

Except Lexa was not sleeping. Juno recognized it as soon as she stepped closer to the quiescent body. The black stain engulfing her shirt. The static diaphragm. The pendulous shoulders. Her peaceful face...

Hoping she was mistaken, Juno inched nearer. "C'mon, Lexa. We gotta keep going."

But the same blank expression she had been exposed to countless times before was here yet again. The only difference being that it was always on the *other* end of Lexa's knife.

Standing just above her unmoving guardian now, Juno felt her heart being squeezed by a phantom hand, trying to pluck it like innocent fruit still clinging to a tree. Her eyes tingled, her lips quivered, her cheeks felt the sting of tears. "This isn't funny anymore, Lexa."

She kicked a stationary foot.

Nothing.

She kicked the other one.

Nothing.

When it was clear that Lexa would make no attempt to resist, Juno's entire body immediately unraveled and collapsed to the forest floor. Out of sheer anguish, she started pounding on the unbreathing chest with desperately clenched fists. "Get up!" Juno yelled between gasps for air. "Get up!"

But the outlash had not brought Lexa back to light. Nothing would. So Juno just stopped. She was empty. Her life was just as over as her companion's. The only thing left to do was curl up into Lexa's lap and sob into a puddle of despair.

"You said we were almost there...*Sniff*...You can't leave me now... *Sniff*...I still need you..."

Every plea pestled more and more into an incomprehensible whimper. Even the tears eventually ran dry. All that remained inside Juno was emptiness.

Sniff...

Sniff...

Shhhck...

Come in...

Shhhck...

Cautiously, Juno untangled from Lexa's body to look around. It was hard to see through her flooded eyes. "Who's out there?"

Shhhck...Come in...Shhhck

Come in...

Shhhck...

The voice was a woman's. Nearby, yet skewed and tinny, like it was stuck inside an empty can. Juno sat up and wiped the snot from her nose. "Hello?"

Shhhck...

Is anyone out there?

Shhhck...

No one else was around.

Lexa, come in...shhhck...please respond...

That time Juno cranked her head toward the source. *My bag?* She crawled over and plunged her hand inside, pulling out the two-way radio. Curiously, she yelled back at the device. "I'm here! I'm here!"

Shhhck...please, if anyone is out there, we need you to respond...

"I said I'm right—"

Juno paused. They could not hear her. She rotated the radio in her hand until she came across a black button on the side with a picture of a face and some lines etched into it. She squeezed it and shouted, "It's me, Juno! I'm right here!"

Nothing followed. Her heart sank for the second time that morning. Had they given up already?

Shhhck...Juno! Thank heavens you're alright! My name is Pan...

She knows me? Juno pressed the button again, cutting off the other side. "Hi Pan! It's...um...nice to meet you!"

Shhhck...Likewise. Is Lexa nearby? I need to speak with her...

Juno's eyes swelled. She looked back at her fallen friend and felt the devouring despair swiftly return.

Shhhck...Juno?

"She...didn't make it."

There was a long pause.

Shhhck...I'm sorry. Can you tell me where you are right now?

"I'm on a mountain." Juno looked outwards, and added, "There's a city below me."

Shhhck...What does the city look like? Can you describe it?

Juno held her hand up to her brow again to shield the sun. "Um... there's a lot of buildings. They all look pretty run-down. It seems like it was built next to a huge flat area at the edge."

Shhhck...Any defining features? Any landmarks?

"Um..." Juno squinted, trying to find something that stood out. "Oh, yeah! At the middle there's this big dome looking thing."

Shhhck...Perfect! That dome is Arcadia. Lexa was sent to find you, to bring you here, and now you are almost home...

Home. That word sounded so foreign to Juno. Like it was formed by an ancient language to describe something that no longer existed.

Shhhck...But you must hurry. There's an incoming storm on the horizon.

Tangled up in all the emotional turmoil of that morning, Juno had not even noticed the climbing wall of sand, dust, and debris forming to the north. It was growing angrily, swallowing mountains whole on its path to the city, ready to blot out the sun.

Shhhck...Can you make that distance?

Alone? Juno doubted herself. She had journeyed alone for a few days, but that was still knowing Lexa was just around the corner, ready to lead her on. Her Polaris. Now Lexa would no longer be anywhere. Only in memory.

Shhhck...Juno?

Juno looked back at her fallen friend. Still composed. Still elegant. Further behind, littered across the leafless forest, were countless scabbed bodies that were as hollow in death as they were in life. Their skin charred like the trees around them. So much fear, so much anger, so much suffering. And for what?

Shhhck...Juno, can you make it?

And yet, in the wake of all that senseless destruction, there was a silver lining. A reason to continue on. It was Lexa's final gift to Juno. Life. She looked back to the radio with a grave understanding of what that sacrifice meant, and nodded to herself. "Yes. I can make it."

Shhhck...We'll await your arrival. Make haste.

Juno stuffed everything back into her backpack and zipped it up. As she was slipping on her duster jacket, she felt something missing. Her knife! It had snapped while breaking Lexa free from the chains. There was no way she would make it through a potentially populated city without a weapon. Panic pushed sweat from her pores once again.

But then she glanced over at the tree. There it was, still strapped to her chest, secured tightly inside its sheath, like always. Even in death, Lexa still had one more gift to give.

After adjusting the leather straps of the holster down to her own size, Juno slipped it over her head and arms and fastened it in place. It felt taught, but not too tight. Dependable. There was a heft to it that let her know it was ready for combat, but would not weigh her down. She pulled the angled blade of the kukri knife from its home and held it in her hand for the first time. It felt graceful and dangerous, just like Lexa. Juno knew she would have to treat it with respect if she expected any in return.

Locking the knife back in place, Juno geared up for what came next. Duster to protect her from the storm, backpack of essentials to last her through the night if she got trapped, and a sharp weapon in case worse came to worst.

But before leaving Juno took a bit of time to gently lay Lexa on the ground. She unflapped the blanket that had been given to her on their second night together and laid it over Lexa's body. A few logs were put in place at the edges to secure it from the wind. Finally, she tore a sheet of paper from her notebook, wrote a few words, and slipped it under the cover. At last she could rest.

A tear streaked across Juno's cheek as she took one final look at the third person to fall protecting her right to live. "I won't let you down," she sniffled, then started down the mountain.

Provo was the name of the sprawling city housing the strange domed structure called Arcadia. The town insignia was followed by the words `Welcome Home` on a sign Juno had read when entering the outskirts. She hoped it was true.

The sky had gone from a piercing blue to a murky tan as she made her way through a neighborhood not unlike the one at the edge of Denver. There were nice houses—well, once nice—with colored doors and interesting architecture. Juno stopped briefly at a yellow one and ran her fingers through her growing hair. How quickly everything reminded her of Lexa now. Even the frustrations.

Deeper in, the buildings turned blocky and rundown. Some had bricks missing, some had lost their roofs, but most just sat in piles of old rubble, creating a surprising amount of open space that Juno would not want to be caught in when the storm reached Provo.

But a few structures still stood strong in the wake of humanity's collapse. One such establishment was a plain brick building that Juno rushed beside to get out of the increasing wind, to catch her bearings. A few swipes of white paint spelled OASIS on an outside wall, but Juno had not noticed while she was digging for her binoculars. Unfortunately, they too must have fallen victim to the previous night because she came up empty handed.

Settling for the use of hands cupped around her eyes, Juno scanned the distance. She had lost the domed structure in the silty, darkening sky. All she could make out were dust-covered streets, a couple of wobbling signs, a few scarce buildings that had lost their features in the haze, and then the rest just…ended. She could see nothing beyond a certain point. It was like looking down into a lake; light only traveled so far until everything disappeared into—

Wait, is that the wall?

A swirl of sand suddenly blew the hood off of Juno's head, stinging the fresh wound across her cheek. "Ow!" she yelped while slipping around the Oasis's corner to shield herself further from the wind. Another gust immediately sent an old plastic bucket spiraling past where she had just been standing. She scrunched up her neck, happy to still have it. But she had also been too slow. The storm was here.

Returning her hood with one arm, and shielding the sideways-blowing sand with the other, Juno spotted a red door down a set of stairs. *Maybe I can hide in there*, she thought, but, just as she approached, three men burst from the Oasis, laughing between themselves, stumbling upwards. They were drunk.

Juno froze. Could she trust them?

The last one to the top of steps slapped his friend on the arm and pointed in Juno's direction. "Hey, boy! You lost or somethin'?"

She started to reply, but the shapes of their bodies told her not to.

All three of them were fixated on the small stranger now. Another spoke up. "Nah, that ain't no boy. That's the girl the Scab King has a bounty on!"

"Well, well, well," the third added. "It's our lucky day, fellas!"

Juno took a step backwards. "Leave me alone!"

They started to spread out and marched in her direction. "'Fraid we can't do that," the one in the middle said. "You see, I could stay drunk all year for the price on your pretty little head."

Juno kept moving backwards. She witnessed a wall of sediment towering behind the Oasis roofline; the biggest she had ever seen. A blinding crack of lightning was immediately consumed by the howling sand. Not a single one of them would survive it out in the open.

"Hey boys, get a load of this!" One of the men had already made it behind Juno and ripped off her hood for the second time, revealing her short hair and freshly scarred face. "She looks just like a mini Lexa!"

The other two laughed in unison and continued closing in. The imminent storm did not seem to bother any of them in the slightest. Juno, on the other hand, was trying to keep her heart from beating through her chest as she backed farther out into the open.

"Whoever brings her in'll definitely get that bounty. Maybe He'll even let us have a go at the girl as a prize!"

"Stay away from me!" Juno screamed as a chain of lightning crawled across the last visible section of sky. It was engulfed as quickly as the first.

A shadow crawled over the four of them at a jarring speed, dousing out the sun like dirt tossed onto a fire. Night absorbed mid-afternoon. In the distance, a rusty sheet of metal flapped free from a CamChem billboard and disappeared into the daunting cloud of debris. The storm bellowed as it swallowed the casualty whole.

When Juno's eyes adjusted to the sudden darkness, the three men were nowhere to be found. Had they been swept away too? No, she could still hear them snickering in the shadows. *I really wish Lexa was here...*

"Boo!" one cackled as he jumped out of nowhere.

Screaming, Juno slapped the man across the face as he lunged into her bubble. When she turned to run, another man appeared from the swirling dust and grabbed her arm. "Oh no, you're comin' with us!"

In a frenzied panic, Juno sent her worn boot into the space between the man's leg as hard as she could. He released his grip on her immediately and dropped to his knees.

"You little bitch!"

Juno only had a few seconds to think. The man she slapped had already recovered, and the man she kicked was lurching back to his feet. Her luck had definitely evaporated this time.

Suddenly, the missing third man leaped from the gloom and pulled her to the ground. They both landed with a thud and rolled. Before Juno could bounce back, he had already scurried over and grabbed her leg. She slid across the sandy ground kicking and screaming. Her free foot eventually connected with the man's face and he let go cupping his nose.

There was nothing left to do but run. Anywhere.

Against her better judgement, Juno cinched the hood tightly around her head and dashed into the roaring storm. She was running blind against the fragments of dirt and debris peppering her coat like shotgun pellets. Every step brought with it more of the stinging soot.

Another bolt of lighting blasted off the corner of a nearby building, sending bricks and sparks into the air. Juno ran in the opposite direction as chunks landed in the footprints she left in the sand behind. A whipping sound came from her left and she ducked just before a plastic chair took her head clean off, only to be slurped up by another blinding bolt like a vengeful straw. Then she turned again and forgot which way she was going to begin with. She was disoriented. Lost. To make matters worse, the only discerning landmarks had all been swallowed whole. Juno hunkered down and hugged her jacket even tighter to her body. She would just have to wait and hope to survive nature's wrath in one piece.

After a few moments of peppering pain, she peeked out from behind her hood to look for an end to the bloodthirsty storm. She saw none. Every direction was as dark and skewed as the last, save for three oddities that were even darker. Angrier. Advancing. The shadows of the three men emerged from the maelstrom of sand and fury with compasses fixed directly on Juno.

"There she is!" one cackled.

No...no...no...

The three men kept moving forward, seemingly unaffected by the particles tearing at their skin.

Trembling, Juno had now run out of options. She could run, but to where? They would just keep coming. Even after the storm. Even if it were three other men. They would alway chase her. She was destined to live inside this vicious, inescapable circle until the day she died.

Unless...

Juno shifted and the handle of the kukri knife pressed against her arm. Like a nudge from Lexa herself, the weapon told her it would have to be now or never. She had practiced, learned, watched, and practiced some more. Maybe she *was* ready. Maybe this is what Lexa had prepared her for all along.

All three of the men jerked their heads to follow a small duster jacket flapping away into the storm. As their attention returned, the young woman had assumed a peculiar stance with a large, angled knife held out in front. They laughed.

"Careful," one taunted. "You'll poke yer eye out with that thing!"

Another moved in. "Now be a good girl and give us the knife."

Ignoring the attacking tempest chewing at her bare arms, Juno staggered her feet and slightly angled her body; balancing weight while displaying the least amount of surface area. The large kukri knife danced out in front of her. "Come and take it from me!"

That sent all three into a recoil of surprise. She studied as they exchanged looks between themselves and uttered some words that were taken by the wind. Gazes turned back to her. The one in the middle stepped forward and cracked his knuckles with a grin.

Juno took a deep breath in, closed her eyes, then exhaled. The man started running at her. She opened her eyes and absorbed his movements, watched his drunken weight sway left and right. He lunged for her outstretched hand. Methodically, she slid her rear foot out and turned inwards. He stumbled right past and fell to the soot-covered pavement.

"Why you little..." he gritted as he hopped up and spat out a mouthful of sand. He launched his assault once again.

Juno could not describe what she had done next. His body flung forward and she spun around it as if Kareem was twirling her in the living room of the Zeiss Home. So fluid and steady. When she resumed her stance, she gracefully danced right by once again.

Then again.

And again.

Blinded by rage, the man bombarded Juno head-on with his arms spread wide. His entire torso was exposed. Juno thrusted towards him. When their paths crossed she jammed the angled part of the blade into his stomach, just under his ribs, and held on tight as the kukri knife glided through his skin until exiting near his spine. As if hitting a brick wall, he halted in broken disbelief. Then he dropped dead to the barren earth.

Since Juno had to replicate her small victory twice more, there was no time to celebrate. She turned back to the other men and readied herself.

The next two approached together; one on each side. Juno swallowed, trying to watch both with eyes being sprinkled with sand. Left side lunged. She ducked under his arm, then scurried a few steps away.

Right side darted after her. She turned, but tripped over something hidden in the built up sediment. She landed on her back. Flipped around. He was close. Then—

Crack!

The man fell right on top of Juno, pinning her to the ground. His dead weight pressed the air from her lungs and did not allow it to return. She tried to push him off, but he was too heavy. She could not breathe. Blobs of blood from the hole in his head dripped warmly onto her shirt. *Huh?* But there was no time to rationalize. The final man had already made his way over.

"Fuck the Skab King! I'm gonna enjoy choking the life outta—"

Crack!

Down he went, too.

Nothing was left but the storm and Juno and the body on top of her. Able now to focus on releasing herself, she wriggled to the side until her arm could prop up his shoulder. She pushed with great effort until there was enough relief to slide out from underneath. A deep breath was well earned, but there was still the matter of, *What just happened?*

Once Juno was upright, she was reminded just how much the sand stung her skin. So, in the haze, she returned the kukri knife to its home, decided she would never see her duster again, and set out walking until she found shelter.

However, it was not long before three new shadows hovered in the storm. It appeared her prediction had come true, only a lot sooner than she had hoped. There would always be more...

Then Juno noticed something unique. The shape and gait of these new figures was far different than the demented lumbering of drunk men. She decided to take a chance. She had to.

"Hello?" Juno called out, clutching the kukri knife.

One shadow emerged from the chaotic storm near enough that Juno could see it was a woman's body shrouded by a long, pale cloak. The woman came right up to her and, without a word, draped a thick blanket across her shoulders. She felt immediate relief.

"Can you walk?" the woman shouted over the final howls of the wind.

Juno squinted at the other two shadows standing motionless inside the tiring wind. Each was holding a long gun. "Yes."

A hand reached out and Juno took it. She and the woman rejoined the other two and together they all moved swiftly through the sandy air. Before long, they approached an area where the streets and structures of Provo seemed to end abruptly. Something was in front of them that could not be seen around or over, and was barely discernible from the hazy atmosphere itself. Only when the structure before them rumbled to life and split at the center did Juno realize it was the wall she thought she had seen when the storm began.

"This is Arcadia," the woman said in the fading wind, her voice now recognizable as Pan from the two-way radio. She looked down to Juno gazing into the emanating light, and placed an inviting hand on the young girl's shoulder. "Welcome home."

When the massive steel gates of Arcadia sealed, a final wisp of dust storm swirled into the courtyard and disappeared with a puff. Juno's neck craned immediately upwards, trying to grasp the magnitude of her new haven. From the inside it was clear that the dome was not really a dome at all. Instead, it was a series of hexagonal panels arranged in a dome-like fashion, almost exactly like schutes on a tortoise shell. Silently, the schutes shifted this way and that, allowing outside air and light to enter with boundless precision.

While Juno stood gawking at the ceiling, a strikingly yellow insect buzzed over and landed on the tip of her nose. Tiny fuzz tickled her skin just before her frightened hands swatted it away with a gasp. It flew off without a concern to her or the world.

"Oh, don't mind the bees," Pan said kindly. "They're necessary for pollination."

"Pollin—" Juno started, but could not finish the word once the magnificence of Arcadia came into full view.

A lake, no, an entire ocean of spectacular greens, yellows, purples, reds, and oranges grew from the ground in perfectly manicured sections throughout every inch of the walled-off world. Trees with flourishing leaves waved comfortably in a light breeze without any spine-curling moans or cracks. Water as clear as fresh glass trickled up and down pre-dug paths, giving life to the foliage like veins in a body. Women and men alike—some with tools, others with baskets full of colorful produce—tended to all of the plant life harmoniously.

And at the center of it all stood an intricate, temple-like structure the likes of which Juno had never seen before. At the base was a staircase leading up to a standard-looking rectangular building; albeit overgrown with crawling green vines that seemed to produce something that a woman just plucked off and ate. Above the rectangle was a ring of windows, about one person in height each, that went around the entire building. Supported on top of the windows was a beautiful marble-white arrangement of tall, rectangular slabs in the same ringed fashion. Jutting out from the roof, a steeple ten times the height of the one Juno had witnessed in Silver Plume stood proudly. Finally, at the very tip of the spire, there rested what looked to be a basket made hastily out of loose twigs. Juno was squinting to make out what the basket was for when two creatures popped up from inside. They had white heads and golden...*beaks?*

"Impressive, aren't they?" Pan commented, admiring alongside Juno. "The last two bald eagles in existence. We hope they decide to mate soon."

Just then, two women approached from across the field. One was wearing a long white coat and the other was dressed in something that would have belonged in Lexa's wardrobe. Though her skin was closer to Kareem's, the rest of her might as well have been déjà vu.

While the one in white spoke briefly with Pan, the other took notice of Juno staring at her. "Hey kid," she said, followed by, "I like your hair," and a wink.

Juno blushed. A hand touched her shoulder again and she looked at Pan.

"Please excuse me for a moment," she said concisely. "Something requires my attention. Feel free to look around. Once I return I'll escort you to your new room."

And with that, Pan and the two women left towards the temple-like building.

Juno was alone. Again. But she did not mind so much with this new land of wonders to occupy her mind.

Another insect fluttered past her face, this one much larger. It was deep orange with white dots on the tips of its wings. Juno recognized it immediately as a hundred-mile-per-day monarch and followed it curiously towards a bush of vibrant purple flowers. The butterfly, unnoticing of its new pursuer, landed politely on a stalk of petals and began feeding. Juno crouched down close to watch the insect uncurl a long black tongue.

As she admired the orange wings closing and opening, an indescribable smell waltzed into Juno's nose. The scent was fresh and earthy, sweet and pungent, femanine and subtle. Yet she had smelled something similar before. She was taking her warm clothes out of the drier in the Zeiss Home and...*Lavender!* For the first time she was smelling the authentic version of something that grew from the ground. And it was even better in real life!

Celebrating the feast inside her nose, Juno took a deep breath in, felt a tickle, then sneezed hard enough to spook the feeding butterfly. It flew quickly over to the next selection of flowers without a second thought.

"Gesundheit," said a nearby voice timidly.

Gah-zoon-tight?

Juno stood up to find the source of the strange word. There was a small person, about her size, kneeling down in some short emerald grass of some kind. Every working adult was too far away to have heard her sneeze, so it must have been them.

"Hi," Juno greeted after she approached from around the bush of lavender. "My name is Juno."

"Hello," they replied. The person stood up, brushed off their knees, turned to Juno, and flashed a warm, almost infectious smile. He was exactly the same height as her. His medium hair was dark and tousled, his eyes were as richly green as the ground below, and he had a little patch of freckles on each cheek. He also looked exactly like Lexa. "I'm Rodan."

The sight of Lexa's unmistakeable features on the face of a boy the exact same age as herself froze Juno to the bone. She was rendered completely immobile by the shock of this impossible moment. *Is this what heaven is like? Did Lexa seriously keep her younger brother a secret from me the whole time? Did she even know?*

An awkward smile eventually stretched Juno's face. Then her cheeks suddenly burned red hot as doubt reared its ugly head. Her appearance must have been hideous! Her hair was buzzed off, her clothes were torn apart, she was covered in who knows what, and she probably smelled like—

"Do you want to meet Shelby?" Rodan added innocently.

Fortunately, Juno was able to snap out of her self-doubt just long enough to reply. "Uh...sure?"

The boy turned around and started searching through the grassy floor. While his back was shown, Juno quickly wiped her face with the bottom of her raggedy shirt, forgetting about the fresh scar on her cheek until she grazed it. "Ouch!"

"Are you alright?"

Rodan was already back with something resting in his cupped hands. The top of the shell was dark, bearing a multitude of yellow streaks that created a wonderfully geometric pattern. Scaly legs were tucked tightly between the top and lower shell, which was almost entirely yellow. Juno dropped the edge of her shirt and gasped. "I'm...I'm fine."

"Do you want to hold her?"

Juno nodded wide-eyed. Carefully, the tortoise was transferred over to her calloused hands. She held it with care. At first it was afraid, clammed up inside its shell where nothing could harm it. Where nothing could get in. But with the absence of pain, soon came acceptance, and eventually trust. Cautiously, Shelby's neck extended until it was out in the world once again. It was then, looking into the reptile's curious eyes, that Juno finally understood what Lexa had sacrificed, what her mother had sacrificed, to bring her to Arcadia.

Rodan placed a red, seeded berry next to Shelby's head. The tortoise blinked, opened its mouth as wide as it could, and tried to fit the entire fruit in its little mouth with one bite. Juno smiled. Everything was going to be alright. No matter what.

, , ,

EPILOGUE

Final Entry

Wow! It's been quite a while. Welcome back, um...me?

I couldn't sleep tonight so I decided to rummage through this old desk of mine. Just like old times, huh? At the back of the bottom drawer (where the best things always are) I found a cloth satchel filled with many wonderful items I found at the bottom of my old backpack. Inside was a postcard from Leadville, a Taco Bell Menu, a couple of silver batteries, a single straggling shotgun shell, and, of course, this old dust-ridden journal.

Flipping through these pages brought back so many beautiful and painful memories. All treasured. However, when I reached the end of my own entries, I found that I hadn't quite filled it up! And what better way to spend a sleepless night than writing from the heart?

So my story needs a fitting conclusion, but I'm also tight on space, and I'm literally wasting it right now (Ha!). But twenty years have also gone by. Where do I even begin?

I guess I'll start with Arcadia. Oh, Arcadia! It's such a magnificent and inspiring place. It never ceases to amaze me. At first I was furious that not everyone in the wastes could experience this haven, but, over time, I learned about everything required for Arcadia to remain a safe, self-sufficient research facility. (Still a little bitter, though.)

I'll give you the shortest version.

Water first. Want to guess where it comes from? There used to be a body of it at the edge of Provo named, quite fittingly, Utah Lake. Well, someone a long time ago had the foresight to flush the entire thing underground into a (wo)man-made aquifer. Over time, the brilliant minds who were able to escape Friedrich's factory of terror (more on that later) migrated here to construct Arcadia around an ancient landmark called Provo Temple.

Powering and protecting agriculture was figured out with clever solar panelling and various geo-thermal solutions. So then they had water, irrigation, and sun, but nothing would grow. It turns out insects are kind of a big deal; pollinators especially. The first step to bringing YOUR food back is to bring your food's food back first.

The solution? Gradually introduce species - insects, plants, animals - one at a time, tailor the ecosystem to thrive off of itself, and then start cultivating the land. Arcadia is actually quite delicate. Remove just one of those pieces and the whole system comes crumbling down.

Here's some fun news: Since I arrived here we've been able to add watermelons, frogs, verbena (the hummingbirds love them), and even a couple of cats (they keep the rodent population down and are nice to have on your lap). It turns out life can still be found out there if you're patient and know where to look.

But, above all, Arcadia is a research facility devoted to returning the necessities we enjoy in here back out into the wild. Every day we try to develop more robust strains of plant life, brainstorm ways to redirect fresh water, desalinate ocean water effectively and efficiently, and, the biggest head scratcher, figure out how to bring back the rain. I'll be long dead before that last one's checked off.

    Which brings me to why I'm spending my sleepless night outside in the cool desert air. It's the anniversary of my arrival in Arcadia. I'm sitting on top of an eastern-facing cement wall that overlooks Provo. The city is more or less the same as it always has been. As is the mountain where, well, where it all happened twenty years ago. I come out here every year to reflect on how far my life has come. To appreciate everything that has been given to me; sacrificed for me. Rodan told me this was always their secret meeting spot. Seems fitting.

    Speaking of Rodan, he's such a sweet man. An amazing father, too. Every day he tells me I'm gorgeous despite my facial scarring or buzzed hair (I never could get used to it being long again). Together we've (me) beared thirteen beautiful, healthy, and fertile children. And, before you ask, of course there is a Lexa, a Kareem, and a Maia (But we love them all equally!).

    Each member of our family has the essential built-in immunity that refuses the gene-altering chemicals contained in plastics (Phthalates and BPA are big ones, but there are literally thousands). We contain in our DNA a missing piece that Pan was never quite able to formulate artificially, despite her best efforts. From what we can tell, Rodan was blind luck. In a way, I suppose I was, too. Though now that I'm a mother myself I think, despite her "failures", Pan may have benefited immensely from mixing a little love in with her science.

Anyways, in a few days I'm finally leaving Arcadia. Given that my children are now old enough to survive on their own (i.e. dad's watching them), and statistically they can repopulate effectively if I happen to die, Pan has agreed to let me off the leash. I'll return, of course, but I've been itching to get back out into the world.

And when I heard the next mission involved a study of Zion National Park, you can bet I was the first one in line. According to our geological survey, there may still be pockets of fresh water inside the unique network of caves there. Our operation is straightforward: visit the area, scout for water, initiate contact with remaining tribesmen, and, fingers crossed, return with new allies and a little more hope for the future.

Though I'm mostly going along as an annoying third wheel, I have to see the incredible formations Kareem had described so beautifully all those years ago. Zion was the one place he had wanted to visit the most (other than the Rocky Mountains). When we get there I'm going to take a day to myself while the other girls do their science thing. I won't be alone, though. I plan to find a place high up in a mountain, watch the sun fall slowly behind the horizon, and sing "Stand By Me" with Lexa and Kareem at my side.

Oh, Lexa. How I miss you.

Not a day goes by where I don't look at Rodan's face and think of you scowling at me (kidding!). If only you knew what you've allowed for me, what you've allowed for all of us. I wish I could tell you that you succeeded. I wish I could remind you that I saved you from the mountain first! And I wish there was some way you could know that on this night twenty years ago, you single-handedly thinned the Scab King's army SO MUCH that Pan was able to send in a unit to destroy that forsaken, monster-making factory once and for all. You made it so he can never come back.

And despite both of us being in danger every second of every day, you were also able to teach me how to be me. You showed me I could be SO much more than a frightened little girl. I thank you for helping me realize my true power; not only as a woman, but as a human being.

I asked you long ago why you thought it was called "mankind". We both had a laugh, but I still spotted the redness of recent tears behind your eyes. You saw men as only one kind; each equal to the other. To you they were inherently corrupt, incapable of compassion, born with evil in their hearts. Our antithesis. It was all you ever knew.

But I've seen differently. Evil does not exist in nature. It is something that is molded out of fear; out of desperation. Friedrich was so afraid of losing his power in life that he created the Scab King in his own self image, literally, so he could clutch onto it forever. Over time his insatiability consumed him, then was nurtured into countless abominations.

    But think of Rodan. Think of Kareem. Both are proof that the love and care of others can produce the most amazing outcomes. Proof that laughter and compassion burns brighter than the darkest shadows of uncertainty. Proof that, even in the face of all the suffering bestowed on us by this hot, polluted, destitute world, the kindness of man could always be one infectious smile away.

ACKNOWLEDGEMENTS

A massive thank you to everyone who was able to read through the rough draft of *Man, Kind* and provide me with feedback. Your insights, suggestions, and criticisms were overwhelming—in the best way. Without your help, my debut novel would have just been a lumpy rock, casually picked up from the pile and carelessly skipped into a lake. Now, because of you, *Man, Kind* is a more interesting, more thoughtful, and more gripping story, baring more semblance to that of a polished gemstone. One that has value. And one that will hopefully be kept and cherished by many readers to come.

A NOTE FROM THE AUTHOR

First thing's first, thank you—yes, you!—so much for reading my debut novel, *Man, Kind*. Seriously. I hope you enjoyed every page and took as much away from it as I put in.

If you liked, or even loved, my work, there is no greater gift that you can give than to publish an honest rating and review on Amazon and Goodreads. Sadly, independent authors like myself are slaves to the almighty algorithm. The more reviews I get, the more books I can sell, and the more time I can spend crafting epic adventures for you to read!

Secondly, the pages you just devoured depicted an awful reality that is, unfortunately, an awful lot closer to you and I than one might think. While the existential dangers of climate change are visibile by merely glancing out your window, those of microplastics are not so easily detected. Yet, they're everywhere. In your yard, in your clothes, in your water, in your food, and in your food's food.

Now I'm not here to paint another portrait of doom and gloom, but I do want to draw some awareness. I want you to be mindful. Though there are simple steps we can all take to reduce plastics in our daily lives—reusable bags, store food and drinks in glass or metal containers, go back to good 'ol bar soap—there is really only one language Big Plastic can understand: Cold. Hard. Cash.

To put it plainly, let the packaging of products influence what you buy. Do your research on a company's sustainability goals. Hold them accountable to the "green" policies they claim to implement. And while we'll never get rid of all the plastic currently polluting the world, there is a still a way to limit the amount that Big Plastic continues to pump out. If you speak their language, they'll listen.

RESOURCES

If the topic of plastics—specifically microplastics in the body—interests you, and you want to learn more, below are some easily accessible and digestible resources that also helped me in writing this book.

. . .

"Sperm Count Zero" by Halpern, Daniel Noah
    GQ Story - 4 September 2018
    www.gq.com/story/sperm-count-zero

"Point Comfort" episode of Dirty Money
    Season 2 - Netflix Series

"Fertility" episode of Sex, Explained
    Explained - Netflix Series

"Mechanisms of phthalate ester toxicity in the female reproductive system"
    by Tara Lovekamp-Swan and Barbara J. Davis
    PubMed Central (PMC) - February 2003
    www.ncbi.nlm.nih.gov/pmc/articles/PMC1241340/

Made in the USA
Columbia, SC
07 May 2021